Praise for Shaun Hamill's

A COSMOLOGY OF MONSTERS

"[*A Cosmology of Monsters*] is an object lesson in truly effective horror storytelling, proving that the best way to make you afraid for a character is to make you care about them first."   —The A.V. Club

"Uniquely weird and wonderful. . . . The writing is simply haunting, the story full of heart. . . . Hamill has built a rich world full of complex characters and he successfully delivers in showing how the horrors of real life can be just as terrifying as any monster."
—The Nerd Daily

"Unique and wonderful."
—C. J. Tudor, author of *The Chalk Man* and *The Hiding Place*

"A mesmerizing, meandering, dark tale of growing up and finding monsters all around you."   —*Houston Chronicle*

"A magnificent tribute to Lovecraft's vexing achievement, *A Cosmology of Monsters* redeems . . . the master's flaws. Hamill's heart-stopping debut novel features exceptionally graceful language and a set of characters we come to worry about, take delight in, grieve for and love."   —*BookPage*

"Exquisitely written, *A Cosmology of Monsters* is both beautiful and haunting. Shaun Hamill has crafted the best sort of horror story: one full of love and dread that will have you rethinking your definition of what a monster is."   —Jennifer McMahon, *New York Times* bestselling author of *The Winter People* and *The Invited*

Shaun Hamill

A COSMOLOGY OF MONSTERS

A native of Arlington, Texas, Shaun Hamill holds an MFA from the Iowa Writers' Workshop. He currently lives in the dark woods of Alabama with his wife, his in-laws, and his dog. *A Cosmology of Monsters* is his first novel.

A COSMOLOGY OF MONSTERS

A Cosmology of Monsters

Shaun Hamill

VINTAGE BOOKS
A DIVISION OF PENGUIN RANDOM HOUSE LLC
NEW YORK

FIRST VINTAGE BOOKS EDITION, AUGUST 2020

Copyright © 2019 by Shaun Hamill

All rights reserved. Published in the United States by Vintage Books,
a division of Penguin Random House LLC, New York, and distributed
in Canada by Penguin Random House Canada Limited, Toronto. Originally
published in hardcover in the United States by Pantheon Books,
a division of Penguin Random House LLC, New York, in 2019.

Vintage and colophon are registered trademarks
of Penguin Random House LLC.

The Library of Congress has cataloged the Pantheon edition as follows:
Name: Hamill, Shaun, writer.
Title: A cosmology of monsters / Shaun Hamill.
Description: First edition. | New York : Pantheon Books, 2019.
Identifiers: LCCN 2018050831
Subjects: GSAFD: Horror fiction.
Classification: LCC PS3608.A654 C67 2019 | DDC 813/.6—dc23
LC record available at https://lccn.loc.gov/2018050831

Vintage Books Trade Paperback ISBN: 978-0-525-56392-1
eBook ISBN: 978-1-5247-4768-8

Author photograph © Rebekah H. Hamill
Book design by Michael Collica

www.vintagebooks.com

Printed in the United States of America
10 9 8 7 6 5 4 3

This book is for my mother, Patrice Hamill; my mentor, Laura Kopchick; and my wife, Rebekah H. Hamill.

He was someone who acted out our psyches. He somehow got into the shadows inside our bodies; he was able to nail down some of our secret fears and put them onscreen. The history of Lon Chaney is the history of unrequited loves. He brings that part of you out into the open, because you fear that you are not loved, you fear that you never will be loved, you fear there is some part of you that's grotesque, that the world will turn away from.

—Ray Bradbury

Upon retiring, he had an unprecedented dream of great Cyclopean cities of titan blocks and sky-flung monoliths, all dripping with green ooze and sinister with latent horror. Hieroglyphics had covered the walls and pillars, and from some undetermined point below had come a voice that was not a voice; a chaotic sensation which only fancy could transmute into sound, but which he attempted to render by the almost unpronounceable jumble of letters, "Cthulhu fhtagn."

—H. P. Lovecraft, "The Call of Cthulhu"

Part One

The Picture in the House

I started collecting my older sister Eunice's suicide notes when I was seven years old. I still keep them all in my bottom desk drawer, held together with a black binder clip. They were among the only things I was allowed to bring with me, and I've read through them often the last few months, searching for comfort, wisdom, or even just a hint that I've made the right choices for all of us.

Eunice eventually discovered that I was saving her missives and began addressing them to me. In one of my favorites, she writes, "Noah, there is no such thing as a happy ending. There are only good stopping places."

My family is spectacularly bad at endings. We never handle them with grace. But we're not great with beginnings, either. For example, I didn't know the first quarter of this story until recently, and spent the better part of my youth and young adulthood lingering like Jervas Dudley around the sealed tombs of our family's history. It's exactly that sort of heartache I want to prevent for you, whoever you are. For that to happen, I have to start at the outermost edges of the shadow over my family, with my mother, tall, fair-skinned, and redheaded Margaret Byrne, in the fall of 1968.

Like me, my mother was born somewhat late into her parents' marriage. Unlike me, however, she reaped the benefits of being born to financially successful parents. Her father, Christopher Byrne, was a women's clothing buyer for Dillard's department stores, and had a close personal relationship with William T. Dillard himself.

Margaret didn't know her father well; she thought of him as a handsome stranger who smelled of cigarettes and who always brought home gifts from trips to New York—mostly original cast recordings of the Broadway musicals he saw while away—but she never wanted for anything. She grew up in a big house in the suburbs of Memphis, Tennessee, and always had a generous allowance, nice clothes, cars, and, when the time came, tuition at her parents' alma mater: Tilden University, a small conservative Christian school in Searcy, Arkansas.

You'll never have to worry about money, Margaret's mother told her, and in 1965 that seemed true. My grandfather had been so successful at Dillard's that in 1966, as my mother matriculated for her freshman year of college, he left the company to open his own store. However, by the winter of 1967, the store was off to a slow start, and in the summer of 1968, while Margaret was home for summer break, her mother broke the news: the store was failing. The Byrnes would pay Margaret's tuition for another year, but would have to take away her car, her monthly allowance, and the dorms.

When Margaret reminded her parents that she would need at least two more years to finish her bachelor's in English, never mind her master's in library science, her mother said, "I'd suggest you speed up work on your M-R-S before you worry about your B.A."

Only somewhat daunted, Margaret did her best with a near-impossible situation. When she returned to Searcy in the fall, she'd secured a job at Bartleby's, the town's only bookstore, and rented a room from the owner, Rita Johnson, a widow whose only religion was the written word, and whose politics were more Betty Friedan than Richard Nixon. Mrs. Johnson lived in a cozy two-story house near campus, charged a pittance for rent, and laid down almost no rules. She didn't care what hours Margaret kept as long as she didn't bring boys to the second floor of the house, and Margaret could use the TV and the record player as much as she wanted as long as she kept the volume low.

All of this new freedom was an abrupt, almost startling change from the stringent rules of the old residence hall. Margaret had never wanted to come to Tilden, with its mandatory signed morality pledges and heavily enforced attendance at Sunday morning worship services. She'd enrolled because it was the only school her father would pay for. She'd suffered through all the religious ritual in the hopes of a college degree, a career, and a life of her own. And now, living with Mrs. Johnson, she got her first taste of what that life might look like.

Margaret loved her new quarters, her new freedom, and, best of all, she loved the dim lighting and narrow aisles of Bartleby's. She loved stocking the new arrivals, setting up themed displays, and helping her customers, kindred spirits on the hunt for stories. The only burr in her work life was a young man named Harry, who came in maybe twice a week and asked her questions to which she suspected he already knew the answers: *Who wrote* Great Expectations*? Where do you keep your biographies?* He always thanked Margaret for the information, but regardless of what he claimed to be interested in, he would inevitably camp out on the floor in the science fiction section, where he read books without ever buying anything.

He looked young, about Margaret's age, and she assumed he must go to Tilden as well. She wondered how he found time to read so much *and* go to school. Also, if he went to Tilden, he could probably afford books. Why loiter? It got on her nerves, but whenever she confronted him about it, he replaced the unpurchased merchandise on the shelf, apologized, and left.

For a while, she worked thirty-two hours a week at the store, attended class, and studied in the downtime, but this routine proved more difficult than she'd anticipated. Work—even relatively easy work, in the tranquility of Bartleby's—was draining. After a full shift, her feet ached and her brain felt like a wrung-out sponge. All she wanted to do was lie down on Mrs. Johnson's couch and watch TV. On the nights she did force herself to study, she found it a slow, repetitive, laborious process. She had trouble focusing, and had to read paragraphs (or single sentences) over and over again to glean any approximation of meaning. She felt tired all the time, overslept, missed classes, and turned in assignments late or not at all. By late September her grades were worse than ever.

Her safety net, sewn by her mother's phantom, taunting voice, came in the form of Pierce Lombard, a boy from her Western Civ class. Tall and skinny with close-cropped hair ten years out of fashion and heavy-lidded eyes underscored by dark bags, he looked perpetually sleepy and about a decade older than his actual age (twenty), but he asked Margaret on at least one date a week and he came from a wealthy family of chicken tycoons. If you did your shopping at grocery stores in the southern United States in the mid–twentieth century, chances were you'd purchased at least one Lombard chicken. Pierce sometimes tried to explain the business to Margaret, but every time he did, her attention wandered.

They didn't go to the movies often, because Pierce disapproved of most films (he was conservative and devout even by Tilden standards), but when they did go, he sat at attention, and never smiled or laughed. Sometimes, in the dark, Margaret watched him instead of the film. He looked thirty now. What would he look like in another ten years, or twenty, when the pressures of chicken entrepreneurship began to wear on him?

He was polite, always opened doors for her and said "Please" and "Thank you." When they took his Mercedes someplace to neck, his kisses seemed mathematically calculated to ride the line between passion and good manners, his hands on her waist, stomach, or face. Margaret, a "good girl" and still a virgin, imagined that real love ought to be a full-contact sport, intense and dangerous, the kind of thing that happened on railroad tracks or forest floors, two bodies struggling to express purity of spirit. She wondered if Pierce, a "good boy" himself, was waiting for her to show a spiritual kinship before demonstrating that kind of passion, so one night in early October, she reached into his lap and squeezed his groin. He startled, pushed her away, and retreated to the far corner of the driver's seat.

"Why did you do that?" he said.

"Because I wanted to," she said.

"That's not the point," he said. "We shouldn't."

He took her home after that and didn't kiss her good night.

She'd always assumed that religion was something you did in polite company, not in private. Surely nobody actually believed any of the stuff they agreed to on Sundays. Pierce was a boy. Shouldn't he push for more, trying to see what he could get away with? Did anyone think Jesus Christ gave a damn how they used their private parts? Pierce should be overjoyed that she'd shown some interest in his penis, shouldn't he?

Pierce stopped calling after Margaret groped him, and sat far away from her in class and worship services. Her newfound free time didn't help her grades; she failed three tests in a row. When her Algebra professor handed back her midterm with a big F− on the front page, he murmured, "Get it together, Miss Byrne."

She felt a growing directionless fury at the unfairness of it all. Why was it her problem her father was a bad businessman? Why was it her responsibility to convince some sleepy-faced pinhead to enjoy her body? How was anyone supposed to succeed in these circumstances?

The day she got the Algebra exam back, she carried her anger to her shift at Bartleby's. Mrs. Johnson read the emotional weather and left her alone to restock the science fiction section, which would have been fine, but Harry was blocking the aisle with his back to the shelves, a hardcover book open in his lap, a Please Don't Read the Books sign hanging directly over his head.

She crossed her arms and glared at him. The sun came through the window behind her, and her shadow stretched forward down the aisle, shading him.

"Hi, Margaret," he said. He smiled at her. "I've been meaning to ask—do you have anything by Philip Roth?" When she didn't return the smile, he said, "What's the matter?"

"Can you read?" she said. "Do you understand the words on the pages you're turning? Or do you sit here because you want to look smart for passersby?"

"I can read," he said.

"Then why don't you—" She tore the Please Don't Read the Books sign from the shelf over his head and tried to pitch it at him. The flimsy paper fluttered through the air between them like a fallen leaf, making its lackadaisical way to the floor. Harry watched it land before looking up at her.

"Why don't I what?" he said.

"Why don't you—you—*you read it, you bought it*!" She grabbed him by the shoulder. "Get up."

Perhaps surprised by the force of her anger, Harry did as commanded, and allowed Margaret to march him to Mrs. Johnson at the front counter, book still open in his hands.

"Harry's ready to check out now," Margaret said. She pushed him toward the register.

He gave her a plaintive look but put the book on the counter. It was a big glossy hardcover, something you might find on someone's coffee table.

Mrs. Johnson took the book and checked the price on the front flap. "Are you sure, Harry?"

He grunted an affirmative. Mrs. Johnson rang up the total. He grimaced when she read it off, but pulled out his faded, cracked wallet and paid. Mrs. Johnson put the book in a bag for him. He mumbled his thanks and left.

She watched him go before speaking to Margaret. "What was that about?"

"Nothing," Margaret said.

"Actually nothing, or you-don't-want-to-talk-about-it nothing?"

"Take your pick, Mrs. Johnson."

"Watch your tongue, young lady."

Margaret returned to work stocking the shelves. As her shift wore on, her anger ebbed away until it disappeared altogether and left her mystified by the strength and force of her outburst. Certain details kept presenting themselves to her, things she'd never noticed about Harry before: the ragged sleeve on his button-down shirt, the fabric rough from too many washings; the faded knees of his jeans; some vague, greasy smell she couldn't place, inescapable when in his proximity.

By the time her shift ended that evening, she felt a dull shame, which only intensified when she found Harry waiting in the parking lot. He sat cross-legged on the hood of an old, beat-up Chevy, hands in his lap. She almost never saw cars that old on campus. Maybe he was a scholarship kid? Or, like her, trying to work his way through school? Face hot, she forced herself to approach.

"That was an expensive book," he said.

"You can return it. If you have the receipt you can get cash."

He made a face. "I couldn't do that to Mrs. Johnson. She's always nice to me."

"Can I pay you back?" she said. She dug for her wallet in her purse.

He moved his head from side to side as though arguing with himself. "I *was* going to go to the movies tonight. I guess if you really want to set things right, you could buy the tickets."

"You want me to go to the movies with you?"

"I'll drive," he said. "You pony up for admission."

"What do you want to go see?"

"*Rosemary's Baby* just opened in Little Rock," he said.

Margaret had heard of the film. The preacher had denounced it in chapel last week, with broad, exciting terms: *blasphemous, profane, hideous*. Any student caught attending the film (or reading the Ira Levin novel on which it was based) would be expelled. But nowhere in Dr. Landon's warning (or the memo posted all over campus) was the film described in any detail. What made it profane? What made it blasphemous?

If Margaret had still lived in the dorms, she wouldn't have even considered the idea. But Mrs. Johnson wouldn't rat her out; the proprietor of Bartleby's thought all stories ought to be accessible to everyone, regardless of inherent morality. She'd be proud of Margaret for making up her own mind.

However, Little Rock was a fifty-mile drive from Searcy, and Margaret still had unfinished Chemistry homework, which she told Harry.

"I'll drive fast all the way there and back," he said.

She looked down at her plain sweater and the skirt she'd worn to class that morning. Not exactly a prime first date ensemble, but this was about reparations, not romance. The clothes would help set his expectations accordingly.

"Let's go then," she said.

3

It was a horror picture starring that girl from *Peyton Place*, about a young married couple that moves into a new apartment and ends up ensnared by the elderly, doting Satanists next door. Margaret bought the tickets, and Harry paid for the popcorn and soda. Their fingers touched in the popcorn bucket a few times during the movie, but Harry didn't try to hold her hand or put an arm around her. He stared at the screen, engrossed.

The movie wasn't jump-out-and-scare-you terrifying, but unsettling on a deeper, more primal level. Margaret found herself identifying with the title character as Rosemary was bullied and isolated by her husband and neighbors, raped by the devil, and helpless to do anything in the end but be a mother to the spawn of that unholy union. As Rosemary rocked her baby in its black bassinet and the credits began to roll, Margaret sat back in her seat, stunned. Were movies allowed to end this way? With the devil triumphant, and the heroine defeated?

The film's spell lasted until Harry broke the silence in the parking lot. "If we speed, I can have you home by ten thirty."

Margaret let him open her car door and studied his face. He had a long nose over a small mouth and pointed chin, and brown eyes capped with thick, dark eyebrows. She wouldn't have noticed him across the room at a party, but his face *was* pleasant, genial. She felt the haze of the movie dissipating.

"Are you hungry?" she said. "I'm starving."

"I could eat," he said.

He took her to a McDonald's a few blocks away, probably the only open place in town. As they climbed from the car, Margaret grabbed the Bartleby's bag from the seat between them.

"I want to see what cost me so much study time tonight," she said.

"You might want to wait until you're finished eating before you dive in," Harry said. "It's kind of gross."

He asked her to go find a seat while he ordered. She took a booth by a window, pulled the book from the bag, and laid it flat on the table: *Visions of Cthulhu: Illustrations Inspired by the Work of H. P. Lovecraft.* The cover featured a painting of a great, hideous beast, roughly human in shape, with thick, muscular green arms and legs, its hands and feet ending in talons rather than fingers and toes. It had the head of a nightmarish squid, bulbous and many-eyed, ending in a mass of tentacles, which hung down over the creature's chest and giant, round belly. A pair of sharp but somehow fragile-looking wings sprouted from the creature's back, and Margaret wondered how such an obese creature could possibly take flight.

"I hope you're still hungry for this stuff." Harry stood next to her with a tray of burgers, fries, and sodas.

Margaret tapped the cover of the book. "Is this Cthulhu?" She pronounced it *kit-hooloo,* and knew from his smirk that she'd said it incorrectly.

"One artist's rendition, yes," he said. "And it's pronounced *kuh-thoo-loo.*"

She pulled the book toward herself, making room for him to set down the food. "He doesn't look scary. Just sort of gross, like the monster version of a fat Buddha from a Chinese restaurant."

He laughed and angled his head for a better look. "Yeah, I guess he kind of does."

"Is he supposed to be scary?"

He sat down across from her. "In the story he's scary. But maybe it's one of those things you can't translate without losing some essential piece. Like, it only works in the imagination."

She opened the book, flipped to a random page, and found a painting of another monster—this one more indefinite and amorphous, a single mass of flesh with four black eyes; a glowing, vulva-shaped mouth lined with sharp teeth; and a mass of tentacles waving from its back. It floated among the stars, dwarfing a small planet in the foreground.

"And this fellow?" she said.

"Azathoth." He picked up a cheeseburger and unwrapped it.

Margaret closed the book with some reluctance and laid it on the seat next to her. She plucked a fry from one of the greasy little sacks on the tray. "So, every picture in the book is based on a story by this Lovecraft guy."

Harry nodded, chewing his food.

"It's a thick book," she said. "He must have created a lot of monsters."

Harry covered his mouth with one hand and spoke around his food. "A bunch. And they're all connected, too."

"What, like they're related to each other, like family?"

He swallowed and took a drink of his soda. "Some of them are, yeah. But I meant that they all exist in a shared world. Sort of like those movies where Dracula meets Frankenstein's monster, you know?"

She shrugged. "I saw the one where Abbott and Costello met the Wolfman."

"Same basic idea. They're all out there, sharing space, breathing the same air. Like how so many of William Faulkner's books take place in the same county."

"You ever make that comparison in an English classroom?"

"Not for a while now," he said. "I learned my lesson."

"Professors don't care for it?" she said.

He started to say something, then stopped and shoved a fry into his mouth.

4

They arrived back at Mrs. Johnson's a little before midnight and sat in the car trying to figure out what to say to each other.

"Well," Harry said, at last. "Thanks for the movie."

"Thanks for buying an expensive book," Margaret said. "We appreciate your business." She laughed at her own joke, the sound shrill and too loud.

He stared straight ahead, mouth piled up on the left side of his face. "I guess I'll see you at the store."

"Good night, Harry." She slid across the seat and kissed his cheek. It was rough with new stubble.

She got out of the car and walked up the drive, trying to decide if she was relieved or happy he hadn't tried anything. This train of thought quickly collided with homework stress—her American Lit paper still unstarted, her Chemistry equations in math limbo.

"Hey!"

She turned to see Harry running toward her, something clutched in one hand. He stopped about a foot away and extended a small paperback with a cracked spine: *The Tomb and Other Tales* by H. P. Lovecraft. The cover was black with white type and featured a picture of a man's forehead split down the middle, red bugs pouring from the place where his brain ought to be.

"So you can try him out," Harry said. "My mom gave me this book for my thirteenth birthday."

Margaret took the book. "Okay, sounds good—" she started to say, but he cut her sentence short, closing the distance between them, grabbing the sides of her face, and kissing her. It ended before Margaret had a chance to think about what was happening. He jogged back to his car and left her to wander, dazed, up the stairs to the house, fumbling with her keys and wishing she'd asked for a burger without onions.

5

Margaret stayed up all night to finish *The Tomb,* as though the book's cast of geniuses, madmen, and near-indescribable horrors held the key to deciphering the strange young loiterer with whom she'd shared a brief, oniony kiss.

The book didn't help. Harry didn't seem like a madman, a monster, or, no offense, a genius. All she learned about him was that he had a taste for the macabre, and an extraordinary patience for dry, over-wrought prose. She found Lovecraft almost unreadable. The stories had characters inasmuch as there were named people who existed on the page, but they never grew or changed or engaged in any mean-ingful human interactions. Whenever they spoke, they sounded like anthropomorphized textbooks from alternate dimensions. Most of the stories seemed to be about a single survivor relating the tale of an exploration of some ancient ruin and going mad as he realized that the ruin had been built (and was sometimes still inhabited) by some primordial horror. It was all florid, adjectival language, with nothing approaching the awesome horror and dread of the paintings in *Visions of Cthulhu*.

On the other hand, many of the tales had a compelling sense of dark revelation, the gradual realization by the narrator that the comforting "real world" humans inhabited was in fact nothing but weak gauze ready to be pulled aside to reveal an abyss of terrors underneath. It was sort of the opposite of Moses and the burning bush, or Paul on the road to Damascus. The same basic concept as religion—*the world is not the world*—but twisted.

She was still wrestling with this idea when she staggered into Western Civ the next morning, and didn't notice Pierce approach until he sat down beside her.

"You're talking to me again?" she said.

He sighed, and his nostrils flared. "I admit maybe I overreacted. But what you did—"

She leaned back in her chair, eyebrows raised. This ought to be good.

He put a hand to his brow. "I'm trying to apologize." His forehead creased, and it looked familiar somehow.

"You're amazing at it. Spectacular."

"Can I take you out tonight? And have a real, adult conversation? Please?"

For the first time in almost a week, Margaret felt the uncomfortable tug of her mother's voice at the base of her skull. The letters M-R-S burned in her mind's eye like a brand. She was too tired to say no.

He took her to Searcy's most expensive restaurant, a surf and turf place named Captain Bill's with old fishing nets and harpoons hung from the walls and ceilings. He encouraged her to get whatever she wanted and ordered the lobster to prove his point. Margaret ordered a salad. She'd never eaten lobster. When she watched her parents do so, she found the whole messy business—the bibs, the excess of fluid, the cracked shells with paltry meat inside—revolting. Her mother and father might as well have eaten giant red bugs. The thought put her in mind of the cover of *The Tomb* and made her glad for her salad all over again.

She finished her food before Pierce finished cracking and digging and dipping and chomping. His forehead shone even in the low restaurant light, and she tried to decide if he was already going bald. Also, had he worked up a sweat over lobster? That couldn't be good, right?

When the waiter brought the check, Pierce set it down in the middle of the table as he pulled his wallet from his jacket. She looked from the bill to Pierce and caught him watching her, making sure she'd seen the total. He pretended not to have seen, threw down several bills, and told the waiter to keep the change.

He's trying, she scolded herself.

After dinner (and a handful of complimentary mints), they drove out to the parking lot by the city park. It was a clear night with lots of stars. The constellations put Margaret in mind of Azathoth from *Visions of Cthulhu,* the vagina monster propelled through the heavens by tentacles. She sleepily wondered what Harry was doing right now, and wished she could have napped before the date.

She'd almost drifted off when Pierce said, "You don't have to sit so far away." She started as he patted the space next to him.

She scooted closer. He put an arm around her, and she made herself lean into his body. It wasn't so unpleasant. There was something comforting about it. Human.

"Are you still angry at me?" he said.

"No."

"I understand if you are. I acted like a real dingbat."

"It's fine." She patted his chest. Honestly, she realized, she didn't care.

He took a deep breath. "The truth is, it scared me when you—did what you did. We haven't been seeing each other for very long, and it happened so soon. I didn't handle myself like a man. Instead, I ran away like a little boy, and hid from you. I asked God, 'Why would she do this? She's a good girl.' And finally, He answered me: *She did it because she loves you.*"

Margaret's body went rigid. "You talk to God a lot?" She never prayed outside of church or meals with other Christians, and even then she only bowed her head, closed her eyes, and said *Amen* when appropriate. Her mind wandered during prayer. She assumed everyone's did, although you weren't supposed to say so.

"All day, every day," he said. "Anyway, my point is, God told me that you love me, and furthermore, that the reason I ran away was that I love you, too, and I wasn't ready to admit it." He shifted in his seat and peered down at her, his forehead nearly blinding in the moonlight. A vein stood out near his scalp. Was it pulsing? Was he okay? "I love you, Margaret. I know it's fast, but my parents say that when you know, you know. If you're ready to get serious, then so am I. I want you to come home with me during the Thanksgiving holiday. I want you to meet my family."

Margaret sat up. Pierce smiled at her with a sort of benevolence—an expression she associated with her father's face on Christmas morning, the look of a man bestowing a great gift.

"That's—that's a big step," she said.

"I love you, Margaret," he said. He leaned down and kissed her. She let him push her down on the seat and crawl atop her. She accepted his kisses and clumsy hands. As he bit her ears and neck, she caught something out of the corner of her eye—something at Pierce's window.

When she moved for a better look, though, it was gone. She tried to settle back into the rhythm of necking, put her hands on his face, kissed him, let him push his tongue into her mouth like a fat, slimy worm. She opened her eyes, and this time the vein on his forehead really was pulsing as he worked himself into a passion on her mostly passive body. She looked up, away from him, and saw something else outside, this time on her side of the car—a large shape with wide, hunched shoulders, and two eyes that glinted orange through the glass.

She made a muffled sound of panic, put her hands on Pierce's shoulders to try to push him off, to get his tongue out of her mouth so she could warn him, but he only moaned and fumbled at her harder. The vein on his forehead had stretched across his brow, dividing it into two separate planes of sweaty, pale skin. She wriggled, trying to get free. Something moved beneath the skin of his forehead. The vein pulsed twice and then burst.

Pierce's head cracked open, and hundreds of tiny red insects came spilling out onto her face, into her hair, down the cracks between her dress and her flesh, thousands of tiny legs wriggling in a bid for freedom. She kicked Pierce off of her, screamed, and scrambled backward, swiping at herself. She had to get them off, she had to get out of the car, she was going to die in here if she didn't get out—

She grabbed the door handle behind her and pulled. The door popped open and dumped her on the ground outside. Pierce came crawling across the seat toward her, and she tried to get up and move, to get away before she had to see his face, to see spiders digging into his eyes, flooding his nostrils, and pouring into his mouth to eat him from the inside out—but she was too tired from her all-night reading marathon, too winded from screaming, and moved too slowly. When his face emerged into the moonlight, she couldn't help but look.

He was a little sweaty and flustered, his face flush with interrupted arousal (and possibly alarm), but otherwise okay. The vein had vanished, leaving his waxy forehead plain and flat.

"What's wrong?" he said. He got out and knelt in front of her.

She blinked a few times, breathing hard. "I'm fine," she said, as much to herself as to him. "I'm okay."

6

She explained that she hadn't gotten much sleep the night before, and might have had some sort of waking nightmare. He played the part of the concerned boyfriend and didn't ask too many questions. She did find herself hungry again, however, and, eager to avoid any further necking, asked Pierce if they could get drive-through.

And so she found herself at a McDonald's for the second night in a row, staring out the window of Pierce's car while he ordered fries and a milk shake for her at the drive-through. Her face felt raw, as though she'd been nuzzling sandpaper. She didn't want to talk, didn't want to think. She only wanted to stare out the window and drift. Let Pierce deal with the disembodied voice at the drive-through speaker. Still, even this innocuous conversation, an exchange of less than fifty words, made her uneasy. What was it? Why the vague panic in her chest? She turned in her seat and surveyed the car, trying to discern the source of her discomfort. It wasn't until they pulled up to the window that she understood. Harry opened the folding glass to take their money.

His eyes met Margaret's across the car, and his mouth opened in apparent surprise.

"You sure you want this?" he said, smiling a little as he offered the shake. "It might have tannis root in it."

"I'm sorry?" Pierce said.

Margaret shook her head a little. Harry looked from her back to Pierce.

"Nothing, sorry," Harry said.

"How much was it, again?" Pierce said.

Harry told him, and they made the exchange. Harry counted the money and shut the window, and Pierce drove away. On the ride to Mrs. Johnson's, Margaret held the milk shake with two hands, but she couldn't bring herself to take a sip. When she got back to the house, she took it to the kitchen and dumped it into the sink before heading upstairs. Tannis root indeed.

She fell asleep almost at once. She dreamt about baying sounds, as if some wolf or hound was in great pain nearby.

7

Margaret's mother cheered when Margaret called to tell her the news about Thanksgiving. She was so loud Margaret had to hold the phone away from her ear.

"That's my good girl," Mrs. Byrne said.

"My grades are in bad shape," Margaret said. "I'm behind in all my classes."

"You only have to hang on long enough to seal the deal," Mrs. Byrne said. "You can do this, princess."

"Mom."

"What?"

"It doesn't feel."

"It doesn't feel what?" Mrs. Byrne said.

It doesn't feel right, Margaret thought. What she said instead was "It doesn't feel real yet."

"It *will*," Mrs. Byrne said, as though reading the subtext in her daughter's voice. "Just practice being in love and wait it out."

As she got ready for school in the mornings, Margaret repeated the mantra again and again. *We are in love. We are in love.* As she brushed her teeth, she tried to picture Pierce next to her, the two of them taking turns spitting into the sink. As she fixed her hair and got dressed, she tried to miss Pierce, to wonder where he was, what he was doing. She tried to pine, to look forward to Western Civ. She ran along with the kite of their relationship held over her head, trying to get it aloft on its own. It always seemed to need a little extra help.

Harry stopped coming into the store. She could understand why he would stay away—he'd withheld the fact of his job from her, and not only had she found him out, but she'd done so on a date with another man. A man who drove a Mercedes. Margaret would have stayed away, too. Poor Harry. But still she had his copy of *The Tomb*, which had been a gift from his mother. He would want it back, and Margaret was eager to get rid of it. Even two weeks after her freak-out in Pierce's car, she continued to have nightmares about lurking figures and distant howls. She was almost positive that it was the book's fault. *The Tomb* contained a story entitled "The Hound," about a pair of grave robbers who dig up a centuries-old dead wizard only to find something inhuman in the coffin, "with phosphorescent sockets and sharp ensanguined fangs yawning twistedly in mockery of my inevitable doom. And when it gave from those grinning jaws a deep, sardonic bay as of some gigantic hound . . . I merely screamed and ran away . . ."

She borrowed a bicycle from Mrs. Johnson's garage and rode across town to the McDonald's. She arrived during the lunch rush and found Harry at the register, working his way through a long line of customers. He didn't notice her when she joined the line; all his attention was focused on whoever stood right in front of him. He looked happy, as though each customer were precisely the person he was hoping to see. The look lasted until Margaret reached the front of the line, at which point he appeared to become fascinated by the cash register.

"How can I help you?" he said.

"I want to give you back your book."

"So give me back my book."

"When's your break?" she said.

"I already had it."

"When is your shift over?"

He sighed. "I'm off at three."

She checked her watch. It was 1:45 now. "I will take"—she opened her purse and examined its meager contents—"your smallest order of fries. For here."

He rang her up, then handed her a tiny sack of fries on a tray. She took them to a table in the corner, sat down, and ate as slowly as possible—so slowly that the final fries were cold and soggy before she was done. It still took only fifteen minutes. Her attention wandered to the window, to the bright blue sky outside, and to Harry taking orders at the register. How could anyone be so consistently cheerful?

Finally, at five past three, Harry shambled over and collapsed on the other side of her booth with a groan. As he sat, a wave of cooking oil smell rolled off him, and Margaret's stomach growled. He fiddled with his little white McDonald's hat while they spoke.

"What can I do for you, Margaret?" he said.

She pushed *The Tomb* across the table. "I wanted to make sure you got your book back."

"I appreciate it, but you didn't have to."

"But your mother gave it to you. It was a birthday gift."

He rubbed his face and squinted at the ceiling. "Oh yeah. That."

"What do you mean?"

"Nothing. Just—if you check the publication date, it's only two years ago. The math doesn't add up. Unless you think I'm fifteen."

Margaret snatched the book back and checked the copyright page. "Why lie about it?"

"I thought it would improve my chances at a second date." He appraised her. "But that's not why you're here."

She shifted in the booth and tried to decide how to answer this.

"It's okay," he said. "I get it. I saw your boyfriend's clothes and his car. It's an easy choice to make—the college boy, or the townie who runs a register for a living?"

"I didn't realize you didn't go to Tilden," she said. "I thought you were like me—broke and working your way through."

"I guess I could have clarified that," he said. "But again—second date."

"So you're not in school? Then why aren't you in Vietnam?"

"My dad's dead and my mom is a paranoid schizophrenic," he said. "I have a deferment." He spun his hat around one index finger. Margaret moved her mouth around, but no words emerged, and he said, "It's really okay. You don't have to explain anything to me."

"Can we be friends?"

The hat spun off his finger and landed on the floor. He bent to pick it up. "How would Captain Mercedes feel about that?"

"His name is Pierce," she said. "He's a good person. A good Christian."

"Is that important to you?"

"I go to a Christian school," she said. "Don't you believe in God?"

He dropped his hat on the table. "Never met the guy."

She made a scoffing noise.

"So your family's rich enough for Tilden, but not rich enough for you to not have a job," he said.

"Daddy always said we were well-to-do, but not rich." She regretted the words at once, hated the way they sounded.

He shrugged. "I guess there's rich and then there's rich. From down here it all looks the same."

She shrugged back. "If you say so. Anyway, we don't have any money anymore. That's why I had to get a job."

"I've had a job since I was fourteen," he said. "I worked through high school."

"Try doing it in college," she said.

"College? You mean when you're only in class twelve hours a week?"

"There's more to it than that," she said. "Homework. Papers. Essay midterms and finals."

"What are you studying?"

"Marketing," she said, surprised by the spontaneity of the lie.

He rolled his eyes. "Do you and the good Christian boy both plan to get marketing jobs after you're married? Do you see all your hard work paying big dividends in the next ten years, when you're a house-wife with three kids?"

Her face felt hot. *"His name is Pierce,"* she repeated.

"Good for him."

"So." She drummed her fingers on the book. "You're a grown man who still reads ghost and monster stories."

"You already knew that about me," he said.

"I guess I didn't think about it until now," she said. "You don't feel sort of ridiculous? Like maybe you should be reading books for grown-ups?"

"I think horror is the most important fiction in the world," he said.

She almost told him about the thing outside Pierce's window, the red bugs, the weeks of nightmares. She almost yelled at him for encouraging the night terrors into her head with the stupid book. Instead, she took a turn laughing at him. "That?" She pointed at the book. "It's self-important, unreadable junk."

He took the book back. "What do you want from me, Margaret?"

"Nothing. I only wanted to give your book—your *book of lies,* as it turns out—back."

He laughed again, but it didn't sound mean this time, only surprised. "What?" she said.

He held up both hands in surrender. "Nothing. I like the way you phrase things when you're mad. I can see why you want to study marketing."

"I actually lied about that," she admitted. "I'm studying English."

He leaned forward, put his face in his hands, and laughed harder.

"You don't have to make fun of me," she said. "I'm already embarrassed."

He wiped tears from his cheeks, trying to regain control. "Why are we so desperate to impress each other? Listen, I'm sorry for what I said about you being a housewife with three kids and no job. I was raised by a single mother working two jobs. She taught me better than that." He checked his watch and grimaced. "Speaking of, I need to get home and check on her."

They both stood. Margaret glanced at Mrs. Johnson's bicycle, chained to the railing outside, then at Harry. "Can I get a ride?"

8

When they arrived at Mrs. Johnson's, Harry got out to help Margaret unload the bike from the trunk.

"So you and the good Christian are pretty serious then," he said.

She punched his arm. "Stop it. And yes. I'm going to meet his family for Thanksgiving."

"It's not even Halloween yet," he said. "Thanksgiving is a long way off."

"So what?" she said.

He shut the trunk and leaned back on it, arms crossed. "My mom never stopped dating until she and my father were married. She went on a date the night before her wedding."

"No she didn't," Margaret said.

"My hand to God—"

"Whom you don't believe in—"

"She said she wanted to be sure."

"What's your point, Harry?"

"You're not married yet. It's not even Thanksgiving. Maybe we could see each other a few more times before then."

She made a face. "I don't think Pierce would like that."

"Then I'm glad I'm not asking him," Harry said. "Who cares what he wants? What do you want?" When she didn't answer right away, he said, "Let's at least try one more time."

"You're not going to change my mind," she said.

"Probably not," he agreed. "But I'm not ready to give you up yet, either."

We are in love, Margaret repeated to herself, trying to picture Pierce in her head. *We are in love.*

9

On their second date, Harry took Margaret out of Searcy and again followed all the signs for Little Rock. Once in the city, he pulled a scrap of paper from his shirt pocket and read from it as he navigated the downtown area. They entered a run-down residential neighborhood lined with old houses in various states of decomposition—broken windows, sunken porches, dangling rain gutters. They'd probably been beautiful once, but Margaret wondered who could live here anymore.

They stopped at the corner of one of these streets, in the shadow of a turreted two-story house with a sign planted in the yard: SPOOKY

HOUSE! A line of people started at the base of the porch and stretched down the sidewalk.

"What is this place?" Margaret said.

In 1968, a year before the Haunted Mansion opened at Disneyland, and well before the proliferation of copycat attractions around the country, Harry didn't have the easily understood cultural shorthand *haunted house* available to him, and had to reach for the closest available equivalent.

"It's supposed to be like a fun house at a carnival, or a ghost train ride," he said, as he circled the block and hunted for a parking spot. "But it's a real house. So this is what it would actually be like to go into a haunted place." He leaned past her, opened the glove compartment, and removed a folded-up newspaper. Margaret caught a headline (LOCAL BOY MISSING) before he flipped it over and handed it to her and pointed to a small ad in one corner.

Margaret angled the paper so she could read by the streetlight as he backed into an open spot across the street from the attraction. The ad was a small square of black featuring a generic, cartoonish ghost with bold white print beneath: "Come to Spooky House—AND EXPERIENCE A TRUE-LIFE NIGHTMARE!"

"This sounds like fun to you?" she said.

"If you don't want to go, that's okay," he said. "We can see a movie, or I can take you home." She heard the strain in his voice. He wanted this bad, but also wanted to be a good sport.

"No, let's do it," she said. "How often do I get a chance to live out a true-life nightmare?"

They joined the line and shuffled closer to the door every twenty minutes or so, as groups of laughing people emerged through the fence around the side of the house. Finally they stood before the ticket taker, an older, heavyset woman with limp gray hair and a cigarette wedged in one corner of her mouth. Harry paid. The woman made change, and then pointed inside.

"Should we— How does it work?" Harry said.

"Go in. You'll see," the woman said, her voice the sound of stones scraped together.

The front door stood open, but dangling orange streamers obscured the view. Margaret and Harry pushed through into a dimly lit entry-way with a flickering bulb overhead and orange fairy lights strung around the banister, twisting up into the darkness of the second floor. Margaret leaned forward and peered up the stairs. Something moved, a shape distinguishing itself against the darkness, retreating from view. Margaret stepped back and bumped into Harry.

"You okay?" he said.

"Fine," she mumbled. Maybe this had been a bad idea.

A group of four teenagers came in after them, two couples giggling and leaning into one another, their energy palpable and reassuring. Harry and Margaret moved aside to let the kids take the lead. They followed them down the hall, which opened on the right side into the living room. Four people sat on a severe, uncomfortable-looking couch, wearing weird (but not exactly scary) costumes. They appeared to be family—the father dressed in a suit and sporting a thick black mustache; the mother with long, straight black hair and a tight, form-fitting gown; a chubby boy in a striped T-shirt with a chili bowl haircut; and a little girl in a black dress, dark hair braided on either side of her grumpy, dour little face. They stared at a television screen covered in static.

"Welcome!" the father said, with a wave. "We're watching the weather report on TV."

"Looks like snow again, Gomez," the mother said to the father.

Gomez? How did Margaret know that name?

"It always looks like snow," the little girl said.

"You know, Wednesday, that's an excellent point," Gomez conceded.

Wednesday? Gomez?

"Oh, it's like that TV show," one of the teenage girls said. "The uh—what was it called?"

"*The Addams Family,*" Harry said, so quiet only Margaret heard. She caught his eye and he made an apologetic face. She studied the Addams impersonators. She saw it now, sure—but wasn't *The Addams Family* a sitcom that made fun of monsters? Wasn't it a comedy of errors, not horror? The ad in the paper hadn't seemed to be advertising funny.

"Since we're snowed in, you'll have to join us for dinner," Gomez said. "Lurch!"

A slightly-taller-than-average figure shambled up the hallway toward the visitors. He wore a tuxedo and makeup that made him look like Frankenstein's monster. He groaned in the tone of a question.

"Lurch, show our guests to the dining room, will you?" Gomez said.

The tuxedoed monster groaned again. Margaret, Harry, Gomez, and the teenagers followed him down the hall into a large, candlelit dining room, where a long table had been set for twelve. Lurch walked around the table and pulled out six chairs. When no one moved to accept the invitation, he leaned forward and removed the lid from a serving dish in the middle of the table. He gestured toward the contents, a mass of black that seemed to be writhing in the flickering light.

Still no one came forward. Lurch reached into the dish, grabbed a handful of whatever was inside, and pitched it at the guests. The mass broke apart in midair and Margaret had time to register spindly limbs, a plastic shine. The teenagers shouted as the black stuff hit them and bounced off, thumping to the floor. Margaret squinted at the shapes. Rubber spiders. Lurch was throwing rubber spiders at them. At least they weren't red.

"Oh, brother," Harry said.

"Lurch, what have I told you about playing with your food?" Gomez said. He stood much closer than Margaret would have liked, and his breath stank of cigarettes. "Now we have to clean our guests!" She was grateful when he pushed to the front of the group and led them to a door at the end of the hall. Smoke drifted out from the crack between the door and the floor.

They shuffled into a kitchen so full of fog Margaret couldn't see the floor. A man in goggles and a white coat stood in the center of the room and stirred a smoking pot.

"It's alive!" he wailed. "Alive!"

Harry's shoulders slumped a little and his face dropped into his hands.

"How's the soup, Henry?" Gomez said.

"It's coming along swimmingly, Mr. Addams," the man in the lab coat said. He used the metal spoon to beat at something in the pot, splashing water onto the stove.

"Glad to hear it!" Gomez said. "Do you by any chance have clean towels? We had a mishap in the dining room."

"Nothing clean, sorry," Henry said. "That is, unless—does *bloody* mean the same thing as *dirty*?" He held up a white towel soaked crimson. The teenagers moaned with disgust.

Gomez turned to address the visitors again. "I think we have some towels in the upstairs bathroom if you want to head that way."

"We're not dirty," Harry said. "Can we go back out the way we came?"

"Nonsense," Gomez said. "We recently remodeled the upstairs guest bedroom. You simply must see it. Lurch?"

Lurch reappeared in the kitchen doorway.

"Take our guests upstairs for some clean towels," Gomez said.

Lurch grunted and gestured everyone back into the hall. Margaret went first, Harry right behind her.

"It's a small house," he whispered, close to her ear, hot breath on her neck. "There can't be much more." Then, a second later, "I'm sorry."

Margaret led the trek up the stairs and moved aside at the landing to make room for the rest of the group. They stood in a narrow, dimly lit hall lined on both sides with closed doors. There was also, incongruously, a tall potted plant on the wall opposite the stairs. Margaret leaned over the railing and looked down at the first floor. She thought about the shape she'd seen staring down at her from this spot when she walked in. That part hadn't felt hokey, or like it was part of a joke. It had felt real. She pushed away from the railing and faced the huddled group.

"Where now?" one of the teenagers said.

The door at the far end of the hall swung open. Lurch turned and went down the stairs, leaving them alone.

They walked forward. No ghouls or demons sprang out. The house sounded quieter than before. Empty.

The room at the end of the hall was doused in sickly-pink light, and had been dressed like an old woman's bedroom. An old vanity stood on the left side of the room, and a twin-size bed sat in the opposite corner. The bed rested on a metal frame, head- and footboards so tall that it resembled a cradle for adults. A lump lay beneath the blankets, unmoving.

Old black-and-white photographs hung on the walls: small children smiling and laughing on a summer day at the beach; a portrait of a soldier in formal wear, hat cocked at what must have been considered a jaunty angle; a newly married couple running from a church, heads ducked and hands raised against an onslaught of rice; an accident photo, one car T-boned into the other, the passenger side of the first car crumpled and caved in, the rear bumper of the second dominated by a Just Married banner and a train of empty cans. A second accident photo hung next to the first, this one depicting a body beneath a sheet that was soaked through with blood on one side. A single hand hung free and visible, white lace stopping at the wrist, diamond wedding ring glinting in the sunlight. Margaret stared at this one a long time. Was it real? Was it staged?

"I don't get it," one of the girls said. "It's creepy, sure, but what's the gag?"

"And what does this have to do with *The Addams Family*?" Margaret said.

"I don't know," Harry said.

One of the girls pointed at the lump on the bed. "What's that?"

"Go see," said the other.

"No way."

They argued for another moment before the taller, broader of the two boys volunteered to investigate. The smaller boy followed, a step or two behind, his torso bent away from the bottom half of his body as though restrained by its own good sense.

The tall boy stood over the lump on the bed, his back to the room. He shook the stiffness from his hands and reached for the covers. Margaret licked dry lips, thought of the shape watching her through Pierce's car window. She reached for Harry and his hand caught hers.

The tall boy took hold of the covers and yanked them off. His friend shouted, the girls shrieked, and Margaret took a step toward the door.

The tall boy stood unmoving, blanket in hand, gazing down. Margaret still couldn't see what he was looking at.

"What is it?" Harry said. He let go of Margaret and stepped forward for a better look. The tall boy dropped the blanket and picked the lump up off the bed. He turned around and held it so everyone could see that it was a pillow with a childish drawing of Dracula on it. The girls laughed, and Harry returned to Margaret's side.

"This place is officially the pits," he said. "Want to leave?"

"Yes, please," she said.

They exited the room, leaving the teenagers alone. When they returned to the potted plant on the second-floor landing, though, they found the way down blocked by a sliding metal gate.

"I didn't notice that on the way up," Harry said. He tugged on it. It rattled a little, but didn't budge.

"Now what?" Margaret said.

"Let me see," Harry said. He began fiddling with the gate. Margaret looked back toward the pink room and realized the house had grown quiet again. What were the kids doing in there?

She strained to hear, listened for the telltale noises of necking. She concentrated so hard on her eavesdropping that she didn't notice the potted plant moving until it had her in its grasp.

She screamed. In her terror, she twisted back and forth, trying to tear free, and the plant, perhaps surprised by her alarm, let her go all at once. She pitched forward into Harry, and he crashed into the gate. They both bounced off and hit the hardwood floor.

Margaret shoved herself up off Harry, tried to stand, tangled her legs in his, and went down again. Her head smacked against the floor, and pain flashed white behind her eyelids. She blinked a few times, trying to focus, aware in some distant way of her body moving through space, hands on her arms pulling her to her feet.

"C'mon," Harry said. His hand closed over hers and he dragged her to a newly opened door at the end of the hall, away from the pink room, the plant, the stairs, and the gate. This room was bare, lit by a single bulb, and had a black hole where the window ought to have been.

Harry let her go, walked to the black hole, and looked inside. He looked back at her, mouth open, eyes suddenly far away and blank. Before Margaret could ask what was wrong, a figure stepped into the doorway behind them and stopped any further intelligent thought. Tall and hunched, wrapped in a crimson cloak, the figure had a long, furry face and a snoutful of giant fangs. Instead of hands it had paws with long, curved claws. Its eyes glowed a bright orange. The creature pointed at Margaret with one talon and bellowed an inhuman, animal noise.

Margaret shrieked. Harry grabbed and lifted her, and when she looked into his eyes, he appeared present again. He smiled and said, "Trust me," as he tossed her into the black hole.

She hit black plastic and sped down through the dark, her body squeaking against the texture of the slide. She heard something behind her, rushing up fast, big and noisy and impossible to see. As she turned her head to try to catch a glimpse, to see if it was Harry or the beast in red, the slide ended and she hurtled out into the crisp, clear night air. She hung there, weightless for a moment, before she landed with a *whump* on something big and soft.

She lay on a giant pillowy mat in what appeared to be the backyard of the house. There was a teenager out here, too, shouting at her. Her heart pounding, her head still clearing, it took her a moment to understand what he was saying: *Move out of the way*. So she was still horizontal on the mat when the slide ejected Harry, and he landed right on top of her.

In that moment in 1968, as they lay missionary style outside Spooky House, my mother looked into Harry's face and felt a comfortable life with Pierce disintegrating. In its place, she saw a different, harder span of years stretch out before her: a small, anxious wedding, too many children, life in a blue-collar neighborhood, aggressive penny-pinching, hand-me-down clothes, thrift-store shopping. She felt powerless and unwilling to stop it from becoming a reality.

She didn't tell my father any of this. Instead, she put her hands on his face and said, "My mother's going to hate you."

The Turner Sequence I: Margaret

When Margaret enters the fluid waking dream of the City,
that mix of memory and nightmare, she thinks she's in
the tiny apartment she shared with Harry in the poorer
part of Lubbock—that shabby one-bedroom affair with ratty
carpet and wood-paneled walls, although you can hardly
see the walls behind the stacks of boxes that line the
room—boxes full of Harry's paperbacks and comic books
and pulp magazines.

Harry's things are everywhere. The kitchenette table
is buried beneath his typewriter and stacks of school
papers and doodles of metropolitan skylines she never
recognizes. He always promises to clean up the mess, but
never seems to get around to it. It's a stressful way to
live, tiptoeing around someone else's belongings, never
truly comfortable in your own home.

Thump.

The sound seems to come from the bedroom, and Margaret
leaves the overfull living room to investigate. When she
opens the bedroom door and passes through, she finds
herself in bed. Harry is asleep beside her, his mouth
slightly open. He wears her sleep mask so she can leave
the light on to read. The mask is lavender and fringed
with frilly lace, but Harry never complains about using
it, and Margaret loves him for that.

Thump.

This time it seems to come from somewhere inside the
room, but she can't tell where. *Thump. Thump-thump.* As
though the room itself is inside the sound. She sets the

Part Two

The Tomb

By the summer of 1982, Margaret and Harry Turner had been married for thirteen years. In their mid-thirties, both were softer of face and body, not fat yet but beginning to widen and buy new clothes in bigger, more forgiving sizes. They lived in a brick house in a good neighborhood in Vandergriff, Texas, with their two daughters: Eunice, newly six, and Sydney, age ten (I wouldn't arrive on the scene for almost a year). Harry worked for the Fort Worth highway department, and Margaret had been a homemaker since dropping out of Tilden and marrying Harry in the spring of 1969. Things weren't exciting, but everyone seemed more or less content—until the morning Margaret woke up from an uneasy pink dream and found Harry's side of the bed empty.

It was a thumping sound that woke her. Foggy-headed and confused, Margaret sat up on one elbow and looked around the dark bedroom. According to her bedside alarm clock, it was 4:00 a.m. The bedroom door, usually left shut at night, stood open. She got up, put on her slippers, walked down the hall past the girls' bedrooms, both still quiet, and into the living room, where she found the sliding glass door to the backyard wide open.

Harry stood in the unmown grass, barefoot and naked and unmoving, his back to Margaret.

"Harry?" she called.

He gave no indication of having heard. She crossed the yard to stand next to him. His eyelids drooped, half-closed, and he stared with empty eyes at the wooden fence marking the border of the yard.

"Harry," she said again.

He grunted. Was he still asleep? He'd never sleepwalked before, although the expression on his face looked somehow familiar. She put a hand on his arm.

"It's seen me," he said. "It has my scent." The words came clear but uninflected and gave Margaret the creeps.

"Why don't we go inside?" she said.

"A labyrinth," he said.

She pulled on his arm, and he didn't resist as she guided him back to their bedroom. "It's too early to be up on a Saturday," she said, and pushed him gently down onto the bed. "We should sleep in, right?"

"I have a headache," he said in that same flat, dead way.

"Sleep some more and see if that doesn't help."

He closed his eyes and lay still. Margaret got into bed next to him, but although he was softly snoring a few minutes later, she was fully awake. She got up, made a pot of coffee, and started getting ready for the day.

Not long after, my sisters woke to the sounds and smells of Margaret in the kitchen: Sydney, who had my father's dark, almost black hair, small mouth, pale complexion, and heavy-lidded brown eyes; Eunice, with my mother's red hair, green eyes, and ruddy (almost blotchy) skin. Sydney, brash and stubborn, frequently angry. Eunice, docile and easy to manage. Sisters you wouldn't mark as sisters if you didn't know, both awake now, wolfing down breakfast and helping Margaret run through a checklist for Eunice's sixth birthday party.

Harry woke for the second time around eight. He showered, dressed, poured himself a cup of coffee, finished it in a few quick gulps, then announced that he was off to pick up the birthday cake. He didn't kiss Margaret goodbye when he left. She and the girls stood in the kitchen and listened to the car start and back out of the driveway.

"Is Daddy okay?" Eunice said.

"He's sad it's your stupid birthday," Sydney said.

"Apologize," Margaret said.

"I'm sorry Daddy doesn't like you, Eunice."

"Sydney," Margaret said, warning in her voice.

"I'm only joking," Sydney said. It was the closest to an apology she would offer, but it seemed to satisfy Eunice, so Margaret let it go.

2

Margaret would never have described Eunice as popular, but the party had a good turnout anyway. Mr. and Mrs. Henson from down the street brought their daughter, Krissy, and Mr. and Mrs. Sangalli came with their small, asthmatic son, Hubert. A couple of Harry's work friends, Rick and Tim, brought their kids, and Sydney had invited a few friends as well. The older girls hid out in Sydney's bedroom to avoid what Sydney kindly referred to as a "baby party," but they all brought gifts and made sure to say hello and happy birthday to Eunice before vanishing.

To Margaret's surprise, the childless couple from next door showed up as well. Daniel and Janet Ransom had moved in a few weeks ago, and Margaret had invited them out of politeness. Daniel was the new drama teacher at the high school, and Janet taught ballet at a studio in town.

"It's so nice of you to come," Margaret said to them, when she had a moment. "I didn't imagine you'd have much interest."

"We won't always be childless," Janet said. "We thought it might be good to get the lay of the land, you know?" She was small and fine-boned like a bird and slender like a boy, her brown hair a tight bun at the back of her head. She looked the way Margaret had always imagined Kitty from *Anna Karenina*: a beautiful, delicate porcelain figurine. Margaret had never been skinny like this, and now, wider and heavier than ever before, she felt awkward and ugly next to Janet and her handsome husband.

"Don't believe her," Daniel said. "She's on the hunt for future clients."

Margaret laughed. Janet looked embarrassed.

"I do have a few pamphlets for the studio, if you think Sydney or Eunice would be interested," she said. She gave Daniel an ugly look.

He rubbed the back of his neck. "You sure have a lot of horror books," he said, and gestured to the shelf against the near wall, stocked with Stephen King, Angela Carter, Peter Straub, Shirley Jackson, William Peter Blatty, Ira Levin, James Herbert, Ramsey Campbell, Thomas Tryon, and, of course, H. P. Lovecraft.

"You should see what we have in storage," Margaret said. They kept a unit at the U-Haul downtown full of boxes of old paperbacks, pulp magazines, and comic books. Harry had been loath to physically part with his beloved collection but agreed that they didn't have space for the time being.

"So, Margaret, what do you do?" Janet said.

"I'm a stay-at-home mom," Margaret said. "But now that the girls are getting older, I'm thinking about going back to school." She'd been talking about reenrolling since 1969 but had never seemed to get around to it.

"I don't know if I could handle being home with kids all day," Janet said. "I think I'd want to kill myself."

"Believe me, there are days," Margaret said.

It sounded less like a joke than she'd intended, and, when no one laughed, she excused herself to make the rounds. The other adults leaned on kitchen counters and sat at the dining room table, sipping from plastic cups, and pulling pizza from a stack of Domino's boxes. The kids were all outside in the punishing August heat, playing in and around the rented bounce house in the yard. Harry sat outside, too, with Rick and Tim, ostensibly preventing any life-threatening mischief.

Margaret paused at the glass door to look at Harry. He stared into the middle distance now, as Rick and Tim laughed on either side of him. His beer bottle dangled between the fingertips of his right hand. He'd remained withdrawn and silent even after he returned with the cake. Did he remember the sleepwalking? Was he feeling all right? This version of Harry was so unlike the man she was used to.

He got up from the chair and started toward the glass door. Margaret waved to him and gave him a sympathetic smile. He seemed to stare straight through her. His movements were stiff and somewhat jerky, like he was sore from some great labor.

At that same moment, Eunice bounded out of the bounce house, wearing the smile of every overwhelmed, happy birthday child, red hair flying behind her like a wave of summer flame. Harry didn't see or hear her, and so when she threw herself onto his back, he had no chance to prepare. Margaret reached for the door handle as Harry lurched forward and dropped his beer. The bottle burst against the concrete patio, a little nova of green glass and foam.

Eunice let go of him and dropped to the pavement as Harry righted himself. He rounded on her and grabbed her shoulders.

"What the fuck is wrong with you?" His shout was muffled but still loud through the door.

Tim, the bigger of Harry's work friends, pulled a startled Eunice away. Rick grabbed Harry's arm and started to speak in the low, calm voice of a man who's had to break up a good many drunken fistfights. Harry jerked away and punched Rick square in the nose. Rick's hands flew to his face and he stepped into the broken glass, grinding it under his sneakers.

Margaret's body finally unlocked. She yanked the door open, ran outside, and put herself between Rick and Harry. For an instant she thought she'd made the worst mistake of her life. Harry's eyes were wild, panicked, and furious.

She put up both hands, murmuring, "Hey. Hey. You're okay. You're okay."

Harry licked his lips and rocked on his feet, breathing hard, fists clenched. Sweat rolled between Margaret's shoulders and gathered near the base of her spine. Her flesh itched in the muggy air.

"Harry," she said, in her most soothing tone. "It's okay. Everything's fine. You were just startled."

He blinked, and some essential piece clicked back into place. He became Harry again. He looked around, at the bounce house and its frightened inhabitants, at Rick in a patio chair with bloodstained fingers closed over his nose and mouth, at Tim patting a wailing Eunice on the back, and Sydney and her friends, gathered at the sliding glass door like zoo patrons.

Margaret grabbed Harry by the arm and guided him inside for the second time that day, past the girls, down the hall and into the master bedroom.

"Lie down," she said.

"I'm not tired," he said.

"I don't care. You've lost your backyard privileges for today." She slammed the door on her way out.

She made vague excuses about Harry not feeling well and promised an impending doctor visit that would answer their questions, all while guiding guests to the front door. Eunice gaped at the dissolution of her party, and fled to her room, face red and tear-streaked. Sydney sat on the couch, blank-faced, and watched a movie on TV while Margaret swept up the glass on the porch, threw away the paper plates, emptied the plastic cups, and carried all the trash out to the garage. She left the balloons and streamers up, although they looked out of place now, a false front on something ugly.

She sat on the couch with Sydney and put an arm around her shoulders. Sydney remained stiff beside her and wouldn't look away from the TV.

"Leave me alone," she said.

Margaret let her go and got up to check on Eunice. She found her younger daughter in bed, turned toward the wall. She sat down and massaged Eunice's back.

"My party," Eunice said, her voice thick.

"I know, sweetheart. I'm sorry, but Daddy's not feeling well, and I—" She stopped, not sure what to say. "I didn't want Daddy to get anyone else sick if he's contagious. He's taking a nap right now. Why don't you lie down for a little while and then we'll finish your party tonight?"

"What about my bounce house?"

"I don't see why we can't keep it an extra day." She would bully Harry into it if she had to. It was the least he could do. She kissed Eunice on the cheek and then went to the master bedroom.

Harry was still in bed, staring at the ceiling. He rubbed his right hand, the knuckles swollen. Margaret shut the door and leaned back on it.

"I know," he said. "I know."

"*Crazy* barely scratches the surface," Margaret said.

"I don't know what happened."

"You were sleepwalking this morning. Do you remember that?"

She could tell from his startled face that he'd had no idea. They'd been on the lookout for something like this for the entirety of their relationship. Because of his mother, Harry had been tested for schizophrenia multiple times, but had always received a clean bill of health. It was late for symptoms to emerge now, but not impossible. Margaret couldn't shake the image of his face this morning—that dead-eyed, distant expression. Why did it look so familiar?

"Look—I don't think anything else will happen," he said. "It's not—it's not what you're worried about. I don't know what it is, but it's not that. If—*if*—something else does happen, I promise to see a doctor, okay?" When she didn't answer, he said, "Margaret, please. Let me try it my way first."

3

They reconvened in the late afternoon to finish Eunice's birthday party. Harry played with the girls in the bounce house while Margaret warmed up leftover pizza. She and Harry let the girls have their pizza and cake at the same time, with generous scoops of ice cream on the side. After dinner, they unleashed Eunice on the pile of gifts on the coffee table, and she tore into the shiny wrapping paper in a wide-eyed sugar rush. They sat in the living room, surrounded by new toys, games, and clothes, and watched a movie on TV. Margaret lay on the couch and Harry lay on the floor, the girls nestled into him on either side. From time to time, Margaret ran a hand through his hair, savoring the way it curled between her fingers.

That night, after the girls went to bed happy and relieved, Harry and Margaret made love. The walls in the house were thin, so they had to move slowly and keep quiet. It gave Margaret time to study Harry's face, to see the bedrock of gentleness and kindness reassert itself. His soft kisses seemed to insist that the afternoon had been a fluke, that everything was fine. And afterward, as they lay next to each other, sweaty and slick, he said the old words:

"I love you until the end of time, and whatever comes after that."

It was a bit of doggerel he'd coined on their wedding night, such a dramatic proclamation that Margaret had laughed in his face. It had since become shorthand between them, part of the internal language of marriage, a phrase both ironic and sincere, something uttered with a roll of the eyes and a thump of the heart.

"And whatever comes after that," she agreed, and laid her head on his chest.

4

In the weeks following the party, Harry covered the insurance copay to get Rick's nose fixed, signed Sydney up for ballet lessons at Janet Ransom's studio, and bought Eunice a Commodore 64 computer and a stack of floppy disks to go with it.

Margaret feigned excitement and chimed in with the girls' delight when Harry delivered these gifts, but as soon as she and Harry were alone, getting ready for bed, she said, "I know you feel bad, and paying Rick's medical bills is the stand-up thing to do, but I wish you hadn't spent so much money on frivolous things for the girls."

Harry looked at her over his copy of *The Dead Zone*. "This is the kind of thing the girls will remember in twenty to thirty years. This is the stuff that *makes* a childhood."

"That computer was almost six hundred dollars," she said, rubbing moisturizer into her hands. "That's not even taking into account all the games you bought."

He dropped the book on his chest. "What do you want me to do? March into Eunice's room and take the computer away?"

"Please, no more big purchases. We still have Christmas to pay for."

She watched him work himself down from fury to calm. When

had he gotten so angry? What was he so angry about? "You're right. I should have talked to you about these things first."

But the next day, he was an hour late getting home from work, and when Margaret met him in the garage, she found the back of his station wagon full of lumber and bags from the hardware store.

"What the hell is this?" she said.

"I'm building a haunted house for Halloween," he said.

Although Halloween was Harry's favorite holiday, and he always celebrated with the girls, as far as Margaret knew, he'd never gone to another haunted house since their trip to Spooky House in 1968. To say Margaret was surprised by the proclamation would be an understatement.

"We agreed," she said.

"This is awesome," Sydney said. She pushed past Margaret into the garage, opened the back of the car, and began to unload it.

"Sydney, stop it," Margaret said. "Daddy's taking all of this back to the store."

Sydney stopped halfway between the car and the door into the house, a plastic bag in her arms. She looked at Harry.

"I'm not taking it back to the store, sweetheart," he said to Sydney. "It's okay."

"Girls, go to your rooms," Margaret said.

They ducked their heads and hurried out of the garage.

Margaret pointed at the lumber in the station wagon. "We agreed, no more big purchases," she said.

After a moment, he extended his hand. "Come outside with me."

She let him lead her through the house and into the yard. The grass poked at her bare ankles as they walked. He stopped in the center and turned a slow circle, pulling her around in his orbit.

"What do you see?" he said.

"It's time for you to mow," she said.

"I keep waiting for fall to start and kill the grass, but it keeps not happening."

The knot of frustration in her chest loosened a little. "You're the one who wanted to move to Texas."

"No, Texas is where I found the job," he said. "But tell me—what else do you see?"

She closed her eyes, took a deep breath, and reopened them. She studied the yard, a large, flat, slightly sloping square of grassy earth, bounded on three sides by a tall wooden fence. A small concrete patio sat right outside the back door, with the grill, a table, and a few plastic chairs arranged on it. A water hose lay coiled in the grass, still attached to the faucet protruding from the brick wall of the house. She realized that she and Harry were standing exactly where she'd found him sleepwalking a couple of weeks ago.

She didn't say this to Harry. Instead, she said, "I see an average yard."

"I get it," he said. "That's how I felt until the day of Eunice's party. But then, sitting on the porch, staring at the bounce house, something flipped in my head, and I saw all of this as the foundation of something else. Something grand. And now I can't get it out of my head." He touched his temple and winced. "It's like this dull ache that never goes away."

"Is that why you lost your mind and started screaming and hitting people?"

"I'm not sure." He dropped his hand and frowned. "But whether it is or not, I have to admit that something's missing. It's nothing to do with you, or the girls," he hastened to add, and reached for her hand again. The gesture felt perfunctory, automatic. "No, it's like—I get up every day, put on the shirt and tie, go fight through traffic to an office where I spend most of my waking hours, and then I come home too exhausted to do anything but watch TV for a little while and fall asleep. And sometimes I think that, best-case scenario, this is all I have to look forward to until I retire, when I'll be too old and broken to do anything but waste the last few years of my existence in front of the TV and waiting for the mail and hoping for a call or visit from one of my grown children. And then I'll die, and that's that."

"Some people would consider that a pretty successful life," Margaret said.

"Would you?"

She almost lied and told him yes, it would be a great life, and he should shut up about it. But most of the anger had ebbed off, and that cold sensation in her middle was too powerful to ignore.

"You know me better than that. I had a chance at a safe, 'successful' life, and I chose you. I wanted the adventure."

"You're smarter than me," he said. "I saved so much money for school, but then I majored in engineering. I wanted to prove that I could take care of you, that we wouldn't be poor. I should have been brave, like you."

A haunted house. Margaret associated haunted houses with that wolflike creature she'd seen right at the end of Spooky House—the one with orange eyes and a red cloak, that had pointed at her as though singling her out, right before Harry tossed her down the slide. The creature she'd seen outside Pierce Lombard's car window right before she hallucinated a plague of bugs bursting from his forehead. She'd never discussed either of these things with Harry. Nor had she ever told him about the dreams of howling and wolves and strange babies. Now didn't seem the time to bring those things up.

"So tell me," she said, strengthening her grip on his hand. "How does building a haunted house in the yard change anything?"

"I'm not sure," he said. "But it feels important. Like if I do it, I'll understand the next thing."

She turned his face toward her. "I'll make you a deal. You want to build something and be irresponsible. I want something in return."

"What's that?"

"I'm not happy, either," she said. She took a deep breath and then said what had been rankling her since her first conversation with Janet Ransom. "I want to finish my degree. I can't do that unless we don't have to worry about money. That means you have to have a job, Harry, even if it's one you hate. So here's the deal: you can build this thing, but you have to keep putting on the tie and fighting through traffic until I graduate and find a job. Can you do that?"

Something flickered across his face, difficult to read in the failing light. "I think so," he said, and she suddenly realized why his sleep-walking face had looked so familiar. It was the exact same face he'd made at Spooky House, the night Margaret had seen the thing in the red cloak. The expression that seemed to indicate a complete vacancy behind the eyes.

5

She let Harry retrieve the girls and give them the news in the living room while she warmed up his meat loaf in the kitchen.

"You're going to build a whole *house?*" Eunice said.

"It won't be a whole house, dummy," Sydney said. "Just like the bounce house for your birthday wasn't a whole house."

"Sydney, don't call your sister names," Margaret said.

"She's rude, but she's right," Harry said to Eunice. "It's only a name. I'll build everything in the garage and we'll put it together in the backyard."

"So it will be more like a haunted yard," Eunice said.

"Technically, yes," Harry said. "But if we do it right, people will forget it's our yard while they're inside it. They'll think they're actually seeing monsters and ghosts."

"Why would we want to scare people?" Eunice said.

"Because it's fun to be scared sometimes," Harry said. "And I think we'll be good at it. I'll do most of the design and construction myself, but you can both design a room of your own and I'll build it."

"I can make up whatever I want and you'll build it?" Sydney said.

"Within reason," Harry said.

"I can make the costumes," Margaret said, surprising herself. She hadn't meant to volunteer, but now found herself wrestling with the central problem of her adult life. She'd never wanted children. Harry had. She'd hoped that the arrival of her first baby would somehow transform her into a natural mother, the sort of woman who glowed with pride over her brood. Instead, both Sydney's and Eunice's births had left her cold. She did her duty, nursed, played, sang, read to, and fed, but she never felt the deep wellspring of fierce love for her children that she felt for Harry. It would have been comforting to think that maybe all parents felt this way, that it actually took years to fall in love with your children, but Harry had cried when each girl was born, and seemed genuinely excited to see them every day after work. He didn't seem to mind the erosion of his personal time and space, and Margaret thought the girls somehow instinctively understood the difference between his heart and her own. She always felt at a disadvantage with them, eager to demonstrate an appropriate level of love.

"Are you sure?" Harry said. He looked surprised and grateful.

"Yes," Margaret said.

For the rest of the evening, they all sat around the kitchen table and drew up plans on graph paper.

My father the engineer was an obsessive collector and fastidious record keeper, so most of these designs survive. I keep them in a notebook in my desk, along with my sisters' drawings of their own ideas: a room full of doll heads, a room where a mummy could chase you around, and, my favorite, a room that looks ordinary, like maybe you've come to the end of the haunted house, but then the lights turn out and disembodied voices begin to whisper ugly truths. Eunice's notes on this drawing call it "The Bad Secrets Room."

At the end of the evening, Harry took all of these disparate ideas and laid them out on the kitchen table. He rubbed his chin and frowned.

"Right now we have a bunch of random scary things," he said. "What we need to do is pick one big scary idea, and let all the little scares come from that big thing. I think," he said, tapping his eraser against his papers, "I think we should do a cemetery. We can make fake grave markers and a pointy black fence for the front of the house, and then, in the backyard, we'll build a tomb. Each room can be a different kind of tomb or crypt. Maybe we do an Egyptian tomb with a mummy, and another could be like one of those aboveground burial places in Louisiana."

"Why do they bury people aboveground in Louisiana?" Sydney said.

"Because Louisiana is one big swamp," Eunice said. "When they try to bury people underground, the bodies wash up out of the earth. They won't stay down."

Both Margaret and Harry looked at Eunice in surprise. She appeared startled by the sudden attention.

"Is that true?" Sydney said.

"Yes," Harry said. He remained focused on Eunice. "How did you know that?"

She cast a guilty glance at the bookcase in the living room, then stared at the table. "I don't remember."

6

Life rolled on. Harry went to work in the mornings, and Margaret sent off for an application packet for the University of Texas at Vandergriff. In the evenings, Harry turned his pile of lumber into modular walls, ceilings, and floors. Sydney kept him company in the garage, wearing child-size safety goggles and doing her homework while he measured and cut.

Sydney started ballet lessons, and Janet Ransom said she was a natural. Whenever Margaret caught Sydney moving through the five positions in front of her bedroom mirror, she noticed an expression of fierce concentration on her face, a sort of ecstatic agitation. She seemed driven to perfect the poses, to execute them with grace. Eunice took to her new computer with a similar fervor. She retreated to her room every day after school, parked herself in front of the bulky brown keyboard, and didn't move unless ordered to do so. Harry had made good choices with his gifts. Margaret would never have thought to do either of these things herself. It stung to realize that even though he spent the workweek away from his daughters, he still somehow intuited their needs and desires better than she could.

As far as his own needs, Harry ran out of lumber before he finished the basic skeleton of the Tomb and took to trolling the neighborhood after work, for unattended construction sites, for homeowners tearing down fences. He accumulated so much wood that he ran out of room in the garage and had to leave a large pile under a tarp beside the

gouges ran through the brick to the right of the window, and the left side of the screen frame had been bent outward by at least an inch.

She grabbed hold of the window frame to steady herself, turned her head, and vomited into the grass. Her fingertips scraped against the unyielding brick as her body convulsed and her chest burned.

7

When Harry got home from work, she made him climb up and look for himself. He ran his fingers over the brick, touched the window, and glowered.

"You see it, right?" she said from her spot on the ground.

He climbed down. "I see some imperfections in the brick, and the screen is out of joint, but neither necessarily means anything. Every brick has little flaws, right? That one could have been like that when they built this place. And the screen could be normal wear and tear. I don't know. I haven't kept up with maintenance out here like I should."

"So you're saying—"

"I'm saying I don't see any reason to panic." He folded the stool to carry it back inside.

"I know how it sounds," she said, following him across the patio. "But after what Eunice saw last night, don't you think—"

Harry pitched the stool against the house and turned around so fast that Margaret took a step back.

"Jesus Christ," he said. "Will you fucking drop it?"

She took another step back.

"Do you have to *invent* new problems for me to solve?" he said. "Are you that bored?"

"Are you out of your mind?" she said. "In what world is this a made-up problem? Eunice saw something, and the window looks weird. I don't think that makes me hysterical."

He closed his eyes and rubbed his temples. "No, you're right," he said, the fight going out of his voice. "But I didn't find anything else last night, so unless something flew in, I don't know how there could possibly have been anyone out there. Eunice is a kid. We can't let her nightmares dictate our waking hours." He picked up the stool and carried it inside.

Instead of following him, Margaret sat down on a patio chair. It was the first time he'd ever raised his voice to her without apologizing. How could he say he saw nothing wrong with the window? Was he crazy? Was she?

8

Even working every weeknight from dinner until bedtime and all day on weekends, Harry continued to fall behind on the Tomb. In the first week of October, he started working late into the night and sleeping on the couch when he slept at all. He made papier-mâché masks, built rubbery monsters, painted the modular walls, and argued with the girls about their room ideas until they settled on an orphanage tomb for Eunice, and a vampire ballerina tomb for Sydney.

He brought home cans of spray webbing, little packages of toy bugs and plastic vampire teeth. The accoutrements of Halloween accumulated in the garage and spilled over into the kitchen, where Margaret had set up her sewing machine at the table. She'd never done much sewing before—her mother had taught her how, but had also given Margaret the impression that it was "low" work, that Margaret ought to find herself sewing only in an emergency (i.e., a torn shirt while on vacation, or extreme poverty). Margaret was surprised and delighted to discover a real knack for it, her first few costumes coming out as well as or better than the patterns from the fabric store.

"Wow," Harry said, when she showed him the artfully ragged white suit with long coattails that she'd made for him. The fabric, though new, somehow conveyed over a hundred years of decomposition, and the stitching was just crooked enough to unsettle the eye. "You could do this for a living."

She couldn't quite enjoy the praise. She was throwing up almost every morning now. She'd done the math: she was two weeks late. She sewed and put off thinking about the issue.

Harry began outdoor construction. He turned his modular walls into a labyrinth of rooms and corridors in the yard. He worked past sundown every night, duct-taping two flashlights to a hard hat so he could see as he hammered and drilled. When his work stretched past eight, then nine, the neighbors began to complain. Instead of changing his work habits, Harry recruited them to help build, cast them as characters, or, in Janet Ransom's case, brought her in as a "movement consultant" for the actors. He flattered his new coconspirators about their heretofore unsuspected talents, and they were suddenly okay with (perhaps even excited about) the construction noise.

In addition to the work in the yard, Harry started to build a flat platform atop the peaked roof of the house to make space for a beacon.

"I want the whole neighborhood—the whole city—to see it and show up on Halloween," he said.

As Margaret fell asleep at night, she heard his voice muffled above, and footsteps stalking back and forth over her head, an impatient guest waiting to be invited inside.

9

Two weeks before Halloween, Harry took a day off and drove the family out to Tyler to visit his mother, Deborah, for her birthday. The drive took most of the morning—a distance Deborah Turner had objected to when Harry and Margaret had first proposed moving her to Weirwood Home.

"You'll never come visit," she'd said. "It's too far away."

She hadn't been wrong. Margaret and Harry were lucky to make it out every couple of months, but Weirwood was the nicest long-term mental health care community in Texas. It had spacious single-resident quarters; lush, well-manicured grounds; an activity-heavy schedule;

and staff to help with things like money management and health and fitness.

Margaret had also been hesitant to put Deborah in Weirwood. When she and Harry first moved to Texas, Margaret had suggested that Deborah come live with them.

"Isn't that the more loving solution?" she'd said.

Harry had put both hands around his coffee mug and stared at the dregs. It took him a long time to answer. "It's kind of you to offer, but it wouldn't be the way you think. I think you—" He broke off and scratched his chin. He tapped the pamphlet for Weirwood on the kitchen table before him. "Trust me, this is for the best."

Deborah had taken to the place right away. She made friends, decorated her apartment, got really into knitting. She seemed content when Harry, Margaret, and the girls came to visit, her only complaints being about how much the girls grew in the intervals between.

"Oh no!" she'd say, as she cupped their faces. "Stop it right this instant!"

This visit started no differently, with the ritual embraces and exclamations, followed by barbecue and cake at a picnic table on the lawn. After lunch, Harry and the girls ran around with one of the home's resident dogs, a golden retriever named Daisy. They threw a tennis ball to each other and Daisy ran between them, trying to snatch it out of the air. Margaret and Deborah sat at the table and watched, drinking soda. Margaret cast surreptitious glances at Deborah until the older woman said, "What's on your mind, sweetheart?"

"What?" Margaret said, startled.

"I'm old but not stupid," Deborah said. "Or blind. Something's been bothering you since you got here."

Margaret had to force herself to say the words. Saying it out loud somehow conjured it into being, made it real.

"When did you first know," she said, "that you were—that you weren't well?"

Deborah turned to face her. "Is there something wrong with Harry? Or the girls?"

"The girls are fine, I think," Margaret said. "But Harry's been . . . strange, lately."

"I started having bad days in high school," Deborah said. "Some days the lights were too bright, and sounds were too loud. It was like being hungover, but without the drinking. Sometimes I would stay up for a week, and then sleep for three or four days straight. I couldn't make or keep friends. I had crazy mood swings. I felt nothing at all on my wedding day, and got the giggles at my husband's funeral. Sometimes when I spoke to other people, they told me I wasn't making any sense. When Bill was alive, he helped me manage and hide it. After he was drafted, when it was only me and Harry, it got a lot tougher. I started to feel like people at the supermarket were all staring and talking about me. Reading the ingredients on a can of soup, or looking at the bottom of my coffee mug, I saw hidden messages." She took a sip of her drink. "I kept a scrapbook—food labels, newspaper clippings, a bunch of memos from the office where I worked. I was so *sure* someone was trying to tell me something, if I could only figure it out. And then, one night the police picked me up on the shoulder of the highway, ten miles from home, barefoot in my nightgown with no idea how I got there. Harry had woken up alone in the house and made the call. I must have been sleepwalking. Who knows what might have happened otherwise? You probably know the rest. Hospitals, medication, Harry living with his aunt and uncle for a while."

"Harry never told me any of that," Margaret said.

"I'm not surprised. It was a bad time for both of us," Deborah said. "No child should have to deal with a mentally ill parent on his own." She blinked at her lap, and Margaret took her hand. She couldn't make herself say anything about Harry's recent behavior now. Whatever came next, Margaret would bear alone.

Instead, she asked, "You don't feel like you're getting secret messages anymore?"

Deborah gave her a tight, humorless smirk. "No."

"What did you think you were supposed to do? Back when you were still getting them."

The older woman considered for a moment. "Nothing that made any sense. That's why they call it crazy."

IO

They left for Vandergriff around five. The girls napped in the back while Margaret and Harry listened to the radio up front. Margaret thought about her conversation with Deborah, turning the older woman's answers over and over in her mind. She was so preoccupied that she took little notice of Harry frowning and rubbing his temples, sucking air through clenched teeth. Then, about ninety minutes from home, he gasped, swerved onto the shoulder of the road, and slammed the car into park so abruptly that Margaret jerked forward against her seat belt.

"What's——" she started to say. Harry's arms flew up off the wheel. One banged against his window and the other struck Margaret on the side of the head. She rocked to her right, more startled than hurt, as the girls woke and began to shout. His legs twitched and his feet stamped the pedals, revving the engine. Little gurgling sounds came from the back of his throat. He sounded like he was drowning. He arched his back, head banging against the headrest.

Seizure. Her mind grasped the word, held on to it like a life preserver. What should she do? In movies people always put something in the person's mouth—like a wooden spoon—to keep them from biting through their tongue. Where was she supposed to find a spoon? Fuck. Fuck. Fuck. The girls were shrieking now, and it made everything so much worse.

"Shut up!" she shouted at them. "Shut up so I can think."

Harry's body went limp and he slumped forward, chin to chest, eyes closed. The girls fell silent. Tears ran down Sydney's face, each breath rattling with snot. Eunice was dry-eyed but pale. Harry took shallow breaths through an open mouth. He wiped at his face with the back of one sleeve. Margaret realized she had one hand to her chest and the other hovered over Harry's shoulder. She let it drop there.

He opened his eyes, took a shaky breath, and looked at Margaret. "Where are we?" he said.

11

Margaret drove the rest of the way home. She dropped Eunice and Sydney with the Ransoms, and then took Harry to the emergency room at Vandergriff Memorial. They sat for hours in the crowded waiting room before being led back to an exam room. It was 3:00 a.m. by the time a doctor poked her head in and promised to be with them as soon as possible.

"Go pick up the girls and get some rest," Harry said. "I'll call you when it's time to come for me."

She didn't want to admit it, but she was happy to leave him there. She needed space. She kissed him on the forehead, her lips dry, his brow salty, and left to retrieve the girls. She brought them home, reassured them with bland promises, put them to bed, and set an early morning alarm so she could call the school and keep the girls home.

She couldn't sleep. She hunted for something to watch on TV, but found nothing. Against her better judgment, she took an anthology called *Great American Horror Stories* from Harry's bookshelf. Glancing through the table of contents, she found a title she recognized too well: "The Hound" by H. P. Lovecraft. She knew she should put the book back on the shelf, but she couldn't stop herself from reading the story again for the first time since 1968. This time, one passage in particular struck her:

Our lonely house was seemingly alive with the presence of some malign being whose nature we could not guess, and every night that daemoniac baying rolled over the windswept moor, always louder and louder. On October 29 we found in the soft earth underneath the library window a series of footprints utterly impossible to describe.

"You have to help Daddy."

She started, jerked out of the story, and dropped the book into her lap. Sydney stood in front of her. Margaret hadn't even felt her enter the room.

"You shouldn't sneak up on people," Margaret said. "And I am helping him. We all are. He's with the doctors, and the best thing we can do for him right now is rest, so that when he comes home we can take care of him."

Sydney gave Margaret a businesslike, unsympathetic look, more annoyed supervisor than child. "That's not what I mean."

"Tell me what you mean, then."

She scowled, some complicated thing working itself out on her face. "Why don't you love him anymore?"

"You're ten years old, Sydney. You don't even know what love means."

"This is bullshit." Sydney stormed out of the room. Margaret was too surprised to retaliate. She accepted her daughter's curse and pondered it. The living room felt tiny, pressed close on all sides. Her stomach cramped and she pressed her hands to it, wincing, before picking up the book and finishing the Lovecraft story. During her first reading, she'd rolled her eyes at the hysterical melodrama, but this time, the final sentences stuck to her mind and wouldn't shake loose:

Madness rides the star-wind . . . claws and teeth sharpened on centuries of corpses . . . dripping death astride a Bacchanale of bats from night-black ruins of buried temples of Belial. . . . Now, as the baying of that dead, fleshless monstrosity grows louder and louder, and the stealthy whirring and flapping of those accursed web-wings circles closer and closer, I shall seek with my revolver the oblivion which is my only refuge from the unnamed and unnamable.

"Where are you?" she hissed into the silence of the house. "What do you want?"

12

The hospital kept Harry until nearly dinnertime the next day. When Margaret and the girls retrieved him, he was waiting for them at the dropoff/pickup curb, looking bone tired but otherwise fine. He walked to the car and collapsed into the passenger seat with a sigh of relief. He leaned his head against the window and closed his eyes as Margaret started the car.

"So what's the story?" she said.

"No story yet," Harry said. "They want me to see a specialist. Get more tests." He produced a business card from his shirt pocket but stowed it again before she got a good look.

"That's it? They didn't even make a guess?"

Harry shook his head. "They don't want to make any premature diagnoses. It could be any number of things, so it's best to wait until we know more."

It was like being given permission to pretend there was nothing to be concerned about, and if my mother jumped on it a little too eagerly, I can't exactly blame her.

Now several weeks late, she bought a home pregnancy test and took it during the hours she had the house to herself. Here's where I enter the story, still offstage but evident from the color of a vial of water in the Daisy 2 test kit. My mother sat on the side of the tub and put her face in her hands. A baby. What an awful thing to happen.

She rubbed her stomach at the spot where she imagined I floated, subdividing, gaining mass and shape. "I'm sorry, baby," she murmured. I wish I could have responded, could have put my hand on the wall of her womb and reassured her. But I went on happily ignorant in my perfect little world, there but not there with her in her despair.

Nor was I the only problematic new development. Five days before

Halloween, Margaret received a phone call from a Wilma Cabot at the UTV admissions office, who informed her that the check for her application fee had bounced.

A cold stone settled in Margaret's middle. "I'm sure there must be a mistake."

"I'm sure," Wilma said, and her kindness layered more ice over Margaret's insides. "But the fact remains that your application fee has not been paid."

"Is my application dead then?" How could the check not have cleared? The balance in her checkbook sat close to a thousand dollars. The fee was only ten dollars.

"No, ma'am," Wilma said. "If you can get us a valid check or money order before the end of November, we can still process it."

Margaret promised to be by in person with the money in the next couple of days, thanked Wilma, and hung up. She went to the desk where she kept all their financial records and reviewed the last few months. As far as she could tell, nothing was out of place.

Harry was late coming home, and when he arrived around six thirty, he was riding shotgun in Rick's truck as Rick backed into the driveway. When Margaret opened the garage door, she found the two of them unloading a polished silver coffin from the bed.

"What the hell is this?" she said.

"Hi, Margaret," Rick said. He looked sheepish, as though he'd been caught doing something wrong.

"Not now, Rick," she said, and turned her glare back on Harry. "I thought you were going to build a coffin?"

"We're almost out of time," Harry said. "This makes more sense."

"How much did it cost?" Margaret said.

"Nothing," Harry said, but Rick looked at the ground, uncomfortable, and he added, "I got it from the community theater downtown."

"And they just let you take it?"

"For Chrissakes, yes," Harry said. He scratched his neck. Rick went out to the driveway and leaned against the hood of his truck, his back to them. "Okay, it cost a little bit."

"How much?"

"A hundred dollars."

"Harry!"

"What?" he said. "I'm giving it to the high school drama department when we're done. Daniel Ransom's going to help with line control. If he sticks around, he's probably going to be a big part of Sydney's life in a few years. She's going to want to be in plays." He studied her reaction, didn't seem to like what he saw. "What's the big deal?"

"I got a call from UTV today," she said. "My application fee *bounced*."

"It did?" She couldn't tell if his surprise was feigned or genuine.

"We had a deal," she said. "But now our checks aren't clearing and you're spending a small fortune on a single prop to convince our neighbor to spend two or three hours as a ticket taker?"

"Will you calm down? I get paid on Friday. Call the office and ask if you can bring in the check next Monday."

"That's not the point," Margaret said. "I shouldn't have to worry what you're spending behind my back. We're not supposed to be that couple."

Harry ran both hands through his hair. "The money is spent, Margaret. I'm sorry that for all the years I supported you and encouraged you to go back to school, you sat on your ass, stayed home, and did nothing. I'm sorry that after over a decade of waiting on you, I decided to do one fucking thing for myself, and I'm sorry that it happened to coincide with your sudden interest in your education. I've already offered a fix for the problem, so tell me, please, what else you could possibly want from me."

She wanted life the way it had been even six months ago. She wanted to be able to worry about her husband, wanted to feel uncomplicated, unambiguous love, so that no part of her hoped he really was sick, or crazy. She wanted not to worry about the question of whether to bring a baby into this disintegrating family or set it free back into the ether. She wanted all of these things, but couldn't find a way to say any of them.

"Nothing," she said. "I don't want a single thing from you."

13

As a baby, Eunice ran my mother to the edge of sanity with her insomnia, and Mom couldn't get her down for a whole night until she was two years old. Even then, I don't think Eunice slept. She got good at quietly entertaining herself, looking at her books, teaching herself to read by flashlight, and sometimes sneaking into the living room to watch TV after everyone was asleep.

After Dad bought her the Commodore 64, though, she never risked the TV again. For a few weeks she played the games Dad had gotten her, but she quickly tired of the simple, repetitive tasks—matching words to images, solving easy math problems, fighting dragons and spaceships—and started teaching herself to type in the word-processor program. She wrote at night, careful to keep her keystrokes quiet.

Being only six (if an advanced, exceptionally bright six), she hadn't mastered all the niceties of formatting and grammar, so her electronic diary from 1982 has no paragraph indentations or breaks, which makes the whole project difficult to read, but this juvenilia makes an interesting prelude to her later work, an important glimpse into a time I can only ever reach through photographs, journal entries, newspaper articles, and the broken, incomplete memories of the surviving members of our family. I mention all this now to draw your attention to a note Eunice wrote during the week before Halloween:

```
Daddy doesn't feel good. He is sick a lot of the
time but he does not want anyone to know. Mommy
is sad but she pretends that she is not. Mommy and
Daddy are both pretending all the time. Yesterday I
asked Sydney if she thought Daddy was weird now and
she said I am stupid. But I do not know if I can
trust Sydney. Once I asked her who she wanted to
marry and she said she was going to wait until Mommy
dyed and then marry Daddy. So Sydney is pretending
```

because Daddy is pretending and Sydney wants to be
good for Daddy. Today Daddy fell down and shook like
that day in the car. We were in the back yard. Mommy
and Sydney were at the store and I did not know
what to do. It was over fast though and Daddy made
me promise not to tell. So now I am pretending too.
I hope Halloween is over soon so we can all stop
pretending.

This is worth noting for two reasons. First, it's proof that my father was withholding information about his health from my mother. Second, and perhaps more important, it reminds me that Eunice was probably not sleeping at the time she claimed to have seen a man at her window. She would have been wide awake, tapping away in the dark, when she glanced over and saw something watching her.

14

The day after the fight over the coffin, Margaret went to her gynecologist for confirmation: she was indeed pregnant. She tried to take the news stoically, but the doctor provided her with the address and phone number for a Planned Parenthood in Dallas, "Just in case."

When she got home that afternoon, she found Harry in the front yard, putting up a rickety, crooked fence.

"You're home early," she said.

"I took some vacation time," Harry said, not looking up. "Where have you been?"

"Fabric store," she lied. And then, to account for the lack of shopping bags: "I didn't find what I wanted." He didn't press her on this point, but went on working. She dropped her purse inside and then walked to the school to retrieve the girls. When they returned, Harry had finished with the fence and was planting Styrofoam tombstones in the grass. If you've seen a haunted house like this, you know the gag.

The grave markers have funny names on them—Frank N. Stein, Dr. Acula, and so on. But Harry either didn't know or didn't care about proper fake cemetery etiquette. His tombstones all bore the names of people he knew: Daniel Ransom from next door, Rick and Tim from the highway department, himself, Margaret, and, on two little crosses near the front door, Eunice and Sydney. When Eunice spotted the cross with her name on it, she started to cry.

"Why did you do this?" she said.

He stopped in his work. "It's supposed to be a signature, like when you write your name on your homework. I wanted people to know who worked on the Tomb."

"Why do you want me to die?" Eunice said, apparently not processing Harry's explanations.

"I think it's a great idea," Sydney said. "Thank you, Daddy."

Eunice lowered her head and slammed it into Sydney's chest. Sydney landed on her back with a croak, and Eunice jumped on her. She pinned Sydney's arms with her knees and pummeled her with open hands.

"Shut up!" Eunice shouted. "Shut up, shut up, shut up!"

Sydney, bigger and stronger, squirmed her right arm free and punched Eunice on the side of the head. Eunice swayed to one side but kept her balance and continued her barrage of open-handed slaps.

"Harry," Margaret said. "Help me!"

Harry, who had continued to plant his tombstones in neat rows in the grass, finally abandoned the work and walked across the yard, where he swept his backhand across Eunice's face. Eunice tumbled off Sydney and landed on the grass. She lay there, curled into a ball, hands over her head. Sydney stood and ran past Margaret into the house.

"Why the hell did you do that?" Margaret shouted at Harry.

Harry blinked, looked at Eunice, then at Margaret. Something like regret danced at the edge of his expression before he shrugged. "You wanted help," he said.

"Don't you *ever* lay a hand on any of us again," she said. "Or I will kill you myself. Do you understand?"

For a moment she thought he might hit her anyway. He stood,

breathing hard, jaw working, then crossed the lawn, picked up the tombstone where he'd dropped it, and returned to work.

Margaret helped Eunice up and led her inside to examine the damage. She had a busted lip but otherwise appeared okay. Margaret wrapped some ice in a washcloth and pressed it to her face.

"I'm sorry," Eunice said. "I was scared."

"I know, sweetheart." Margaret had never seen Eunice fight anyone before, even in preschool. Lots of firsts today, none of them good.

"I'm scared all the time now," Eunice said.

Margaret looked down the hall toward Sydney's shut bedroom door. She thought she could hear Sydney crying.

"Does Daddy still love us?"

Margaret forced herself to look back at Eunice. "Of course he does."

Eunice wouldn't meet her eye after that. She stared at the table and let the ice melt against her face. Margaret ran a hand over her daughter's limp red hair, and it came to her all at once: she would leave Harry. She'd be smart about it, would make her moves silently—get the abortion, enroll in school, find a job—but she'd be out of this suffocating, awful house as soon as possible, away from the monstrous shade of the man she'd once loved, and on track for a better life.

She massaged the back of Eunice's neck. "I'll fix this," she said. "I'll fix it all. Just hang in a little longer."

15

She called Planned Parenthood the next day while Harry worked in the yard. The first open appointment was November 9, and would cost $150 out of pocket. The woman on the phone told her that she would need someone to drive her home after. Margaret said no problem and hung up.

Afterward, she sat at the kitchen table and crunched numbers. One hundred fifty dollars for the abortion, plus another ten dollars for her UTV application fee. Several hundred for the deposit and first month's rent on a three-bedroom apartment. How was she supposed to come up with that kind of money? She wouldn't call her parents and ask, couldn't let her crone of a mother know that, yes, her marriage was failing, burning down spectacularly, if you wanted to know the truth. She couldn't ask a friend, because she didn't really have any. Hell, she didn't even know who to ask for a ride home from the clinic.

She chewed on the end of her pencil, looked across the kitchen and into the living room, at the bookcase full of horror novels. All of Harry's old magazines and comics were still in a storage unit downtown. Boxes and boxes full of things that must be worth something. Harry would never miss a few items, and, if he did, he'd assume something had been lost in one move or another. She hoped she'd be long gone by then.

She called around to a few comic book shops in the area, asked if they bought old pulp magazines. Most did not, but one store gave her the contact info for a local collector named Jamie White, who agreed to meet her at the storage unit the following afternoon.

The next day, Margaret stole the spare key to the unit from Harry's key ring in the garage and drove to the storage facility, off the highway on the far end of town. When she arrived, she looked around for an older man, someone who might match the voice she'd spoken to on the phone, but the only person in the parking lot was a woman leaning against the side of a car. The woman stood up and approached as Margaret parked and got out. She seemed younger than Margaret, but not by much, her light brown hair tied back in a ponytail. She wore jeans and a Mickey Mouse sweatshirt. Mickey was dressed like Gene Kelly in *Singin' in the Rain,* hanging from a lamppost.

"Margaret?" the woman said. She offered her hand, which Margaret shook. "Sally. I think we're supposed to be meeting."

"I thought I was meeting Jamie White."

"Jamie's my uncle," Sally said. "He wanted to come himself but got delayed with another client. Sometimes I help him out."

Margaret's mouth twisted and she clenched her fists a couple of times. She already felt nervous, and deviating from her plan even in small ways made her feel worse.

"I promise I know what I'm doing," Sally White said. "I deal with this kind of thing all the time. But if you don't feel comfortable, I'm sure you can reschedule with my uncle—"

"No," Margaret interrupted. "No, it has to be today."

"Okay," Sally said, her voice surprisingly gentle. "Lead the way."

Harry's unit was on the fourth floor of the climate-controlled building. Sally whistled as Margaret rolled up the door and revealed the pristine white boxes stacked floor to ceiling, front to back. "May I?" she said, gesturing to one of the boxes.

Margaret helped her pull it down from the top of the stack and set it on the corridor floor. Sally sifted through the contents, gingerly handling everything she touched, occasionally shaking her head or swearing under her breath. She showed Margaret a copy of *Weird Tales* cover-dated February 1928. It featured a man in a trench coat with a gun in one hand, and a fainting woman in a ball gown collapsed against his side. "The Ghost Table, by Elliot O'Donnell" it read.

"Would you believe this was the first publication of 'The Call of Cthulhu'?" Sally said. "And it's not even the *cover*." She smirked, disbelieving. "That's like publishing an issue of *Action Comics* without Superman on the front. Although they did that, too, in the early days."

"I don't know much about comic books," Margaret said.

"Look," Sally said. She pointed to a list of names near the bottom of the cover: H. P. Lovecraft, Ray Cummings, Seabury Quinn, Frank Owen, Wilfred Taiman, John Martin Leahy. "Maybe the single most important piece of Weird fiction, and its author is a footnote. Nuts."

Sally gazed into the unit, at the remaining tower of boxes. "These are all full of the same stuff?" she said.

"Magazines and comics. Film posters. Stuff like that."

Sally made a face, seemed to be arguing with herself.

"What?" Margaret said. "What's wrong?"

Sally sighed. "My uncle sent me here today with a check. He told me to offer you somewhere between fifty and two hundred dollars if I thought there was enough here to justify it, and if you'd agree to sell him everything."

"Everything?" Margaret surveyed the unit. Whatever her feelings about him now, she couldn't forget the years of love and care Harry had put into building this collection, and how hard it had been for him to remove it from his home and store it across town. This assemblage of boxes was how he built his worldview, his personality. It was how he dealt with his mother's sickness and his father's death. She hated herself for this pang of sentiment, but it was there, all the same.

"My uncle had no idea what I would find here," Sally said, "and if he'd come himself, he might have offered you, I don't know, maybe five hundred or a grand."

That sounded like a fortune to Margaret, an instant problem solver. "Can you call him and ask?"

"The problem," Sally said, "is that you could probably get five hundred for what's in this box alone, if you knew what you were doing. Usually it's my job to trick people who don't know what they have into selling me things that we then sell for much, much more. Usually I'm happy to do that, because it's only a comic or two here, a box of magazines there, but this"—she waved at the storage unit—"this is too big. You need to catalog it, find out what it's really worth, and then either sell it yourself or let someone like my uncle or me make an honest offer."

At another time Margaret would have thanked this woman for her candor, but right now she wanted to scream.

"It's sweet you're trying to help me out," she said patiently, "but I need money today. Why don't you take this box, write me a check for two hundred dollars, and we'll call it even?"

"I can't," Sally said.

"Please," Margaret said, desperation creeping into her voice.

Sally studied her a moment. Margaret didn't like the shrewdness in the look, which made her feel exposed.

"Something pretty serious, then," Sally said. It wasn't a question.

Margaret gave a tight nod. Sally searched through the box in front of her again, pulled out about ten magazines, and set them on the floor. She picked up her purse, pulled out a pen and a folded-up check. She flattened it on one knee, filled it out, and handed it to Margaret. It was made out for two hundred dollars.

"I'm still cheating you," she said. "But not as much."

"Thank you," Margaret said.

Sally took another scrap of paper from her purse, scribbled something on it, and handed it to Margaret. "This is my home number. I meant what I said. If you actually want to sell this stuff, I can help you get a fair price. I need time to figure out what you have."

"Thank you," Margaret said again.

Sally stood, helped Margaret return the box to its tower, and shut the rolling door. They shook hands.

"Call me," Sally said. "I'll work for ten percent of the final sale. That's cheap, by the way."

16

Margaret cashed the check at a Western Union and hid the money in an old aspirin bottle at the bottom of her purse. She drove to the admissions office at UTV, paid her admission fee in cash, and put the rest away for the second week of November. She'd worry about the cost of the apartment after Halloween.

Work on the Tomb grew frenzied. The family pulled together again. No one mentioned Harry's seizures or outbursts. Margaret pushed thoughts of doctors away. It was like they'd made a silent agreement: no more shouting, fistfights, or confrontations until November. It gave them permission to get along and to be courteous to one another, if not warm.

The house was messy, chaotic, more a backstage area for the attraction in the yard than a home. Sydney, who would later have some experience with high school theater, first became acquainted with the strange bouquet of backstage smells in the fall of 1982, in her own house—fabric, glue, sweat, and dust all hanging stale in the air like the ghosts of old shows.

Then, on the morning of Halloween, Harry planted a sign in the yard, which read FREE HAUNTED HOUSE TONIGHT in dripping, bloody red letters. Eunice took a picture of my parents crouched next to it, which I salvaged before I left home for the last time.

In the photo, Mom and Dad hunker on either side of the sign, with the house and fake graveyard behind them. The sun was too bright, and Eunice forgot to turn off the flash, so the picture looks over-exposed, faded, like it was taken at the onset of nuclear winter. Dad's wearing jeans and a Texas Tech sweatshirt. I can make out the dark bags under his eyes, even through the fade. Mom wears jeans and a denim jacket, and looks embarrassed in the universal manner of all moms before a camera lens, but both she and Dad are smiling, and in their smiles I see none of the manic energy and false cheer described to me later. I see only my parents, happy. I see why they could have loved one another to begin with.

Later that morning, Balloon World (the same folks who had supplied Eunice's birthday party bounce house) arrived with a giant balloon, which they helped Harry install on his roof platform and inflate. It took shape over the neighborhood, rising like a horror from beyond the stars, a giant white ghost visible from far away in the flat, still-undeveloped city of Vandergriff. Around town, children dropped their toys and stopped their games as the beacon entered their field of vision and announced itself, a signal from the spirit world that All Hallows' Eve had begun. The streets would soon be awash in dark magic and the world beyond the world would show its face.

17

By midafternoon, a crowd of people had gathered on the sidewalk—not only children and parents, but teenagers and college kids as well. The friends and neighbors who'd agreed to help arrived around dinnertime and found a stack of pizzas waiting for them ("We can't pay them, but we should at least feed them," Harry had said). These "Tomb Players" scarfed their food and then stepped into the living room to be made up as vampires, werewolves, and the ghostly dead.

Mr. and Mrs. Ransom were on line detail, and already frazzled. The line out front stretched down the block and around the corner.

Back inside, Margaret made panicked, last-minute alterations to costumes while Harry applied makeup. When Mr. Haggarty's monk costume ripped (he'd put on a few extra pounds since she first measured him), Margaret ran out of thread repairing it. She sent Eunice to find more, but Eunice returned a moment later, unable to locate any.

"I think we're out," she said.

"Hold this," Margaret said. Eunice took hold of the split fabric and held it together over Mr. Haggarty's belly while Margaret dashed into the bedroom. There was a small chance she'd left an emergency sewing kit in the dresser. She proceeded to rip drawers out and dump the contents onto the floor. When she finished with her own, she started on Harry's. She dumped his folded-up shirts, found no sewing kit. Next, she dumped his socks and underwear. Again, no sewing kit, but something else, a quick fluttering at the corner of her eye so brief that she almost missed it. She paused, set the empty drawer on the bed with its fellows, then pushed apart the socks and underwear to see what she'd found.

It was a glossy pamphlet that had been folded in half, as if to fit in a pocket. Margaret picked it up and unfolded it. "Glioblastoma and Malignant Astrocytoma" was printed across the top, above a few photographs of generic faces: serious but tough, showing the viewer that they weren't going to let this thing (whatever it was) beat them. A logo at the bottom informed Margaret that this was a publication of the American Brain Tumor Association.

She paged through the pamphlet, trying to take it all in at once, focusing not on sentences, but on paragraphs, pictures, diagrams of brain cells that she didn't (couldn't) understand. Individual words glommed on to her mind: *surgery, radiation, headaches, seizures, disinhibition*. On the last page, she found a sticky note with another few words scribbled in Harry's small, blocky handwriting: *inoperable, radiation, antipsychotics, personality change, 6 months–1 yr.*

She sat down on the bed among the upended drawers. Harry had been to the specialist. He had been diagnosed. Glioblastoma. Brain tumor. A hound lurking out of sight, driving the hero mad. It all made sense. The disappearing money. The crazy behavior, the shouting, the hitting, the cruelty. The haunted house, the fanatical determination to get it right no matter what the cost. Six months to a year.

"Oh, Harry," she said.

"Mom!" Sydney called, yanking her into the present moment.

"Coming!" she shouted. She dropped the pamphlet and walked through the house on wobbly legs. She braced herself against the living room doorway. Everyone was standing in a circle around Harry. "I couldn't find any more thread," she said.

"We'll have to do without it," Harry said. He looked around at his assembled cast and crew. "Okay, everyone. Have fun tonight, but also keep in mind that we're doing important work." Noting the skepticism on some of his audience's faces, he held up a hand. "Hear me out. Human beings are small and insignificant in a big, scary universe, and in a horror story—be it a movie, a book, or a haunted house—we have to face that fact. But no matter how scary things get, no matter what the audience has to confront or endure, there's always a happy ending. When the credits roll, or the reader closes the book, or when our guests walk out tonight, their lives will go on. Because they faced the dark, the sun will shine a little brighter tomorrow, and the real-life monsters won't seem so bad. For a day, or an hour, or even a moment, life will be better." He seemed like he might say more, but instead shook his head. "Sydney, get everyone into their places. Mom and I are heading to the gravedigger's shack."

The crowd of players dispersed. Margaret and Harry made their way to the garage. It looked like a set from an old movie: rough wooden walls, an old calendar; a cardboard stove in the middle of the room with an orange lightbulb inside to simulate fire; a small desk near the front door, some papers scattered on it; a pair of shovels leaning in one corner; and in the middle of the room, the sleek silver coffin Harry had bought from Theater of Vandergriff. Margaret started to put on her costume, but stopped and stared down into the plush silky lining, torn and faded after years of use.

"Do you want to run your lines?" Harry said.

"No, I'm fine," she said.

"Okay then." He rubbed his temples.

"How do you feel?" Margaret said, zipping up her jumpsuit and putting on a blue cap.

He frowned. "It still feels wrong somehow. I should have done more. The whole thing should be better than it is."

"It'll have to do," Margaret said. "Want me to help you into the coffin?"

She held his hands as he lowered himself in. She leaned over, to close the lid.

"Listen, Margaret—"

"I'm pregnant," she said. She hadn't intended to say it. As far as she knew, she was still planning on an abortion in a little less than two weeks. The confession popped out of its own accord, the only thing she could think of to delay the real conversation. An announcement of life, to stave off one of death.

My father's reaction to my impending birth was one of poorly concealed pain. "Are you sure?"

"Positive."

He opened his mouth to say something else, but was interrupted by a loud bang on the garage door. He looked away from her, to the door, then back.

"What was that?" he said.

"Maybe it's Daniel Ransom, trying to hurry us up," Margaret said.

The bang sounded again, twice more.

"Maybe," Harry said. "Margaret," he said again, and looked frightened.

She didn't want to hear it. Not tonight. Tomorrow they would deal with glioblastoma. They would discuss and debate round after round of punishing treatment, the possibility of her handsome, kind, loving husband reduced beneath the force of radiation, dulled by medications meant to stop seizures and prevent him from assaulting his children. Tomorrow they would discuss what to do about me, the parasite gathering mass in Margaret's womb. Tomorrow they would face the thing on the doorstep, demanding to be let in. But not tonight.

She leaned forward and kissed him.

"I love you," she said. "Until the end of time and whatever comes after that."

He reached for her, as if to keep her close, but she stood straight, affixed her fake mustache to her face, and walked toward the door. The banging was insistent now, unceasing.

"Let's give these people a scare," she said.

The Turner Sequence II: Sydney

When Sydney enters the City, she arrives in terror, a
scream still echoing in her heart. The fear fades almost
at once, however, as she finds herself outside the house
she lived in for the first half of her childhood, the
house she associates with love and plenty and safety.
She's standing in a line that stretches down the block
from the garage. Everyone is in costume, Sydney included.
She wears a rumpled, dirty pink tutu, and white makeup
is caked on her arms, shoulders, and face. A giant
inflatable ghost sways back and forth on the roof,
summoning visitors. It's ominous against the darkening
sky, and a thrill of delight courses through her. It's
the haunted house she built with her father when she
was ten years old—the last thing the family did together
before Daddy got sick.

The garage door is open, but a false front has been
built into it, so it looks like the entrance to a little
hovel—an aging, weathered wall with a door on the right
side and a foggy little window on the left.

Mr. Ransom, from next door, stands in front of the
garage, counting out groups of people to go inside. There
are six people in front of Sydney who want to go in
together and are willing to wait, so Mr. Ransom has them
step aside and beckons Sydney and the person behind her
up to the door.

Shouldn't you be inside? Mr. Ransom says. Sydney
prepares for a scolding, but he winks. *I won't tell,* he
says. He turns the knob and pushes the door open.

Sydney and a group of strangers shuffle into the gravedigger's shack. A small worktable and chair stand to the right, and a large coffin dominates the middle of the room. Sydney's mother, Margaret, sits at the worktable, dressed in a blue coverall and cap, wearing a gray wig and fake mustache. She's bent over some paperwork, a metal thermos lid full of coffee at one side. She looks up and feigns surprise.

Well hello there! she says, her voice twisted and scratchy but still not exactly manly. *I wasn't expecting visitors so soon, but welcome all the same. In fact, if you want to know the truth, I could use a second opinion on a couple of things. Think you might be able to help me out?*

Okay! says a small boy in the group.

Let's take a walk, the Gravedigger says. She stands and gestures to another door at the back of the room. *There's something queer afoot here, and I'm not sure—*

The lid of the coffin flies open and a man in a white top hat and tuxedo sits up and roars. The group screams, and Sydney starts a bit, too, even though it's only Daddy in makeup. He looks inhuman.

See now, that's exactly the sort of thing I'm talking about, the Gravedigger says. She opens the door—the door that would typically open onto the kitchen but instead opens on a black tunnel of modular walls that leads through the house and into the backyard. The tuxedoed ghoul howls after Sydney and the visitors, but doesn't give chase.

I had to break both his legs with a shovel so he'd stay put, the Gravedigger admits, leading the group down the hall. Panels open in the walls. A tentacle emerges near the baseboard and gropes at Sydney's leg. It's cold and slimy through her tights. She doesn't scream, but shakes the tentacle off and follows the group into the next room.

As she does, the group disappears, and she finds herself out of costume, out of the haunted house, and on the living room couch. The house is still wrecked from last week's Halloween prep. Mom has made some cursory attempts at cleaning, but rolls of fabric still lean in the corners, and makeup and prosthetics still cover the dining room table. The whole family is still exhausted, moving through life in a sleepy stupor.

Eunice sits next to Sydney on the couch. Mom and Daddy are on the love seat catercorner, holding hands. They're getting along better since Halloween, and Sydney's not sure how she feels about that. She's not sure Mom deserves Daddy's forgiveness.

Mom says, *We have news.*

Good news or bad news? Eunice says.

Both, Mom says. *First, we're having another baby.*

Is that the good news or the bad news? Sydney says.

Mom scoffs. *Good news, smart aleck.*

What's the bad news? Eunice says.

Daddy licks his lips. *I have cancer.*

What's cancer? Sydney says. She's heard the word on TV and she knows it's bad, but she doesn't know why.

It's a disease, Eunice says. *A bunch of abnormal cells divide and destroy your body tissue. It's like being eaten alive.*

Both Mom and Daddy give Eunice a look somewhere between astonishment and disgust.

You'll get better, right? Sydney says.

Her parents exchange a glance. *I have good doctors and they're hopeful*, Daddy says, but it's a lie. Grown-ups are always lying to Sydney. They tell her Santa Claus is real and monsters are fake, that they still love each other when they don't, that they're doing their best when it's clear they don't care. Here's another falsehood to add to the pile.

Eunice gives Mom and Daddy a weak smile. Sydney wants to puke. *Excuse me,* she says. She runs out the back door, away from these liars, but she finds herself back in the Tomb on Halloween night, in a group of visitors following the Gravedigger into a room that is completely dark. The group titters nervously.

The perfect darkness is broken by a single instant of blinding light, and the sense of something moving, too quick to track before the room plunges back into darkness. The other visitors gasp. One person yelps.

The light returns, this time in two pulses, then three. Sydney can make out a figure on the far side of the room, small and lithe, and she recognizes herself—the version of herself that performs on Halloween night. She watches her double work through the five positions, and she feels her own muscles stretch and flex even as she stands still among strangers. She's become both audience and performer, and as music begins to pound from a boom box hidden in the corner—a light but driving piano medley joined by ringing bells and a low bass line—her smooth movements are chopped into a series of stills by the strobe light: arms raised, leg kicked high; head bent forward, arms out at her sides; standing on her toes, spinning across the room the way Mrs. Ransom taught her.

That peculiar calm settles over Sydney, the calm that comes only when she performs. The watching version of Sydney fades away, merges with the dancing Sydney. She raises one leg like a bird, *croisé derriere,* spins once, twice, three times, and on her third rotation, she finds herself sitting on the bed in Eunice's room while Eunice sits at her desk and reads aloud from a comically large library book.

Glioblastoma is a tumor that arises from astrocytes—those are the star-shaped cells that make up the supportive tissue of the brain, the glue that holds everything together. It's a highly malignant tumor—

What does malignant *mean?* Sydney interrupts.

Life threatening, Eunice says. *Very dangerous.* She starts reading again. *It's a highly malignant tumor because the cells reproduce quickly and they're supported by a large network of blood vessels. There are two types of glioblastoma. There's primary or "de novo," which forms and makes its presence known very quickly. Then there's secondary, which has a slower, longer growth period but is still very aggressive.*

Which type does Daddy have? Sydney says.

Primary, Eunice says.

Sydney and Eunice sit in silence, trying to find a way to live with the apocalyptic implications of this information.

You believe me, right? Eunice says. *About the man at the window?*

Sydney gets up and leaves the room, but as she passes through the door, she finds herself in a hospital room. Daddy's in the bed, his hair gone, his body wasted and sunken. Mom has her chair pulled up next to him. She looks grotesque next to Daddy, as though gaining mass at the exact rate he's losing it. Like she's draining him to feed the new baby. Sydney and Eunice sit on a couch in the corner, watching a TV show with the volume turned down. It seems like it's about fishing.

Mom holds a notebook balanced on her lap, making notes and sketches based on Daddy's dictation. They're working on next year's haunted house, as if it's something Daddy will be around to do. Daddy's idea is a whole city, and now he and Mom are populating it with buildings.

It's a hotel, Daddy says now. *Not remote, like in* The Shining, *but downtown, fancy—and it's been abandoned. The windows are open and the curtains are billowing, snow's blowing in, and there's weird Christmas-slash-clown stuff everywhere. Like fun house meets Winter Wonderland.*

Mom holds up her sketch pad to him. *Like this?*

Daddy snatches the pad and pencil from her. He flips the page and makes quick, violent pencil strokes. *I swear to Christ, Margaret, I would rather die alone than spend another minute with you.*

Eunice puts her face in her hands, but Sydney keeps her head up. He's sick. He doesn't mean it when he says awful things—although in this case Sydney secretly agrees with him. Mom is weak. Sydney can see pain written across her mother's plain face. She's not strong enough. She doesn't deserve him. She's ready for him to die.

Sydney thinks that she'd also die if it was a choice between that and spending life with Mom.

And suddenly she finds herself back on the stage in the Tomb. Turn, turn, turn. Tinkling bells and plinking piano with underlying bass and an occasional bright burst of noise interrupting the music like a jump scare in a slasher movie. Tumor from astrocytes. Star-shaped cells, somehow lovely to picture, like marshmallows in sugary cereal. Short, controlled breaths. Don't let the audience see how hard you're working. Be the performing Sydney. Make it look effortless. Turn. Turn. Turn. Disinhibition, radiation, antipsychotics. Seizures, personality change, inoperable. Turn, turn, turn, faster now, because even though Sydney is strong, she doesn't want to see the rest.

She does anyway. Despite the dance, she loses the calm, becomes the small, sad Sydney, and is dragged back into the scene.

She's in the room with Daddy when it happens. It's been two weeks since her younger brother, Noah, was born. Daddy was too weak to hold him, and he didn't seem interested anyway. Sydney understands. Why bother getting to know a baby you won't raise? Eunice is with Mom and the baby in a different room. Sydney visits them seldom. She wants to be with Daddy. She's always enjoyed being alone with him, getting him all to herself, but for some reason, even when it's just the two of them in a room together lately, she feels another presence. Something she can't see, watching them both.

As if this creepy feeling weren't enough, the last few days have been bad. Although Daddy was writing and drawing a lot, he no longer has the strength. He stares into space, his breath ragged, and Sydney stands beside him and holds his hand. He doesn't seem aware of her, seems trapped in his own mind, alone with himself. But then his hand suddenly tightens on hers. He takes a sharp breath, as though experiencing some great pain.

He turns to look at her, his eyes aware, and present, and terrified.

Eunice was right.

Daddy? she says. It's the only answer she can scrape together under the sharp focus of his gaze, harsher than any spotlight.

Margaret, he says.

Sydney. It's Sydney, Daddy.

The drawings. The designs. It's all there. You have to, he says.

Have to what? Sydney says.

It's seen us. It has our scent.

Daddy closes his eyes. His breathing is deep and untroubled. She calls to him a few more times before she notices that his chest has stopped moving altogether.

Turn, turn, turn. Sydney's back on the stage at the Tomb and running short of breath herself. She slows down into a Vaganova fourth arabesque, and then she's at her father's funeral with Eunice, Mom, Mr. and Mrs. Ransom, all the neighbors, Granny and Granddad Byrne, Grandma Turner, all of them gathered around an open grave while a minister speaks over Daddy's casket. Noah is crying and Mom hands him to Sydney, asks her to take him away until he quiets down. Sydney wants to ask why Grandma Turner can't take him, but she knows why. The old woman looks awful, skin waxy, eyes sunken. In another six months she'll overdose on sleeping pills. Everyone will say it's an accident and know that it wasn't.

But that's later. Now Sydney carries Noah across the cemetery, saying all the worst words she knows in her softest, most soothing voice: *Fucker. Asshole. Bitch. Motherfucker. Shit. Goddammit.* She studies each tombstone she passes. They all look sharp and hard. How easy it would be to shut Noah up forever. No one would miss him except maybe Eunice, but Eunice likes everyone anyway. She probably misses her snot after she blows her nose.

Sydney doesn't drop Noah. She walks him back and forth, pats his back, swears at him and rages at her mother for sending her away in the middle of her goodbye to Daddy. It's the latest in a long series of Mom's failures. She's selling the house and the family is moving into an apartment like poor people. They're losing everything.

Sydney finds herself on the stage again. Turn, turn, turn. Fast as she can, faster than that. The performing Sydney needs to be the only Sydney. She'll figure out what Daddy needed. She'll do the right thing. She'll make him proud.

Part Three

The Thing on the Doorstep

I

"Take it off, Noah."

"Let him have his fun. What's the big deal?"

"He looks ridiculous."

"No one will care."

"Where did he go? Noah, get out here. We don't have time for this."

August 1989 and I was six years old, hiding behind the yellowed living room curtains in our crappy, run-down apartment while Mom, Eunice, and Mom's business partner, Sally White, argued about my clothing choice for the evening. We were already running late for Vandergriff High School's production of *The Sound of Music,* but I wanted to wear a costume: a cheap, flimsy mask and cape knockoff produced to cash in on that summer's Batman film. I'd been wearing it nonstop in the week since Sally bought it for me.

I was paying only vague attention to the conversation. The living room curtains hung before the sliding glass door to our apartment's little atrium, and I'd turned to look out at it. Every unit in our complex had a ten-by-twelve space, open to the elements up top and closed in on three sides by walls of the unit (in our case, it was my bedroom window on one side, the blank wall bordering my mother's bathroom opposite, and catercorner to both, the sliding glass door to the living room), with a fourth wall separating your atrium from your next-door neighbor's. Think of it like the poor person's version of the back porch or balcony, a patch of sky to call your own but no view of your neighborhood, or even a parking lot. A more generous soul might try to talk up the privacy such an atrium provided, but in my own experience, it was hard to ever feel anything but incarcerated on that little spread of cracked concrete.

"Noah, I can see your sneakers," Mom said. "Come out now or you'll have to stay home and miss the play."

I shuffled back into full view. Mom, Eunice, and Sally stood in the middle of the stained beige carpet, Mom with her arms crossed, Eunice wearing a backpack, Sally hiding a smile behind one hand.

"Take it off," Mom said again.

"Eunice gets to bring her backpack," I said.

"Eunice is bringing homework."

"Everyone in the play is wearing costumes," I said.

"Off, now."

I untied the knotted string around my neck and pulled the mask off my head. The whole thing slumped to the floor behind me.

"Your hair is a fright," Mom said.

"Margaret," Sally said. "No one is going to care if he looks a little tousled."

Mom pinched the bridge of her nose. "Fine. Let's go."

2

The high school parking lot was a study in chaos by the time we arrived, and Mom had to park far from the entrance, carefully guiding her wheezing old Ford Torino among clumps of slow-moving people. She glowered and huffed as she dragged me across the parking lot, and I had to run to keep my footing. The high school looked gargantuan and sophisticated compared to my elementary building, and I marveled at the endless trophy cases and lockers as we hurried toward the auditorium, with its plush folding seats and midnight blue stage curtain. We found four seats together near the stage.

"Don't take your mom's mood personally, kiddo," Sally said, leaning close as we settled in. "We had a rough day at the store." She was referring to Bump in the Night, the comic book/memorabilia shop they'd opened in 1984, using the proceeds from the sale of my late father's extensive horror collection. If Mom's moods were any indication, every day was a rough day at the store.

On my other side, Eunice had already unpacked her bag. She scowled at the open textbook on her lap and scratched numbers into a spiral notebook.

"What are you working on?" I said.

"Algebra," she said.

"Is it hard?"

"Only when people interrupt me." She winked to show there were no hard feelings.

An excited hush fell over the crowd as the auditorium dimmed. Bells began to ring in the orchestra pit, and a chorus of female voices rose from my left and right. Two lines of nuns floated down the aisles, candles in hand, singing a solemn, beautiful song whose words I couldn't make out. Their voices drifted over us, lovely and haunting. As they reached the bottom of the auditorium, they mounted the stage, faced the audience, and broke into a joyful chant of "Hallelujah." They filed off into the wings as their voices faded, leaving the stage empty and dark.

A moment later, a spotlight crept up, revealing a single figure before a painted backdrop. She wore a simple postulant's dress and held a wooden bucket with both hands. Sydney, age seventeen, as Maria. Unlike Julie Andrews's chaste, motherly Maria, Sydney had left her hair long and brown, tied back in a ponytail, and despite the loose, baggy dress, she glowed in the bright light as she began to sing:

My day in the hills has come to an end, I know.
A star has come out to tell me it's time to go.

The orchestra strings rose to meet and accompany her as she spun slowly across the stage and let the song unreel. It wasn't a Julie Andrews or Mary Martin impression, but something uniquely Sydney: wounded, wondering, and raw, something private made public. I clamped my hands over my mouth and tears tickled my knuckles as they rolled past. I didn't want to make a sound and break this delicate spell.

"Hey," Eunice whispered. She dropped something into my lap. I reached down and felt the cheap, slippery fabric. My bat cape and cowl. I bunched it in my hands, fingered the slight points of the floppy bat ears. It was still agony to watch Sydney sing, but something loosened in my chest. It became endurable.

3

The cast received a standing ovation during curtain call, but the auditorium went nuts when Sydney emerged and led the final bow. Afterward, families hung around the auditorium to wait for their respective cast and crew members, and also to talk to the show's director, Mr. Ransom. By 1989, seven years after he and his wife had moved in next door to my family's old house and he'd helped my father run the Tomb, Daniel Ransom had rounded out and his dark hair had thinned, but he still had a deep, authoritative voice and a quick laugh, and when he smiled at me, I always felt like I was personally putting light into the world.

"Look at that ham," Mom grumbled, watching him beam as he accepted congratulations, his laughter echoing in the auditorium.

"Keep your distance and don't make eye contact," Sally said.

"Here he comes anyway. Daniel," Mom said, shaking his hand.

"It was a wonderful show," Sally said.

Mr. Ransom waved the compliment off, bashful and pleased with himself at the same time. "Did Sydney tell you the opening with the nuns in the aisles was her idea?"

"I'm not surprised, if that's what you mean," Mom said.

His smile calcified, turned false. "She's a special kid."

"They're all special, right?" Mom said. "At least, come fund-raiser time."

The smile slipped. "I'm not asking for money, Margaret. I just think a lot of your daughter."

"I'll let her know you said so," Mom said. She opened her purse and began digging around inside.

"While we're on the subject, though," he said, either missing or ignoring the obvious dismissal, "Halloween is right around the corner. Have you given any more thought to my proposal?"

"You already have my answer," Mom said.

I winced as Mr. Ransom tossed off a tiny salute. "Always a pleasure, Margaret. Sally, Eunice, Noah," he said, nodding to each of us. He retreated into a crowd of admirers.

"You know he's having a rough time," Sally said.

She was referring to the collapse of his marriage, which we all knew about but talked around, using phrases like *rough time* or *troubles*.

Mom rolled her eyes at Mr. Ransom's back. "Boo hoo." She glanced at me and scowled at the cape clenched in my hands. "Where did you get that?"

4

Sydney went to dinner with some friends after the play, coming out only to get our congratulations and announce her plans before she disappeared backstage again. Mom complained about the wasted time, but there wasn't much gas left in her fury tank. She was tired.

When we arrived back at the apartment, Sally kissed us all on the cheek and left, and Mom bid us good night and disappeared into her own room, leaving me and Eunice alone in the living room.

"It's a school night, mister," Eunice said, dropping a hand on my shoulder. "And way past your bedtime. Go brush your teeth and put on pajamas."

"Will you read to me?" I said.

"For a little bit, but only if you hurry," she said.

I did as ordered, and, after hanging my cape in the closet, I climbed into bed. When Eunice came into my room a little later with a paperback in one hand, she had to do a bit of a dance to get to my bed, crossing the minefield of scattered toys and dirty laundry on the balls of her feet, and even after she reached the bed and urged me to scoot over, she had to pull spaceships and action figures from beneath the blankets to make enough space for herself.

"How can you sleep with so much junk in here?" she said, setting a Ghostbuster on my nightstand.

I always had trouble drifting off at night, and because I wasn't as smart as Eunice had been at my age, I played rather than read or wrote myself to sleep. I scooted against the wall to make room. She settled in next to me and pushed her glasses up her nose, her bony, freckled arm cold against mine. She opened her copy of *The Dream-Quest of Unknown Kadath* and began to read:

> There presently rose ahead the jagged hills of a leprous-looking coast, and Carter saw the thick unpleasant grey towers of a city. The way they leaned and bent, the manner in which they were clustered, and the fact that they had no windows at all, was very disturbing to the prisoner; and he bitterly mourned the folly which had made him sip the curious wine of that merchant with the humped turban. As the coast drew nearer, and the hideous stench of that city grew stronger, he saw upon the jagged hills many forests, some of whose trees he recognised as akin to that solitary moon-tree in the enchanted wood of earth, from whose sap the small brown zoogs ferment.

We'd been reading *Kadath* for a few nights now. I had trouble following the story, with its skimpy characterization and preponderance of goofy words like *zoogs*, but I liked listening to Eunice's voice. Her slow, careful way of speaking, the way she seemed to handle each word like a delicate, precise thing, always soothed me. I'd already started to nod off against Eunice's shoulder when she shut the book for the night and got up to tuck me in.

"Who do I love most?" she said.

"Me," I said, waking up a little.

"And who do you love most?"

"You," I said.

She kissed my forehead. "Sleep tight, little prince." She turned on my night-light, switched off the overhead light, and made to leave the room.

"Eunice," I said.

She paused.

I worked my mouth for a moment, struggling for words. I wanted to communicate my fear, my need for her to stay close, but I was also afraid that if I said anything, she might decide that the Lovecraft was too intense for a bedtime story, and stop reading it to me.

"Nothing," I said. "Good night."

"Night." She shut the door behind her.

The scratching began as soon as the door closed, a quick, insistent scrabbling against the glass of my bedroom window. It had been happening for weeks now, and I'd safety-pinned the curtains together so no one could see inside, even though the window only looked out on our apartment's closed, private atrium. A small sliver of space remained visible between the panels, and through it I saw only darkness.

The scratching grew in intensity, a panicked, screechy song. I wished I'd hidden my Batman cape under my pillow instead of hanging it in the closet. With my cape, I could feel brave, and safe, but to get to it now I would have to cross in front of the window. Instead I stuffed my head under my pillow and waited for the sound to stop. It seemed to go on for hours.

5

On their best, most pleasant days, Mom and Sydney kept an uneasy peace—polite and deferential, but never warm. Most of the time, though, they fought. Eunice and I got a break in the weeks leading to a dance recital or play, but once Sydney had a chance to rest, the cycle started all over again. Case in point—the week after *The Sound of*

Music, all of us in the car together after school, Eunice and me in the
backseat, Sydney and Mom up front, Sydney exploding after several
minutes of quiet:

"Mr. Ransom told me what you said about me."

"And what's that?" Mom said. She sounded tired. Bored, even.

"You said I'm not special," Sydney said.

Mom slouched over the steering wheel. "I'm going to run that man
over with my car."

"Good luck sneaking up on him in this death trap," Sydney said.

"I didn't say you weren't special. I was making a joke. I know you
can't see this now, because you're seventeen, but it's unprofessional
of him to twist my words and rile you up. I should have a talk with
your principal." Mom often made this threat, but it was empty and
Sydney knew it.

"He also said you turned him down again," Sydney said.

"I always do," Mom said. "Why would I change my mind now?"

"Change your mind about what?" I said.

"What if you didn't have to be a part of it?" Sydney said. "You could
give me Daddy's old papers and I could do it."

The car fell silent again. No one ever talked about my father in
front of me—not even Eunice. If I asked about him, she occasionally
dropped information (he was tall, he had dark hair like me and Sydney,
and he'd died of cancer), but usually she changed the subject or tried
to distract me. I understand why Mom would avoid the topic, but not
Eunice and Sydney. Maybe the pain of his illness and death had made
its own marks on them, and silence became the family's way to carry
on. I'm not sure. Living with a family wounded by a loss you can't
remember is like sitting behind a tall person at a movie theater. The
people around you are laughing, crying, reacting to something, but
you have no idea what.

"You know better than to ask me that," Mom said quietly.

"Those papers are as much mine—" Sydney said, her profile ugly
in its frustrated anger.

"What papers?" I said.

"Noah, hush," Eunice said, squeezing my arm so hard it hurt.

"Sydney, I advise you to back out of this conversation," Mom said.

Anger rolled off Sydney in hot, palpable waves. The car felt warmer. Was that possible? I leaned toward my open window, trying to catch more of the breeze. The car shuddered and jerked, and I bumped my head against the window frame.

"What's happening?" Eunice said.

I rubbed my head. Mom took her hands off the steering wheel and raised them like a criminal surrendering to the police. Sydney stared at her, anger ebbing into confusion.

"I'm not sure," Mom said. "I—"

A bright jet of orange light burst from the hood of the car, choking off the end of Mom's sentence and sending a fresh, stifling sheet of heat through the car.

"What's happening?" Eunice said again.

The orange light began to sway and dance. The hood of the car was on fire.

A man appeared at Mom's window, slapping the glass. His hands were crusted with grime, and a bandanna held a filthy mass of hair out of his face. I think we were all too surprised to scream.

"Get those kids out of there!" he said, voice muffled.

Eunice leaned over and unclasped my seat belt with one quick motion. Mom and Sydney got out of the car and opened the rear doors. Mom yanked Eunice out by the arm, and Sydney lifted me like a baby, clasping me to her chest. She took several steps backward and nearly tripped over the curb while Mom and Eunice ran to the opposite side of the street.

The man at the window had stopped his blue VW bus right behind Mom's Torino. He threw open the sliding door, rummaged through an impressive array of fast-food garbage and dirty laundry, and located a bright red fire extinguisher. He read the instructions on the side of the can, murmuring to himself, then crossed back to the front of the Torino, braced his feet, and squeezed the trigger. White foam coated the hood of the car, suffocating the fire.

"Holy cats!" the man said. He still held the extinguisher toward the car, as though he expected it to reignite. "You buy one of these things because, y'know, safety first and all, but you never think you'll actually use it." He glanced at us, still on either side of the street, Mom and Eunice holding hands, me in Sydney's arms. "Everybody okay?"

We'd stopped on a residential street, deserted except for our family and the disheveled amateur firefighter. Sydney seemed to realize she was still holding me and leaned forward to set me on the ground.

"I think we're fine," Mom said.

The man walked back to his van, tossed the extinguisher into its bed of junk, closed the sliding door, hopped into the driver's seat, and waved to us. "Have a blessed day," he said. He drove away, leaving us alone in the street with our dead car.

6

Mom had the car towed back home and called Rick, who Eunice told me was an old friend of Dad's from the highway department. Here was another tenuous link with my own secret origin: a potbellied good old boy in cowboy boots who sometimes came over to help with handyman things but who also wouldn't talk to me about Dad even when I managed to get his attention.

I didn't get a chance to bother him that day. When he arrived in his pickup, Mom met him in the parking lot with a beer in hand. He popped the Torino's blackened hood while my sisters and I sat on the front porch. Mom stood next to him, arms crossed. He spent only a few moments poking around before he stood and wiped his hands with a rag. He shotgunned the beer and then gave his prognosis. Mom's head drooped.

"Looks like bad news," Eunice said.

"The car was on *fire*," Sydney said.

"Do cars catch on fire a lot?" I said.

"Almost never," Eunice said.

Mom shook hands with Rick. He waved to us and got back into his truck. Mom watched him drive away, kicked a bit of loose gravel, and then trudged up our front walk.

"Well?" Sydney said.

"I have to make some phone calls," Mom said.

She carried the phone to her bedroom and stayed there for hours. Eunice made hamburger steaks and macaroni and cheese for dinner while I stood on the step stool next to her, handing her whatever she asked for. Mom still hadn't come out when the meal was ready, so we fixed her a plate, put it in the microwave, and ate without her.

She emerged late, not long before my bedtime, and sat at the table while we gathered around her. She ate half her food before she spoke:

"The engine in the car is obliterated. Rick would have to rebuild it from scratch."

"What happened?" Sydney said.

Mom took a long drink from her water glass. "The fire destroyed any evidence, so we'll never know for sure."

"But he *can* fix it," Eunice said.

"Rebuilding an engine costs a lot of money," Mom said.

"How much?" I said.

"A lot more than we can afford right now." She clenched her hands into fists. "I just had the oil changed."

"What will we do?" Eunice said.

"Sally can drive you and Noah to school, and she'll take me to and from work. Sydney, you'll need to get rides to school and rehearsals with a friend."

Sydney already did this most of the time anyway, but still asked, "For how long?"

"A while," Mom said. "Money's tight and I don't see it changing anytime soon."

"It doesn't have to be that way," Sydney said.

"Sydney," Mom said. She pressed the heels of her hands into her eye sockets. "I'm having a rough day. Can you, this once, stop pressing my buttons and get on my team?"

"I'm trying," Sydney said, matching Mom's frustrated tone with impressive accuracy. "This isn't about your feelings anymore. We've put up with the crappy apartment, the C-grade ground chuck and cruddy pasta, the rattling, flaming car—we've done it your way for years, and this is where it's landed us. Will you please entertain the notion that it might be worth trying something different this one time?"

Mom put her elbows on the table and clasped her chin. She looked at the half-finished food on her plate, then around the room. Her eyes settled on me and her brow furrowed. I shrank under her gaze—she usually looked at me this long only when I'd done something wrong. As a result, I've never really liked being looked at.

She sighed. "Tell Mr. Ransom I'm willing to have a conversation about a haunted house."

Sydney got up and went to the phone.

"That's all I'm promising," Mom said. "A conversation."

If Sydney heard, she gave no sign.

7

On Saturday night, Sally drove us all to Mr. Ransom's for dinner. He still lived next door to my family's former house, and I insisted on sitting by the driver's side window so I could get a good look when we arrived. Another piece of our family history I'd heard about but never seen. Sometimes, driving around town, I'd look at random houses and try to imagine my sisters playing in the yard, Dad mowing the lawn, Mom reading in a bay window, all of them spread out in an overwhelming abundance of space, where you could go a whole day without seeing another person if you wanted.

As we pulled into Mr. Ransom's driveway and Eunice pointed out our old home, I was disappointed by the reality—a brick house with a tree in the overgrown yard and a rusting van in the driveway.

"That's it?" I said.

"The lawn looked better when it was ours," Mom said.

Sydney, sitting behind the passenger seat and facing resolutely the other direction, said, "It was a nice place to live. Nicer than where we live now."

Mr. Ransom's house didn't look great, either. We traversed a walkway bordered with scraggly grass, stepped over waterlogged newspapers, and ducked under a low-hanging tree branch before we reached the door. When Mom rang the bell, Mr. Ransom answered in a button-down shirt, bits of bloody toilet paper stuck to his neck where he'd cut himself shaving. His collar was crooked as he beckoned us in.

The inside of the house felt nicer—framed prints on the walls, decorative scarves over the lamps, furniture upholstered in pristine white fabric and protected by shiny plastic covers—but smelled stale and dusty, like a place where people hadn't lived in a while.

"I ordered in," Mr. Ransom said, leading us to the kitchen table, which was stacked with pizza boxes, paper plates, and plastic cups and plastic silverware. It looked like the setup for a sad kid's birthday party, lacking only pointy hats and a decorative tablecloth.

"This is—quite a spread," Mom said.

"It got here a lot sooner than I thought it would," he said. "So it might be cold."

"We can warm it up in no time," Sally said. She opened one of the boxes, touched the crust, then moved into the kitchen like she owned the place.

"Do you have a bathroom?" I said.

"Wouldn't be much of a house without one, would it?" Mr. Ransom said, then smiled to show he was joking. "At the end of the hall on your left."

I crossed the dusty living room and headed down the hall, too shy to admit I didn't yet know left from right. I found three doors, picked one, and opened it. I knew as soon as I flipped the light switch that I'd entered a boy's bedroom. Masters of the Universe bedsheets, Superman curtains, and a Batcave play set in the middle of the room, Batman action figure facedown in front of it, as though abandoned midplay.

Because money had been so tight this year, I hadn't gotten many new toys. As the flood of Batman merchandise had crashed onto store shelves, I'd had my hands on plenty, but owned none of it, and the Batcave was the holy grail: a hunk of gray molded plastic made to look like stone, with red stairs and blue platforms for Batman to stand upon and brood, a Batcomputer with a huge monitor where he could solve mysteries, and, on the backside, a holding cell for criminals, and a trick platform that could dump a villain (or hero) into a deep pit.

I bent over the Batcave, mouth dry with longing, and picked up the Batman. I shoved my free hand into my pocket, gauging the available space. Would anyone notice the lump? It wasn't really stealing—Mr. Ransom's family had left, and who would miss a single toy?

"Get lost?"

I dropped the toy and almost shouted. Mr. Ransom stood inside the room. I clasped my hands behind my back. "I don't know left from right. And then I saw all the toys."

"It's my son Kyle's room," he said.

"I thought he didn't live here anymore."

"I'm hoping he'll come back someday, at least to visit. I want his room to be just the way he remembers it."

"That's very nice of you, Mr. Ransom," I said, shame burning my face.

"The bathroom's across the hall," he said. He ushered me out of the room and shut the door behind us. I opened the bathroom door and he started back down the hall, but before I could enter, he called to me.

"Your left side is the side with your heart," he said, putting his hand to the spot. I mimicked him, and we faced each other for a moment like we were saying the pledge of allegiance.

I've thought about this moment a lot in the years since. In the old days, your left side was considered your sinister or bad side. Left-handedness used to indicate a moral failing. Teachers would smack you with a ruler if they caught you writing with your left hand. So it seems appropriate to me that the heart, the symbol of love, the organ supposedly driving the major decisions of our lives, beats on the left side of the body.

When I got back, everyone had settled down to reheated pizza.

"Here's the deal," Mr. Ransom said, as I hopped into a chair beside

Eunice. "The theater department overspent on our summer production of *The Sound of Music,* and we only have enough money to put on maybe one more show this year. The problem is, we're supposed to do *four* more."

"So we both have money problems," Mom said.

Mr. Ransom rubbed his goatee. "Your family has already demonstrated a talent for a particular kind of production design, and I have a little money and a department full of kids dying to get in front of an audience. So we thought"—he gestured at Sydney—"that the department could collaborate with your family on a haunted house this year. We'd go fifty-fifty, and if it works, my department earns enough money for another year of plays, and you can afford to fix your car, or maybe even buy a new one."

Mom ran a fingertip along the rim of her wineglass as she considered. "You have the money and the kids. It sounds like you don't need my help."

"We need your family's vision or else it's just another crappy haunted house," Mr. Ransom said.

"That 'vision,'" Mom said, throwing air quotes around the word, "was my late husband's. I only made costumes."

"Eunice and I did some design work, too," Sydney said. "It wasn't all Dad."

"You drew funny pictures and your father indulged you," Mom said.

"Bullshit," Sydney said.

"Sydney," Sally said.

"Bite me, Sally," Sydney said.

"*Sydney,*" Mom said.

"Be that as it may," Mr. Ransom said, raising his voice, "I understand Harry left behind a lot of unused designs?"

"Those are off-limits," Mom said.

"They're not yours to keep," Sydney said.

"They absolutely are," Mom said. Sydney looked ready to dive across the table. Mom stared her down. "Test me and I'll set them on fire tonight."

I stuffed pizza into my mouth. I wasn't hungry—felt kind of sick to my stomach, actually—but I had to do *something*.

"Maybe this was a bad idea," Mr. Ransom said. "I didn't mean to cause trouble. I'm sure you have another plan for getting back on your feet."

Mom took a huge bite of pizza. After she swallowed, she finished her wine in a single gulp. "If I had another plan, I wouldn't be here. Sally, do we have the money?"

Sally emptied the remains of the wine bottle into Mom's glass. "We'll make it work."

"It'll cost less than you think," Mr. Ransom said. "We have a scene shop at the school, so we can pitch in with building materials. Students will work for class credit, so you don't have to pay them, and we can sell tickets at the school to a captive audience. You can keep the sets, props, costumes, and half of any profits."

"You really think there will be profits?" Mom said.

"I really do," he said.

8

That night, I sat on the girls' bedroom floor, my back against their shared dresser, feet pressed to the foot of Eunice's bed. Their room, although larger than mine, felt much smaller with two beds crammed into it, the walls decorated with programs from Sydney's shows and a giant Paula Abdul poster. Eunice's only decoration was a photo of Ursula K. Le Guin, hanging directly over her bed like a crucifix or dream catcher. The girls passed back and forth over me a flurry of pajamas, makeup removers, moisturizers, face creams, and toothbrushes.

"Why did Mr. Ransom's family move away?" I said. Although I'd heard about the split when it happened, I hadn't started thinking of the Ransoms as people—as a family—until I visited their quiet, empty house, and felt the tug of the missing people on Mr. Ransom, who cut himself shaving and couldn't even get a warm pizza meal together.

"None of your business," Sydney said. She shooed me away from the dresser. "I need in the bottom drawer."

I got into Eunice's bed, and paged through her heavy algebra textbook. The impossibly complex series of letters and numbers printed inside looked like an alien language, dizzying to behold. I shut the book again.

"Yeah, but why?" I said.

Eunice swept in from the bathroom and hopped into the bed with me. She took the alarm clock from the nightstand between their beds and pulled it into her lap to set it. "Sometimes people marry the wrong person, and, when that happens, they either stay together and hate each other, or they do the right thing and break up."

"Don't make excuses for her," Sydney said. She pulled a tank top out of the drawer.

"Did Mom marry the wrong person when she married Dad?" I said. "Is that why she won't talk about him?"

"Don't ever let me hear you talk about Dad that way again," Sydney said. She stalked out of the room and slammed the bathroom door.

9

Later, after spacing out for ten pages of *Kadath* before bed, I asked Eunice, "What's a haunted house like?"

"I've never been to one myself," she said. "Only the one we made with Mom and Dad when I was your age."

"Was it scary?"

"Not for me, but since I helped make it, I already knew everything that was going to happen. I think it was scary for the people who came to visit, though."

"What about Mom and Dad?" I said.

"They both seemed angry and worried most of the time," she said. "They fought a lot."

"Then why would Mom want to do it again?"

She made a face. "She doesn't want to, Noah. She has to. Sydney's the one who wants to."

"Why does Sydney want it so much? And why doesn't Mom want to use Dad's old designs?"

"I don't know," Eunice said. For the first time in my life, I didn't believe her.

IO

There was no scratching at the window that night, just a loud crack that startled me awake. I opened my eyes and sat up. The apartment was dark and quiet around me, which meant everyone was in bed. Either I'd dreamt the sound, or it had come from the atrium.

I got out of bed, opened the curtains, and pressed my face to the glass. A few toys lay scattered where I'd left them, and something small and black lay in a rusty lawn chair, almost invisible in the dark. Still half-asleep, I unlocked the window and slid the glass panel open as quietly as I could.

The concrete felt cool and rough against my bare feet, the air humid and reeking of automobile exhaust. I walked over to the chair and picked up the object: a Batman action figure, as shiny and pristine as if fresh from its package. The toy I'd almost stolen from Mr. Ransom's house. I turned a slow circle, but found no figures lurking in the shadows.

II

Mom and Sydney set up shop at an old warehouse on the far side of town. Mom sold a rare run of *The Amazing Spider-Man* to pay for the lease, and the weekend after signing, my family made a trip in Sally's car to our old storage unit. Mr. Ransom and a couple of theater kids met us there, and together we unpacked all the props, costumes, and sets from the Tomb. I watched with simultaneous wonder and disappointment as it shambled piece by piece back into the light—wonder, at finally seeing this obscure bit of family history, and disappointment at how cheesy it all looked under the unforgiving fluorescents: flimsy sheets of wood painted to look like limestone brick in a mummy's tomb; flaking papier-mâché monster masks; intentionally raggedy costumes with stitching that might drive a Lovecraftian hero into hysterics. I'd erected vast nightmare chambers in my imagination, and the actuality was, like my family's former house, a letdown. Mom, Sydney, and Eunice, on the other hand, looked uneasy and troubled.

Once everything was loaded and strapped down—the whole unit fit into two pickup truck beds—we drove out to the new warehouse, which sat on the town limits at the end of a long, narrow, tree-lined drive. Sydney got out of the car to unlock the gate, and we pulled into a massive parking lot before a rectangular box of a building, dull and gray as cinder block. Mom led us through the glass front door and into a reception area with a large desk and a few dusty chairs pushed against the wall, then through a set of double doors into the warehouse proper, a big open space with a concrete floor and exposed rafters, a pair of restrooms in one corner, and, along the wall facing the parking lot, a series of rolling garage doors. Dust billowed under our feet, and the hot, stuffy air stung my nose.

They opened two of the dock doors and moved everything inside, spreading it across the empty floor. While the theater kids drank soda in the parking lot, Mom, Eunice, Sydney, and Mr. Ransom surveyed everything, assessing what could be reused and what ought to be thrown away. They realized quickly that Mom's initial idea—reconstruct the Tomb, freshen the paint, and add a couple of chambers—wouldn't work. For one thing, much of the wood Dad had salvaged during construction had either rotted or cracked, rendering it unusable. For another, it all looked small and cheap arrayed in such a large, well-lit space.

"If we ask people to drive out here for this"— Mr. Ransom said, gesturing at the flattened set—"they're going to feel ripped off."

"This won't do at all," Mom said.

"So we have a few weeks to dream up something from scratch," he said. He ran both hands through his hair.

"Not necessarily," Sydney said. She unzipped Eunice's ever-present backpack and removed a small portfolio, from which she pulled a stack of paper. She passed sheets around to everyone. The page I received featured a picture of a group of teenagers huddled together in a bedroom, shining a flashlight under the bed while something peered at them from its hiding place in the closet. As we traded drawings, I realized that each featured the same group of teenagers in a different scene. In one, the kids moved through a morgue, while behind them a body sat up in an open drawer, still draped in a sheet. In another, the kids walked across a small pond, stepping from stone to stone, while a scaled, webbed hand reached out of the water toward one poor girl's ankle. In yet another—a rich man's study, lined with animal heads—this same girl had been snatched by the monster, and it dragged her away while the rest of the kids hugged one another in terror. In each picture, the kids shared a single flashlight.

"You did these?" Mom asked.

Sydney nodded.

"I had no idea you could draw," she said.

"How come there's always one flashlight?" I said.

"That's the concept," Sydney said, looking relieved at the change of subject. "We take some of the simplest, most mundane scare rooms— the easy ones we can throw up in a few weeks—and we add a chase element. So in addition to the regular scares, there's a monster tracking you, and you're trying to escape before it finds you. We only let people through in groups of four, and the only lighting in the place is a single flashlight. Maybe we even plant one of our own people in a group every now and then, and the monster could 'get' that person. It would be cheap, and we wouldn't have to reinvent the wheel in a few weeks."

Everyone else handed Sydney's drawings back to her, but Mom held on to hers. Her face looked tight, as though the flesh had been yanked taut.

"How did you come up with this?" she said.

Sydney fussed with the stack of pages. "Mr. Ransom always says that necessity is the mother of invention, right? I just tried to think up what would be easy." She held out her hand for the picture.

"These drawings are good," Mom said. "More than good." She sounded miserable about it and handed the drawing back to Sydney with obvious reluctance. "Is this *really* what you want?"

A moment of silence followed, broken only by Mr. Ransom's snort. "Jesus, Sydney," he said. "I'd hate to be you when I go to sleep at night." He looked around at us, half a smile on his face. It faded when none of us laughed.

"Speaking of, should Noah be here for this conversation?" Eunice said.

"What?" I said. "What did I do?"

"Nothing," Eunice said. "But I don't want you having nightmares."

Mom pointed over our shoulders. "Eunice, take your brother to the office while we talk."

"I want to help," I said.

"Go play with Eunice," Mom said.

"I'll take him up front, but I'm coming back," Eunice said. "I'm part of this."

Mom considered. "Fine," she said. "Don't touch anything!" she called as Eunice tugged me away.

12

"This isn't fair," I said, as Eunice tucked me in that night.

"Life isn't fair, buddy," she said.

"Mom would have let me help if you hadn't said anything."

"Mom isn't paying proper attention," Eunice said. "But I am, and you have to trust me when I say this will be too scary for you." She leaned over and kissed me on the forehead. "Who do I love most?"

It was too early for that question. "Wait—aren't you going to read to me?"

"I'm sorry, but I have to get started on the script tonight. Mr. Ransom's making me work with this girl from his playwriting class, so I have to come up with some ideas before I meet with her tomorrow. Maybe I'll have time in a couple of days?" She hurried across the room and flipped off the light switch. "Good night, little prince."

I lay fuming in the dark. Why did my family always exclude me? Why wasn't I ever a part of things?

When the scratching at the window started, instead of fear, I felt a hard ball of anger in my stomach. I climbed out of bed and yanked aside one of the curtains. The anger dissipated at once, replaced by wonder.

My first impression was of dark stone blocking my view of the atrium, tall and monolithic, but roiling dark on dark like flirting clouds of smoke. I leaned forward, trying to gauge the object's size, and it moved, its top sweeping down. A face drew level with mine, elongated and furry, its snout pressed to the glass and exhaling blasts of fog. Its eyes were bright orange.

I started to flinch back, but then realized that I was only doing it because I was supposed to. It's what people on TV and in movies did when they saw a monster. I wasn't actually afraid. I wanted to see this thing.

The creature kept still, as though understanding and obeying my desire. I let my gaze linger on its tufts of brown fur, orange eyes, and protruding snout, its talons on the glass, its garment like a living shadow, shrinking and bending from the light, sometimes black, sometimes red.

I put a hand to the cool glass and spread my fingers. The creature tilted its head to one side, then mimicked my movement, placing its long-taloned paw opposite mine. It looked at our hands, then back at me. I couldn't shake an impression of a dog, and laughed a little. The creature exhaled hard, fogging the glass. Startled, I stepped back. A dog, maybe, but dogs could still bite.

I shifted to look through unfogged glass. The creature had also drawn back into its cloak, so only its snout remained visible. It peeked at me from inside, an orange gleam in its eye sockets.

I leaned forward, held up one finger. "Wait a minute," I said. "Do you understand?"

The creature held up one digit, then nodded slowly, as though trying out the gesture for the first time. I moved my finger to my lips to signal for quiet. Again it mirrored me.

I let the curtain drop and crossed the room to my toy box. I opened the front panel as quietly as I could and thrust my arm through all the sharp plastic edges to the very bottom, where I'd hidden the Batman action figure. Next, I grabbed my Kermit the Frog flashlight off my nightstand. I unlatched and opened the window wide enough for me to wriggle through.

I stood on the concrete of the atrium, barefoot. The creature kept its distance. Extended to its full height, it looked at least seven feet tall, most of its considerable length obscured by the amorphous cloak. I turned on the flashlight to get a better look, but the creature held up its claws and looked away.

"You don't like that," I said.

It shook its head. *No.*

"I'm sorry," I said, and switched it off.

The creature faced me again, its breath heavy and wet. I grew uncomfortable beneath the bright, unwavering gaze. I wasn't used to being so visible, or noticed. I held up the Batman toy.

"Did you bring this?" I said.

It nodded.

"Why?" I said.

The creature crouched and picked up a chunk of sidewalk chalk. It made several slow, unsteady scratches on the ground. I shone my light on the space and read a single word written in jagged, barely legible letters: FRIEND.

"Friend," I said. "You want to be friends?"

The creature nodded.

"Why?" I said.

It remained crouched before me but made no response.

I held up Batman again. "You didn't steal this, did you?"

The creature shook its head. *No.*

Behind the creature, the living room light came on. Had someone heard us? The creature cringed without turning around, as though even this veiled illumination hurt.

"I have to go now," I whispered. "Bye."

I turned to my open window and crouched to crawl back inside. One of the creature's claws landed on my shoulder. I had the sensation of drifting, the way you do in the moments before sleep, everything around me soft, comfortable like a blanket—

I bumped my head against the window and found myself back in the atrium, squatting outside my window with a monster's paw on my shoulder. I shrugged it off, embarrassed, as though I'd been caught naked.

"What do you want?" I said.

The creature scratched out another message with sidewalk chalk, and I shone my light on the ground to read it: INSIDE?

If it had made the request before it touched me, I probably would have acquiesced, but now, waking from the sweet fog, I declined.

"I might get in trouble," I said. And then, after a second's internal debate, I added, "You can come back tomorrow if you want."

It didn't try to stop me as I wriggled back into my room, but stared as the glass slid closed between us.

"Good night," I whispered, putting my hand to the window. The creature—my monster, My Friend—put its paw opposite mine and scratched the glass, whining just a little.

13

With their concept decided upon, my family and the Vandergriff High theater department began work in earnest. I wasn't allowed back in the warehouse, so I saw none of it. Instead, I spent my afternoons and evenings in the back room of Bump in the Night, doing homework and entertaining myself. Sally picked me up from school and brought me back home at night. She checked my homework, put me to bed, and stayed until Mom, Sydney, and Eunice returned.

I saw my family only in the mornings, sleepily shuffling past one another as they prepared for the day. I missed Eunice, but My Friend visited every night, arriving sometime between Sally's kind-but-rote good night and that strange floating place between wakefulness and sleep, its scratch at the window as gentle as a shake on the shoulder. If I'd been older, or a little more careful, or if adults had paid more attention to me when I was small, I might have worried about getting caught out there. But I was used to being invisible, and anyway it was tough to worry about anything once My Friend arrived. At first, we played with action figures, but the creature's strong, clumsy hands popped off heads and arms. Next we tried board games, but the creature seemed to have trouble remembering the rules, and winning every time grew tiresome, so we started working through my collection of books. First I read to it, and then we copied out sentences and pictures. The creature's penmanship remained atrocious, but when we tried to copy illustrations from *Danny and the Dinosaur,* the creature's facsimiles actually resembled the contents of the book.

"You're good at this," I said, frustrated as I compared our work on the pavement to the book. My own pictures were crude and incomprehensible blobs of color. "I wish I could draw like you."

The creature offered me a fat blue cylinder of chalk, which I took. It stepped behind me, put one paw on my right shoulder and the other around my left wrist, and began to guide my hand on the ground. Again I was flooded with that incredible sense of drifting bliss, of warmth and comfort and desire fulfilled. I was vaguely aware of the concrete in front of me, the same way you're aware of the road through a streaked and filthy windshield.

When the creature let go, the feeling receded, and I rounded on it, frustrated and disoriented, chalk raised in one hand as though ready to strike. My Friend looked a bit woozy, too, its head bobbing from side to side. It gave me a questioning look.

"I'm sorry," I said. "I didn't mean to."

The creature pointed over my shoulder. I picked up my flashlight and shone it where I'd made my guided drawing: a vast, sprawling city in miniature, as if seen from a hilltop, stretching out in concentric circles of towering skyscrapers, and, at the center, the nucleus of this strange cell, a tower reaching into the heavens. It looked familiar, someplace I'd been before.

"I did this?" I said.

The creature pointed at me, then at itself, then interlaced the digits of its paws. We'd done it together. It bent forward and scratched its nightly question on the pavement: INSIDE?

I gave my nightly reply: "Not tonight."

I didn't tell anyone about the creature, although I wasn't entirely sure why at the time. Call it instinct. Looking back now, I wasn't worried about seeming crazy, but I was happy to have something entirely my own, something my family couldn't hide or take away from me.

14

Construction on the haunted house (christened The Wandering Dark) ended in mid-September, but Mr. Ransom and the theater kids stayed later and later past my bedtime for rehearsals. Since Sydney's arrival at home (signaled by the living room light behind the atrium curtain) was my new bedtime alert, I stayed up later and later with the monster. My performance in first grade, never stellar, began to slip. Sally made sure I finished my homework and turned it in, but I failed tests and slept in class. I didn't cause any disruptions, so my teacher, Mrs. Column, didn't expend much energy trying to keep me awake. My days took on a dreamy, distant quality, somehow unreal, as though I was watching a long, boring, poorly projected, and hard to understand movie. When I did see my family, they were preoccupied. All they wanted to talk about was The Wandering Dark, which they would do only in oblique terms in front of me. Even Eunice was distant. I missed her, and was jealous of this new enterprise that had stolen her from me.

Finally, one night, fed up with being left out of things, I asked the monster, "How do you get here every night?"

It tilted its head, but didn't respond.

"Do you fly?"

It either didn't understand or refused to answer.

I ran a hand through my hair and sighed. "Can you take me someplace else?"

The creature bent forward, picked up the piece of chalk, and scratched a question on the pavement: WHERE?

"I want to see the haunted house," I said. "Take me to The Wandering Dark."

My Friend stood and stepped back. It extended the talons of its right paw. It felt more like the hand of an adult human than like that of some unspeakable horror, and, as the creature pulled me into its embrace, I felt warmth and sturdiness. It held me fast to its middle and drew its cloak closed around me. Beneath the cloak, the creature wore a baggy, rough tunic that scratched my face.

The creature's leg muscles tightened as it squatted, and then the ground fell away beneath my feet, replaced with empty air. I caught glimpses of the world below, interrupted by rippling fabric: the atrium shrinking, revealing the building of seven units we lived in, and then we tilted forward, the angle changed, and I saw nothing but the purple-black of the light-polluted night sky over Vandergriff. Worry was distant, like a faint radio signal from another state. Pressed flush against the creature, I drifted, a little cold but soothed, comforted and far from the world. The creature had a distinctive smell, something fragrant but also earthy, like the garden department at Walmart, and my mind filled with an image of an immense field of flowers beneath a heavy, dark sky, and, beyond that, a vast skyline, spires and towers and coliseums that seemed to exist only in silhouette.

I was startled out of my reverie by our landing, as My Friend swept its cloak back and released me. I stumbled away, my legs rubbery, my head dizzy and clouded. I fell forward and scraped my hands on the pavement. The pain cleared my head. We were in the parking lot in front of the warehouse. Mr. Ransom's pickup truck was parked near one of the garage doors, and a Styrofoam skull now framed the front door. It looked eerily convincing beneath the parking lot lamps. The creature approached, and I waved it off.

"I'm okay," I said. After a moment of breathing the open air, I felt the dizziness pass. I approached the skull door. My Friend stayed where we'd landed.

"Aren't you coming?" I said.

It shook its head. I tugged at the front door handle, but it didn't budge. I was about to turn around and tell My Friend to forget it, that we should go home, when the door gave way. There was no click or magic spark. One moment it wouldn't move, and the next it swung open.

The lights in the front office were off, and I left them that way. Instead I turned on my flashlight. The room had been cleaned since I'd last been here, the layer of dust scrubbed off everything. The front desk and waiting area chairs had been removed, and the double doors leading into the warehouse were obscured behind a black wall with a white door at its center, the brass knob dull and dented. It turned easily in my hand, and the door opened inward without a sound. I walked down the black hallway, which made a right turn before opening out onto a study—the kind of place where doctors and professors in old movies often conferred. A red and gold rug was spread on the floor, and a cracked leather couch stood across from a huge, ancient-looking desk. Behind the couch sat a fake fireplace, dark and empty. The walls of the room were lined with taxidermied animal heads: deer mostly, occasionally interrupted by a moose or mounted fish.

Above the fireplace hung an empty mounting board with a hole in its center. I peered into it, trying to see what lay beyond, but the darkness remained remote, impenetrable. I thought about Sydney's initial pitch for this place: a monster stalking you through a dark labyrinth, and the visitor with a single flashlight to find the way. I knew it was all pretend, for fun, but knowing didn't help when I was right in the middle of the thing itself, or when there was a real-life monster waiting for me in the parking lot. A monster that had refused to accompany me inside. Who knew the real rules anymore? I moved on, deeper into The Wandering Dark.

After the study came a long, rectangular chamber lined on either side with what I took to be filing cabinets. The floor was blue tile, with drains placed at regular intervals. Two metal examination tables stood close together in the center of the room, both empty, and at the far end there was a wooden door with a frosted glass pane and a phrase I didn't understand: CORONER'S OFFICE. A tall potted plant stood to the right of the door.

I approached one of the big drawers on the right side of the room. It had a small white label right in the center, and printed on it in small, neat type were the words RANSOM, J. I tugged at the cold metal handle, but it wouldn't budge. I let go and continued shining my light on all the names on the drawers: Vogler, Goldman, Daniels, Price. I read each aloud, sounding the words as quietly as I could, enjoying the sounds they made when translated into speech: Sangalli, Smith, Stephens, Turner.

This last one stopped my mindless recitation. Turner, H. As in Harry Turner? I grabbed the handle and tugged. This one opened for me.

I shone my flashlight into a rectangular box about seven feet deep, containing a narrow cot on rollers. On the cot lay a large lump, roughly human in shape, beneath a white sheet. I reached for it.

A peal of laughter exploded through the building, boisterous and cheerful. It drove the lump under the sheet right out of my head. I left the drawer open, walked past the potted plant and through the CORONER'S OFFICE door into a large, relatively well-lit space with a hardwood floor and a stage covered with instruments. A single microphone stood in a spotlight, beneath a banner reading WELCOME HOME, BOYS! in red, white, and blue. Balloons were scattered about the floor, and two figures were entwined on a folding chair in the middle. Even from behind I recognized Mr. Ransom's form, his beefy arms wrapped around the shirtless teenage girl in his lap. She pushed his face into her cleavage, her head thrown back, eyes closed and mouth hanging open. I recognized her, too: Sydney.

"Say it," she said.

Mr. Ransom moaned, making hungry sounds like a pig at a trough. She grabbed his hair and yanked so he had to look at her. In a dirty movie, she'd have been smiling, taunting. Instead, there was something wounded and vulnerable in her face.

"Say it," she said again.

"I love you," he said, breathless, voice hoarse.

She tightened her grip on Mr. Ransom's hair. "Again," she said. Maybe it was meant as a command, but she sounded like she was near tears.

"I love you, Sydney," Mr. Ransom said.

With her free hand, Sydney reached back and unclasped her bra. The straps slid from her shoulders and down her arms. He made another muffled, hungry sound against her chest, and she cried out, as if in pain. The sound startled me, and I lost my grip on my flashlight. It hit the floor with a clatter, and Sydney's eyes snapped open, bright with surprised fear.

She released her grip on Mr. Ransom's head as her gaze locked on mine. "Noah?"

Mr. Ransom began to turn around. I bolted. I heard them moving as I scrambled back through the maze of rooms and into the parking lot, but I was small and fully clothed and terrified, and I emerged uncaught, untouched. My Friend remained where I had left it, and I ran into its embrace.

"Take me home," I said. Warmth enveloped me as the creature swept its cloak shut and my feet left the ground.

We landed what felt like seconds later. The creature opened its cloak, and I stepped back into the familiar atrium. I leaned forward, dimly aware of the creature crouched next to me, scratching something on the ground with sidewalk chalk. My head began to clear, and I reached for my window, meaning to open it, but the creature's paw landed on my shoulder, and things grew immediately fuzzy again. I shook free.

"What?" I said. "What is it?"

It pointed at the ground, and I squinted to read what it had written in the dark: INSIDE?

"No."

The creature huffed and scribbled two more words before looking back at me:

FRIEND
HELP

The creature underlined the second word three times, and the chalk broke on the third stroke. I read plaintiveness in My Friend's slumped posture, the hard curve of its neck.

"*No,*" I said again, shaking my head harder.

It didn't try to stop me as I pushed my window open and clambered through, and it was gone by the time I turned around to push the window shut again.

At some point Sydney let herself into the apartment. She came to my bedroom door, the shadows of her feet visible in the crack beneath it, her breath oddly loud and labored. She sounded like she'd just finished a marathon, taking deep, almost wheezing gulps of air, her exhalations jagged and uneven. Eventually she walked away.

15

I moved through the next day on autopilot, spaced out during and after school. I spent the afternoon in the back room at Bump in the Night, reading an old *Archie Double Digest* with bleary eyes until I heard Sally talking to someone up front. The person she was talking to laughed, and I recognized him as Mr. Ransom at once. I looked around the room for a way out but remained rooted in my chair as Sally said, "Sure, go on back."

Mr. Ransom lurched into the break room, carrying a large box. "There's the guy!" he said, voice booming with theatrical cheer. The box looked big enough to stuff a kid into, if you got creative with how you packed the body. He stood in front of me, blocking my view of the doorway. "I'm glad you're here. There's something I've been meaning to give you." He set the box on the table and stepped away from it. "Go ahead," he said.

I put my comic down and stood on my chair. As I reached for the loose flaps of the box, I hesitated.

"It's not going to bite," Mr. Ransom said, annoyance creeping into his tone.

I forced my hands forward and opened the flaps. I gasped at the contents. It was the Batcave play set. The toy I'd lusted after for weeks, right in front of me.

"Do you like it?" Mr. Ransom said.

"Isn't this your son's?" I said.

"It was," Mr. Ransom said, "but he has too many toys anyway, and I saw you take a shine to it when your family came over for dinner." He raised his eyebrows, waiting for me to say something in return.

I pulled my hands out of the box. "This is very nice of you, Mr. Ransom, but I don't have a Batman figure anyway," I said. It was a lie, but what probable explanation could I have offered regarding how I'd received the toy? "All I could do is look at it."

He sighed. "I meant to bring you Kyle's Batman, too, but no matter how hard I looked, I couldn't find it. I know Kyle didn't take it with him, and I haven't had any guests in my house since your family came over. So do you still want to stand there and tell me you don't have it?"

"I didn't steal Kyle's Batman," I said.

"I can keep a secret if you can. Can you keep a secret, Noah?"

I looked at the new toy and didn't answer.

"What you saw last night," he said, "with me and Sydney—it was something private, for older people. If you were to tell anyone about it, both your family and I could get into a lot of trouble." He walked around the table and squeezed my shoulder with one massive, bearlike hand. "You don't want to make trouble for your family right before your new business opens, right?"

"Right." I would have agreed to anything if he would just stop touching me.

He started to walk out, then stopped and turned around. "Noah," he said.

"Yes, Mr. Ransom?"

"How did you get to the warehouse?"

As long as we were keeping each other's secrets, I saw no reason to lie. "I flew," I said.

He gave me a strange, searching look, and then left.

16

At home, I hid out in my room, curled up with the blanket over my head. I told Sally I wasn't feeling well and she left me alone. Eventually, Eunice came home and let herself into my room. She sat next to me on the bed and put a hand on my shoulder.

"What's wrong?" she said.

"Nothing," I said.

"You never used to lie to me."

I remained hidden beneath the blanket, pondering the secrets I now kept: Sydney's; Mr. Ransom's; my own. I started to cry.

"Noah," she murmured, running her hand up and down my back. "Noah, Noah, Noah. It's okay. Whatever it is, it's okay."

Still I didn't unburden myself. Although we still went through the ritual I love yous at bedtime, an invisible wedge separated us. Her affection felt rote, and I was now a liar.

As I lay in bed, I wished my family had never decided to make a haunted house. I didn't care if it meant we were poor forever, if I could have things back the way they were. When the scratching outside my window began, I threw the blankets off the bed and picked up the Batman from the floor. My Friend stood outside, dragging its claws against the glass. I motioned for it to step back, and it obeyed. I unlatched the window and climbed out.

When I stood, the creature tried to bridge the distance between us. I stopped it by holding up Batman. "Did you steal this from Mr. Ransom's house?"

The creature shook its head. *No.*

"Are you lying?" I said.

Its head drooped.

"Why did you do it?"

The creature picked up a piece of chalk, and drew a box around the words it had scratched the night before: FRIEND. HELP.

"Help?" I said. "Help? How does this help anything?" I boiled with the unfairness of it, the way I'd been trapped and burdened. "I could get in a lot of trouble because of you. Go away."

The creature stood, chalk still gripped with odd delicacy in its talons. It tilted its head in apparent puzzlement.

"I know you understand me," I said. "Go." I made a shooing motion. The creature stood still. I pitched the Batman, and it struck right above the creature's left eye. Its head jerked back and it dropped the chalk. Its eyes lit a brighter shade of orange. A low growl started in its throat. Behind it, the sliding glass door went bright as the living room light came on. The creature turned, noticing it as well. I ducked back through my window and pulled it shut right as I heard the latch on the sliding glass door, the pleasant rumble as it moved along its track. I kept still behind the curtains, waiting for startled screams or even violence. Instead I heard the distinctive pad of my mother's footsteps on the concrete, pausing outside my window, then retreating inside. If she saw the writing out there on the ground, she never said anything to me about it.

I was still awake when Sydney let herself in around midnight and headed straight for the bathroom. She shut the door and turned on the faucet, but I could hear her harsh, broken voice over the roar of the water. Sydney, hyperventilating, crying by herself in the middle of the night.

17

Two days before The Wandering Dark opened for business, Mr. Ransom invited my family to his house for another dinner, promising "honest-to-goodness home-cooked food." Sally didn't come with us this time, but she lent Mom her car for the trip. When we arrived at the Ransom house, we found a Ford Fiesta parked next to Mr. Ransom's pickup in the driveway.

"Who else is coming to dinner?" Eunice said.

"He didn't say anything to me," Mom said.

Sydney faced forward, silent in the front seat, and I tried to divine meaning from the back of her head. We'd been avoiding one another with great success since I'd caught her with Mr. Ransom, and this was the first time in over a week we'd been in the same place for more than a few minutes.

The lawn had been mowed, the newspapers removed, and the errant branch clipped so it no longer blocked the walk. When we rang the doorbell, a small, thin woman, barely taller than Eunice, answered. If not for the laugh lines around her mouth, I might have mistaken Janet Ransom for a girl as she pulled Mom into a hug.

"So good to see you, Margaret!"

Mom returned the hug a second too late, her surprise and discomfort apparent in her posture. Mrs. Ransom let her go, then pulled Eunice and me into a wiry, painful embrace.

"Eunice, you've become a young woman," she said. "And, Noah, you look just like a miniature version of your father. It's uncanny."

No one had ever told me this before, and I was still processing it as Mrs. Ransom pulled Sydney into the deepest, longest hug yet.

"Oh, Sydney," she said, clutching the back of my sister's head like a baby's.

Sydney was also late to return the embrace. "Oh, me," she agreed.

Mr. Ransom appeared inside the doorway, wiping his hands on a dish towel. "Surprise," he said, voice weak.

"Don't blame him, it was my idea," Mrs. Ransom said. "Come in, come in!"

The air inside the house had been renewed, turned fresh and fragrant. The lights were bright, and the layer of dust had been swept from the furniture. A boy sat on the living room floor, playing a Nintendo that had not been there before.

"Kyle," Mr. Ransom said to the boy. "Manners!"

The boy sighed and stood. He shook hands with everyone.

"You're Noah," he said when he got to me, boredom turning to open hostility. "You have my Batman and Batcave."

"Noah, did you steal Kyle's toys?" Mom said. Over a week the Batcave had been sitting in a box in my bedroom and she hadn't noticed.

"Mr. Ransom gave them to me," I said.

"Did he?" Mom said. She looked into the kitchen, where Mr. Ransom moved back and forth, checking the oven, stirring the contents of a large pot.

"Daniel's grown very fond of Noah," Mrs. Ransom said, "and I guess he was feeling generous one day." Her smile seemed too wide, as though, despite the words coming out of her mouth, she absolutely thought me guilty of stealing from her child.

Mom's stare at Mr. Ransom turned into a frown. "Still, if Kyle wants his toys back, I'm sure Noah would be happy to return them."

"Nonsense," Mrs. Ransom said. "We're not about to take back a gift, are we, Kyle?"

"No," Kyle said glumly.

"Why don't you show Noah your room?" she said.

"Come on," he said, and I followed him down the hall.

His room looked much the way it had the last time I'd been here, only less dusty and missing its Batcave. A lot of Ghostbusters toys were scattered across the carpet.

"You like Ghostbusters?" I said.

"I like Batman better," he said.

"I'll give it back."

He looked as though nothing would please him more, but knew better than to agree. "I'd get in trouble. It's so dumb. Mom got so mad at Dad when she found out about the Batcave, but she won't let me have it back, either. Dad bought me a Nintendo to say sorry. Mom got mad about that, too."

"Does she get mad a lot?"

He smiled a little. "All the time."

At that point Mr. Ransom summoned us to the dinner table. Kyle and I sat next to one another, the air between us now open rather than hostile. We ate together in companionable silence while the adults talked.

"So," Mom said, after we'd all settled in and made the usual comments about how good everything looked and smelled. She gestured at Mr. and Mrs. Ransom, sitting at the head and foot of the table. "This *is* a surprise."

"How long has this been going on?" Sydney demanded.

"Sydney, manners," Mom said.

"About a month, I think," Mrs. Ransom said.

"A *month*?" Sydney glared at Mr. Ransom. He glanced at her, and then caught my eye. Kyle looked around the table, confused by the sudden tension. I stuffed food into my face, pretending obliviousness.

"Sydney, what is the matter?" Mom said.

Sydney squeezed a balled-up napkin in one fist. With her thumb and forefinger, she tore tiny shreds of paper from one end and dropped them on the table. Her breathing also seemed a little labored, but I don't think any of the adults noticed this tiny alteration in the movement of her shoulders, chest, and back. Sydney was good at performing. It was the sort of subtle change that only a sibling could sniff out.

"I see you every day, Mr. Ransom," Sydney said. "You never said anything to me."

"It's not Mr. Ransom's job to tell you about his personal life," Mom said. "He's your teacher, not your friend."

Mr. Ransom took a sip from his wineglass. "It didn't seem appropriate, Sydney," he said.

"Daniel tells me great things about the choreography you've put together for the dance hall in the haunted house," Mrs. Ransom said. She reached across the table to hold Sydney's hand. "I'd love to come take a look and maybe give you some pointers."

Sydney swallowed hard, and I saw her bring her breathing under control. "Of course," she said. "I'd love some advice." Something about the glassiness at the edges of her eyes, briefly visible before she hardened her gaze again, fractured me deep inside.

18

When we got home, Sydney remained in the doorway while the rest of us went to the living room to remove our jackets and shoes. She stood silhouetted against the open door, arms pulled tight around her middle.

"Sydney?" Mom said, hands poised over her sneaker laces.

"This is all wrong," Sydney said.

"What do you mean?" Mom said.

Sydney gave a tiny shake of her head. "I mean I quit."

Mom paused in the act of pulling off a sneaker. "You quit what?"

"The Wandering Dark," Sydney said. "I quit. I'm done. It's all wrong and I don't want to do it anymore."

"We open the day after tomorrow," Mom said.

"Not my problem," Sydney said. She walked up the hall to the girls' bedroom.

"It's absolutely your problem, young lady," Mom said. She stood to storm back through the apartment after Sydney, but stumbled over her untied shoes. She caught herself with one arm against the hallway wall and pushed forward into the girls' bedroom with overlong, careful strides. She didn't shut the door behind her, so Eunice and I heard the ensuing conversation:

"We did all of this—this whole stupid, painful, *foolhardy* project— for you," Mom said. "It's your baby, your concept, your dream. You don't get to quit."

"You handicapped the whole fucking thing from the start!" Sydney said. "It's not my fault that you kept Daddy's designs to yourself and ruined it."

"There *are* no designs," Mom said. "There never were! There's a collection of nonsense that your father drew while he was dying of a brain tumor. It was something we did to pass the time while we waited for the end. There's nothing there."

A silence drifted out of the room and up the hall, long enough that Eunice and I had time to look at one another rather than the hallway.

"You're lying," Sydney said at last, her voice small.

"I'm not," Mom said. She matched Sydney's lower tone, gentle like you'd expect of a mother comforting her kid. That gentleness set off a pang in me, an honest yearning. Mom almost never used that voice.

"Then why keep any of it? Why not let anyone see?" Sydney said.

"I don't have to answer either of those questions," Mom said, still in that gentle voice, but with the familiar steel beneath it.

"And I don't have to work at this shitty haunted house anymore," Sydney said. "You and Mr. Ransom go have fun."

I'm not sure who slammed the door as Mom left the room. She started back up the hall toward the living room and tripped over her shoelaces again. She didn't catch herself this time, but instead fell forward onto the linoleum floor with a curse. She landed on her hands and knees, sat up, and tore her sneakers off, pitching them into the living room. She followed them a moment later, fuming. I cringed as her fiery gaze landed on me, and then Eunice.

"Do either of you have any idea what's going on right now?" she said.

"No," Eunice said, sounding genuinely surprised.

I nearly cracked and told her what I'd seen. I longed to unload the information, to let an adult deal with it, but I'd promised. I'd even taken payment in exchange for my silence.

19

Mom and Mr. Ransom replaced Sydney with another girl from the theater department. Sydney spent most of the two days before opening in her room, in her pajamas. She didn't ask about The Wandering Dark, and stopped fighting with Mom altogether. If Mom told her to do something, she did it without comment.

Even though she was now my de facto babysitter, we still avoided each other. I stayed out of the girls' room, where it sounded like she was speaking for hours at a stretch, in a voice too soft for proper eavesdropping. I didn't know if she was on the phone, or reading her favorite plays out loud, and I kept my distance. When she emerged to watch TV, I retreated to my room. I tried to play with my new Batman and Batcave a few times, but the experience was sour, joyless. It was my first experience with getting something I wanted the wrong way, thereby ruining the thing gotten.

On opening night, Mom and Eunice both hugged me and made me promise to behave for Sydney. Sydney told them to break a leg. Again Mom gave Sydney a queer, searching look, as though she knew something was wrong, maybe even suspected the nature of the wrong thing, but was afraid to ask and find out for sure.

After they left, Sydney sat next to me on the couch, where I was watching TV. When I got up to leave, she put a hand on my shoulder and asked me to stay. We sat in silence for a while, and I got so absorbed in the show that I was startled when she finally spoke.

"There's one thing I don't understand," she said. "How did you get to the warehouse?"

I didn't answer. She rolled her eyes and made a disgusted sound as she threw herself to her feet. She headed for the girls' bedroom as a knock sounded at the front door.

"Get that, will you?" she said.

I answered the door, but found the porch empty. I stepped outside to look around. The parking lot appeared deserted as well, nothing but unoccupied cars beneath flickering lights. It was quieter than I'd ever heard it, too. Usually you could hear traffic, or the sounds of neighbors on their porches. Now it was like a TV with the volume turned all the way down.

"Hello?" I called, my voice loud in the unnatural quiet.

Inside the apartment, Sydney screamed.

I ran back inside, leaving the front door open behind me. I threw open the girls' bedroom door. The room was a mess—drawers hanging open, clothes in untidy piles, beds unmade, books open and facedown—and, aside from me, empty. The curtains drifted slightly, in front of an open window. The window looked out on our front porch. Had it been open when I answered the door? I couldn't remember, but I didn't think so.

I walked back to the front door and looked at the open window from the outside. Aside from being open, it looked perfectly normal. No blood, no dropped objects or broken glass.

"Sydney?" I called.

Behind me, all the lights in the apartment went out. I stood still, listening. A new sound began, so faint I could barely hear it outside the silent apartment: *skritch-skritch-skritch*.

I went to my room. *Skritch-skritch-skritch* against the window, soft and hesitant. As I drew closer, the sound grew louder, more excited. I pulled my curtains apart. My Friend stood in the atrium, hunched over, palms spread on the glass. It looked frightened, somehow conveying worry with its dim orange eyes. I put my hand on the glass opposite its, and felt its incredible warmth through the barrier.

I unlatched the window and pulled it all the way open. I stood back and gestured inside.

"Friend," I said. "Help."

The Turner Sequence III: Eunice

When Eunice arrives in the City, they put her to work
at a desk. In her mind, she sees it as several desks.
First, she sees it as the one in her room at the old
house where she lived while her father was alive. She
thinks she's up late, hammering away at the keyboard of
her Commodore 64. She loves the sound her fingers make,
a quiet clacking music that carries her thoughts along
with it. Sometimes she closes her eyes because the words
flow better in complete darkness, free from her judging
gaze. Other times she leaves her eyes open but looks
away, to give her vision a break from the piercing light
of the screen. Now, in this facsimile of her old bedroom,
she turns her head to the right, toward her high, narrow
window—and that's when she sees the face peering in
at her.

In real life, she screamed and jumped into her bed, but
now she stands and approaches the window for a better
look. No matter how close she gets, though, the shape
remains an inky blot on the other side of the glass, a
vague suggestion. It seems to flicker, frozen between
two positions, like an image on a paused videotape. It's
trapped somehow. She should feel relieved, but instead
she feels heavy. Low. Bad in a way she can't quite
name, like she's sick but without symptoms—no fever, no
headache, no nausea, but low all the same. The feeling
grows as she stares at the shape in the window.

Uneasy, she walks back to her desk and sits down, but
as she lands, she finds herself in a large, well-lit

area. Instead of the stiff wooden chair of her childhood desk, she sits in a folding metal chair, and the desk and computer have been replaced with a collapsible card table and an ugly brown electric typewriter. She's sitting in the middle of her family's warehouse in the late summer of 1989, writing the original script for The Wandering Dark.

If she were working alone, Eunice would have set up in the front office, where things are quiet, but her writing partner, Merrin Price, wants to be out here. This is, after all, a group project, and Merrin thinks that they'll write a better script with all their fellows around and inspiring them. Eunice doesn't know if she buys it, but Merrin's older, so Eunice lets her take the lead.

Eunice has always been the writer in the family, so it offended her when Mr. Ransom insisted that Merrin serve as coauthor. She can't shake the feeling that Merrin's being pawned off on her. The older girl is a little too plump to play lead roles and has a brittle voice that breaks when pushed too hard. When she acts onstage, she seems overwhelmed, and whatever is unique or special about her flattens out, especially when compared with Sydney.

Eunice can identify with this last bit—all her life she's been watching the world part and make way for her sister like the Red Sea, while Eunice hurries along behind, hoping she won't drown. Even so, she's not eager to have Merrin at her shoulder while she's trying to write. She doesn't complain, because she never complains. With Mom and Sydney at perpetual war, it always falls to Eunice to keep the peace, regardless of her own feelings.

Eunice shifts in her chair and sees Merrin next to her. Merrin smiles, and something dislodges in Eunice's chest. Breathing gets easier. The dark shape at her bedroom

window fades from her thoughts. The memory takes on a
light, faded quality, like a bad photocopy from a machine
running low on toner.

Where do you want to start? Merrin says.

Eunice faces the typewriter, lays her fingers on the
home keys. She takes a deep breath, closes her eyes,
and begins to type. Each keystroke sounds like a tiny
gunshot, and the carriage rings every time she reaches
the end of a line:

*You the visitors are let into a warehouse by a
bouncer of sorts. He counts your group out, and if
you're at a prime number (three, five, or seven), he
picks up his walkie-talkie and utters a single word:
Innsmouth. As you enter there is a girl standing just
inside.*

*"There were too many people in my group," she says.
"I hope it's okay for me to tag along with yours. I'm
Katie," she says. She smiles. No one would think of
refusing this girl.*

*Your group enters a dark room. The bouncer shuts
the door behind you, sealing you in complete
darkness. You're left this way long enough to notice
the eerie quiet. Your friends' breathing becomes
loud. You wonder if you've been forgotten, or if you
ought to move forward without the benefit of sight.
You hear a click, and a single beam of light bursts
on, pointed right in your face, blinding you.*

*"You shouldn't be here," a voice says. It runs like
an ice cube dropped down the back of your shirt.
This is THE GUIDE.*

The typewriter bell rings, signaling the end of
another line. Eunice hits Return, and the carriage flies

back to its starting position. She shakes the stiffness
from her hands and looks over her shoulder at Merrin.
Merrin's eyes move from the page to Eunice's face.

You just gave me chills, she says. Eunice notices for
the first time that Merrin's eyes are blue.

The room changes again, and now Eunice sits at the
breakfast table at home, across from her younger brother,
Noah. She sees him only in the mornings now. She still
gets him up for school, still makes sure he's dressed and
fed, but she doesn't have time to read to him, or answer
his litanies of questions about the world. For whatever
reason, he's stopped asking for those things. He's a wan,
silent presence now, with dark bags beneath his drooping
eyes. It's strange. Eunice feels fuller than before,
like there's more of her somehow. She wonders briefly if
somehow her ascension is linked to her little brother's
descent.

She doesn't like the thought. She turns her gaze away
from him and finds herself back in the warehouse, in
front of the typewriter. As she and Merrin write, the
building fills with the whine of saws and drills, the
thunder of hammers. They're joined by the rattle of
sewing machines, the metallic hiss of scissors cutting
fabric. The bones take shape around the authors of this
production: morgue, study, dance hall, and an endless
series of corridors. Eunice's chest feels full of light,
so bright it must be shining through her teeth. She
didn't know it was possible to feel this way. She didn't
understand how muted and gray and tired and bad she felt
until now, sitting next to Merrin and dreaming up ways
to scare and delight strangers.

Really, she's dreaming up ways to scare and delight
Merrin. If Merrin reacts to an idea or line—if she
laughs or gasps, or slaps Eunice on the back—Eunice knows

it's good. The first time Merrin touches Eunice, Eunice jumps in her chair and tattoos some nonsense onto the page.

I'm sorry, Merrin says, and backs away.

If you don't count accidental jostling from strangers in public, it's the first time in years that anyone other than Noah has touched Eunice.

It's fine, Eunice says, warmth traveling up her shoulder to her cheeks and ears. *I was just concentrating and you surprised me.*

Sorry, Merrin says. *Won't happen again.*

No really, it's fine, Eunice repeats. She settles in her chair and faces the typewriter. *Here. Try again. Pretend I wrote something superlative.*

For a second, nothing happens, and she worries that she's made things irrevocably weird. Then Merrin's hand lands on her shoulder.

Superlative work, Eunice, she says, her mouth right next to Eunice's ear. Eunice burns.

They take their breaks at the typewriter, eating their lunches from brown paper bags. The AC is on, but the bay doors are open, and the air is thick and still. Perspiration gathers in the hollow of Merrin's throat, shining, and Eunice worries whether she's sitting too close or too far away for Merrin's liking.

Do you have a boyfriend? Merrin asks.

Eunice shakes her head. *Not yet.*

How old are you?

Thirteen.

Merrin nods, chewing a grape.

What about you? Eunice says. *I bet you've had lots of boyfriends.*

Merrin laughs, a surprised, throaty sound. *Not many boys want to date a fat girl.*

You're not, Eunice says, because it's what you're

supposed to say when someone says something
self-deprecating.

Merrin waves the statement off. *It's okay. I've come
to terms. But you—you're skinny, so I imagine it's only a
matter of time.*

Eunice bows her head to look at her body. She is
skinny, flat-chested, narrow-hipped, and small-bottomed.
When Sydney was thirteen, her shape changed, curves
breaking up the smooth planes of her body, pushing
it toward womanhood. Eunice's body remains stubbornly
boyish.

She looks back at Merrin, watches Merrin's mouth
working around the fruit. Merrin holds the next bite in
one hand and crosses her other arm over her middle, as
though trying to hide herself. She wears a black T-shirt
and blue jeans that hug tight to her wide, generous
body. Her fingernails are painted red, but the polish
is chipping. Her eyes are bright blue, her cheeks round
and pink and flush, her dark brown hair cut short and
framing her face. Eunice takes in the soft slope of
her shoulders, her wide, round bottom, and thinks that
Merrin's body is the opposite of her own, expressly,
aggressively feminine.

Merrin notices Eunice's stare and stops chewing. *What?*
she says, mouth still full of food.

If I were a boy I'd want to date you, Eunice says. Her
face feels hot and she bows her head, but the room has
changed again. She's still sitting at a table, but now
her typewriter is gone and she's surrounded by other
people. It's audition day, when Sydney and Mr. Ransom
will cast the characters Eunice and Merrin have written.

Eunice has never had to listen to anyone else perform
her work, and she cringes often as the hopefuls read her
lines. She makes endless notes on how to fix her many
shortcomings as a writer (and a human being). When it

comes time to cast the role of the Guide, Eunice looks up from her notepad to find a dance hall full of people staring at her.

What? she says.

Merrin says you want to read for the role, Mr. Ransom says.

When Eunice opens her mouth to protest, Merrin gives her a little shove. She walks to the middle of the room, everyone staring, and she wants to bolt, wants to run screaming, and she's furious with Merrin, how dare Merrin do this, but then Eunice catches Merrin's eye and Merrin winks.

Whenever you're ready, Mr. Ransom says.

Eunice clears her throat, glances down at her copy of the script, and begins to read.

You're not supposed to be here. She clears her throat again, or tries to. Some obstruction refuses to move. *How did you get in? The walls here grow thin, ever more confused. There are doors where there used to be walls, and darkness blooms in place of light. The only way out is through, to the other side. I cannot go with you, but I can offer help.* This sounds like bad Tolkien. Who wrote this? Who could be expected to speak this out loud? *A single beam of light, to show you the path. Use it wisely.* She makes a vague gesture to simulate handing the flashlight to a visitor. *Oh, and a word of caution. A great evil, once safely contained, is now loose. It roams freely, regardless of walls, doors. So I must caution you: no matter what you see or hear, try not to make too much noise. Sound will attract the creature. Good luck.*

Eunice looks up, back at the crowd of watching faces. If only she had the ability to disappear.

Thank you, she says, waiting to be dismissed.

Mr. Ransom and Sydney exchange a glance, then face her again.

Eunice, do you want this part? Mr. Ransom says.

Eunice looks past Mr. Ransom, past the assembled faces, to Merrin. Merrin gives her a thumbs-up.

I think so, she says.

Mr. Ransom says, *It's yours.*

Eunice walks back to the table. Merrin slaps her on the arm and beams. What would it take, Eunice wonders, to feel this way every day?

Eunice turns to look at Merrin, to say something, but again the room changes. Now she stands in a small, enclosed, stiflingly hot, dark space, next to a table with flashlights on top and bottles of water on the floor beneath. She looks down at herself. She wears a white, hooded robe. She's in the entryway of The Wandering Dark on opening night, playing the Guide.

It's been a fraught couple of days. Sydney quit at the last minute and they had to recast her role, so now Merrin is performing the big jazzy number in the dance hall. Noah still isn't looking well, and she's worried— but it's a distant worry, because, somewhere not too far away, Eunice can hear guests laughing and screaming, and she knows that The Wandering Dark is working. People are having a good time. She imagines herself a playwright, hiding in the lobby of the theater, listening to her show through closed doors. She takes a bow in the dark, facing toward the center of the building. She wishes her father could be alive to see this.

Look, she thinks. *Look what we did for you.* She wonders how things are going for Merrin, over in the dance hall.

Later, as everyone washes the makeup off and changes back into their regular clothes, Eunice finds her typewriter in a corner of the dressing room. She pauses in the act of changing to lay a hand on it. Merrin approaches and hugs Eunice from behind.

Fondling your typewriter? Merrin says.

We should have it bronzed, Eunice says, leaning into the hug. *Did you hear that audience tonight? Is this what it's always like? Putting on a play?*

On the good nights, Merrin says, before releasing her. *So listen. What are you doing now?*

Nothing, Eunice says, trying to sound casual even as her heart pounds. *Why, did you want to do something?*

Merrin licks her lips. *Brian Smith and I are going back to his house to hang out for a little while. He's got a little brother about your age. I thought maybe you two would hit it off?*

Eunice does her best not to look completely crestfallen. *Oh, wow. That's really nice of you, Merrin.*

What's wrong? Merrin says.

It takes Eunice a humiliatingly long time to think up an answer. *Nothing's wrong. But I promised Noah I'd tuck him in tonight. It's been a while, you know?*

What did I do? Merrin says.

Eunice hasn't quite scrubbed her face clean of all the makeup, but she heads to the rack where her street clothes hang. Merrin follows.

Will you please tell me what I did wrong? Merrin says.

Really. I promised Noah, Eunice says. She takes off her robe, hangs it on the rack, and starts to dress.

Another time, then, Merrin says.

Sure. Eunice feels Merrin looking at her, waiting for her to turn around, but she doesn't. She keeps her back to Merrin until Merrin leaves.

Eunice suddenly can't stand up. She walks back to the typewriter and sits down. She doesn't cry. Not here. She closes her eyes and tries not to see Merrin, tries not to even think of her. Merrin meant no harm. She thought she was doing a good thing. Eunice just wanted a different favor. She wanted to hear Merrin say the forbidden words,

to make okay the rotten thing at Eunice's core that makes
her ashamed and afraid of herself.

When she looks up, she's in a different room. At first
she has trouble understanding what she's seeing. She gets
the impression of a large chamber with vaulted ceilings
and a wide, empty marble floor reflecting moonlight. The
walls seem to be made of some writhing black material,
like tentacles sliding past one another. But then she's
back in the bedroom at the old house, and she's six years
old again, and the typewriter has been replaced by her
old Commodore 64. She looks at the words on the screen: *A
great evil, once safely contained, is now loose. It roams
freely, regardless of walls, doors.*

She turns to look at the window, and there's that
shape, the flickering mass outside the glass, looking in
with bright orange eyes.

She looks back at the screen. Her hands remain in her
lap as another line of text appears on the screen:

*No matter what you see or hear, try not to make too
much noise. Sound will attract the creature.*

From somewhere close by, she hears laughter, and here
in the City, where she exists both in and out of time,
she recognizes the sound. It's Noah, her little brother,
making way too much noise for this time of night. She
looks at the window again to see if the figure there has
also heard it, but the figure is gone.

She feels a sharp pain in her chest. Merrin's face
leaves her mind's eye, replaced by an image of Noah. *A
great evil, once safely contained, is now loose.* What,
Eunice wonders, has she set loose?

Noah laughs again. Eunice knows she should get up to
check on him, to see what might be at his window, but
a low, heavy feeling is upon her—a sickness without
symptom, the exhaustion that no rest can quench. She

feels her face sinking toward the desk. She lifts her hands to try to hold herself up, and her fingers land on the computer keys. They begin to type without her permission, as her face drifts closer and closer to the screen:

Loose.

Loose.

Loose.

Part Four

The Whisperer
in Darkness

"Are you sure you know what to do?" I whisper-shouted.

Mid-August of 1999 and I was sixteen years old, crouched on the roof of my family's house, drenched in sweat, my hair stuck to my forehead. From my vantage point, I could see into the backyards of our neighbors on three sides—the bright blue of a swimming pool to my left, a yard littered with toys on my right, and a gazebo and fancy deck in the yard opposite ours.

Floating in the air a few feet from the edge of the roof, My Friend extended its arms.

"I'm trusting you," I said.

My Friend clapped its paws twice, then extended them again, like a dad trying to convince a kid to jump into a swimming pool. I took three steps back, wiped perspiration from my face with my shirt, and took a running leap. Arms spread like a bird, I rose, the earth briefly falling away—and then I jerked to a halt in midair as the creature caught me beneath the armpits.

We hovered together, face-to-face. The creature's mouth dropped open in a dopey grin, and I scratched behind its ear. It leaned its head into my hand.

"Good job," I said. "But is there a way to do this that doesn't hurt so much? I'm going to get bruises under my arms."

My Friend drifted over to the rooftop and set me down again. It backed up to its previous spot and clapped twice before extending its arms. *Come on.*

I shook my arms, trying to ward off the ache around my shoulders. I took two deep breaths and closed my eyes. Even at this pitifully low height, a mere two stories up, I couldn't prevent visions of shattered bones or a broken neck. I would have to learn fearlessness if I wanted to play this game more often.

I backed up to the peak of the roof and ran down the slope. This time I bent my legs a little and put more push into my jump. Again I rose, arms spread, and again I began to descend. Panic tried to bloom, but I closed my eyes and pictured myself a figure out of myth: Daedalus, escaping the prison island of Crete on feather-and-wax wings, arms spread, head up, silhouetted against the moon. This time instead of an abrupt stop, I had a quiet sense of weight shifting, like it might in water. The creature caught me gently and spun me in a slow circle. I opened my eyes and meant to speak, but something in the creature's countenance stopped me. For a moment—probably less than a second—I had the impression of looking at a person's face rather than an animal's. This happened occasionally, like catching something out of the corner of your eye, and, like those things that flit at the edge of vision, this impression disappeared as soon as I tried to focus on any specific detail.

"Good job," I said now, and gave it another scratch behind the ears. "Let's call it a night."

We let ourselves back into my bedroom window. The creature flopped onto my bed, and the springs groaned with its weight. I went downstairs, made myself a sandwich in the kitchen, and then brought it upstairs to eat. When I came back, I found an envelope that must have been slipped under my bedroom door. I picked it up and took it to my desk, where I sat to read it while I ate my sandwich:

Dear Noah,

Today I was in my geology lab, staring out the window, and I started thinking about all the layers of the earth, and how as we dig/drill/what-have-you, we pull up all these things that are new to us, but are actually ancient. I wonder if human beings aren't the same? Like every tic of personality, every talent or shortcoming is already in place, waiting to be discovered. My love of writing, for example: Did that already exist, as soon as I was born? Or did it take shape after Dad bought my first computer? I like to think it was already there, and Dad was just smart enough to know where to dig.

Of course, not all prospectors are so kind. Most people in your life are digging at you for things they want—sex, attention, a smile, permission to change lanes on the highway. They're hunting for things to take, not give.

When this occurred to me, I started feeling low. How long until the world hollows me out?

I know I haven't been at my best for the past few years. I've gone to my doctors and taken my Paxil like a good girl, and for the most part I'm able to get out of bed and function every day. But I feel less me, Noah. I don't get as sad as I used to, but I never feel really happy, either. Maybe I'm already hollowed out?

Yours (albeit numbly),
Eunice

We all dealt with what had happened to Sydney in our own ways. In 1989 Mom had reported Sydney's disappearance to the police, and even faithfully related my story of screams, dimming lights, and a ransacked bedroom. Soon after, news vans were camped outside our apartment. We stopped watching TV because our faces were all over the local (and, briefly, national) news. But as weeks turned into months without new leads or clues to my sister's whereabouts, public interest waned. The news vans moved on. The police still called it an active investigation, but I discerned no further activity on their part.

Eunice experienced her first major depressive episode at about this time. Mom had her briefly hospitalized and then medicated. The doctors helped some, but no matter how they adjusted Eunice's medication and dosages, she still had trouble functioning in the world. She couldn't keep a job for more than a few weeks, and while she continued to test extraordinarily well, she couldn't completely focus on anything. She graduated from high school a year later than planned and bombed out of a full scholarship at the University of Texas in Austin after one semester. Since then, Eunice had been living in her old bedroom again and chipping away at an associate's degree at Vandergriff Community College, taking one or two classes a semester and working sporadically at Bump in the Night and The Wandering Dark when she wanted spending money.

It was during this span of years that the "suicide notes" began to appear. I don't know why I kept them. I guess I was hungry for Eunice's company, even if only on the page. Every now and then she floated the idea of suicide, like something she kept in her back pocket, but I couldn't imagine my kind, funny sister hurting anyone, least of all herself.

I read this latest note twice and then stuffed it back in its envelope. I put it in a shoebox beneath my bed with the others. I let my hand linger against the envelopes, felt the dry, springy comfort of my stash, and then closed the box. My Friend grumbled as I climbed into the bed beside it, but scooted over and made space for me.

"Thanks ever so much," I said. In response, it wiggled toward me until its back was pressed into my front. Its warmth through the cloak and my clothes didn't help with my general sweatiness, but there was still a sweetness, a comfort to the touch, a sense of coming home. It pulled me swiftly down to sleep, even as I tried to make a mental note to check on Eunice in the morning.

2

As a cruel booby prize in exchange for our loss, my family's financial situation underwent a vast improvement after Sydney vanished. The Wandering Dark drew heavy crowds in its first couple of years, and Bump in the Night, buoyed by the comic book boom of the early 1990s, turned profitable for the first time. We were able to move out of the apartment and into a four-bedroom house. Sally White let her share of the store's success carry her even further: although she tried to keep her hybrid friendship-partnership with my mom going after Sydney's disappearance, she eventually grew tired of Mom blowing her off and shutting her out. She sold off her half of Bump in the Night and moved to Indiana with a boyfriend in 1993. Although we received an invitation to the wedding, my family didn't attend.

We weren't happy, but we were financially solvent, which, after my early childhood in poverty, nearly amounted to the same thing. And, in 1999, Mom finally agreed to hire Kyle Ransom and me as paid employees at The Wandering Dark. As our first on-the-payroll assignment, we had to go see Kyle's father's production of *The Crucible* at Vandergriff High, a ripe spot to pick up new talent. Mom handed us a stack of audition flyers and practically shoved us out the door on opening night.

I've always hated *The Crucible*. It's an interminable, joyless affair, and the most interesting idea in the play—that witchcraft may be afoot in Salem—is reduced to a metaphor for McCarthyism. Also, call me crazy, but I hate "poor innocent man falsely accused by sexy young girl" narratives.

Mr. Ransom erected an interesting set—a giant tree that dominated the stage, with all the judges sitting in the branches—but the actors looked lost as they milled about and shouted blank-faced accusations at one another. The girl playing Abigail, who was so blond her hair looked almost silver in the stage lights, did an okay impression of Sue Lyon in *Lolita*, but by the time the acne-ridden John Proctor elected to hang rather than sign a false confession, Kyle and I sat with our chins propped on our fists, praying for curtain call.

After the play, we found Mr. Ransom at the base of the stage, shaking hands with well-wishers. He'd suffered a heart attack not long after Sydney's disappearance, and after surgery and some severe diet changes, he'd lost a lot of weight, but the change made him look even less healthy. His skin hung around his face and puddled at his waistline like a half-melted candle, and his ruddy complexion had been replaced with a pallor that made him look more fungal than human. He was the only participant in the opening season at The Wandering Dark who hadn't been asked back after 1989.

As we approached him now, flyers in hand, I didn't see Mrs. Ransom anywhere. When I mentioned it to Kyle, he looked uncomfortable.

"She teaches a class on Thursdays," he said. "She'll come to the Saturday show."

"It's an important story," Mr. Ransom said, shaking hands with what appeared to be someone's grandfather.

"Absolutely," the old man said, "but I wonder if teenagers will agree?" He glanced up at a mostly empty auditorium behind him.

Mr. Ransom smiled tightly. "Thanks so much for coming out," he said. He turned to us and forced the sour look from his face. "Boys. What did you think?"

"It was intense," I said.

"Very dark," Kyle said.

"Very faithful to the text," I said.

"This is one of the great American plays," Mr. Ransom said. "Who am I to chop it up?"

The girl who had played Abigail emerged from the backstage area, out of costume but still caked in makeup. Up close she was *very* pretty, with glowing hair and bright blue eyes. She stopped when she saw Kyle and me.

"Hi, Kyle," she said. She nodded to me. "Hi, Noah."

"Do we know each other?" I said, taken aback.

She punched me on the arm. "Come on, quit it."

"Quit what?"

She widened her eyes a little in disbelief. "We sat two rows apart in Mrs. Thurston's English class. For like all of eighth grade." She put her hands to her chest. "Donna Hart?"

"Oh yeah," I said, but it sounded like a lie. "Sorry, I'm kind of a space cadet."

We stood in awkward silence until Kyle piped up: "The play was intense."

"Very dark," I agreed.

"Superfaithful to the text," Kyle said. "And you were great!"

"The best part," I said, because I wanted to make up for hurting her feelings.

She punched me on the arm again. "Quit it," she said, obviously pleased.

"Hey, while we've got your attention," Kyle said, handing her a flyer. "You should come audition for The Wandering Dark in a couple of weeks."

"It's this haunted house my family runs," I said.

"I know what it is," she said. "I'm no rube." She studied the flyer.

"We always need actors," I said.

Kyle tugged on my arm. "We have to get going."

I took the hint. "See you around, Donna Hart."

"Sure," she said. "Who knows, maybe you'll even remember me next time."

We started up the steps to the stage. When we were out of earshot, Kyle stopped me.

"How have you never noticed that girl?" he said.

"I noticed," I lied. "I just didn't remember her name."

"How do you forget anything about a girl like that?"

It was a good question. She was charming and easy to look at, but even now she was sort of fading from my mind.

"I've got a lot on my plate," I said.

"Like what?" I didn't answer right away, and he scoffed. "I don't understand you, not one bit. If I were in a class with that girl, that's all I would think about. In fact, I will think about nothing else henceforth." He closed his eyes.

"Kyle," I said.

"Shh," he said. He handed me the stack of flyers with his eyes still closed. "You go ponder whatever you're so busy with and hand out flyers. I'm thinking about Donna for the both of us."

3

When Kyle and I got back to the house, there was an unfamiliar Honda CR-X parked in the driveway behind Eunice's station wagon. The hatchback was covered in stickers for bands like AFI, Bikini Kill, MxPx, and the Misfits, and a giant bumper sticker reading PORNOGRAPHY RAPES THE MIND. As I walked through the front door, I heard a sound so rare I didn't recognize it at first: Eunice laughing.

We found her at the dining room table next to a wide, squat girl with spiky blue hair. The girl wore a hoodie with patches safety-pinned to the sleeves. She and Eunice were bent over a textbook, and both looked up as I entered the room. The punk girl had half a smile on her face, but Eunice was flush with laughter, eyes watering.

"Noah," she croaked. "How's it going?"

"Fine," I said. "I handed out most of the flyers." I set the remaining stack down on the table.

Eunice gestured to the stranger beside her. "This is Brin. She's in my English class."

We traded hellos, and I offered Brin a flyer.

"A haunted house?" she said.

"It's the family business," I said. Eunice looked uncomfortable, as though she wished I hadn't said anything.

"Well," Brin said, digging in her purse, "as long as we're trading flyers." She handed me a crumpled-up quarter-sheet of paper. At first glance, I thought it was an ad for a punk rock show—it had that washed-out xerox quality, and the background was a giant nautical star with a banner across it, but this banner read REDEMPTION BIBLE CHURCH. And beneath it, in almost illegible white text, instead of a list of bands, there was a schedule of worship services and events.

"You go here?" I said.

"You can, too, if you like," she said, looking at me and then Eunice. "Maybe change your mind about your livelihood."

The discomfort on Eunice's face increased, but she smiled. "Yeah, maybe."

Before I could give a (probably rude) answer to this invitation, Mom came into the room, her mouth set, complexion paler than usual.

"Mom, this is Brin—" Eunice started.

"We handed out most of the flyers," I said, but Mom waved both of us off.

"Noah, it's time to say good night. Kyle, you should probably head straight home. Your mother will want to see you. Brin, it might not be a bad idea for you to go, too."

"What's going on?" Eunice said.

Mom's mouth worked for a moment, and when she spoke, her voice broke. "A little girl went missing today."

By the next morning, the story would be unavoidable on both local and national news, but Mom related the vital facts to all of us in the room: earlier that morning, Maria Davis, age nine, and her five-year-old brother, Bobby, had ridden their bikes to an old, closed Winn-Dixie store a few blocks from their house. Twenty minutes later, Bobby turned around and went home, but by dinnertime, Maria still hadn't returned. When Maria's parents drove to the store, they found her bicycle on its side in the parking lot, but no sign of Maria herself. They called the police, who called the FBI.

Mom stood behind a chair at the head of the dining room table as she told us all of this, gripping the back with white knuckles. After she finished, we all sat in a sort of stunned silence—Brin and Kyle included.

I spoke first. "They don't think it has anything to do with Sydney, do they?"

"They don't know yet," Mom said. "But the police wouldn't have called me if they didn't think it was a possibility."

Kyle and Brin both said their good nights to us. Brin and Eunice exchanged a lingering smile I didn't know how to read, but I had more pressing things to worry about.

Mom, Eunice, and I sat together in the living room for almost two hours after that, staring at the TV and not talking. I don't think any of us knew what to say, or even think. We'd never really let go of the hope that Sydney had just run away, that her parting scream had been some sort of elaborate prank, exactly the sort of thing that an angry teenager with a penchant for haunted houses might do. I'd secretly hoped she was out in L.A., that I might go to the movies someday and either see her on-screen or maybe read her name in the end credits. But now, with another girl missing, it was a lot more difficult to entertain that fantasy.

When Mom sent me up to bed, Eunice followed me upstairs and even came into my room, which she almost never did anymore. She took a seat on my bed and watched as I pulled off my shoes.

"You okay?" she said.

"I guess so."

She sat for a moment, running her hand back and forth on the blanket.

"What about you? Are you okay?" I said.

She considered. "What do you think of Brin?" she said.

It wasn't what I'd expected. "That girl from earlier? I don't know. She's fine, I guess. Seems kind of religious."

"She says she mostly just goes to church for fun these days," Eunice said. "A lot of her friends from high school still go there. They have a punk rock praise band or something."

"You like punk now?" I said.

Eunice smiled at the floor, then stood. "I should let you get your rest. Good night, Noah." She gave me a quick kiss on the cheek and left.

I waited until I heard her bedroom door shut down the hall before I called to the monster.

"Are you in here?" Usually, at this summons, My Friend would emerge from the closet or from beneath the bed, but tonight I received no reply.

This happened sometimes. Some nights the creature arrived late, right before I went to sleep, and other nights it didn't come at all. But I could have used the company that night, some comfort from someone who wasn't suffering like my family was. I fell asleep sitting next to my bedroom window, waiting for My Friend to come home.

4

In the days that followed Maria Davis's disappearance, as the national news became more obsessed with the case, there was a definite change in the emotional weather in Vandergriff. It had never been an idyllic town where everyone smiled at one another, but now there was a tightness in everyone's jaw, a crease in the brow. There were fewer kids out playing in the parks or front yards in the afternoons, and the street outside our house was quieter at night. I heard less laughter around town, although I heard a lot more in the halls at school. We were all tense and drowning in hormones, and still too young to take anything seriously. There was an assembly in the school auditorium, where a local police officer explained that we'd be seeing cops in the building and stationed in the school parking lot to keep an eye on things. This same officer reminded us not to take food or rides from strangers, as if we were still in grade school. She showed us a poster with a phone number on it and implored us to call that number if we ever saw anything suspicious.

"Even if you're not sure if it's worth reporting, let us know. The life you save may be your own."

The whole presentation had the tone of a bad joke being told by someone who knows they're telling a bad joke but can't stop. Like any of this would help bring Maria home, or prevent another disappearance. There'd been school assemblies and national news coverage after Sydney vanished as well.

Mom, Eunice, and I had several discussions about whether to open The Wandering Dark that year. Although I wanted us to stay open for purely selfish reasons, I had to admit that there were good reasons to consider not doing it. After all, most of our employees were high schoolers, and we might have trouble filling all those roles if parents didn't feel safe sending their kids out into the night for six weeks straight. Every time the subject came up, we talked in circles and then tabled it again, but I could feel the chances of our 1999 season slipping away.

Aside from work talk, my family and I didn't speak much. We kept to our own corners of the big house—Mom downstairs in front of the TV, Eunice in her room, I in mine. I missed the monster like crazy. I'd almost given up hope of ever seeing it again when, a week after its last appearance, I snapped awake to a scratching at my bedroom window. The creature was crouched on the roof outside, running one talon up and down the glass.

I unlatched the window and pushed it open. I stepped back and tried to put on a stern face as the creature climbed into my room. I meant to yell at it, scold it, demand an exact accounting of its whereabouts for the last week. What I actually did was fall into its arms and hug it tight around the middle. It hugged me back, and that old sense of comfort and bliss washed over me, mingled with the scent of its musty cloak and fur. My anger dissipated, and I felt relief.

"I missed you so much," I said, into its chest. "I was so worried." I meant to say more, but My Friend tightened its grip on me, and my feet left the carpet. We were in the air, the creature's head inches from the ceiling.

My Friend carefully maneuvered us out the window and into the balmy summer night. My first thought was that it meant to play another round of jump and catch, but instead, it shifted me so that I was pressed against its side and rocketed into the sky. The wind whistled in my ears and tore at my hair. The town shrank below us, an increasingly small constellation of lights, as the air grew colder and thinner. I had to take deeper and deeper breaths to fill my lungs.

The monster stopped our ascent high in the night sky and hung in place, turning a slow circle. Off toward Dallas I saw Reunion Tower, and toward Fort Worth, the sturdy rectangle of Burnett Plaza. Vandergriff's own Fun Mountain amusement park sat directly below, the parachute drop lit up even though the park was closed at night.

Without warning, the creature released its grip. The park flew up at me like a bit of zoom photography as I tumbled through the sky, the parachute tower rising like a sword thrust up from the earth. A scream burst from my throat, and I flailed my arms as if there were something to grab on to.

Oh, Christ. Oh, Christ, oh, Jesus, this was it, I was going to die, and worst of all it was going to *hurt*—

But before I shattered every bone in my body against an amusement park ride, the creature caught up to me, clasped me around my middle, and flew me in circles around the tower, neon lights a strobing blur in my periphery. My wail of terror became a cry of delight. Energy surged through me. I howled. I laughed. The creature tightened its grip, and waves of warmth pulsed from our point of contact. The world took on a golden hue and my heart galloped in my chest. Then the creature released me again.

I didn't plummet this time. This time, I rose. I wasn't going particularly fast, but, I realized, I was making a loose spiral of ascent on my own. My Friend remained just behind and below, keeping pace but not touching me. I was flying under my own power. I turned around to face the creature.

"How did you do this?" I said. "This is amazing!"

As usual, it didn't answer. I flew away from the tower and out over the highway. I moved more slowly and clumsily than the creature—as it turned out, learning to fly wasn't so different from learning to swim—but managed to stay aloft and propel myself in the correct direction. Suddenly, all the worry and anxiety of the last week didn't matter. All that mattered was this ascent, this sensation of complete power and freedom.

The exhilaration eventually faded, subsumed by a delightful exhaustion. By the time we arrived back at the house, my temporary ability to fly was wearing off. I bobbed and weaved through the air like a drunken insect, and stumbled onto the roof, landing on my hands and knees. The creature landed next to me, more felt than heard, a gentle shift of wind. "It's hot out here," I said. "Are you hot?"

I didn't wait for the creature's response. I climbed into my bedroom and stripped to my boxers. Even bared, my skin prickled with unnatural heat. My face was hot to the touch, and, I noticed, my shorts were tented with my own tumescence. I braced myself against the desk, and took a couple of deep but useless breaths. I couldn't cool off. I turned around and found that the creature had followed me inside.

"I think maybe you gave me too much pixie dust," I said. "I feel . . . hoo . . ." My head swam.

The creature's look turned to one of concern. It touched my face and my chest, letting its paw linger there. My heart continued to race, and my face throbbed with heat. The creature picked up a pen and sheet of paper from my desk and wrote:

FRIEND HELP?

"Can you?" I said. My voice sounded remote, and distorted, as though processed through a synthesizer.

The creature set down the pen and paper. It put one paw on my shoulder, and used the other to guide my hand to my groin. The room thrummed around us, and my gut clenched again. The world grew dimmer, less *there* somehow.

"Are you sure you want to be here for . . . for this?" I said, both embarrassed and excited at the prospect.

The creature nuzzled the side of my face with its wet snout, its fur brushing my burning cheek. I dropped my boxer shorts around my ankles, gripped myself, and began to tug, feeling both inside and outside my body. It didn't take long. As I tensed in preparation for climax, My Friend clamped down on my shoulder. My inner eye refracted into dozens of fragments, a kaleidoscope suffused with golden light, every distorted version of myself writhing in ecstasy out into infinity.

I slumped forward when it was over, and would have toppled to the floor, but My Friend caught me and held me against the musty smell of its cloak. It laid me down on the bed and climbed in behind me, one arm over my middle. The warmth no longer felt trapped inside me, but circulated between us now, an individual burden transformed by touch into a shared comfort.

"Thank you," I said. I drifted away on the fading pulse of my orgasm, washed out to the sea of sleep with the fleeting impression of being kissed on the cheek by soft, human lips.

5

I woke the next morning with an idea for how to keep The Wandering Dark open and make sure our employees were safe. We would institute a system that would require minor-age employees to call in when they were either coming to us or heading home. Mom liked the idea, and so we were back in business. We started the work of getting the place ready for the 1999 season that week.

The Wandering Dark had grown considerably since 1989, from six rooms to fifteen. Four of the new rooms were on a second "floor" we built in 1995, so even counting the employee break room, the costume shop, the dressing rooms, bathrooms, security surveillance room, and the monster's labyrinth, we were still only using about two thirds of the available floor space. I'd already started sketching ideas for how to use the remaining third. My working title was Chain Saw Chase Party, and I was excited that Mom hadn't said no yet.

Kyle and I spent our afternoons and evenings sweeping and dusting the attraction, then running the lights and mechanical pieces (like the vertigo tunnel) through their paces, repairing or replacing as needed. Eunice, in one of her more energetic phases, agreed to come help, provided that Brin could come, too.

"She's agreed to check the place out if I'll go to her church with her sometime," Eunice said.

"Why would you want to go to a church?" I said. "Especially a punk rock church? You hate both of those things."

"I'm trying something new," she said. "How about you try and be nice?"

As soon as Brin walked into the building for the first time, she made a face of mild revulsion.

"You're okay taking people's money for this?" she said.

"No one's forcing you to be here. You grasp that, right?" I said.

"Come on, let me show you around," Eunice said. Brin allowed herself to be led into the labyrinth and out of sight. As Mom and Kyle and I worked, we were continually interrupted by echoed laughter, Brin sending my sister into shrieking hysteria with joke after joke.

"What the fuck?" I said, after the first hour of this nonsense.

"Language," Mom said, tone mild as she marked something on her clipboard. We stood in the Professor's study as Kyle dimmed and brightened the orange bulbs in the fireplace. "Eunice has never had many friends. Let her enjoy this one, even if she is sort of rude."

"Is anyone paying attention to my remarkable bulb work?" Kyle said, crouched in front of the fireplace.

"Yes, you're doing excellent work," Mom said, without looking. "Now shut up, both of you, so I can think."

Auditions took place the weekend after we finished repairs. Mom and I sat at a table in the dance hall set while Kyle ushered in the usual bevy of hopeful theater kids. Donna Hart was the first through the door. She performed Abigail's "I cannot bear lewd looks no more, John" monologue from *The Crucible,* and sang a verse of "I Don't Know How to Love Him," from *Jesus Christ Superstar*. She played it big, her performance pitched toward the exit signs at the back of the high school auditorium across town.

Mom kept her eyes on the clipboard, scribbling notes for a good ten or fifteen seconds after Donna finished singing. When Mom looked up, she rubbed her nose with the back of one hand and said, "How's your scream?"

"Fine, I guess," Donna said, worrying the pleats in her skirt.

Mom made a little gesture. "Go on, then."

Donna cleared her throat and unleashed a pure, crystalline scream.

Mom returned to her clipboard. "Thank you, Donna. We'll be in touch."

Donna smiled at me on her way out of the room. I smiled back, because it felt like the polite thing to do, and after checking to see Mom wasn't watching, I gave her a thumbs-up.

After the rest of the auditions, Kyle, Mom, and I sat in a circle in the dance hall and compared notes.

"First order of business," Mom said, "is to figure out your roles."

Kyle leaned back. "Oh, man. I've been waiting so long to be

asked this question." He closed his eyes. "Professor. I want to be the Professor. And I want tenure."

"We'll see how it goes this year," Mom said. "Noah?"

I'd also been waiting for this question. I'd known my answer for a while now, but I felt weird saying it out loud, admitting that I wanted this thing, because I wanted it bad, and was afraid I wouldn't get it. I was also afraid what my family might think of me for asking.

"Monster," I said. "I want to play the monster."

Kyle made a sympathetic face. "The poor homely boy. It's his only option."

Nobody laughed. My face burned, and I stared at the floor.

"Monster it is," Mom said, her tone neutral.

6

Later, on the drive home in Kyle's Pinto, he returned to his favorite subject: Donna Hart.

"You lucky, stupid motherfucker," he said. "She likes you."

"No she doesn't," I said.

He gave me some serious side-eye. "Why do you do this?"

"Do what?"

"I get that you're shy, but at some point you've gotta go out with *somebody*. I mean, you're not gay, are you?"

"Fuck you," I said. In Vandergriff in 1999, there were few scarier suggestions. Less than a year ago, Matthew Devries, a gay man in his early twenties, had been tied to the back of a truck and dragged for miles down a stretch of two-lane highway. It had happened in Artemis, about twenty minutes from our town.

"Look," I said. "If I promise to flirt with the pretty girl, will you shut up about it?"

He clapped his hands and held them up over his head like he'd scored a point.

"Hands at ten and two, Super Dave," I said.

I wanted to talk to Eunice about it, but when I got home her bedroom was empty. She was probably out somewhere with Brin. Without really thinking about what I was doing, I wandered past Eunice's room and into the room at the end of the hall.

The fourth bedroom in the house was what Mom called the "home office." It had a filing cabinet, a desk, a computer, and a fake plant in one corner. The room was supposed to be for Mom, but I could count on one hand the number of times I'd found her in here. More often it was me or Eunice using the computer for schoolwork or games. Mostly the room sat empty, as if we all knew its true purpose and were waiting for an excuse to move out the furniture and make space for its real occupant.

It was also the only room in the house where we kept a photograph of Sydney. It sat atop the filing cabinet, an eight-by-ten school portrait in a gold frame. Sydney in a sundress, hair big with hair spray, her brilliant stage smile turned toward the camera. I'm not sure why Mom picked this photo to display. It had been taken at the start of Sydney's senior year, a mere two months before she went missing, and it was the photo that inevitably accompanied any stories about her in print or on TV. This photo had become the thumbnail avatar for her disappearance from our lives.

I picked up the picture, careful not to smudge the glass with my fingers. I wondered if Maria Davis's parents were going through something similar right now; whether they had a photo of their daughter that would perfectly encapsulate their loss, regrets, pain, and perceived failures as parents.

I told myself to stop it. That Maria could still be alive and out there somewhere. That Sydney could, too. I didn't *know* anything about either case. Not really. I set the photo down, walked back past Eunice's bedroom, and into my own. My Friend was sitting on the floor, frowning at an open comic book in its lap. It marked its place with one taloned digit when I came in, and pointed at the night sky. *Outside?*

"Not tonight," I said. "I have some work to do." I got up and got my pencils and some paper from my desk. The creature gave me an inquisitive look. "I have to design a new monster costume for The Wandering Dark. I thought I'd base the design on you."

The creature's gaze grew cloudy and momentarily troubled. It set the comic book down and reached for the paper and pencils, which I handed over. It wrote: YOU WANT TO LOOK LIKE ME?

"Well, yeah," I said. "You're awesome. Why wouldn't I want to look like you?"

It pondered the question for a moment but didn't seem able to come up with a good answer. Still looking slightly troubled, it handed the pencils and paper back. I sat down opposite the creature on the floor, my back against my dresser. It went back to reading, and I started sketching. I sketched for several hours, only vaguely aware of other sounds in the house—Mom moving around downstairs in the kitchen, then settling in front of the TV.

I've never been a great artist, so it took me several tries to draw anything that even approached a resemblance to the creature. I wanted to capture its bulk, its matted fur, the way its eyes glowed with menace and pathos, but everything I drew looked like a dog in a hoodie. I was still huffing over my pad when a knock came at my door, and Eunice entered before I had a chance to invite her.

"Hey," she said, then made a face. "You okay?"

I glanced at the creature's spot on the floor, which was now empty, then back at Eunice. I swallowed and licked my dry, cracked lips.

"Fine," I said. "You startled me, is all."

She let herself in and sat on the bed. "Your bed's really warm."

"Yeah, that's why I moved to the floor," I said.

She ran her hand over the blankets, looking concerned. "Do you have a fever? It feels like you left a fired brick in here."

"I'm fine," I said.

She glanced at the open window, and for a second seemed ready to say something, but then she frowned and looked slightly pained.

"Did you need something?" I said.

She blinked a few times and stood up. "You're right. It's late."

"You don't have to leave," I said. "Where'd you go tonight?"

She stood still in the middle of the room with that strange, pained look of concentration on her face for another moment. A small, unsure half smile emerged from it, and she glanced to the side as if she might find an answer in the corner of my room.

"I went with Brin to her church," she said, and sat back down on my bed.

"On a Friday night?"

"They do some kind of service or event almost every day or night of the week," she said. "Brin says that they want to appeal to people with nontraditional schedules, who maybe can't get off every Sunday morning or Wednesday night."

I leaned back against the desk. "What was it like?"

Again that shifting gaze, the refusal to look at me. "It was . . . weird. First, the church is in a storefront in a lousy strip mall, between a nail salon and a tax prep place. The front windows are painted black, so no one can see in or out, and the inside looks like a punk rock show venue—just a bunch of folding chairs in front of a small stage with colored lights and a black back wall.

"Everybody who showed up for the service looked like Brin—tattooed, spiky hair, patches on their jackets—but they were all carrying Bibles. It was like something from *The Twilight Zone*. They all wanted to shake my hand and welcome me 'to the flock.' There was a praise band that played a bunch of really loud, fast punk rock music, and I didn't understand any of the words, and everybody ran to the front of the room and started moshing around . . ."

"Did you mosh?" I said. As bony and fragile as Eunice looked, I imagined she'd shatter like glass in a mosh pit.

"I didn't," she said. "I sat in my chair, but Brin moshed. And then, after everybody got worked into a frenzy, the pastor came up and the room got quiet. He has this really calm, soothing voice, like someone talking you down off a ledge. He starts off about how happy he is to see everyone, and how blessed we are to have this space to be together and worship the Lord. But then it got sort of weird. He got on this riff about how he noticed that not all of us were moved to dance by the Holy Spirit, and I swear he was staring *right at me*.

"'I hope you'll find the strength to let go and let the Spirit move you in the future,' he says. I just tried to laugh it off. Like maybe it was his way of being friendly, you know? Encouraging me to participate.

"But *then* he starts talking about people who have left the church and started attending elsewhere, and he rants about disloyalty. He starts naming people one at a time, and revoking any blessings they'd ever received through the church. Like 'Jane Dunlop, who met her husband at this church, and who had her baby baptized here—I revoke your marriage and your child's salvation. You are damned.' He did this for like twenty different people. And, Noah, everybody there seemed *fine* with it. They were shouting 'Amen!' and 'Praise Jesus.'"

"Even Brin?" I said.

"Not Brin," Eunice said. "She just sort of sat there. Afterward, I told her that the sermon seemed weird and wrong to me, and she was like 'Now you know how I feel about what your family does for a living.' So we made a deal. I'm going to take some time off from The Wandering Dark this year, and she's going to try and find a different church. One that's not so . . . hostile. And in the meantime, she and I can hang out without feeling weird about it."

"Wait," I said. "What do you mean 'take some time off'?"

"It's not like I've been superinvolved so far this year anyway," she said. "It's been a tough semester, and I think I deserve a year off."

"Yeah, but letting some Jesus freak bully you into quitting? Eunice, that's wrong."

She still wouldn't meet my eye. "It's not quitting. It's just . . . taking some time." She stood again. "Anyway, it's late. Good night, kiddo. Don't stay up all night." She kissed me on the cheek and left.

I waited up, but My Friend didn't come back.

7

I gave Mom the new sketch the next day at the breakfast table, expecting her to sign off on it without much reaction. Instead, her expression went from preoccupied to something like outright alarm.

"Where did you come up with this?" she said.

I pretended to study the picture. "I don't know. I made it up. Why?"

She seemed on the verge of saying something. "What?" I said.

"Nothing," she said.

"Mom, it's obviously not nothing." Why was she freaking out?

She ran her fingers over my sketch and then glanced at me. "You're not—you've never seen this thing before?"

Now my own curiosity was piqued. "Have *you*?" I said.

The tight line of her mouth assumed a few different shapes before she shook her head. "No. No, of course not. This Maria Davis business has me on edge is all."

I didn't know how to respond to that. What did a monster costume have to do with Maria Davis?

"Sorry," Mom said. "This thing gives me the creeps."

I could tell she was going to give in and let me have my way, so I didn't pursue the topic further.

"That's the idea," I said.

8

I refused to join rehearsals until I had my costume. I would've felt silly trying to drag people away in my street clothes, and once my coworkers had seen that ridiculous image, how would they ever take me seriously in a costume? No matter how good the finished product, my victims would always remember regular, sweaty Noah. When they saw the monster for the first time, it needed to be the monster.

So while my fellow cast members learned lines and blocking, I memorized the monster's warren, a series of passages alongside the attraction that allowed the monster to track visitors unseen and emerge at random to terrify and/or drag away our audience "plants"— characters always named Brad or Katie. I ran laps, my feet echoing on the concrete floor and wooden stairs, rattling the walls of the flimsier sets. I needed to be able to move through this space in a heavy costume and a mask that obscured my vision—and to do it in the dark. So I ran and ran. By the end of the first week I could travel it with my eyes closed.

On breaks, I sat at an open dock door, guzzling water and soaking up whatever breeze the day had on offer. Sometimes Donna (who'd joined the cast as a Katie) and Kyle sat with me. Kyle played the part of the "wacky friend" in these little scenes, making jokes and talking me up in front of Donna. I did my best to play the part of "interested, normal dude."

The new costume was ready by the end of the second week, and we introduced it to rehearsals that Friday. Without showing it to anyone ahead of time, or letting them know what we were doing, Mom announced that the cast would start rehearsing with the lights off. The Brads and Katies, clumped together and playing "the audience" would be given a single flashlight to navigate the warehouse.

For this first lights-off rehearsal, Mom gave me free rein to show up wherever and whenever I wanted. As the Brads and Katies moved through the attraction, I silently kept abreast. With the lights on, they had moved with bored arrogance and surety. Now, in the quiet and shadows, their laughter turned anxious.

"Jesus," one of the Brads said, as I peered into the Professor's study. "I know it's fake, but Jesus."

Donna swung the group's flashlight back and forth, but still I held back. I followed them into the morgue, and then into the dance hall, where the band started their big brassy number and other bit players waltzed around the room, blocking the Brads' and Katies' way, forcing them to navigate a sea of dancers. The room, with its dim lighting and wide floor, should have been a relief from the unbearable tension of the small, dark rooms preceding it, but it left my prey feeling edgy and exposed. They shuffled through the room, flashlight turned off for the moment, a knot of nervous energy, and reached the double doors marked EXIT on the far side. Passing through, they found themselves pitched into darkness again.

"Donna," one of the Katies hissed. "Flashlight."

Donna turned the light on and found her nose inches from my snout.

"Boo," I said.

Her scream made me glad for the muffling barrier of the mask. The whole group shouted in terror. I ducked through one of my secret exits and back into my labyrinth.

"Noah, you asshole!" someone called.

9

That scream, that moment of terror I had created, made me so giddy that, in a fit of manic glee, I decided it was time to make a move on Donna. When My Friend arrived after sundown that night, I said, "I need the best flower you know of. Something hard to get."

The creature picked up the pen and pad on my desk. WHY? it wrote.

"Never mind why," I said. "Will you do it?"

It sighed. FRIEND HELP, it wrote. BACK SOON. It trudged to the open window and flew out into the night.

I paced the room and waited. My Friend returned about half an hour later, carrying a long-stemmed black flower. The heart of the plant glowed faintly, like a tea light about to flicker out. The illumination was ringed with thorns.

DON'T POKE THE MIDDLE, the creature wrote. DON'T STARE AT IT EITHER. YOU MIGHT FALL IN. It pointed to the flower. WHAT FOR?

I found myself reluctant to say, "A girl." My face felt hot, but I pressed on anyway. "I need another favor, too. I need you to make me fly again."

The creature stared at me.

"What's wrong?" I said.

NOTHING WRONG, it wrote. FRIEND HELP.

A moment later, after getting a fresh charge of energy from the creature, I soared through the sky, the black flower clenched to my chest. The monster trailed me at a distance to make sure I didn't plummet to my death. I'd looked up Donna's address on her application for The Wandering Dark, but since I'd just gotten my driver's license, I still had only a hazy idea of the town's layout and kept having to fly low and check street names. I eventually found myself over a one-story house on a street full of near-identical homes. As I hovered above it, the creature stopped beside me.

"I'm trying to guess which window is hers," I said.

The creature drifted around the left side of the house and pointed at a window right behind the fence.

"You're sure?" I said.

It nodded.

I followed it and drifted down to the ground. "Hang around but out of sight, okay?"

The creature hung in the air over my head, glowering, then floated into the yard behind the house. I rapped on the glass, stepped back, and held up the flower. The curtains rippled and parted a fraction of an inch. I felt like I might puke. Why had I thought this was a good idea? What girl would find this romantic? This was what a crazy person would do.

Donna's face appeared between the curtains, eyes cloudy with sleep, hair pulled into a golden bun atop her head. She wore a T-shirt and pajama pants. She mouthed my name as a question: *Noah?*

"Sorry," I whispered. "I'll go."

She held up a finger to say *One minute*, then disappeared. When she came back, her jaw was working. She was chewing gum. She unlatched the window and slowly pushed it open. When she got it halfway up, she bent down and stuck her head out.

"What are you doing here?" she whispered.

"I came because—" I stopped and cleared my throat. I could have used some water. "You're doing a great job at work and I wanted to say thanks."

She smiled. She was happy to see me at least. "In the middle of the night?"

"We *are* a haunted house," I said.

She pointed at my chest. "What's that?"

I remembered the flower. "This is for you," I said, looking at its dim glow instead of at her. "Sort of a congratulatory—whatever."

"Are you going to give it to me or just stare at it?" she said. I tore my gaze away from the hypnotic light and handed it to her. She peered down into its folds, her face lit orange. She *was* pretty. Why did I keep forgetting how pretty she was? Why didn't her face cling to my mind's eye?

"It's beautiful," she murmured. "What is it?"

"An ebon kindness," I said, delighted with my own spontaneous creativity. "NASA engineered it in a lab—they're experimenting with plants they can take on spaceships, or plant on asteroids to foster breathable atmospheres."

It seemed to cost her some effort to look back at me. "You're messing with me."

"I would never," I said. "But for real, don't touch the thorns in the center. They're poison."

"Are you bringing flowers to all the Brads and Katies?"

"Only you," I said.

She grabbed the front of my shirt and pulled me forward. My first kiss was quick, firm, and over before I had a chance to react. Donna released her grip on me, and I staggered back a step.

"See you at work?" she said.

"Yeah, cool," I said, running a hand through my windswept hair. "I have to fly home now anyway."

She laughed. "You're so weird." She shut the window and pulled the curtains together. I watched the orange glow of the ebon kindness recede. A strange memory popped into my head—the nuns, floating down the aisles with candles in their hands during the overture to Mr. Ransom's production of *The Sound of Music* in 1989. With that thought, the elation of the previous minute was over, and a heaviness had set in again. I trudged through the overgrown yard until I stood almost beneath My Friend.

"A little help?" I said.

With a loud sigh, it drifted to the ground and grabbed my shoulders. A rush of energy passed between us, my stomach tight, heart racing. When it let go, I bent my legs and pushed up into the air. The creature kept its distance on the flight home, and looked away whenever I glanced at it. When we arrived at the house, I flew through my open window, but My Friend remained outside.

"Are you mad about something?" I said.

It hesitated, then shook its head.

"You're not mad."

It shook its head.

"So are you coming inside?"

It shook its head again and, turning its back, flew away into the night.

I shut the window and walked down the hall to Eunice's room. I wanted to talk to her about Donna, to share the night's triumph, but when I knocked on her door, Brin answered with a flushed face, her spiky hair out of alignment.

"Help you?" she said.

"Are you being funny?" I said. I leaned to one side, and she moved to block my view.

"Just a second, Noah," Eunice called, somewhere out of sight. She sounded winded, and I understood what they must have been doing before I knocked. My realization must have shown, because Brin tilted her head and raised her eyebrows.

"Forget it," I said. I walked back to my own room, undressed, and went to bed. I replayed Donna's kiss, trying to pull more details from the memory, but it remained a startling blur. There was pleasure commingled with the surprise, but more an intellectual pleasure at the fact of having kissed a girl than in any physical delight, or desire for the person who gave it to me.

Muffled laughter sounded from down the hall—Eunice and Brin playing behind a closed door. I guessed their deal—no church, no haunted house—was working out fine. I put my pillow over my head to block the noise, and eventually was able to sleep.

When I woke the next morning and went downstairs for breakfast, I found Mom and Eunice on the living room couch, wan and almost unblinking before the TV set. They were watching the news.

"What is it?" I said.

Eunice looked away from the TV slowly. "It's happened again."

10

The second abductee in the fall of 1999 was a twelve-year-old boy named Brandon Hawthorne. Brandon had gone to bed at home the night before as usual and his parents had watched late-night TV and fallen asleep without incident. Around three in the morning, Brandon's father woke up, went to the bathroom, and then decided to check on the boy. He found Brandon's window open and bed empty. The Hawthorne family had called the police, but so far, the search had turned up no clues. The boy was just gone.

It would have been impossible to ignore the similarities between this most recent disappearance and that of Sydney ten years before. My sister's name and picture started to pop up on newscasts again, and reporters called my mother at home and work to request quotes or interviews. She didn't say anything to me about it, but I heard the messages on our answering machine, and I agreed with the reporters. There was something weird going on.

Ten days went by without the monster coming to visit. It had been a month since Maria Davis had been taken. No witnesses had come forward, and if there were any new leads, the police weren't telling the press. I had dreams of flying over Vandergriff, the wind making a rat's nest of my hair. I had dreams of golden light, of desire rising and being fulfilled. I had dreams where Sydney screamed again and again. I dreamt of open windows, but I never dreamt about Donna.

At work, the cast began to wear costumes during rehearsals. The Brads and Katies took turns as my victim. I got good at moving in the suit, adapting to their patterns of defense and collapse. Nobody moved like Donna. She wriggled and thrashed against me as I pulled her out of sight. In the dark of the labyrinth, she remained pressed to me even after I put her down.

Sometimes she tried to talk to me. "So this is the monster's lair. I have to be honest, I'm a little disappointed. I thought it would look like something from *Buffy* or *Aliens*." Another time: "You know that flower you gave me? I forgot to put it in water for like two days and it still hasn't died."

I never took the conversational bait. If Donna thought my behavior strange, she didn't say anything. We ate lunch together at school and held hands in the hall between classes. She rode with me and Kyle to rehearsals in the afternoons. From the outside, we probably looked like a normal high school couple, but everything she said sounded like it was coming from far away, down a distant hall.

I wanted to talk to Eunice about it, but every time I stopped by her room, I could hear her in there with Brin, and I knew better than to try to interrupt again. Instead, I waited for Eunice to come to me—which, on the last Friday night before The Wandering Dark opened, she finally did.

I was supposed to go to Donna's for movie night, but I called her and pretended to feel sick to get out of it. Eunice and I took her station wagon to the high school, where Eunice let me get some practice in with my new driver's license. Afterward we went to an all-night diner for soda (for me) and coffee (for her).

"So," she said, dumping creamer into her mug and stirring the black liquid to a light brown. "I hear you've started a romance with a Katie named Donna."

I smiled a little and bit my straw. I'd missed how funny she could be when she was feeling playful.

"I don't know," I said. "I guess."

"It's okay, you don't have to be embarrassed. I'm glad you're finally out in the world, meeting people. I was starting to worry that my antisocial tendencies were rubbing off on you."

"It's not that I'm embarrassed," I said. "I mean, Donna's nice, but . . . I've been having trouble thinking about anything besides Maria Davis and Brandon Hawthorne."

Eunice stopped futzing with her coffee to regard me. She seemed to really take in my face for the first time all night.

"Because of Sydney?"

I shrugged. "I guess so. Do you think it's the same person taking the kids now?"

She took a sip of coffee. "I don't know. I haven't put much thought into it."

"Seriously?"

"I know it's selfish," she said. "And I hope they find those kids, and that they're okay. Hell, I hope we get closure with Sydney. But none of those are problems I can solve. I've got my own stuff going on now."

"What—" I hesitated, because I worried what it might mean to acknowledge it in the open. "You mean Brin?"

Her cheeks turned pink and she stared into her coffee, but she did nod.

"Where is she tonight anyway?" I said.

"Church retreat," Eunice said.

"I thought she was taking a break from that place," I said.

"This is sort of her 'last hurrah,'" Eunice said. "She's been going to church with some of these people for years, and they pretty much begged her to come to this weekend. It's a chance to say goodbye." And then, either not noticing or choosing to ignore my skeptical expression, she pushed on. "You know, I didn't realize how lonely I was until I wasn't anymore. It's funny. She gets me. I guess I get her, too."

I swallowed my dislike for Brin. "I'm glad you have a friend," I said.

She looked radiant with embarrassed happiness, hands clasped around her mug. I gently pushed my soda glass across the table until it clinked against her mug.

"Cheers," I said.

11

The Wandering Dark opened and drew strong crowds despite the curfews and real-life nightmare taking place in our town. I stalked strangers, banged on walls, rattled doors, and harvested ripe, full-bodied screams. Sometimes I let a Brad or Katie through untouched, and sometimes I captured them, terrifying the audience. It kept the plants jumpy and heightened the guests' terror, making the catharsis of emerging into the parking lot, in full view of our security guards, that much sweeter. I was a good monster. I loved the work. When I wore the costume, separated from the world by a barrier of fur and fabric and plastic, nothing else mattered.

It was only at the end of the night, when I peeled off my second skin and became Noah Turner, that I felt confused and anxious. Donna and I continued to hold hands and traded the occasional kiss at work, but I didn't feel anything about any of it. I thought a lot about Eunice's suicide note, about people excavating one another in search of things they wanted and needed. I felt like a hollow shell being operated remotely. Mostly I felt a vague, nebulous dread. Like something awful was about to happen, which I was powerless to stop.

It turned out to be not any one thing, but a series.

The Monday after we opened, I got home from school to find Eunice's bedroom door shut. I paused outside, listening for muffled laughter or rustling sheets, but heard only silence. I went back downstairs to fix myself a snack. As I passed through the dining room with my peanut butter and jelly sandwich, I noticed a white envelope on the kitchen table. A new note from Eunice? I sat down to read while I ate. The envelope contained several sheets of paper, but the page on top was a note in a hand I didn't recognize:

"For this reason God gave them over to degrading passions; for their women exchanged the natural function for that which is unnatural, and in the same way also the men abandoned the natural function of the woman and burned in their desire toward one another, men with men committing indecent acts and receiving in their own persons the due penalty of their error. And just as they did not see fit to acknowledge God any longer, God gave them over to a depraved mind, to do those things which are not proper."—Romans 1:26–28

I have repented my sins. If you care about the world after this one, you will, too. Please don't call again.

Your sister in Christ,
Brin

Eunice's note came on the following page:

Dear Noah,

    Love is ridiculous, right? A chemical imbalance, an illness. We catch it, we go mad for a little while, and what do we do when it passes? If we're "lucky," we're saddled with an imperfect marriage, a mortgage, and obnoxious, needy, resentful kids. Our ambitions and dreams and potential greatness are extinguished for want of a little human contact and some orgasms (passing bodily contractions that can easily be achieved on one's own). And yet, 99% of all music, literature, film, and art is devoted to love. The world carries on like this is the best, most natural thing. We sing endless songs about getting sick, and the complex of scars left when the illness fades.

    But you know what's worse than catching love? Having the object of your illness not return the feeling. Hearing them say, "No thank you," when you declare yourself. Worst of all is knowing, deep down, that she doesn't really feel that way, but let some creep scare her into saying it anyway. Why do the creeps of the world have so much power? I don't know.

There was no jokey verdict at the end, no reassuring farewell. The letter just stopped. I went to Eunice's room and knocked on the door. She answered disheveled and puffy-faced.

"What is it, Noah?"

I glanced behind her into the darkened room, and had the impression of a deeper, wide space—a huge fairy-tale ballroom with floor-to-ceiling windows full of moonlight. I glanced at Eunice's tired, impatient face, and then at the room again. This time it looked like Eunice's room—tidy, stuffed with books, and a small TV on the dresser pouring out pale blue light.

I held up her note. "I wanted to make sure you're okay."

"I'm fine," she said.

"You seem like maybe you're not."

"*I am okay,*" she said, emphasizing each word. "I thought you liked reading about what's on my mind, but if you're not mature enough to handle it—" She reached for the note.

"No, no," I said and stepped away. "I guess I overreacted. Sorry to bother you. And I'm . . . sorry about . . . you know."

She made a face. "I'll talk to you later."

12

The following night, I begged off a late dinner with Kyle and Donna after the last guests left and hung back to help Mom close up shop. I found her at her desk, counting cash.

"I'm worried about Eunice," I said.

"Is that so?" she said, without looking up.

I told her my reasons (minus Eunice's sexuality), and when I finished, she leaned back in her chair and rubbed her eyes with the heels of her hands. I noticed the streaks of gray in her hair for the first time, the permanent laugh lines around her mouth. She had turned fifty-one this year, but I hadn't realized until now that she was actually getting older.

"Eunice has always been like this," she said. "A fight with her friend might intensify things, but as long as she's on her medication, all you can do is wait it out. She'll get better when she's ready."

"This time feels different," I said.

She raised her eyebrows. "Different how?"

Was she really so blind? Had she not noticed the change in Eunice when Brin had come into our lives? Had she never suspected?

"Do you really not know?" I said.

She gave me a cold stare, as if daring me to say more, to break the border between us, cross the no-man's-land of Sydney's disappearance, and start admitting things. When I didn't, she resumed her count. "I understand you're worried about your sister, but trust me, it will be fine."

But when we got home, I found a note in Eunice's scribble on the upstairs bathroom counter:

The more he withdrew from the world about him, the more wonderful became his dreams; and it would have been quite futile to try to describe them on paper—H. P. Lovecraft, "Celephaïs"

I don't know if she meant for me to see it or not.

13

The week passed without much incident. My Friend still hadn't reappeared, so I spent my downtime reading and watching TV with the volume low, so I could pay attention to Eunice's movements. She didn't move much—mostly from the bedroom to the bathroom or kitchen. Her hair was greasy and tousled, and her eyes puffy with either too much or not enough sleep. I did what Mom said. I gave her space.

Kyle was home sick from school the following Monday, so Donna and I ate lunch together in the cafeteria without our usual buffer, both of us quiet as we worked through our cold, rubbery school-issue pizza. Even through the fog of worry about Eunice and My Friend, I could feel Donna working up to something.

"The other night, when Kyle drove me home after closing?" she said. "That night you stayed behind to help your mom? Something happened and I'm afraid how you'll take it."

"What's that?" I said.

"We kind of kissed."

"Kind of?" As though these were the two words worth arguing about.

"It wasn't anything we planned." She finally looked over at me. "I invited him inside to see the ebon kindness—which still hasn't died, by the way—and then . . ." She trailed off and shrugged. "I spaced out, and when I came to, we were kissing. I know it sounds like bullshit, but it's like I forgot that I even had a boyfriend for a minute. I've actually been forgetting a lot of stuff lately."

I didn't know what to say—or even how to feel. I felt myself reaching for the tools I'd been handed by every cheating/breakup scene from every TV show or movie I'd ever watched, but I paused when I realized that it would be an empty motion. Donna's admission only created a sense of relief. It could be over and it wouldn't be my fault.

"Don't worry about it," I said. "It's okay." I poked at my pizza. I really didn't feel hungry.

"Really?"

"Yeah. It's okay. We're cool." I left my lunch on the table as I exited the cafeteria, already thinking of something else.

14

That night I stood at the edge of my roof and called softly into the night, "If you're out there, I need you."

The summons worked. Moments later, the monster descended through the air until it floated before me.

"Thanks for coming," I said. "Come inside."

I climbed back into my bedroom, and the creature followed. It didn't take its usual place on the bed, but remained next to the window, as though ready to take off.

"I've missed you for the past couple of weeks," I said. Something softened in its posture. "Where have you been?"

It picked up the pad and pen from my desk and wrote DID YOU WANT SOMETHING?

I noticed the creature's refusal to share its whereabouts, but decided not to remark on it. "I don't know if you keep up with the news," I said, "but two kids have gone missing in the last several weeks. Everybody's pretty freaked out about it around town—and my family is, too. But today it occurred to me that I have a best friend who can fly, and do magic. So I was thinking maybe you could help me, you know, find the kids. Bring them home."

The creature bent to the pad again and scribbled a single word with quick, decisive strokes:

NO.

"No?" I said. The creature had never refused me before. "Those kids need our help. Even if you're mad at me, don't you care about them?"

It underlined its NO three times. Then wrote, ASK DONNA FOR HELP.

"Donna?" I said. "Donna and I are done. I'm asking you."

My Friend regarded me for a moment, and for the first time in years, I felt uncomfortable with the intensity of its gaze, the heave of its shoulders as it breathed. Finally it sighed and wrote, WHAT CAN I DO?

At my request, we flew to the closed Winn-Dixie where Maria Davis's bicycle had been found. After circling the area overhead to make sure no police cars were keeping watch, we landed in the parking lot. It was lined with lampposts, but they'd either burned out or been turned off by whoever owned the property. The only light came from the street, some twenty yards from the storefront. The creature's eyes glinted in the near dark as it gave me a questioning glance.

"Let's look around," I said. "Shout if you find anything."

I turned on my flashlight and headed in one direction while the creature went in the other. The parking lot revealed by the sweeping arc of light was almost preternaturally clean, having already been combed over by an army of federal crime scene investigators. When I reached the edge of the concrete, I switched off my light and turned around to watch My Friend, bent forward and snuffling, nose close to the ground.

I tried to imagine what it must have been like on the day Maria had been taken. Partially cloudy, the sun popping out every now and again between banks of clouds. The not-quite-taboo thrill of riding her bike across an empty lot, a wide expanse of concrete all to herself. Maybe a slight breeze lifting her hair behind her when she got going fast. The curiosity when a vehicle pulled into the lot and drove right up to her. Did she know the driver? Or was it a stranger? Was she talked into the car, or grabbed? When the kidnapper drove away, did his route take Maria past her house? Did she get a last glimpse?

Across the lot, the creature was a dim, bulky outline and the sounds of its sniffing as it walked up and down the lot. But then the sounds abruptly stopped. My Friend had paused near the middle of the lot, facing me now.

"What is it?" I said. "Do you have something?"

It took a couple more sniffs of the ground. Then it looked at me and shook its head: *No*.

"You don't feel anything weird? No bad vibes in the air?"

The creature cocked its head, then shook it again—*No*—and I knew what I should have known—should at least have suspected—weeks ago. The creature was lying to me.

"Do you and my mother know each other?" I said.

It made no response, but I thought I read a sort of surprise in the lessening of its shoulder hunch, a slight drawing back of the head.

"That drawing I made of you for my costume at work," I said. "When I showed it to her, she got weird about it. She's seen you before, hasn't she?"

The creature shook its head.

"Right after I showed her that picture, she started talking about Maria Davis. Why would a picture of you start her thinking about missing children?" I said. "Unless she somehow associates a picture of you with Sydney's disappearance?"

A growl started in its throat, and it turned away from me. The smart thing would have been to let it go, but I was angry now, fully feeling *something* for the first time in weeks, and ready to ride it out. I pursued the monster and shoved it. I caught it off guard, and it actually fell forward onto its knees.

"You can fly!" I said, running to catch up. "You do magic! You somehow know how to find Batman toys, or which window at Donna's house is hers. You go missing every time one of these kids goes missing. You *know things*. I know you know what happened to Sydney, and Maria, and Brandon. So stop lying and tell me!" I reached for the creature's shoulder, and it slapped me away. This time, I fell over and landed on my ass.

The creature bared its teeth at me and snarled, its eyes bright orange. Saliva dripped from between clenched teeth. I closed my eyes and held up my forearms, knowing it was a pitiful defense against slaughter and wondering why I had had to bring the creature here, so far from home, where I could have at least cried for help. I waited to die.

And waited.

When I opened my eyes, the creature had gone, leaving me alone in a parking lot in the middle of nowhere.

15

I walked to the closest gas station and called home from the pay phone. Mom looked livid when she pulled into the parking lot half an hour later, jaw set and nostrils flaring through the windshield of her car. She was still wearing her pajamas.

I hurried from the storefront and slumped into the passenger seat. I felt her gaze burning into me but stared forward.

"I don't even know where to begin," she said.

"I'm sorry," I said.

"What the *hell* were you doing out here? Alone?"

"I snuck out to ride around with some friends and I got ditched," I said.

"What friends? Did Kyle do this?" It was strange how her parental concern seemed to emerge only when she was angry with me. I wish I could say that made her fury more pleasant, but that would be a lie. It still felt like shit.

"No, Mom, it wasn't Kyle," I said. "Kyle's with Donna tonight." I didn't know this for sure, but it seemed a safe bet. Since he was "sick," maybe she'd brought him chicken soup and word of my blessing/ indifference.

"Kyle with Donna?" she said, her voice softening. I crossed my arms over my chest and looked down at my lap. Let her work it out for herself.

"I'm sorry," she said. And then, almost to herself: "Your feelings were hurt so you went out and did something stupid."

"I wanted to see where Maria Davis went missing," I said. It never hurt to put a little truth in. "I thought maybe I could find something the police missed and . . ." I trailed off and shrugged.

"So stupid," she said, the steel returning to her tone. "Christ, do you know how lucky you are to be in *this* car right now, instead of on the news, like your sister and the other two?"

"I do," I said. I thought I knew even better than she did. I risked eye contact, and saw real concern mixed with fury.

"I should fire you," she said. "Make you stay home and sit out the rest of the year at The Wandering Dark. It might be the only thing that could help you understand the gravity of what you did tonight. And if Sydney hadn't disappeared right after she quit The Wandering Dark in 1989, that's exactly what I would do. But I'd rather you be where I can keep an eye on you. So here's how it works: you're grounded for the foreseeable future. You go to school, you go to work, and you come home. And that's your whole life until I say otherwise."

After the night I'd had, I felt like I was getting off light. I nodded and tried to look contrite.

16

Grounded, without a girlfriend, on hiatus from my best friend, and in mortal terror of the monster, I spent a lot more time at home but still saw little of Eunice. She hid in her room, or dominated the family computer. She typed at a rapid clip for hours, and rarely seemed to pause for thought. Mom said we had to give her space, that Eunice would traverse the country of depression at her own pace, but it's hard to live with a depressed person. The depression takes up physical space, swells and seeps under closed doors. It wafts between rooms like poison gas, settling over the house in a fog.

In an act of self-preservation, I decided to try to cheer Eunice up. On the third day of my grounding, I knocked on her bedroom door after I got home from school. I didn't receive an answer but walked in anyway. I found Eunice in bed, tangled in a mess of sheets. She'd pinned a blanket over the window, blocking most of the sunlight, and the room smelled of unwashed human flesh. Dirty laundry littered the floor, and dishes crusted with food were piled on the desk.

I jostled her by the shoulder and startled her awake.

"It's okay," I said, voice soft. "It's me."

Her panicked intake of air came out as a long, annoyed sigh. She opened and closed her mouth with a smacking sound. Her lips curled in disgust at whatever she tasted.

"What time is it?" she said.

"About four," I said.

She groaned, stretched, and kicked a book off the bed. It landed on the floor open and facedown, pages askew. *The Dream Cycle of H. P. Lovecraft: Dreams of Terror and Death.* She lifted her head, seemed to find it too difficult, and dropped it back on the pillow.

"I have the night off," I said. "I'm grounded, but Mom probably wouldn't mind if you rented us some movies."

"I'm not in the mood," she said.

"How about dinner?" I said. "I have money. We could order pizza."

"Invite Donna over."

"We broke up," I said.

She stared up at the ceiling. "Noah, take a hint. I want to be alone. You can't expect me to suddenly be your best friend because you got dumped."

"That's not how it is," I said.

"I get it," she said. "Mom ignored you when you were small, so it was my job to feed you and love you and exclaim over your gold stars and art projects. But you're not a little kid anymore, so how about you give me some fucking time to myself?"

"This isn't only about me," I said, trying to keep my voice even. "I thought some time out of your room—out of your own head—would be good for you."

"I don't get to leave this room," she said. "I have a brain as big as Saturn, but I go to community college because of a chemical imbalance. I'm stuck in a conservative concrete hell, decaying inside and justifying my choices to a C-average narcissist with mommy issues. So please, hear me before you spout any more nonsense about my well-being: I'd be fucking fine if you would fuck off and leave me the fuck alone."

"Eunice."

"Go. Fuck. Yourself."

I started to leave the room, but found myself too angry. I turned back and said, "No, you go fuck yourself. I was just trying to help you get over that stupid Jesus bitch, you—" I looked for something to hurt her like she'd hurt me, and reached for the most vile, low-hanging fruit. "I hope Brin is right and you rot in Hell."

I slammed her door behind me, my whole body shaking. I could've killed someone. I wanted to kill someone. Instead, I stormed downstairs and snatched her car keys from the hook by the front door.

I stole the car as quietly as I could. I didn't peel out or blast the radio. The act of driving, still awkward and new, soothed my nerves. I moved through town without aim, traffic bleeding off as the sun set and rush hour ended. I drove back to the closed-down Winn-Dixie, where My Friend and I had had our last violent conversation.

I parked my car in the lot and stared out the windshield, trying again to picture what had happened, the monster snatching Maria Davis off the bike and secreting her away to—to where? And in broad daylight? Brandon Hawthorne had been taken at night, but not Maria. Did My Friend ever appear anywhere while the sun was out? I supposed it was proof of how little I really knew about the creature.

The sun set, and, despite my inner anguish, I was getting hungry and nervous. I started the car and headed home, going a little under the speed limit, trying to think of what to say to my sister, how to take back the hateful thing I'd hurled at her. I was so preoccupied that, about two miles from the house, as I started a protected left turn, I didn't see the other vehicle coming until light flooded my passenger side window and the world spun, a blur of concrete and streetlights.

17

I came to a crunching halt and sat with my hands on the wheel, breathing hard. Nothing hurt, but my body glinted and sparkled like water in sunlight. Glass. I was covered in broken glass. Through the cracked windshield I saw the other vehicle, a VW bus, also stopped, facing the wrong way into oncoming traffic. One of its headlights was smashed and the sliding panel door hung open.

It took me three tries to unlatch my seat belt. When I opened my door, I tumbled onto the concrete but barely felt it. I stood on wobbly legs and staggered across to the bus. The driver was slumped over the wheel. The world spun. My head throbbed.

"Are you okay?" I called.

The figure at the wheel groaned and moved a little. The side door was open and the cab light inside was on, a soft, calming yellow. I paused in the middle of the street, happy for its reassuring warmth, but had to clamp my hands over my mouth and nose as a putrid, sickly-sweet stench rolled over me. I held my breath and squinted at the contents of the van: empty beer cans, fast-food trash, an overturned fire extinguisher, and, in the middle, a shiny black lump. A garbage bag—no, several garbage bags in a pile, containing misshapen, irregular cargo.

Something grabbed my forearm and jerked me away. I found myself facing a tall, filthy, bearded man with greasy hair. He wore an assortment of mismatched thrift-store castoffs and smelled terrible. He was bleeding from a gash on his forehead. I knew him from somewhere.

"What are you doing?" he said.

"Are you okay?" I said. "You're bleeding."

"Why were you looking in my vehicle?" he said. "That's none of your business."

"I don't—I'm not—I'm sorry," I said. His stench made it hard to think straight. I couldn't help glancing back at the open door.

His hand tightened on my arm. "It's none of your business," he said again.

As I started to look away, something shifted in the back of the van. One of the bags, prompted by some tiny, unseen shift of gravity, rolled forward, tipped out of the cab, and hit the street with a thick, heavy sound. The bag hadn't been tied properly, so there was nothing to stop the pale thing from falling out and lying in sharp contrast to the black bag and gray pavement: a single small hand.

He saw me see. I had enough time to register another glint, this one on serrated steel, but not enough time to do anything as it arced sideways through the air between us, strangely beautiful. I wondered why it had to be so lovely. Before I could come up with an answer, a great weight crashed into me, the world spun again, and I hit the pavement. I heard the knife clatter away.

I sat up a little, feeling my body for wounds and finding none. A hooded figure crouched between me and the other man, blocking my view. It rose and revealed its full height. My Friend, a low growl in its throat. Its crimson robe seemed to float around it, no longer tethered by gravity.

My assailant tilted his head as the creature approached, a look of dim thoughtfulness on his face. He opened his mouth, but before he said a word, something else plummeted from the sky and landed between the two of them. It looked like My Friend, but different, fur more gray than brown, a scar running up the side of its face. It wore a blue cloak rather than red.

Mine wasn't the only one. Here was another, meaner-looking monster. It growled and bared its fangs, protecting the filthy man. My Friend spread its arms and took a step back. The man shouted, "Not your business!" again, and the Gray Beast lunged forward with a roar. My Friend hit the ground and covered its head with its paws. The Gray

Beast tripped over it, snarled its legs in the intermingling cloaks, and crashed in the street.

My Friend rolled to its hands and knees as the Gray Beast did the same. The Gray Beast now crouched between My Friend and me. Both creatures seemed to realize the reversal at the same time, although the Gray Beast was quicker. It galloped at me on all fours and opened a gaping maw of swordlike teeth. The mouth seemed to open wider and wider, filling an expanse of space that ought not to have been possible, creating a starry sky of fangs.

I scrambled backward with one arm up, moving too slowly. I closed my eyes. A gush of something wet hit my face and My Friend howled like a wounded dog. I opened my eyes to see its face next to mine, bright with pain and real fear. It had jammed its forearm between the Beast's jaws. I was glazed in a layer of My Friend's black blood.

My Friend beat at the Gray Beast with a free arm, but its blows looked weak. I scrambled around behind the Beast, pulled myself to my feet, and heaved myself at its back. I wrapped my arms around its throat like a TV wrestler. It was like trying to choke a stovepipe. The Beast released its death-grip on My Friend and spun in a circle, swiping at me. I tried to wrap my legs around its middle, but couldn't find purchase. Its claws grasped at me, first left, then right, and I couldn't duck both arms at once. Its talons caught the left side of my face and dug in. I screamed as the sight in my left eye went red, then gray.

I was torn off the Beast's back, dangled in the air, and then tucked against My Friend's body, its weak arm soaking my shirt with blood. The Gray Beast dived toward us again, and My Friend dropped me, braced itself with bent knees, and caught the Beast by the open jaws. My Friend howled as the Beast's fangs impaled its paws, but it kept its grip. The Beast's long, purple tongue waggled almost comically in its forced-open mouth, flapping against My Friend's paws as though it might be able to knock them loose.

My Friend leaned forward and stood up, driving the Beast to its knees. The Beast slapped at My Friend, its blows bouncing off as its mouth was pulled open wider and wider. I should have looked away then. Instead, I saw My Friend rip the Beast's jaws apart, separating the bottom part of its skull from the rest. It flung the pieces to either side. The jaw joined my assailant's knife in the dark, and the Beast's body collapsed in a pile, a mess of cloth and black blood, its orange eyes extinguished.

My Friend thundered a cry of pain and furious triumph. The remaining glass in Eunice's car and the VW bus burst and the street-lights shattered, plunging the immediate area into darkness.

"Holy cats. None of your business." It was the filthy man, voice small and shocked. "Holy cats. This isn't how it goes. I want to do it again. Start over."

At last I recognized my would-be murderer. I'd seen him only once before—the day Mom's car caught fire in 1989. He'd put out the flames. Holy cats. Small fucking world.

My Friend started toward him, probably meaning to finish the job. Somewhere nearby, sirens wailed. Vehicles with flashing lights were coming, full of people paid to restore at least the illusion of order in the mundane world.

"Stop," I said, and My Friend did. "Leave him." Let him explain the car crash, the monster fight, and the lump of garbage bags in his van. It would serve him right.

My Friend knelt to lift me. It winced and gave me a questioning look. *Where to?*

"Far away," I said. "Not home."

18

The wind tore at us and then it didn't. The air took on a sulfurous smell. I tried to lift my head and look around, but My Friend gently pushed my face back into its chest. I was nearly asleep when we landed in a small clearing in a dense forest, the trees so thick around that I couldn't see anything but darkness between them. The trees and grass were inky black, and, above, the sky was a dark greenish shade that felt somehow familiar. A low, wide, grassy mound stood in the center of the clearing, with a door in one side. The mound was encircled by ebon kindnesses like the one I'd given Donna.

"Where are we?" I said.

My Friend carried me through the door and down a short, winding staircase. The door shut itself behind us, and candles flickered to life, lighting the way to a single large room with a wooden floor and walls. The creature put me on a large bed covered in thick, furry blankets, and moved into what looked like a small kitchen. The walls were decorated with paintings, starting with simple depictions of cars, buildings, and people, and moving on to more complex, abstract pieces featuring meshes of color and shadowy figures out of focus. A rough-hewn easel and stool stood in one corner, and a stained palette sat on the stool, alongside a tankard full of paintbrushes. Canvases leaned in a pile behind the easel. The one on top depicted two hideously distorted faces, layered so that they stood out in three dimensions.

"Is this where you live?" I said.

The creature didn't answer. It worked in a hurry, crunching up something and stirring it into a mug of water. When it turned to face me again, it held two mugs in one paw, its injured arm tucked against its body. It crossed the room and offered me a mug. My arm shook as I reached for it.

The creature set the mugs on the floor and wrapped me in a blanket from the bed. It picked up one of the mugs and put it to my lips. The contents were dry and bitter as dirt. I tried to turn my head but met My Friend's eyes and read angry determination. I forced myself to swallow the dirt tea. Gradually the shakes subsided and pleasant, numbing warmth spread through my body.

When my mug was empty, the creature drained its own. It extended its injured arm and pulled up the sleeve. The hair was still missing, but the wounds had faded to light pink scars. Most of my own pain had faded, but my left eye still showed nothing but gray.

"My eye," I said. "Will it be okay?"

My Friend shook its head.

I started to cry—over the eye at first, but then for my fight with

Eunice, the awful names I'd called her, the accident, the other driver, the lump of foul bags in his van, and the other monster.

"That was them in his van, wasn't it? The missing kids."

The creature nodded.

"So they're both dead," I said.

The creature nodded again.

"That man killed them. Maybe he killed Sydney. And he meant to kill me, too. And even though I accused you, you still saved my life."

The creature touched my face, turned my chin so that our gazes locked. In the space of a few seconds, its frame narrowed and shortened, the broad shoulders drawing in and coming down to my height, the snout retracting, the eyes changing from bright, pupilless orange to a soft green. The fur went last, drawing in through pinkish flesh to reveal a pale woman with high cheekbones, a strong chin, and a small, determined mouth. Her long red hair was tied back in a ponytail.

She cleared her throat. "I love you," she said. "And I would never hurt you." Her voice was hoarse and carried an accent I couldn't place.

Maybe it was the shock of the evening, or the simple declaration of love after our estrangement, the joy of being reunited after a near-death experience. Whatever the reason, I leaned forward and caught her mouth with my own. Her kiss was forceful and confident, her hands cool and callused as she cupped my face. She pushed me onto my back and pulled the blanket off so I could move. I grabbed her face, her hips, her thighs beneath her now-oversize robe, my hands too excited, too hungry to stay still. She straddled me and ground down against my groin. My body responded to the pressure, effortless and free, full of blunt desire.

She opened her robe and let it fall off her shoulders, revealing her alabaster skin, her heavy, round breasts, her thatch of red pubic hair. She bucked into me, pushing against my erection with a gentle smile.

She unbuckled my belt, popped the button on my jeans, and yanked my zipper open. I lifted my ass, and together we wiggled my jeans down around my knees. Then she took me in her hand, gave me a squeeze, and lowered herself onto me.

Like my first kiss, my first sex ended before it really began. I was embarrassed, but the soft, kind look never left the woman's face. She gently rode it out, easing my humiliation on waves of pleasure. When I finished spasming and started to soften and slide out of her, she placed her hands on my chest and said, "Again." Golden light spread in my mind's eye, and I was ready, the suddenness of the erection like a thrust as I slipped back into her. She gasped a little.

The second time lasted much longer. She rode me hard, rubbing herself with her hand, eyes closed, head thrown back. As she came, she shouted words I didn't understand, repeating them again and again until she collapsed against my chest and forced a second, almost painfully powerful orgasm from me.

After, she lay next to me with one arm and leg over my body, and pressed her face against my neck.

"You can change shapes," I said, stroking the milky thigh across my middle.

"Yes," she said, lips tickling my ear.

"Can you turn into anything? Or anyone?"

"No. Just this."

"Why didn't you show me before now?"

She didn't answer, but held tight, as though afraid I would leave. I was too exhausted to move, and happy to stay put, far from the complicated troubles of the real world.

19

There were no windows in the little house, so I had no idea if it was day or night when I woke and found her staring at me, stroking my face.

"How do you feel?" she said.

"Hungry," I said. "Do you have any food?"

"Nothing you'd like," she said. "But I can bring you whatever you want."

"That's okay," I said. "I should probably be getting home. I'm going to be in a world of trouble for wrecking Eunice's car. Also, I need a doctor. And some clean clothes." With reluctance, I climbed out of bed and began to dress.

She sat up and leaned against the wall, unkempt and lovely. "You don't *have* to go."

"Of course I do."

"You can stay here as long as you want."

"What, and just abandon my whole life?"

She cocked her head. "I can bring you anything you want or need."

"Where is here exactly?" I said.

She acted like I'd said nothing, and watched me dress in silence.

"I like you better without your clothes on," she said.

"Will you send me home?" I said.

She stood and walked across the hut, kneeling before one of the cabinets. Watching her naked body perform these casual gestures started my excitement all over again, and I was about ready to go a third time when she returned to me with a small black stone in her hands. It was tied to a thin length of leather.

"Take this," she said, slipping it over my head. The stone lay cool against my chest, and I lifted it for examination. It was perfectly smooth, without flaw.

"Whenever you want to come see me," she said, "just clench the stone in your fist and think of me. No matter where you are, the stone will bring you right to my front door. And when you're ready to go back, clench it again and think of where you want to go. It'll take you there."

"Thank you," I said.

She smiled, but there was something pained in it. "I wish you didn't have to go."

"Me too," I said.

"Do you promise to come back?" She tilted her head down and looked up at me with heavy-lidded green eyes.

"As soon as I can," I said.

20

My first trip using the black stone deposited me on my family's front porch in bright morning sunlight. I could hear dogs barking and kids laughing somewhere down the block. I fumbled for my keys before remembering I'd left them in Eunice's car. Without much hope I tried the door. To my surprise, it opened.

I stepped inside and called, "Hello?"

The word hung in the entryway and died in the still air. I walked into the dining room and found a half-eaten bowl of Cheerios on the table. The cereal was mushy, as though the bowl had been left out for several hours. I found other things amiss—a picture frame that usually hung at the foot of the stairs, lying on the floor, the glass cracked and broken; a single drop of blood in the cream-colored carpet; the telephone receiver on its side at the base of the couch.

I found Eunice's note about halfway up the stairs, where Mom had probably dropped it as she barreled toward the locked bathroom door. The bathroom door was kicked in, the water in the tub pink, the porcelain stained red above the waterline, the razor dropped carelessly on the rug.

I sat on the toilet. My left eye pulsed and the world swam.

Downstairs, the phone rang. Its shrill trilling filled the house. It sounded impossibly far away, a cry for help I could never answer in time.

Eunice's Last Letter

Dear Noah,

 The first thing I want you to do is put this down,
and I don't want you to pick it up again until you've
forgiven me. I mean it. Go.

 Okay. Maybe it's been six months and you're curled
up in your bed, taking a break from homework while Mom
watches TV in the next room—or maybe it's years and
years later and you're sitting in a rocking chair on the
porch of some idyllic nursing home with tall windows
and vast green grounds. Maybe your hair has gone white
and your skin's taken on that spotty, lived-in quality.
I don't know; I can't see it, and that's the problem. I
can't see you. I can't see anything anymore, except
here, now.

 It's October 28 and I'm in the computer room with the
lights off. It's a clear night outside, and a sickly-
green finger of streetlight pokes through the blinds. It
wrestles with the light from the computer monitor on
the floor behind me, fighting for my shadow. I've packed
all my books and CDs and clothes in marked boxes. All
that's left is the final chore. Although there were some
tempting alternatives, I've chosen the old-fashioned
method. I want to leave a little bit of a mess, but not
much. When all the wailing and gnashing is finished, you
can open the drain, run some fresh water, and use the
scrubbing bubbles on the porcelain.

 I did this because I love you.

 Please don't think this is your fault. I'm sorry about

what I said to you, and I'm not mad that you took the car. It's important to say these things, because there's only one word that matters in these situations: *Why?* If you don't lay out your answer (or answers) with lawyerly precision, the people you leave behind blame themselves. People are selfish and self-centered that way.

When I wake up in the morning, I hurt all over. It's like I have the flu, but without the fever and puking. Just an overwhelming ache, and sorrow at surviving another night. I know what you're thinking: *Eunice, we've known about your depression for years now. That's why it's important that you take your medication.* The problem is that the medication doesn't work anymore. I take it every day and still I hurt. When I look in the mirror, I don't see my own face. I see a slowly disintegrating thing with dark circles under bleary, unfocused eyes and cracked lips that bleed when they try to smile. Sometimes when people talk to me, I can't hear them, and when I do, I don't know what to say back. Usually it's the wrong thing. As I demonstrated tonight.

I don't mean to be like this. I've tried to get better, but I'm never going to be normal. There's always going to be something wrong with me. No matter how hard I try, no matter what I do, I will always fail. I won't be pretty or athletic, and boys won't like me. Worse, I won't like boys. Noah, if you ever run into her, and it somehow comes up organically, tell Brin that I'm sorry I wasn't born a boy. Not that I actually want to be a boy, but that I would trade my entire identity if it meant it was okay for me to love her.

I keep pausing whenever I hear a car door. I get up and go to the window, thinking it's you, cooled off and ready to try and talk to me again. I picture our muttered apologies, the worry on your simple, open face, my courage and resolve faltering as we build the awkward

bridge that will reconnect us. I see myself giving in to
your need for everything to be okay, and trudging on for
another day, or week, or month. Maybe trudging through
a whole life for your benefit. But then I look out the
window and it's not you.

Probably not long from now, when you put on my funeral,
some teary-eyed person is going to stand up behind a
pulpit next to my casket and speak at great length
about my selfishness. How dare I? What right did I have?
To that person I say (and I hope you'll pass this on):
shame on you. Kierkegaard said (I think) that society
has always put a taboo on suicide because when a person
kills herself, the people around said person start to
question the value of their own lives, and that makes
them uncomfortable. Figure it out for yourself—what makes
your life so great?

What makes my life so great? The swell of Brin's hips.
Her laugh. The faces you made when I used to read to
you. Seeing Dad make Mom laugh—the way her whole body
convulsed. Seeing Sydney dance, the way the movement
seemed to set her free and make her whole. The way it
felt to type so fast my Commodore 64 could barely keep
up. Brin's mouth on mine.

I'm trapped here, in our family's home office, far from
all those things (except the typing, of course). Trapped
in this body, in the gridlock of linear time.

I had an interesting dream recently. I usually dream
about boring things like losing my car keys or forgetting
to study for a test—but the other night I dreamt that
Brin showed up on our front doorstep and asked me
to take a ride with her. We got in her car and drove
through the night, across strange mountainous country.
The torn pleather upholstery of her car seat scratched
at the back of my neck. The engine puttered along like
the world's most agreeable senior citizen, and the whole

time, Brin just watched the road with a strange Madonna
smile. We didn't stop for food, or gas, or to use the
bathroom. We didn't need to.

Eventually, we pulled up into a gravel parking lot at
the crest of a hill.

"Stay put," Brin said. "And keep your eyes shut."

I did as she said. She came around, opened my door,
and took my hand to help me out. She guided me off the
gravel and into the grass.

"Okay," she said. "Open your eyes."

I stood on the hilltop, the stars bright, fat bulbs
above, a crescent moon tucked into a halo. A brown
tree stump sat to my left. I reached to touch it, and
I realized that I looked like a living Impressionist
painting, the brushstrokes of my body vibrating and
shifting, not smooth in motion but still somehow
pleasing in their disregard for things as simple and
boring as consistency. I looked up at the sky and saw
a beautiful garden of stars, like dandelions caught in
a visible, unfurling wind. They pulsed in sequence, as
though communicating some coded message.

The visible wind above furled and then unfurled.
Furled and unfurled. Furled—held it—then slowly and
luxuriously unfurled. It was moving in time with my
lungs. I looked back at Brin, and she'd changed out of
her punk costume. She wore a black and green dress that
clung to her figure and pushed the tops of her breasts
up toward her chin. Her hair hung free around her
face, a loose confederation of dark curls suggested in
broad strokes that danced around her head, changing its
configuration from second to second.

"Come on," she said, and gestured to a little town at
the bottom of the hill. "I'll show you around."

I followed her down along a path. The nestled
buildings and towering church steeple grew larger as I

approached, and I noticed warm lights in the windows,
figures bustling in the streets despite the late hour. I
heard the hum of conversation, scattered laughter, music.

She led me up the street and into the village, past
closed doors and frosted windows with orange lights
behind them. One of the doors opened and a small figure
darted out—a child, wearing a black cape and cowl. He
ran up the road in front of us, cape fluttering behind
him, and turned a corner, disappearing.

"Was that?" I said, pointing after the boy, sure I'd
recognized him.

"Come on," Brin said, as she pulled me up the road.
"You'll see."

The winding street ended at a sort of town square,
wide and cobbled, with a well in its center. People
clumped around vendor stalls to buy fruit and fish and
bread, children ran, and a man played accordion while
young couples danced. The notes he played were as visible
as the wind, an aurora borealis flashing up from his
instrument. I recognized Mr. Ransom, portly and flush,
selling fish, and Sydney dancing with a handsome man I
didn't recognize, her peasant dress flying around her,
caught in the wind. I began to recognize other people
as well—Merrin Price, my old writing partner from The
Wandering Dark, selling fruit. Hubert Sangalli, my friend
from grade school, buying a hat. Rick, Dad's old coworker
from the highway department, building a stage. While I
watched him hammer a leg into place, I realized that,
as the wind had moved in time with my breath, the world
moved in time with the music. The visible wind flowed
along with the accordion's melody, performing a sort of
interpretive dance. And beneath the music, almost buried,
the sound of tapping keys on an old manual typewriter,
giving the song its rhythm.

"Where—" I said, searching the square for signs of a

typist, but before I could finish the question, Brin pressed her body flush against mine, her right hand on my hip.

"Dance with me," she said, and pulled me into a turn. The world spun around me, slowly at first, then faster. Discernible shapes—people, houses, the well, the shop stalls—lost definition, became a stream of paints squeezed from their tubes and running together, a thick vortex of color. The only thing retaining its definition was Brin, the center of gravity holding me in orbit, spinning me about. Somehow I knew the steps of the dance; my day-to-day awkwardness vanished, washed away in the flood of color, the typing of my feet on the cobblestones. I kept my eyes on Brin. As the song reached its climax, she twirled me into her embrace and kissed me. I lingered on her mouth as she pulled away, leaving my face hanging in empty space. She seemed about to say something else when the little boy in the cape darted through the square again. You, Noah, age six and obsessed with Batman, weaving between people on your way to the doors of the high-steepled church. You grabbed the handle of one of the double doors and pulled. It didn't move at first, so you leaned back and put your weight into it. The door groaned open with obvious reluctance, spilling pure, almost-blinding white light into the square.

I let go of Brin and ran after you as you went into the church, but stopped on the threshold, confused by what I was seeing. Try to imagine two or three different movies being projected on a screen at once, a jumble of competing images, none of them a church. I saw Dad, pushing me on a swing at a park; Mom, giving me an ice pack after I bumped my head at the playground; me and Merrin, writing together at The Wandering Dark; me and Brin in my dark bedroom, nose to nose and covered in sweat, a sheet tangled around us. I saw the Tomb and

The Wandering Dark layered atop each other, the former somehow scaffolding for the latter. I saw the monster dragging away Katies and Brads while I stood by in my white robe, watching. And then the competing images faded, and I saw what appeared to be an art gallery—a wide, dimly lit space, white walls lined with paintings, and in the center of it all, a red-haired woman I've never seen before, in a red dress. You ran up to her, and she put an arm around you, and the door swung shut with a bang. I ran forward and tugged at it, but it was locked against me.

I turned to find Brin next to me, her hands folded in front of her.

"What is this place?" I said.

Brin opened her mouth as if to answer—but then I woke up.

I've been trying to get back to that dream ever since, but it eludes me, and I'm back to my vague dreams about failed classes and misplaced car keys. I can't get that village out of my mind—full of people I know, smiling and laughing, painted as their best, most perfect selves. That church—art gallery, with you and the red-haired woman and all of eternity inside. The dream Brin, about to answer my question—the question that could answer all other questions. After a dream like that, how can I live with the drudgery of being trapped in this ugly, rotting body, going to my shitty college and moving slowly through time in the wrong direction?

Sitting here, typing all this out, I think I finally understand. Dad told me once that every horror story has a happy ending, but he was wrong. Look at how his life ended. Noah, there's no such thing as a happy ending. The songs, books, and movies with "happy endings" all stop at the moment of triumph. They don't tell the whole story. Only the old tragedies tell the truth. Beowulf triumphs

over Grendel and his mother, only to fall fighting a
dragon. Gilgamesh loses his best friend. Achilles, too.
Everyone dies in *Hamlet*. This is the whole truth.

There are, however, good stopping places. I made the
mistake of traveling past mine, is all. I'm like spoiled
milk stuck in the jug. I need to pour myself out and
move on. I need to be free to move through eternity and
infinity, to spend a century on Brin's breast, listening
to her heart pound, and an aeon tucking you into bed,
your eyes bright with love and trust. I'll spend a decade
watching Sydney dance, Dad making Mom laugh. I'll have
eternity with my greatest hits. That has to be what's
inside the church. It has to be the answer. We can't
make new happiness past a certain point, but we can
linger in past joy forever, perfectly captured with the
rememberer's eye.

Remember me, Noah, tucking you into bed, kissing you
good night. Remember the stories I told you. We will see
each other again.

Love Always,

Eunice

Part Five

The Nameless
City

In the fall of 2002, I took a night off from The Wandering Dark to visit a Christian Hell House in Mansfield, Texas, called Inferno. I'd meant to go with Kyle, but he bailed at the last second, citing plans with Donna, so I made the drive to Holy Spirit Bible Church that evening with an Anne Rice paperback for company. The book was a good idea, because the line to get in at Inferno stretched from the church doors all the way across a wide, grassy field, and everyone in said line started staring as soon as I arrived.

I should have been used to the attention. The eye patch made more of a statement than a glass eye, and even without it, I would still have been recognizable as Vandergriff's own Hardy Boy, the kid who inadvertently cracked the case of the child snatcher in 1999. Stares were going to be a normal part of life as long as I lived in or around Vandergriff, but the scrutiny still made me uncomfortable. I didn't like being stared at unless I was in my monster costume at work.

I read in the failing sunlight and ignored the assorted gawkers until I reached the front of the line. There, an employee in an INFERNO polo shirt tacked me onto the odd-numbered church youth group in front of me. The gaggle of teenagers and their thirtysomething chaperone gave me uncomfortable looks as we passed through the rubber-flap entrance together.

A slight figure draped in black robes met us inside, its head tilted down. The lights around us gradually rose and the figure lifted its head, revealing a rubbery, skeletal demon mask. The eyes behind it were caked with black makeup and bright with malevolent glee.

"Welcome!" it said. It was a teenage girl, her voice twisted and cranked up to carry past the rubber mask. "I'm so glad you could make it to this little open house. I hope you enjoy yourselves so much you'll make a permanent residence! But I'm getting ahead of myself. Why don't we go look around?"

We followed her down a long hall, red lights above us, blue lights shining up through a clear plastic floor. Blue fog swirled beneath the surface, hypnotic and tranquil, until a hand sheared through the wisps and smacked against the plastic, fingers spread and scratching. One of the girls in front of me shrieked and jumped back. More hands emerged from the fog, slapping and banging, scattering the haze and revealing wide-mouthed faces crying for help.

"Don't mind them," the guide said. "Just a few of our new arrivals." She cackled and moved along, but I lingered, impressed with the workmanship.

When I caught up with the group, they'd arrived at a house party set. A kid with a long zitty face pretended to DJ, running his hands back and forth over two empty turntables, and colored lights splashed random patterns over stiff, awkwardly dancing teenagers. Two girls stood near the audience, drinking from red plastic cups. One of the girls had long, straight blond hair, a large nose, and big brown eyes. The other had green hair and more of a club-kid look.

"Meet Miranda and Ashley," the guide said, pointing to each girl in turn. "Miranda just moved to town from Connecticut. Cut off from her old church and her Christian friends, Miranda has fallen in with a bad crowd. Ashley grew up with atheist parents and reads Harry Potter for fun. She doesn't see anything wrong with partying and drinking on a Friday night."

"Isn't this fun, Miranda?" said Ashley, the green-haired girl.

Miranda cast a mistrustful glance into her cup and took a sip. "Sure," she said, grimacing. "It's all so new, you know?"

"Look over there!" Ashley said, stepping on Miranda's line. She pointed across the room to boys leering at them and moving their heads in time with the beat. "Trent and Evan. Oh my god, they're coming this way."

"Having a good time, girls?" one of the boys said.

"Totally," Miranda said.

"You know what could make it even better?" the other boy said. "This." He held up a small white pill, cheating it toward the audience. "It'll make you feel amazing."

"I've already had two," said the first boy.

"Sounds great," Ashley said. She took the proffered pill and washed it down with her drink.

"How about you, good-looking?" the second boy asked Miranda.

"I don't know," Miranda said. She looked at Ashley, tortured with indecision. While her head was turned away, the second boy dropped the pill into her cup. Unaware, Miranda downed the rest of her drink.

The boys closed in on the girls, and the Guide swept in front of them, blocking our view.

"What Miranda doesn't know is that she's just taken a date-rape drug," she said, in her faux–Crypt Keeper screech. "She feels good now, but in about thirty minutes she won't feel anything at all."

Further chambers told similar cautionary tales: school shootings, drunk driving accidents, the violent culture of buying and selling drugs, attending a black mass, reading fantasy fiction not written by C. S. Lewis, domestic abuse, et cetera. The scenes grew more viscerally upsetting as they progressed, most ending with the protagonist dying in some horrible way. My discomfort increased, as it was meant to, until we passed into what was obviously supposed to be a teenage girl's bedroom, and Miranda, the girl who'd taken the date-rape drug, wandered in with tangled hair and a dazed expression, arms wrapped around her middle as though she didn't feel well.

"You remember Miranda," our guide said. "So desperate to make new friends that she would try anything with anyone. Of course, now she can't remember what she tried or who she tried it with. Isn't that right, Miranda?"

Miranda sat on the bed and stared into the middle distance. I wondered how they shuttled the actress back and forth between rooms without disrupting the flow of visitors. Was it difficult to muss and unmuss her hair and makeup over and over?

"What's wrong, Miranda?" the Guide said. "Didn't you have a good time?"

"Shut up," Miranda said, voice low and pained.

"It's a simple question," the Guide said. "Unless maybe you can't remember?"

"Shut up," Miranda said, louder this time, rocking herself.

"Remember the day at your old church when you signed an abstinence oath? You were so proud. You felt so sure God would protect you."

Miranda slumped to the floor. She opened a drawer in her bedside table and pulled out a framed painting of Christ.

"There He is!" the Guide said. "Hiding in a drawer, out of sight. Didn't do you much good there, did He?"

"How could you let this happen?" Miranda asked the picture. She dropped it and reached into the drawer again. This time she withdrew a pistol. This girl kept strange stuff in her nightstand.

"Ooh, what's that?" the Guide said.

"I hate you," Miranda said to the picture of Jesus. She pressed the gun to her forehead, cocked the hammer, and pulled the trigger. A loud BANG sounded, and the lights turned from soft yellow to muddy red. The Guide knelt next to her and caught her as she slumped over.

"Good girl," the Guide murmured. "Good girl."

I thought I might throw up.

Next came a mock-up of an emergency room, where a woman covered in blood from "an abortion pill" begged for God's grace and forgiveness right as she died. I followed all of this only vaguely, willing myself not to get sick in the middle of the attraction. It took me until the next room to regain control of myself. This one was lined with golden foil, and ethereal music poured through hidden speakers behind a huge cross. Characters from previous scenes wandered in, faces lit with wonder.

"It's beautiful," said the abortion pill girl. "Like nothing I ever dreamed." She stood so close I could smell the red paint on her pants.

"Is this Heaven?" Miranda asked.

"It is, my child," came a booming voice from the speakers. "Tell me—did you obey my commandments and take my Son into your heart? Did you keep Him there all of your days and repent of your sins?"

Miranda and the others stuttered excuses. They'd been confused, misguided, unsure. They fell silent and parted as the abortion girl approached the cross.

"I went to church as a little girl," she said, "but I stopped going when my parents stopped making me. I grew up outside your grace and love, and I laughed when good people tried to minister to me. But then I had unprotected sex with a stranger, took a pill to keep from getting pregnant, and everything went wrong. I couldn't stop the bleeding, and your Son's name was the only one I could call for help."

"Welcome home, my child," the deep voice rumbled. A door opened beneath the cross and she walked through. As the others tried to follow, however, the entrance slammed shut.

"What about the rest of us?" Miranda said.

"You denied me in life," the disembodied voice said, "and I deny you in death. Get thee gone!" The room plunged into darkness.

"Finally!" the Guide crowed from somewhere behind me. "Payday!"

Red light rose from the baseboards. The characters denied Heaven turned slow circles.

"What's happening?" Miranda said.

"It's time to go home, dear," the Guide said. "Get 'em, boys!"

A horde of monstrous figures dashed out from behind the wall hangings. The damned struggled and cried for help as they were dragged away. Miranda fought hardest, lunged forward and lost her balance. She landed on her hands and knees in front of me and made eye contact. The panic and fear disappeared from her face, replaced with bald surprise. She stared at me, mouth half-open as demons grabbed her arms and towed her out of sight.

"Well, that was fun," the Guide said, "but this is where I leave you. I hope to see you all again soon!" She cackled as she followed her minions out of the room. Another door opened, and a woman in jeans and a T-shirt appeared in the doorway, limned by fluorescent light.

"This way please," she said, her warm, gentle voice a comfort after all the screaming.

The group shuffled into a final room with wood panels and gray carpet. A tall, somber man stood between two doors on the opposite end of the room.

"How y'all doing?" he said.

The youth group exchanged furtive looks, and a ripple of nervous laughter passed over them.

The somber man gave us a look probably calculated to appear sympathetic. "I've been seeing that same look all night, and, believe me, now that you're out the far end of Inferno, I'd like to offer you some relief. What you've seen here tonight is the absolute undying and eternal truth of the universe. Bad things happen all the time. People get hurt. People die. And if they die without Christ in their hearts, they're sentenced to a pit of never-ending pain and suffering." He paused, clasping his hands and surveying our faces. "You could get hit by a drunk driver on your way home. A drug addict could break into your house tonight and murder you for the contents of your piggy bank. Christ could return tomorrow morning and carry the faithful to Heaven before your alarm clock goes off. You can't know. What you have to ask yourself is, if one of these things happened, would you be ready? Could you look Christ in the eye on your day of judgment and truthfully say you lived and died in His grace?" Again he paused, giving us time to reflect on the question. "There are two doors behind me. Through the door to my right, there's a room full of good folks waiting to pray with you, and that room will be open for the next sixty seconds." The gentle-voiced woman who'd brought us to this room opened the door to the prayer room and stepped aside, hands folded in front of her.

I'd had enough. I broke from the crowd and walked through the door to the man's left. It opened out into the cool evening air and slammed shut on the man's voice, some parting shot I didn't hear. There was a hayride shuttle waiting to drive people back to satellite parking, but I elected to walk. I kept my hands in my pockets and my shoulders hunched as I crossed the dark field.

Why would I subject myself to this place to begin with? Because The Wandering Dark was in trouble. Ticket sales had been declining for the last two years, and it was now rare for our parking lot to be even half-full on a Saturday night. Most of our customers were families with young children, and the few teens and adults who showed up seemed dazed and unimpressed, like an audience drugged with Thorazine. Mom wanted to close down, and had even fielded offers to sell the place, but I had asked her to give me a few nights off to scope out the competition. I wanted to see who was stealing our business, and what we might do to win it back.

I'd been to three haunted attractions in the last week—Blood Bath, a gory slasher-themed place in Dallas; House of Scares, a family-friendly collection of mini-haunts; and now Inferno, a Christian Hell House run out of a megachurch in Mansfield, a perversion of the tropes for religious ends. I should have been able to roll my eyes and laugh it off, but I felt shaken, upset. I couldn't dismiss the image of Miranda, the date-rape suicide, pleading with me as she was taken to Hell.

2

Mom was already in bed when I got home. I went up to my room, and as soon as I was inside, I grabbed the black stone that hung around my neck. I closed my eye and concentrated, and when I opened it again I found myself in the clearing in the black forest. The air was thick and fetid, the trees inky and dense as an Impressionist's brushstrokes.

The door opened before I could knock, and there she stood, robe open to reveal a strip of flesh running from the hollow of her throat to the patch of red hair on her mons pubis.

"Leannon si," she said.

Leannon si. Pronounced *lihannan shee.* A nickname, an inside joke picked up from a book of Celtic fairy tales: a beautiful fairy woman who takes a mortal man as a lover. I'd suggested the name Leannon for want of something to call her, to think of her as something other than "the monster," "the creature," or "My Friend," to reframe our relationship outside the bounds of *Danny and the Dinosaur* or *E.T.*

Leannon si, to make it less weird as I carried her down the stairs to her bed. *Leannon si,* as I dropped her on the blankets, lowered myself to my knees, and pushed her legs apart. *Leannon si,* spelled out with my tongue as she pulled my hair. *Leannon si,* her thighs clamped around my head, my nose squashed against her as her body locked and she cried out. *Leannon si* as, gasping, I climbed onto the bed, wrestled my pants off, and slipped into her. *Leannon si,* her teeth on my ear, her ankles around the small of my back. *Leannon si,* holding me and whispering, "Good boy," as the golden kaleidoscope split me into dozens of tiny starbursts. *Leannon si.*

We lay entangled and sweating in the humidity. Three years of this. Three years of visiting this little house in this little clearing in another world, of lingering with her in this bed. Did I think it was weird? I wasn't exactly eager to announce our relationship to anyone, and now, a year and change after high school, I'd started questioning the long-term viability of the arrangement, but only a little. Mostly I'd enjoyed myself, and my passion for Leannon continued to burn hot, lasting in a way no human passion ever seems to.

Now I laid my head on her pale stomach and studied the canvas on her easel, which depicted two figures on a hillside beneath a sky of blended yellows, maroons, blues, and blacks. A crescent moon and an oblong, misshapen star hung in the sky, and a second star lay on the ground. I couldn't tell what the two figures were supposed to be. The one on the right looked like an animal, hunched over and draped in yellow, its purple-gray head shaped like an apostrophe. It had an alien eye, lidded only on the bottom and gazing without apparent expression at the sky. The figure on the left looked like a flower with a wide stem and two stalks culminating in mismatched bulbs, one with wings, the other a purple vulva. Behind the vulva, almost hidden in the paint, was the figure of a woman, hips rising to a pair of round breasts. I thought of Miranda at Inferno. She'd been curvy like that.

"What do you think?" Leannon said, startling me.

I sat up, pretending to want a better look. "I'm not sure I understand it."

She sat up, too, and rested her chin on my shoulder. "It's not a codex to be decrypted. It's a painting. It's okay to say what it makes you think and feel."

"What do you think and feel about it?" I said.

She looked pensive and didn't answer right away. "I think about you," she said. It didn't sound like a lie, but it wasn't the whole truth. It was a balance I'd noticed often. When I'd first heard her speak, I'd assumed the mysteries surrounding her would thin out, but I felt no closer to the heart of things now than in 1999. I still didn't know her real name, how old she was, or even what she was. I didn't know where this house was, or how the stone around my neck helped me traverse the distance from my bedroom to Leannon's front door.

Sensing the conversation flow in a direction she didn't like, she got up and crossed to one of her kitchen cupboards.

"Are you hungry?" she said. "I have food." She retrieved a bowl of apples and set them in front of me.

I took a bite of one of the apples and realized that I was hungry—starving, in fact. I demolished two while she watched. When I finished, she took the cores and remaining apples back to the cupboard. I didn't know what she did with food trash. She always stashed it back in the cupboard, and by the next time I visited, it was gone. Another mystery to add to the list.

As she secreted the apple cores, a low rumble sounded somewhere in the distance. Leannon grew rigid. She grabbed her robe off the floor and fastened it around her waist.

"What—" I started, but she snapped her fingers to shush me. The noise grew louder and deeper. The floor began to vibrate, and then the house began to shake. The easel danced from leg to leg, the painting tilting. The inside of my skull rang. Leannon jumped on the bed and wrapped her arms and legs around me. She felt feverish and hot, her limbs like metal cables. The constant, maddening vibration went on and on until another sound joined it—four slow notes, like sleepy, lazy whale song. The rumbling lessened, then stopped. She moved her hands to my cheeks and let me pull my head free of her throat.

"Are you all right?" she said.

"Fine, I think."

She turned my face back and forth, peering into my good eye. "You're sure? Nothing is—changed? Nothing feels broken?"

"I'm fine."

She let me go and we sat up. The house looked like it had been turned upside down and shaken. The cabinets hung open like slack-jawed witnesses, and the floor was buried in an assortment of broken crockery, rags, dried roots, blocks of clay, pads and pencils. The painting lay next to the bed, intact but dinged on one side.

"Shit," I said.

She sighed but waved a dismissive hand. "It's fine."

"At least let me help you clean up." I started to stand, and she grabbed my arm.

"I don't need help, but thank you for offering." She remained seated, hand clamped almost painfully on my arm. She looked upset. Scared.

"What just happened?" I said.

"I don't know." I didn't read a partial truth in her voice this time. This time I read an outright lie.

3

I slept badly in my own bed, chased through nightmares by some unseen leviathan, and woke with the sun already high in the sky. My bedside alarm clock read 11:30 a.m. I swore at myself. I was supposed to meet Eunice for lunch at noon.

I arrived at the café ten minutes late and found her seated on the patio, reading a Tami Hoag book and drinking a mimosa. She glowered as I took a seat.

"I know, I know," I said, holding up my hands in surrender. "I overslept."

"God forbid you ever need a real eight-to-five job," she said. She downed the rest of her mimosa. "Anyway, thanks for showing up."

"Sure," I said. It was the most positive response I could muster. I couldn't manage *Wouldn't miss it* or *Happy to be here*. Although we were nominally on good terms, things had been strained between us since the night I'd stolen her car and she'd attempted suicide. After two months in a mental health facility on a strong dose of Prozac, she'd dropped out of school, gotten her paralegal certification, and gone to work for a firm in Fort Worth. She moved out of the house and got an apartment close to work, and although she visited every few weeks, our conversation was always cordial, never warm. She complained a lot about her arrogant, know-it-all boss, and kept checking her watch, as though Mom and I were as much a run-out-the-clock situation as any job. She always brought a dessert with her—a pie, cookies, cupcakes—as a gift for Mom, but she usually polished it off herself. I mention this not because I want to judge, but because the constant overeating arrived at the same time the writing stopped. During her visits I usually asked if she was working on anything, and while she made excuses at first, eventually she just said "No," whenever I mentioned it. She delivered the negation with exaggerated casualness, as if I were asking about the weather.

"The voices don't speak to me anymore," she said. "I'm doing my best to move on."

About a year after the hospital, she began to date again. I would have been thrilled, except that Eunice began dating men, and, after a few months, zeroed in on one man in particular: Hubert Sangalli, a long-lost friend from her grade school days. They'd been paired together on a blind date, and after the initial shock of recognition, had embarked on an accelerated courtship, which included a pilgrimage to meet Mom and me after only two weeks. Hubert was tall and thin, with a bad blond comb-over and watery blue eyes. He looked distorted, like someone had pushed him through one of those machines that flattens pennies to stamp on an image, only Hubert's image hadn't quite taken.

The day I met him, he spoke in hushed tones about luck, fate, and destiny. Eunice sat next to him, holding his hand and wearing a thin smirk that looked more like indulgence than agreement. Six months after that, they were engaged, and now the wedding was only a month away. Eunice and I were having lunch to discuss Hubert's bachelor party, for which I, the de facto, reluctant best man, was responsible.

"Does Hubert know we're meeting?" I said. "Normally the groom and best man do this without the bride."

"Don't be a prick," Eunice said. "You know he's shy. He likes you, but you're an intimidating person to be around." She waved to catch our server's attention.

"Bullshit," I said.

She didn't argue the point. Our server arrived, and again I felt a stranger recognize and evaluate me. If Eunice noticed, she didn't say anything. She ordered another mimosa.

"What does Hubert have in mind?" I said, meaning, *What do you have in mind?*

"He doesn't drink, so you being underage won't be a problem," she said. Inside the restaurant, I saw our server talking to another server. Both turned to look at me, then away again when they realized I was watching them.

"What about the other bachelor party staple?" I said, refocusing my attention. "Strip club?" I'd never been to one and was curious.

"He gets nervous when a stranger cuts his hair. I can't imagine how he'd react to a building full of naked women trying to touch him."

"Noble reasoning on your part," I said.

"Fuck off," she said.

"So no drinking and no strippers," I said. "What *does* he want?"

"Fun Mountain," she said. "Mini golf, rides, go-carts, then a nice dinner. Maybe a movie, if anything good is showing."

"He wants a ten-year-old's birthday party?" I said.

"This man will be your brother in a month," she said. "Please just make him happy? And try not to make fun of him to his face while you're doing it. It would mean a lot to me."

"All right," I said, although I couldn't bring myself to apologize. "I'll get it done."

"Great," she said. She gave me a list of other men Hubert knew— not necessarily friends—who I might be able to corral into attending the party. Our main business concluded, she asked about me, and The

Wandering Dark. I told her about how I was spying on our competition for ideas.

"Have you found anything worth stealing?" she said.

"Not yet," I admitted. "What they're doing, we already do better. The only thing these places have going for them is that they're not us. If we're going to innovate, we'll have to do it on our own."

"Any ideas?" she said.

"I'd like to create a more immersive experience," I said. "Beyond a walking tour of cheap scares. A place where people could spend the night, like a haunted bed-and-breakfast, or a motel where weird shit is always happening. And depending on what level of scare you sign up for, you get an experience ranging from 'creepy' or 'vaguely unsettling' to 'genuinely afraid for your life.'"

Eunice tilted her head, inscrutable behind her sunglasses.

"What?" I said.

"Nothing." She pursed her lips. "Dad had a similar idea, right before he died."

It had been years since anyone had mentioned Dad to me.

"I don't know how far they got with it," Eunice said. "It was something he and Mom worked on to pass the time, but he was far gone by then. Mom said it was all just nonsense she wrote down to humor him. Crazy person stuff."

4

I met with Mom later that afternoon in the costume shop at The Wandering Dark. She worked while we talked, repairing the latest iteration of my monster costume, fat threads of black and red holding together strips of fur in various shades, from near black to a faded brown bordering on yellow. Mom's hair had wide streaks of gray now, and she carried permanent bags beneath her green eyes. Crow's-feet and laugh lines had etched themselves into her face. She was fifty-four this year, but the bifocals perched on her nose made her look even older.

I paced as I made my report, telling her what I had told Eunice, and my theory about familiarity being our biggest problem.

"It makes sense," she said. "Imagine running a movie theater that only played one movie every day for thirteen years." She glared at the costume. "The place is falling apart anyway. I swear, the costumes never used to wear out this fast."

"Maybe we could do something all-new then," I said. She set down the costume and leaned back on her stool. "I had an idea for a haunted hotel, and Eunice said you and Dad had a similar idea back around the time I was born, so I thought maybe, if you'd let me look at his old notes—"

She started shaking her head before I finished the sentence. I'd braced myself for an argument, but not what Mom actually said:

"I threw all that stuff out years ago."

I stopped pacing. "Why would you do that?"

She took off her glasses and rubbed her eyes. "Try to imagine a box in your house that exists only to remind you of the worst, most painful time of your whole life. Would *you* want to keep it?"

"You could have hidden it in the attic and given it to Eunice when she moved out. You could have given it to me."

She put her glasses back on. "I did what I did. I can't undo it."

"I've never even seen a picture of Dad," I said. I would see one eventually, but not for another eleven years.

"Look in the mirror and you'll get the general idea. And even if I still had the box, it wouldn't make a difference. You promised ideas to save this place, but come back to me suggesting we build an all-new and completely different place—one that would cost a fortune and might not be legal. But setting aside money and the law, you assume I'm interested in building something new. I got into this business in 1989 to save our family from financial ruin. It turned into a good moneymaker for a while. It meant a lot to you and Eunice, and it's been a nice tribute to Sydney. But now it's stopped making money and it sounds like you don't have any strong ideas for fixing that. My advice to you would be to enjoy your last few weeks here. Soak it in and say goodbye."

5

I stopped my industrial espionage and went back to being the monster. It was still a joy, but tempered now by sadness because it was ending. As with Leannon, I tried to avoid long-term thinking, but it was hard in this case, since I had so little time left to harvest screams and terrify strangers.

One night, about a week after going back on the job, I popped my head through a "porthole" and saw "Miranda" from Inferno amid a clump of visitors in the Professor's study. The strangers jumped and shrieked at my appearance. Miranda did not. She leaned back a little and squinted, as though trying to get a better look. Her lack of surprise startled me, and I backed away, disappearing into my labyrinth. Later, when I emerged in the dance hall, meaning to snatch a Brad, I paused next to her. I sniffed at her elbow and slid my snout up along her arm, past her shoulder and neck, and hung my face right before hers. Her breathing remained calm and steady. She wasn't at all scared of me.

"Hey!" the Brad sputtered, sounding confused but trying to stay in character. "Leave her alone!"

His real name was Jimmy, a skinny, chinless kid who'd been miscast. He put a hand on my shoulder like he meant to shove me, and we shifted into our choreographed tussle. He tried to punch me, and I choked him unconscious before fleeing with him back into my labyrinth.

After we were alone and I'd helped him to his feet, Jimmy said, "I thought you weren't allowed to get so close to guests."

I never spoke when I was the monster, and didn't start now.

"It was super-creepy, but I don't know if it was appropriate, you know?"

Later, as we closed for the night, I found him talking to a couple of girls in the break room. He stopped when he noticed me, and both girls glanced at me, and away again. I was reminded of my lunch with

Eunice, and my wait in the line at Inferno. In 1999 they'd called me a hero, but that shine had worn off quickly, and been replaced with this. The discomfort, the averted gazes. The keen sense of otherness, of being apart from the group. As though I were a lightning rod for tragedy, and no one wanted to get too close.

I wondered now if maybe it wasn't The Wandering Dark that was failing. Maybe it was me. Maybe I was tanking it just by working here. My very presence was making people uncomfortable in the bad way.

I waited until the kids had gone home before I left the building. I was surprised to find Miranda standing alone in the parking lot, shifting on her feet and looking nervous.

"Noah Turner?" she said.

"Yeah," I said, thinking I was about to get a dressing-down from a Jesus freak and knowing I deserved it. It didn't occur to me until later that I'd been wearing my disguise inside, that there was no good reason for her to connect me with the monster. I'd only become inextricably linked with my other skin in my own mind.

Instead of scolding me, she offered a hand. "Megan Gaines."

We shook. "How can I help you, Ms. Gaines?"

"Megan. And—I have to be honest, I work at another haunted attraction in the area—"

"Inferno," I said. "I caught your act last week."

"Right," she said. "I thought you looked familiar." Of course I did. How many customers did she see with an eye patch? Also, she sounded like she was lying, and knew that she sounded like she was lying, and that I noticed it, too. What was happening here? I didn't know, but I felt an automatic instinct to rescue her from her discomfort and set her at ease.

"I was moved by your performance," I said (true), "and impressed with your whole attraction" (not true). "Any chance you want to get coffee and talk shop?"

She worked her closed lips back and forth over her teeth like someone swishing mouthwash.

"I don't drink coffee," she said at last. "But I am starving. Do you like waffles?"

6

We went to a small, brightly lit, and overwhelmingly greasy all-night chain diner, and took a booth by a window looking out on the empty street. Megan ordered a heap of waffles with sausage and orange juice. I ordered an egg sandwich and coffee.

"Was this your first time at The Wandering Dark?" I said.

She nodded. "My mom never let me do Halloween stuff when I was a kid," she said, hand over her mouth. "She always said it was the devil's holiday. A pagan celebration of the occult, co-opted by corporate America and made okay by animated TV specials. Said it was proof of Satan's growing influence in the world."

"I don't know if it's as bad as your mom thinks," I said.

"Thought. She died a couple of years ago."

"Oh. I'm sorry," I said.

She looked down at her food. "Can I ask you a personal question?"

"Sure."

"What's with the eye patch?"

I set my coffee mug down. "You don't know?"

She shook her head. "Should I?"

I waited to see if she would break and admit she was messing with me. It didn't happen.

"It's a long story," I said.

"Do you have somewhere else to be?"

So I told her the official version, the one I'd delivered so often and so consistently that it was generally considered the truth: how Eunice and I had gotten into a fight; how I'd stolen her car for a joyride; how I was T-boned at an intersection by a man named James O'Neil; how I lost my eye in the crash; how I found the lumpy garbage bag in the man's van, containing the decomposing remains of Maria Davis and Brandon Hawthorne; how James O'Neil tried to kill me and I narrowly escaped; how it took me all night to wander home, in shock. I left out some details—how law enforcement let me slide on driving without insurance and fleeing the scene of the accident, since I'd inadvertently solved the case of the missing kids, and also because of my sister's attempted suicide. How, because the prosecution sought the death penalty, I'd had to testify. How I had stared at my lap so I wouldn't have to look at James O'Neil's face while I was on the stand. How the prosecution made the case that James O'Neil had also abducted and murdered Sydney, since he'd seen us the day Mom's car was on fire. About the news vans on our street for a few weeks, and the strange looks I tended to get around town. How, although I was ostensibly a hero, people seemed to get less comfortable around me as the years wore on, as though I carried the onus for both the disappearances and the deaths.

Megan leaned forward in her seat, holding me with her bright brown gaze through the whole tale. When I finished, she said, "I remember seeing something about it on the news a couple of years ago. It's weird to meet someone that something has actually happened to." She looked back at her plate, and I had the impression that she had meant to say something else but chickened out at the last second.

"Out with it already," I said, doing the *hurry up* gesture with one hand.

She took a big draw from her juice before she spoke. "Did you see anything—*strange* that night?"

"Stranger than a crazy man with dead bodies in his van?"

She flinched, and I regretted my tone. She was trying to decide whether to tell me something.

"I don't know," she said at last. "I've never been close to a crazy person before. What was that like? Did he say or do anything extra-strange?" Again, not what she wanted to say. What was she holding back?

"It felt like a dream where everything looks normal, but you know that something is wrong. Like how you can taste it in the air before a big storm hits. Something felt off about him, but he was acting pretty normal, considering the circumstances, until he pulled a knife."

She frowned slightly, but said, "That sounds creepy." It wasn't what she'd wanted to hear.

She got quiet after that. I filled the silence with questions and put together a thumbnail biography: she'd grown up around here, and after her mother died, Holy Spirit Church had helped her with moving expenses to start in the theater program at the University of Chicago. In return, she came back every year to help with Inferno—she got special permission from her professors, somehow managing to classify the trip as both a religious obligation and an independent study. She loved performing, but had few illusions about a future in the arts. She expected to end up teaching theater at a high school or community college.

Our plates demolished, I paid the bill, and we headed for the parking lot.

"I had fun," I said, because I wanted it to be true.

"Me too," she said.

I took out one of my business cards and handed it to her. "If you find some extra time before you go back to Chicago, I wouldn't mind buying you waffles again."

She studied the card and smiled reluctantly. "I'll keep it in mind." I had little hope that she was telling the truth.

It didn't occur to me until I got home that she hadn't asked any questions about The Wandering Dark.

7

During the following days, Megan's bright stare and calm demeanor lingered in my mind. I hadn't realized how hungry I was for someone to look at me in a normal way. How starved I was for even that bit of kindness. I checked The Wandering Dark's voice mail and my own email, hoping she would get in touch, but also feeling guilty about it. After all, I was with Leannon (whatever that really meant). My one meal with Megan wasn't technically cheating, but it was close enough to make me uncomfortable.

I didn't hear anything, so I did my best to move on. I switched flashlight batteries at The Wandering Dark, changed dead fluorescent bulbs, replaced faulty wires in our hidden speaker system—anything that kept my hands busy and my mind off the fact that we were going out of business. I started sending away for college application packets. Maybe I could start over in a new town if I went to school. I also reached out to the men on Hubert's bachelor party list. I begged Kyle to come along so I'd have someone to talk to, and he agreed. He didn't talk about it much, but I think he was eager for any excuse to be out of his parents' house these days. Whenever I tried to bring it up, he shook his head and said, "I don't know what the hell they're doing."

When I finally visited Leannon again, after an absence of nearly a week, she opened the door before I even knocked.

"Leannon si," she said. "I was beginning to worry."

I followed her into the house, took off my shoes, and sat on the bed. I'd brought a sack of fast food with me and unwrapped a burger to take a bite.

"You don't have to wait for me," I said. "You can come visit whenever you want."

She sat next to me. "This is your busiest time of the year."

"Never used to stop you," I said, around a mouthful of burger.

"That was before I taught you to use this," she said, touching the black stone around my neck. "And I've been busy myself." She gestured to a new painting on her easel, a companion to the one she'd been working on the last time I'd visited. This one featured several robed figures against a backdrop of grimy blacks and yellows. The figures huddled together beneath a crescent moon, communicating both fear and conspiracy.

"It's haunting," I said.

She'd cleaned since my last visit. The broken crockery had been disposed of, the roots hung back on their hooks in the kitchen, the paint cleaned from the wooden floor. Only the painting from last time showed any marks of the earthquake. It leaned in a corner behind the easel, a chip of paint gouged from the upper-left corner.

"That's too bad," I said, nodding at it.

"Some things even I can't fix."

My dead eye throbbed in its socket. "Have there been any more earthquakes?" I said.

"No."

"Any idea what might have caused it?"

She stood before the easel and leaned forward so that her nose almost touched the canvas. "What causes any earthquake? Shifting plates or something."

"What about the musical tones when it ended?" I said.

"I'm as mystified as you." She pulled the sash on her robe and let it drop. She regarded me over one pale shoulder. "Did you want to have sex?"

I felt strangely reluctant tonight. "Leannon," I said. "What are we?"

"What do you mean?" she said.

"I mean, are we a couple? Are we married? How does this work, long-term?"

"I'm not sure I understand," she said.

"I mean, what does our relationship look like in ten years? Or twenty?"

She turned around, and I found myself distracted by the contours of her body. "Why does it have to look any different than it does now?"

"I mean, eventually I have to move out of Mom's house. People already look at me strangely around town. They're going to wonder why I don't date. They're going to talk."

"Why do you care?" she said.

"It's not just that. I'm going to start getting older. Maybe I'll lose my hair. Maybe I'll get fat. Life is going to happen to me whether I want it to or not."

She faced the painting again and dropped her head, as though examining her naked form. "Do you want that?" she said. "A regular life?"

Coming here had been a mistake. Instead of clarifying my feelings, it had muddied them further. I tossed the burger in the bag and stood.

"I've hurt your feelings," I said. "I'll go."

She yanked the robe back on and intercepted me before I reached the stairs. "You don't have to leave. We can spend time together and *not* have sex."

"I know," I said. I wanted to push her hand off but didn't. "I'm not in the mood for company."

She let go. "But you and me—we're okay?"

I couldn't quite bring myself to look her in the eye. "Why wouldn't we be?"

8

Mom let herself into my room without knocking the next morning and made a face at all the mess.

"Far be it from me to interrupt your living the dream," she said, "but I have some errands and I wanted to give you this before I forgot." She handed me a folded-up scrap of paper. "A message left for you at the box office last night."

"Thanks," I said to her retreating form. I unfolded the note.

Noah,

I came back for an encore at The Wandering Dark tonight, but they told me it was your night off. Sorry I missed you. Anyway, if you want, you should come to a get-together with me and some friends tomorrow night. I'd love to talk more.

xoxo—Megan

I touched the valediction with my thumb and my heart did a little pitter-pat.

That night I replaced my usual T-shirt-and-hoodie combo with a collared button-down and sports jacket, and then drove to the address she'd specified. It turned out to be a house in one of Vandergriff's infinite suburban housing divisions, all the homes as generic and middle-class as you please. Megan stood in the driveway, wearing jeans and a man's button-down shirt with the sleeves rolled up and the collar wide open.

"Are you waiting for me?" I said, climbing from the car.

She shoved her hands in her back pockets. "I didn't want you to get lost."

"You look nice," I said.

"Thank you," she said, and brushed a strand of hair behind one ear.

We stood in the sloped driveway, her position rendering her momentarily taller than me. I tried to think of something to say.

She worked her lips over her teeth in that way I liked. "You'll be nice, right? You're a nice person?"

"When I'm not in costume."

She didn't look entirely reassured, but led me into the house anyway. It felt like somewhere a grandmother might live: furniture upholstered in out-of-fashion patterns, afghans draped over the couch and easy chair, doilies in bloom across myriad surfaces. A group of teenagers and adults (and one white-haired woman, whom I took to be the owner) were putting chairs in a circle in the living room and setting up snacks on the coffee table. Everyone stopped and stared as we came through the door.

"Hey, everyone," Megan said, her voice loud in the abrupt silence. "This is Noah Turner." She grabbed my shoulders as she said my name.

The room's happy energy didn't return, but a small woman with frizzy brown hair touched the place below her left eye, as though feeling phantom pain on my behalf.

A broad man with a blond beard and a trucker hat crossed his arms across his chest. "Megan, you know the rules."

"Come on, Josh," Megan said. "This is a special case."

He stroked his beard, and everyone else looked to him. He seemed to be the person in charge.

"I would like for him to stay," said the older woman.

"Ellen," Josh said.

"He's already here," the woman (Ellen) said, "and in case you're forgetting, this is *my* house. So unless you'd like to spend the meeting standing in the street, go find him a chair."

He sagged a little. "Fine." He jabbed a finger at me. "But you don't speak unless spoken to, and you can't tell anyone about what you see or hear here. Got it?"

Megan huffed. "He's got it, Josh." She steered me to an empty chair. "Don't mind him," she said, sitting next to me. "Josh is protective of the group. He wants everyone to feel safe, himself included. Himself especially."

"What group?" I said, but received no answer. A dull panic started low in my stomach. What the hell had I just walked into?

Everyone took their seats in the circle. I counted eight people including myself. Everyone looked to Josh. He closed his eyes, and when he opened them again he looked calm and sober. He placed a microcassette recorder on the coffee table and set it to record.

"Welcome to the Texas chapter of the Fellowship of the Missing, a group of people who help each other deal with mysterious and inexplicable loss," he said. "This is usually a closed meeting, but tonight we have a guest. Noah, since you are not a member, we request that you do not speak during the meeting unless we ask you to."

I gave him a thumbs-up. Seriously, fuck this guy.

"We will now introduce ourselves by our first names only. Hi, I'm Josh, from Denton, and I experienced an inexplicable loss."

"Hi, Josh," the room replied. Everyone else introduced themselves in this way: Ellen from Fort Worth, Sarah from Rusk (the small woman who'd exclaimed over my eye), Laura from Athens (a woman with a narrow face and long, straight hair), Hector from Paris (a kid about my age), Eli from Houston (a teenager with spiky green hair), and Megan from Mansfield. Each claimed inexplicable loss.

"The Fellowship of the Missing is a group of men and women who share their experiences, strength, and hope with one another, like any support group," Josh said. "However, unlike other support groups, which help people come to terms with loss, addiction, or a medical diagnosis, we do not preach catharsis through conversation, and we don't share our stories to build fellow feeling only. We believe that catharsis may only be achieved by solving the cause of the individual's loss and confronting the source. We share our stories so our fellows may listen for clues, details that may help us solve our communal problem once and for all." Here he looked at me again. "Remember your promise of confidentiality: what you hear here stays here. Also, no cross talk or interruptions." He consulted a clipboard on his lap. "Sarah, I see you're scheduled to share tonight."

Everyone in the room turned to look at Sarah. Eli, the kid with green hair, gave her a gentle, encouraging smile.

"You all know the story," she said, "but I'll do my best to tell it like you don't." She cleared her throat, an oddly childlike sound. "My brother Stephen went missing when I was in ninth grade and he was in eleventh. He was a nice kid—popular, well liked. He didn't play sports, but he did date cheerleaders. He was a reader. He wanted to teach history." As she spoke, everyone in the circle took notes. Only I remained to witness the story undistracted, my hands folded in my lap.

Stephen had been out on a date with a girl named Daisy the night of his disappearance. He had borrowed their father's car, leaving the house around six. Sarah was watching TV in her bedroom when he left, so she didn't say goodbye, and didn't think about her brother again until the next morning, when Daisy returned in Sarah's father's car, alone. The car was fine, but Daisy looked a mess, hair full of forest debris, makeup smeared and tracked with tears. It took Sarah's parents a few tries to get anything coherent from the girl, and Sarah lingered at the foot of the stairs, eavesdropping as Daisy told the story:

Stephen had picked her up that night as intended. They'd gone out to dinner, but skipped the movie to make out in the parking lot at the park instead. After about twenty minutes, Stephen started acting distracted. He kept breaking off kisses to ask if Daisy heard anything strange. Daisy never did. Again and again he put his hands to his temples and grimaced. He described a sound like a dagger going through his mind, and, despite Daisy's objections, he got out of the car to go investigate. He staggered across the parking lot and past the tree line into the park, hands clamped to the sides of his head.

Daisy waited for the better part of an hour, but eventually got out and followed. She wandered the wooded paths in the dark, shouting for Stephen with no response. Even though she knew the park pretty well, she somehow got turned around in the dark, and it took her until dawn to find her way out of the woods and back to the car.

The next part of the story sounded uncomfortably familiar. Sarah's parents called the police, and there was a search, but despite scouring the park, they found no signs of the boy—not even of his passing through the woods, although there'd been ample evidence of Daisy stomping around. A full-scale investigation of Daisy, Sarah's family, and the surrounding area yielded similarly disappointing results. Stephen was gone, but there was a chilling postscript to the story: two years later, his wallet turned up in a convenience store milk case in Topeka, Kansas. It still had his driver's license, school ID, the receipt from his dinner with Daisy, twenty dollars in cash, and a scrap of paper with a single word scratched on it: *HURTS*.

I was afraid to look at Megan, afraid of what anything on my face might confirm to her. Why had I been invited here?

"Thank you, Sarah," Josh murmured, as he finished writing something on his clipboard. "Was what you said, to the best of your knowledge, true?"

"Yes," Sarah said.

"You didn't embellish or change any details, to try and make us see the story in a particular way?"

"No," Sarah said, after a pause.

Josh leaned back and gestured around the room. "Then we'll open things up for questions."

"Did your brother have a history of migraines?" Hector said.

"As a small boy, but they mostly cleared up by high school," Sarah said.

"What about Topeka?" Laura said. "Did he ever mention Topeka?"

"Never," Sarah said, sounding firmer on this point.

A moment of silence passed, and Josh said, "Are there any more questions?"

Sarah cast a hopeful look around, as though someone might be chewing on a question whose answer could solve the whole mystery. My heart broke a little at the openness on her face, the momentary willingness to hope. I forced my gaze to the floor, afraid all over again of what I might have revealed, what these strangers, uniquely situated by loss, might be able to infer about me.

"Everyone think on this," Josh said, "and if you have any thoughts or ideas, do let us know. Moving on, we should get to Megan's guest."

The room's collective regard landed on me, as I had known it would.

"What about me?" I said.

Josh turned the recorder toward me. "In your own words, why don't you start by telling us about the night your sister disappeared, and then move on to the night you met James O'Neil?"

I tried to catch Megan's eye, but she stared at her journal as though it held some vital, hard-to-parse text.

"Megan says you're a little hesitant to talk about what happened that night," Ellen said. "But believe me, this is a safe space."

"Tell me," Josh said. "How does a shattered window take out a person's eye?"

I stood, pushed between Eli and Hector, and ran out the front door. Megan caught up with me halfway across the lawn and grabbed my arm.

"Please don't go," she said.

I jerked free. "My sister isn't missing," I said. "She was abducted and murdered by James O'Neil. So I'm not eligible for membership in your little club." I got into my car. She stood at the curb as I drove away.

9

I went to see Leannon as soon as I got home, and we had frantic, back-scratching, hair-pulling sex. I tried to fuck out my embarrassment and frustration, and she seemed game, rising to meet my strokes with chafing, bruising intensity. When she pushed me past my edge and I lost myself, consciousness disintegrated like tissue paper in water. She held my head to her chest, stroking my hair.

As my pulse settled and my breathing slowed, I squeezed her around her waist and kissed the top of one breast. She made a soft, happy sound.

With my head clear, I wondered at my reaction to the Fellowship of the Missing's questions. Why had I gotten so angry? Part of it was Josh's condescending attitude, and the way they'd ambushed me. Part of it was embarrassment at my misinterpretation of Megan's interest in me. But none of those things added up to the panic I felt at the beginning of the interrogation, the alarm and ache that started as soon as they mentioned Sydney's disappearance. As though I'd been caught doing something wrong. As though I was somehow responsible for the pain in their lives, and owed them answers. Because I did know a few things. I knew that Leannon's kind existed, and that one of them had been tied up somehow with James O'Neil. But—and I'm being honest—it had never occurred to me to ask Leannon just what that relationship looked like.

"What are you thinking about?" Leannon asked.

"How many of you are there?" I said. "Your people, I mean."

"I don't know," she said.

"If you had to guess. More than a hundred?"

"Sure."

"More than a billion?"

"Good god, no," she said, and laughed a little.

"Do you have a name for yourselves?"

"You're full of questions tonight," she said.

"I want to know more about you," I said.

"You know the important things. You know where I live, what both of my faces look like, and that I love you."

"I don't even know your real name."

"You gave it to me," she said. She pushed me off, stood, and crossed to her easel. It held the painting I'd seen on my last visit, colorful robed figures huddled beneath a black sky and crescent moon, in poses of almost religious terror and supplication.

I sat up against the wall. "I've upset you."

"No," she said, but she kept her back to me. "I'm not hiding any-thing important, but there are things I'd rather not discuss." She finally faced me again. "If I'm not telling you something, it's because I'm protecting you. Will you trust me?"

"I'm sorry," I said, and I was. Weird as it was, this relationship was the only functional one in my life. "I'm all tied up about Eunice's wedding. I have to throw a bachelor party for her stupid fiancé, and pretend that I like him, and that I'm happy about this whole mess." It might not have been the marquee player on my mind, but it still drew a respectable crowd of anxieties.

She softened. "How is Eunice? I haven't seen her in years."

And that quickly, my unease was back. "I didn't know you'd ever seen her at all," I said.

"I slept in your bed most nights for ten years. Of course I've seen her."

"But she's never seen you," I said. "Or if she has, she never said anything to me about it."

"Not everyone *can* see me," she said. "Not unless I want them to."

"So when I saw you for the first time, that was your choice?"

She smiled a little. "No. You saw me right away. You're unique."

"But Eunice—you never look in on her in secret? Or me, or my mom?"

"Why would I?" she said. "You know where I live, and you visit often enough. I would only come looking if you went missing, or I thought you were in danger."

So she had no idea about Megan. Probably best to keep it that way.

10

A few nights later, Hubert was waiting on his front porch when Kyle and I arrived to pick him up for the bachelor party. He sat on the step like an overgrown child in khaki slacks and a button-down shirt. The shirt was covered in tiny squares like a sheet of graph paper.

"There's a man born to be a dad," Kyle said.

"Straight out of central casting," I agreed.

The man of the hour brought a special mix CD for us, entitled *Farewell Freedom Jams,* which he described as "sort of a concept mix," charting the emotional journey of his romance with Eunice. During the ride to Fun Mountain, we listened to excruciating soft rock hits, culminating in Creed's "Higher." Kyle and I studiously avoided looking at one another, knowing that if we did we'd burst into sanity-shaking gales of laughter.

A few of the invitees met us in the lobby of Fun Mountain's arcade, a blue and purple cave full of kids pumping tokens into machines. Each of the guys looked older than Hubert, fellows with beer bellies and the genial good natures of men settling comfortably into roles as fathers, husbands, and office drones. Men with mono- and disyllabic names like Steve, Brian, and Jack, all with firm handshakes and barely distinguishable faces.

I led them to the miniature golf course out back and kept score while they putted and talked shit. Kyle slipped into the flow of the conversation without apparent effort, and it occurred to me how little time I'd spent in the company of men. Although I shared the same basic biology, they felt like a foreign species. Boastful, loud, and rambunctious, even these fat, aging men remained proud and confident, as though they owned the world. Where did that confidence originate? Also, where did they find their innate sense of brotherhood?

On the fourth hole, Hubert hung back to talk to me. "They can be a handful," he said, as Steve bent to place his ball on the rubber tee mat. "But they're good guys. Steve does volunteer work for the homeless with his church, and Jack adopted his daughter from Russia."

I focused on the garish purple and orange scorecard. "They're your friends, Hubert. You don't have to give me their résumés."

He put an arm around my shoulders. "I know. But Eunice told me you don't have a lot of guy friends. If you give them a chance, I think this group will surprise you."

My skin crawled beneath his hand. "I'm sure you're right," I said.

Still he didn't let go. "It's important to me that you and I get to be friends. Your sister—she's everything to me." He blinked, eyes swimming behind his glasses. He laughed and wiped his cheek. "Sorry. It's an emotional time. See, I thought—I was getting used to the idea that I would be alone for the rest of my life, and so, to have Eunice come along and change everything—well—" He finally got too choked up to continue, and wiped his eyes with the back of one hand. I wanted to be disgusted, but I found myself moved against my will. Here was a man thinking about long-term plans. Compared to me, still living at home with a monster on booty call and a job that would disappear at the end of the month, he was a paragon of adult life.

"You two gonna kiss?" called Jack. Everyone laughed, even Kyle and Hubert. At last he let go of my shoulder and headed for the next hole.

"Noah?"

The voice stopped me before I could join the group. Megan stood to my left, putter swung back over her shoulder like a rifle, red ball cupped in her right hand like a grenade. She looked like someone trying to make an impression, sort of embarrassed but giving it a go anyway. Actresses.

"What are you doing here?" I said.

"I didn't like the way we left things the other night," she said. "When I called the number on your card, I got your mom and she told me where you'd be."

"She gave me up to a stranger?" I said.

"I told her it was an emergency," she said. "She *may* think I'm pregnant." Her cheeks pinkened. My face felt a little warm, too.

"So you decided to crash a bachelor party," I said.

"I wanted to apologize," she said. "I should never have ambushed you like that."

"You drove out here to apologize?" I said. "What about the putter?"

"The girl behind the counter wouldn't let me come look for you unless I paid for a game," she said. "Six bucks and gas this apology has cost me so far."

"Noah!" Kyle called, hands cupped around his mouth. "You're up!"

"Gotta go," I said to Megan.

"Are you really walking away from me right now?" she said.

"Noah!" Kyle shouted. "What the hell, man?"

I jerked a thumb in his direction.

"Okay, fine," she said, sighing hard through flared nostrils. "Noah, please don't go. Or if you do, at least give me your home number. I'm not in town for much longer, and I—I'd like to explain some things. And I really wouldn't mind spending a little more time together. For waffles or whatever."

This girl. Turning her charm up to eleven and knowing it was working.

"Wait here," I said. I ran back to the group.

"About time," Steve said.

"Bachelor party is no place for romance," Jack said.

"Bros before hoes, Noah," Hubert said. The words sounded as though he were borrowing the cliché and trying it on for the first time. A couple of the men laughed.

"Kyle, you keep score for a minute," I said, passing him the card. "I'll catch up." Amid a chorus of boos, I grabbed Megan's hand and led her to my car. When I started the engine, Night Ranger's "Sister Christian" began to blare.

She shut her eyes and grimaced. I snapped the radio off.

"Not my music, if that makes a difference," I said.

Driving on autopilot, I took her to The Wandering Dark. It was closed for the night, but Mom had forgotten to lock the gate to the parking lot. My car drifted up to the front door, encased in its chipped and faded Styrofoam skull frame.

"I hop into your car, put myself at your disposal, and of all the places we could go, you bring me here?" Megan said.

I paused with my hand on the key, unsure whether to kill the engine. "We can go somewhere else," I said, though I had no idea where. I spent all my time here, at home, or with Leannon. I worked, fucked, and slept. I had no favorite spots, nothing in the acceptable world to share except my work. Hubert really was better than me. He at least had friends and hobbies.

"No, you had an instinct," she said. "Let's see it through."

We got out and went inside, through the bare, dusty front office and into the warehouse proper. In the break room we grabbed water and granola bars, and then I gave her the tour. When we got to the dance hall, we hopped up on the edge of the stage to eat our snacks, feet dangling. After she finished her granola bar, she turned the foil wrapper over and over in her hands. The crinkling sound filled the still, empty space.

"I promised you an explanation," she said.

"You did," I said, although I was tempted to call it off now, seeing her discomfort and wanting to preserve the calm between us.

"This is hard for me to talk about," she said. "But you deserve to know." She took a deep breath. "Everyone in the Fellowship of the Missing has lost someone they care about. Someone they love has vanished in a way that makes no sense. Except for me. I know exactly where my person is. He's incarcerated at Polunsky Unit in West Livingston, on death row. His name is James O'Neil."

"You know him?"

"He's my father," she said. I must have looked worried, because she put a hand on my knee. "Don't worry, this isn't some *Dracula's Daughter* bit. I'm not out for revenge. I'm just trying to understand, like the rest of my friends."

I lifted my water bottle to drink. It was empty.

"He was never normal," Megan said. "He always struggled with mental illness. Mom left him when I was little, so I didn't grow up around him. He sent cards on my birthday, when he remembered it, and came to visit a few times. He was always nice, but sad. He knew he wasn't fit to be a full-time dad, but he missed me, I think. He never seemed dangerous to anyone but himself. So when he was arrested a few years ago, it didn't make any sense, and when he was charged with three murders and convicted of two, it made even less sense. I went to visit him in lockup, but he kept saying he wanted a do-over."

"It's what he said to me, too," I said. "The night I met him. Maybe he had a psychotic break?"

"That's what I thought," she said. "But then he started sending me letters. Really detailed letters about this demon that had been tormenting him all his life, making him say and do things he didn't want to say or do. He insisted that he'd never touched your sister, Noah, but that this demon did make him kill Maria Davis and Brandon Hawthorne. He wrote me that the demon was dead now and he was feeling much better. Sometimes he sent me pictures of the demon, too." She pulled a sheet of paper from her pocket and handed it to me. I unfolded it and found myself looking at a charcoal sketch of the Gray Beast, the monster that had attacked me and destroyed my left eye. I tried to keep a skeptical (if sympathetic) face.

"At first, I figured it was a delusional person trying to reconcile the terrible thing they had done, and I didn't answer any of the letters. But then, one night, while my mom was dying, I got up and started poking around online. That's when I found the Fellowship. On their message boards, they have pictures that look a lot like this one. And the people in the group are real people. You can look up Sarah, or Josh, and see—they're not full of shit. They really did go through these things. It's public record. And yet, despite all the time we've spent together, all the talking and theorizing, we don't have any real proof of these things"—she gestured at the drawing—"or any idea why they do what they do. I've wanted to talk to you for years, Noah. Mom kept me away from the trial, and made me promise to leave you in peace. She said you didn't want to hear my father's excuses or lies about your sister. But I saved your picture, and when I saw you at Inferno . . . it seemed like there was some spark, some instant connection, and I thought—" She broke off, and blinked a few times. I would come to know the look well. It was her trying-not-to-cry face, and it got its hooks in my heart the very first time I saw it.

I took her hand, and she started, but didn't pull away. "I haven't been entirely honest with you," I said. "The night I met your father? I did see this thing." I nodded at the drawing. "I saw it, and another exactly like it. They were fighting over—over your father, I think. I ran away in the middle of it all, because I was terrified. I never told anyone because I was worried—"

"That people would think you're crazy," she finished.

This seemed to ease something in her. Her shoulders sagged a little, and then she did start to cry. I don't know why I picked that moment to kiss her, but she didn't recoil. She leaned forward to kiss me back. She tasted a little sweet, like a granola bar, and salty, like tears.

11

Fun Mountain was deserted when we returned. I'd half-expected to find the bachelor party outside, arms crossed in parental disapproval, but it was just a couple of cars. Megan leaned over to kiss me before she got out, and then I was alone in the parking lot.

I didn't go home right away, but sat in my car with the dome light on, studying the drawing she'd given me. It really was a perfect likeness. Why hadn't I made any real effort to investigate Leannon and her people? I'd been around her for thirteen years. Why hadn't I been more curious? I'd asked questions, sure, but Leannon always changed the subject or distracted me with food or sex, and afterward my questions didn't seem so important anymore. That was certainly part of it. But there was also the fact that I'd suspected her of kidnapping and killing Maria Davis and Brandon Hawthorne in 1999, and I had been proved completely wrong. In a mode of perpetual apology, I had learned to take what she said to me at face value. I'd made myself believe that James O'Neil and the Gray Beast were exceptions, not the rule. But what evidence did I have of that? How did I know that James O'Neil and I weren't on parallel tracks? Maybe O'Neil and the Beast started as secret playmates, too. Maybe he'd been led by his pleasure centers, manipulated and made to take part in some much darker agenda. But what could that agenda possibly be? Why would the Gray Beast want him to kidnap or kill children? And what if he'd been telling the truth when he insisted that he hadn't killed Sydney? What then? If he hadn't killed her, then where had she gone? And was Leannon somehow involved?

My head had begun to pound again. I set the picture down in the passenger seat to rub my temples. How could I make all of this make sense?

The sun was peeking over the horizon, turning the sky orange and pink when I arrived back home. Eunice's car was in the driveway, and when I came through the front door, tucking the drawing into my back pocket, I found her with Mom, Kyle, and Hubert in the living room, all of them facing me like a small intervention.

"Hi, Noah," Kyle said, in a small voice.

"Where the hell have you been?" Eunice said.

"Out." I shoved my hands into the back pockets of my jeans. "Something came up."

Hubert nodded. "We understand, Noah. We're glad you're okay."

Eunice clamped one hand on his narrow knee, her fingers white beneath her gaudy engagement ring. "After what you did, the only acceptable excuses are kidnapping or murder. The only place I should see your face is on the side of a milk carton or on the news, where they give people a number to call—"

I yanked the drawing out of my back pocket and unfolded it for them to see. "Do any of you recognize this?"

Eunice's tirade came to an abrupt halt, and a faraway, dreamy look came over her face. Mom leaned back on the couch, mouth slightly open. Kyle and Hubert only looked confused.

"You do, don't you?" I said, looking at Mom.

"Sure," she said, gathering herself again. "It looks like your monster costume."

"Come *on*," I said. "How long are we going to play this game? How long are we going to keep lying to each other, pretending everything is fine when it's not? What are the two of you hiding from me? What do you know?"

Hubert gave Eunice a questioning look, and she stared at me with pure hate etched on her face. Mom remained stony, impassive.

"I have no idea what you're talking about," Eunice said. "Stop being dramatic and trying to change the subject. You abandoned your brother-in-law and best friend last night, and—"

I didn't stay to listen. I bounded up the stairs to my room, locked the door behind me, closed my eye, and put both hands to the black stone around my neck. When I opened my eye, I stood in the clearing outside Leannon's house.

12

The sky was brightening here, too, although it remained a dark, mossy color. There were no windows in the house, so I had no idea whether Leannon was awake or not. I thought about knocking at the door, but hesitated. Whatever I was going to find out, I needed to find out on my own, before she could interfere or explain it away.

I turned away from her house and trudged off into the black forest. For want of a better plan, I walked in a straight line. The trees and underbrush were sparse enough to allow my progress, but the forest remained inky black. Every time I tried to get a close look at anything, it danced back into murk, remaining mere suggestion. I walked faster, arms extended before me so I wouldn't run into anything. I dodged around coal black trees and kicked through tangled brush until I came to a break in the darkness, sickly greenish light through the trees.

I passed the tree line out of the woods, into open air again. The ground before me ended in a sharp cliff. I walked out to the edge and surveyed the land below. Instead of more forest, I looked upon a vast network of buildings and streets, concrete and glass and glistening black stone spread for miles and miles. Skyscrapers like teeth against the horizon and, at the center, a cyclopean pillar of black stone so tall it stretched up into the pea-soup clouds. It hurt my head to look at it, like staring through someone else's glasses.

The buildings looked modern in design but ancient in age, weathered and decayed, eerily quiet and apparently empty. The ground rumbled, gently at first, and then with more force. I stepped back and grabbed the closest tree. My fingers closed around gummy bark. The City began to move, entire stretches of street shifting like panels in a children's picture puzzle—no, that's not quite right. The City *slithered*, adjacent streets grinding against one another in opposite directions, a serpent's head of pavement rising from the ground and rushing at me so fast I didn't have time to panic or think. It stopped at the edge of the cliff and lay flat there, bridging the distance between me and it with a flourish of four slow, lazy musical tones.

I waited to see if the street would lash out and strike, but it lay still. This was an invitation, not a threat. I walked down the sloping obsidian pavement and into the City, passing into a canyon of stone and glass. The buildings seemed structurally sound, the windows clean and glossy, the fluorescence behind them yellow-green. Aside from the lack of traffic and the choice of building materials, I might have stepped onto any street of any major financial district in America, except for the feeling that there was something here beyond appearances, lurking just out of sight. What that something was, I couldn't say, but it felt important. Like a promise being extended, an answer to some unarticulated question, just around the next corner.

At the end of the street, I turned right, deeper in. As I started down a second block of near-identical buildings, the ground quivered and rumbled. I stopped, arms out for balance as the buildings at the end of the street, outlining the top of the T-intersection, slid away to the right and revealed a new, different street, lined with black iron lamps. Red cobblestones replaced obsidian, and the buildings were smaller, older-looking, restaurants and cafés with outdoor seating. If I'd been in a sketch of a financial district before, I'd stepped into a sketch of the French Quarter now. An unseen jazz combo played somewhere nearby. A sandwich board to my left promised real beignets and THE BEST AU LAIT IN TOWN. Across the street, something moved behind a darkened plate-glass window. I crossed for a closer look, cupping my hands around my eye to cut the glare on the glass.

The inside looked like an old-fashioned barbershop, with big mirrors, plush red chairs, and a shining tile floor. A man with thick silver hair and a pear-shaped body sat in the middle chair, tilted back like he was going to get a shave.

I rapped on the glass. He lifted his head slowly, like a man waking from a dream, his eyes bleary and unfocused.

"Are you okay?" I called.

Before he could answer, the surfaces of the chair burst and thick black appendages tore out through the fabric. They wavered in the air above him like tentacles with stingers at the ends, and then stabbed down, piercing his forearms and thighs. Blood spurted from the wounds as the tentacles dug in, and he tilted his head back to scream. He struggled against the chair, but it held him fast.

"Jesus," I said. "Oh, Christ." The chair was going to kill him. I ran to the shop door and tugged, but it wouldn't budge. I looked around for something to break the window, but while I'd had my back turned, the street had removed its wastebaskets and outdoor seating. I could only pound on the glass and watch as the man writhed, screamed—and began to change.

It started with his limbs, where the chair had anchored him. His arms and legs lengthened and thinned out like Play-Doh rolled between two palms, until both hands and feet lay loose and boneless on the floor. Then the tentacles began to pulse, as if something were pumping through them, and the man's limbs thickened and inflated. The sleeves of his shirt and the legs of his slacks tore. His shoes exploded as his feet swelled. Fingernails and toenails thickened and curled, and hair burst in tufts from the pale, doughy flesh, covering him in fur. The man banged his head back against the chair, his screams less human and more animal. His nose and chin stretched away from his face into a snout. He closed his eyes, and when he opened them, they had turned orange. He'd become one of them. One of Leannon's people.

The chair released him, and he rolled onto the floor in a furry heap. I stepped back and bumped into something hard. I saw them reflected in the barbershop mirrors: a whole line of monsters in robes, standing right behind me. I turned and faced the one I'd bumped into. It bared its teeth and snarled. I took another step backward, this time bumping up against the glass window. The wolf-thing raised one of its talons as though to strike.

A sharp bark from nearby cut the moment short. The creature threatening me dropped its arm, and the line parted to show me Leannon across the street, wearing her monstrous face for the first time in years. She squared her shoulders and spread her claws, a growl deep in her throat. The gang of monsters opposite her exchanged looks and apparently decided not to fight. They parted, and Leannon extended one paw to me. I walked to her. She yanked me against her body and took off.

It took only a few seconds to get back to her clearing, and she dumped me in the grass before we landed. I rolled to a stop, and she set down in front of me, back in human form. I tried to stand, but she shoved me back to the ground, face white.

"What the *hell* did you think you were doing?" she said.

On my feet again, I fought the urge to shove her back. "What the hell did I just see?"

"That's a private, sacred ceremony," she said. "You had no right to go snooping."

"The City *invited* me in," I said. "It wanted me to see."

She studied me a moment, her fury burning out. She put a palm to her forehead. "It's seen you. It has your scent."

"Is that how you—your people—are made? Is that how you got to be the way you are?"

She didn't answer.

"Is that what you do? Kidnap people, bring them here, and turn them into monsters? Is that what was supposed to happen to James O'Neil? Was that what he meant to do with Maria Davis?"

And then I remembered Josh at the Fellowship meeting, asking me about Sydney. Sydney, who had gone missing around this time of year thirteen years ago.

"What really happened to Sydney?" I said. "Is she dead? Is she here?" I gestured back at the City, where I had just seen a man transformed. "Is that what happened to her? Did *you* do this to her?"

Leannon approached, reached out to me. "I know you have questions, but you have to trust me now, Noah." The way she dodged the question told me all I needed to know. She'd taken Sydney back in 1989 and was trying to distract me, the way she always distracted me.

"Don't touch me," I said, taking a horrified step back. "Leave me alone." I clenched the stone, closed my eye. Leannon was still protesting as I returned to my own room.

The house was silent now, free of my family's scolding. I lay down on my bed and tried to get my shaking under control.

13

I called Megan and asked her to meet me at Fun Mountain again that night. When she arrived, smiling, she found me sitting cross-legged on the hood of my car. She must not have liked what she saw, because her cheer turned to concern at once.

"What's up?" she said.

"I need your help," I said.

The Turner Sequence IV: Noah

The City has seen Noah. It has his scent. So although his
visits are intermittent, and usually brief, it watches
him while he is abroad. His torture isn't anything he
can wake from in a cold sweat, something to be swept
away by a lover's reassuring touch or a bit of late-night
TV. It's the course of his life.

It begins in 2002, as he waits for Megan in the parking
lot at Fun Mountain. He feels uneasy, alone with the
concrete and the sodium vapor lights shining a yellow-
green that's a touch too familiar. Part of him wishes
he'd gone into the dim purple cavern of the arcade. But
for once, he's sick of the dark.

So he waits, cross-legged on the hood of his car,
fingers tucked into the crevice where his calves touch.
He hopes he looks impish and cute, a twenty-first-
century Peter Pan with a pirate's eye patch, come to
lead his Wendy to merry mischief. He keeps reaching
for the stone around his neck, the way he sometimes
does when he's nervous, and he is repeatedly startled
to find it absent. He left it in a desk drawer in his
bedroom, where it can rot for all he cares. He just
wishes its absence didn't make him feel so naked and
exposed.

Here comes Megan now, climbing from her car, wired
from an invigorating night of saving souls, her hair
up in a ponytail. She looks to Noah like a picture of
normality and open wholesomeness. After the day he's had,
he aches for her.

What's up? she says, her smile disappearing as she sees his expression.

He's debated what to say for hours, but settles on the simple, true thing. *I need your help.*

He explains that there's more to his story than he's told so far. She joins him in his car and he tells her about the night Sydney vanished—the scream and the power outage that knelled together. He tells her about the strange sounds at his bedroom window in the weeks before Sydney's disappearance, and about his mother's and his sister's strange reactions to James O'Neil's drawing of the wolflike creature.

He doesn't tell Megan everything, though. Not about his friendship with the creature, or the name he gave her, or that, until today, they were lovers. He wants Megan's feelings about him clear and uncomplicated. She needs to see him as a lovable victim finding the strength to speak up for the first time, not the kid who grew up to fuck the monster.

When he finishes his partial confession, Megan takes his hand, and an hour later the two of them are in Ellen's living room for an emergency meeting of the Fellowship of the Missing. The room looks a lot more cluttered than the last time Noah was here. It turns out that the entire Fellowship has been staying at Ellen's for the past few weeks. They mostly communicate through their message board online, but once a year they make a point of meeting up to talk shop and to be together. From the bowls of popcorn and the paused frame from *The Sixth Sense* on the TV, Noah guesses that he interrupted movie night.

Noah repeats his abridged tale to the gathered members of the Fellowship. Josh gives him the stink-eye the whole time, but doesn't ask any questions. He sits and listens, and even takes notes.

There's only a week left before Megan has to return to school in Chicago and the rest of this chapter of the Fellowship scatters back home. Unable to make himself return to his mother's house, Noah stays with the Fellowship at Ellen's, sleeping on a pallet of blankets on the living room floor. He and the group spend the days and nights going over and over his story, looking for clues. Noah doesn't give them any more information, sticking to his version of events with such rigidity that he can almost believe it himself. The Fellowship is simultaneously frustrated and thrilled. Noah does not share their excitement. He's not interested in knowing *more* about the creatures, or the City. All he wants is to get away from his life and this place. When the week ends and Megan invites him back to Chicago with her, he agrees at once.

He tells his mother about the move over the phone. She's cool and rational about it, but warns Noah that no one person can solve everything for him forever.

Noah doesn't tell Eunice about it at all. They haven't spoken since the day after Hubert's bachelor party.

When Megan drives out of town, Chicago-bound, Noah rides shotgun in her car, the two of them trading nervous but encouraging looks. All he's brought with him is a suitcase full of clothes and a copy of *The Call of Cthulhu and Other Weird Tales* that was given to him by Eli, the youngest member of the Fellowship. It sits on his lap like a talisman as Vandergriff speeds away outside the windows, the car rumbling and squeaking, rain pattering against the roof.

When they get on the highway, however, the sound drops away altogether. It's like the world is on mute. Noah turns to look at Megan, to see if she's hearing this anomaly, too, and sees the parachute drop at Fun Mountain through her driver's side window.

A flash of light splits the gray day, a bolt of lightning seeming to strike the park. In that instant, the parachute drop takes on the visage of a colossal, ink-black tower, smooth as volcanic glass and reaching into the temporarily illuminated heavens. Its surface shines like fresh tar, oily and slick.

As the image fades, sound returns. The world shakes with the growl of something massive, one long ridge of sound that moves the earth. Noah grinds along its edge, teeth clenched, terrified of falling off into some abyss, where he'll be alone with—with—

He manages to look at Megan and sees that she's tossing worried looks at him. She's slowed the car down. The vibrations fade and the audible world returns all at once, a volume knob turned too loud too fast.

What's wrong? she's saying, the sounds scraping his brain. *Should I pull over?*

He realizes that he's pressed against the passenger door, arms braced against the dash and his headrest.

He unclamps his jaw with effort. *No,* he says. *Don't stop. Get me out of here.*

In Chicago, he finds a tiny one-bedroom apartment on the third floor of a drafty old building. He shares a bathroom with everyone else on his floor. It's awful, but it's all he can afford on his savings while he hunts for jobs. Megan stays in her dorm, but visits almost every day and sometimes stays the night. He finds a job at a Barnes & Noble near the university. Although they give him only twenty hours a week to start, he spends his off days there as well. It's warm and well lit and he gets 50 percent off coffee, which makes it preferable to his increasingly frigid apartment. Best of all, although the eye patch still garners looks from strangers, people don't treat him like something to be afraid of. To the people of Chicago, Noah is just another bookseller.

For a few months, nothing happens. Noah does well
at the store, gets more hours, and gets to know Megan
outside the wide shared terrain of grief and loss. She's
kind, but there's something flinty at her core, the
strength of someone who had to deal with too much pain
too early in life. It's the strength he wishes he had
himself.

When they have sex for the first time, it's gentle
and sweet. It doesn't end in a flood of golden light, a
fracturing of consciousness or transcendence of time and
space. Instead it's a series of pleasurable muscle spasms
and a collapse into a muddled grouping of limbs.

Megan touches his cheek as he rolls off her, and finds
his tears. *What's wrong?* she says.

I'm just really happy, he says, because he wants it to
be true. He wants to feel uncomplicated about what has
just happened, like he hasn't just committed infidelity.
He tries to push Leannon from his mind's eye. That part
of his life is over. For the sake of his sanity and his
soul, it must be.

The next day, something happens when he's walking
home from Barnes & Noble. He turns left at the corner of
Blevington and King, and instead of emerging on a wide,
busy street, he finds himself in an alley between two
anonymous brick buildings he doesn't recognize. A metal
door bangs open on his right and a bearded, tattooed man
walks out carrying two garbage bags. He wears jeans and
a T-shirt and pauses to stare at Noah's coat and scarf.
Noah suddenly feels too hot in his clothes.

You lost? the man says.

Noah doesn't answer, but turns around and walks back
the way he came. When he comes out the far end of the
alley, he's on a wide street lined with sagging buildings
made of a brick that seems desaturated somehow, like
someone used a straw to suck out most of the color. The

windows are dusty and cobwebbed, and there are no other people around. He looks back toward the alley, but it's gone. He's standing before a blank wall.

He stops beneath the street sign and raises his head to read it. It's written in a language he doesn't recognize, and the sky beyond it is pea-soup green. A startled sound—almost a laugh—escapes his throat. "Huh." The sort of sound you might hear from a craftsman surprised and impressed by another's work.

Hello? he calls. If anything is listening, it doesn't respond. And then, in a change so quick it makes a blink look long, Noah finds himself back at the intersection of Blevington and King, the leafless trees shivering in an arctic wind, cars parked bumper to bumper at the curb. The street sign has put back on its everyday face, and people jostle him as they hurry past.

He considers telling Megan, but what good would it do? It would worry her, or worse, it might push her away. If she knew, might she not give him up as a lost cause?

So he says nothing that day, and he says nothing about the nights when he awakes around three in the morning, convinced he can hear a woman humming in his ear. And he tells himself that he's not happy about these things, not intrigued by this strange, otherworldly come-on.

In the spring, after midterms, Megan receives a call from her father's lawyer. The execution has at last been scheduled. She and Noah scrape together enough gas money for the drive to Texas.

When they arrive, the prison reminds Noah of his high school: the same painted cinder-block walls and fluorescent lighting, the identical sense of industrial indifference. The only things missing are trophy cases and pep rally banners.

Megan is on James O'Neil's approved visitors list, and goes in to speak to him alone. When she emerges, her face is puffy and she says nothing. She and Noah are ushered into a small room with two rows of chairs facing a plate-glass window. They sit in the front row and the attendant explains that the glass is a two-way mirror. They will be able to see in, but the condemned will not be able to see out. A newspaper reporter and Maria Davis's parents arrive not long after. Nobody from Brandon Hawthorne's family comes. Noah can feel the rest of the room watching him, and his skin crawls. He makes himself face the glass and takes Megan's hand. It rests limp in his, a cold, dead thing.

James O'Neil is wheeled in on a gurney, wrapped in restraints. His right arm is strapped to an extension so that it stands apart from his body, making him look lazily crucified. He's clean-shaven and bald now, his face ragged and pockmarked. His eyes are thoughtful and subdued, lacking the manic energy Noah remembers.

When one of the prison officials behind the glass asks O'Neil if he has any last words, he only shakes his head. Maria Davis's mother begins to cry as a hooded man administers the injections and James O'Neil at last looks away from the ceiling and at the glass. He seems to see beyond it, seems in fact to have singled out Noah for his final sad, distant stare.

Noah is reminded of standing in the City, looking at the man strapped to the chair in the barbershop. He watched through a window then, too, as the chair made that man into something inhuman. Noah barely feels Megan withdraw her hand as O'Neil's lips part. He seems about to say something, but stops at a sound, one he seems to recognize. Noah recognizes it, too: *skritch-skritch-skritch. Skritch-skritch-skritch,* like long talons scratching glass. When it stops, O'Neil closes his eyes and they wheel him away. He might not be dead yet, but the show is over.

Noah and Megan don't touch or speak on the walk back
to the car. They both spend several minutes staring out
the windshield at the building where a man's life just
ended with clinical precision. Noah can't shake the old
man's gaze, and the scratching sound has settled at the
base of Noah's skull, sending shivers up and down. He
grips the steering wheel to keep from shaking. Beside
him, he can feel Megan's heartbreak. Worse, he can feel
a gap opening before him, a hole that he could fall into
if he doesn't watch himself. How long before he's the one
behind the glass, getting the lethal injection?

Let's get married, he says.

It takes her a long time to turn her head and
acknowledge what he has said. *Seriously?*

Seriously.

Like now?

As soon as possible.

They extend their stay in Texas long enough to throw
together a small ceremony at Holy Spirit Church, attended
mostly by members of the congregation and the Texas
chapter of the Fellowship. Noah doesn't invite his family,
or even let them know he's in town. Kyle comes to serve
as best man. When he and Donna arrive at the church,
Donna looks like she has a basketball strapped to her
front. She's due in a couple of weeks. For some reason,
this image, this irrefutable proof of the passage of
time, makes Noah miss Eunice. He missed her wedding and
now she's missing his.

Noah and Megan spend the night in a hotel near the
Fort Worth stockyards, decorated with paintings of cacti
and cow skulls. After sex, Megan cries and won't talk to
him. He gives her space and falls asleep on his side of
the bed.

He wakes around three, parched. He grabs the ice
bucket from the bathroom and ventures out into the

bright hallway. He looks for a sign to point the way
to the ice machine, but sees only doors and cartoonish
southwest paintings stretching away in either direction.
Wasn't there a window at one end of the hall when they
came in? He must be misremembering.

He passes a series of doors, catches the hum of
conversation, the drone of TVs, a whiff of marijuana.
When he turns the corner, he finds a door marked STAIRS.
Maybe he'll have better luck on the next floor down.

His flip-flops make muffled thumps on the carpeted
steps, but there's no door at the bottom of the first
flight, or the second. He pauses at the head of the
fifth flight and leans over the railing, trying to
guess how many are left. A hard ball of mingled dread
and anticipation begins to gather in the pit of his
stomach. He realizes that this feeling isn't strange.
It's so familiar that it's almost a warm blanket. It's
the feeling he gets when he's finally getting to the good
part in a horror story, or entering a new haunted house
for the first time. It's the way he felt the first time
he entered the City.

With only one eye and no depth perception, it's hard
to tell how many flights he has left to go. He looks up,
but, again, his crappy depth perception must be fucking
with him. This hotel is only six stories tall, but there
appear to be dozens of flights above him, receding up out
of sight.

Something moves up there, black silhouette on gray. He
recoils, forgetting the anticipation he felt only moments
before—and also that he's standing on uneven ground. He
flails for balance, flapping his arms like a ridiculous
bird as he tips and falls down the stairs, each one
a bright horn blat of pain. He lands at the bottom in
a heap, breathing hard and waiting for the agony to
subside. Footsteps clomp down from above, echoing so that

he can't be sure if it's one set of feet, or several, or many. *Clomp-clomp-clomp,* louder and louder. The sound grows to a crescendo, and he clamps his hands over his ears. Something closes on his arm.

Don't! he shouts. *Please!*

You're okay. It's only me. He hears the voice as if it's coming from inside his head. Leannon, gentle and soothing.

He looks up and sees the pained expression on her human face. She offers him a hand but pauses before helping him up. She runs her thumb along his new wedding band.

Why would you do this? she says. Her tone remains gentle, but pain seeps in at the edges.

Why won't you leave me alone? he says.

She seems to tear her gaze away from the band with great effort, and licks her lips before she speaks. *That isn't how this works. There is much you don't understand.* She reaches for his face, and he jerks away.

Let me help you understand, he says. *I don't want to end up like Megan's father. I don't want to end up like Sydney. I don't want to hurt anyone, and I don't want to see you anymore. I want to forget I ever knew you.*

Leannon si, she says.

Go! he shouts, and as he does, he finds himself facing an open door, through which he sees the hotel lobby. The clerk at the front desk leans forward, giving him a puzzled look.

Everything okay, sir? the clerk says.

Noah sees his ice bucket on its side a few feet away, still wrapped in a layer of flimsy, rattling plastic. He grabs it, waves to the clerk, and walks through the lobby to the elevators. He arrives back at the third floor and immediately finds the alcove with the ice machine. He fills his bucket and returns to his room.

He drinks his water and gets back into the bed. He lies awake for a long time, thinking about Leannon and the City. He works hard to convince himself that he did the right thing, banishing her. That it wasn't nice to see her again. That it wasn't exciting to slip into the City's grasp for a moment, to not know what he might find at the bottom of a flight of stairs, or around a corner.

He and Megan honeymoon in Ashland, Oregon, home of the Oregon Shakespeare Festival. The town is small and idyllic, like something from a movie, with wide sidewalks and display windows, stores with names like CD or Not CD, and three different playhouses. It seems like the perfect way to cheer up a theater nerd bride. On their first night in town they see a play called *Life Is a Dream* by Pedro Calderón de la Barca. They have balcony seats, and watching the drama unfold feels like spying on colorful neighbors from a high window. The story follows Segismundo, the prince of Poland, who has been imprisoned by his father, King Basilio, because of a prophecy that the prince will wreak havoc on the country. Of course, Segismundo does get free and, in his rage, unleashes rampaging hell before Basilio reimprisons him and convinces him that his brief freedom was in actuality a dream.

As Megan and Noah walk to their hotel afterward, she flips through the *Playbill,* animated for the first time in weeks, pointing to actors' head shots, reading aloud trivia from their bios. Did Noah know that one of the guardsmen played Benedick in last summer's *Much Ado About Nothing?* Noah admits he was unaware. It's tough to speak. The play has pressed itself into his mind like a thumb pressed into a marshmallow, leaving him lumpy and slow to regain his original shape.

Are you all right? she asks, picking up on his mood.

Just thinking about the play, he says.

She takes his arm and leans into him. *I'll protect you, handsome prince. You're safely trapped in the tower of our marriage.* Then she shoves him, and for the second time in a week, he goes pinwheeling off his feet. This time he lands in a hedge at the edge of the sidewalk.

But who will protect you from me? she cries, and runs away laughing.

On the last day of the honeymoon, after a week of plays, tear-free sex, and small-town Shakespearean charm, they eat lunch at a terrible imitation British pub where the food tastes like misery pressed onto a plate. Megan seems subdued again, and Noah worries that the spell of the vacation has been broken.

As she grimaces around maybe her fifth or sixth bite of blueberry chicken, he says, *You don't have to finish it if you don't like it.*

She sets down her fork and touches her napkin to her lips. There's something prim in the gesture, brittle.

I want to ask you something, she says. *Something I've been putting off for a while now. And I need you to tell me the truth, even if you think it's something I don't want to hear.*

Okay, he says, bracing himself.

You heard scratching at your bedroom window as a kid, and then your sister disappeared. Then, ten years later, you saw two of these monster things fight over my dad.

Right.

But as far as I know, that's it. You haven't mentioned any other encounters, or sightings, or even general weirdness. So my question is: Was that really it? Has there been anything else? Anything you haven't told me about?

Heartbreak has written itself across her face. She's hidden it well for the past few days, but it's back and it seems like it might etch itself there permanently. He reaches for her hand, and for a second he worries that she might jerk away, and if she does, he knows that he'll tell her everything, all in one go, every second of the otherworldly he's experienced since they first left Texas together. He'll even confess his years-long affair with Leannon.

Her hand doesn't relax into his, but she doesn't withdraw, either.

I swear to you, that was it, he says. *I think it was just weird coincidence, or fate, or whatever you call it. Maybe divine intervention. But you know everything there is to tell.*

She does pull her hand away, but squeezes back before she does. She does that little headshake and ashamed smile that means she's trying not to cry. He knows better than to try to stop the tears, or encourage them. She prefers to fight this battle alone every time. He sits and he waits.

When she gets control of herself, she says, *If it's okay with you, I don't think I want to do Fellowship stuff anymore.*

Why not?

Because I feel like I have all the answers I'm ever going to have, she says. She swallows hard. *And that's going to have to be enough. That's my closure. I want to move on.*

With me, I hope, Noah says.

Of course with you, she says. *You're my husband.*

They both pause. It's the first time she's said the word out loud since the ceremony, and it still carries its original incantatory power. It strikes him anew that he has gotten married. He has a *wife*. Regardless of what has come before, he's made his choice. Megan is his responsibility.

I am, he says. *And as your husband, I have a request.*

What's that?

I don't want to live in Chicago anymore after you graduate, he says.

Where do you want to live?

Why not here? I mean, not like right here, at this restaurant—

God forbid, she says.

But here. Ashland. A theater town. I could find work in the scene shops, and maybe you could act in a play or two.

This place seems sort of made for us, doesn't it? she says.

She graduates the following May, and they move into a second-floor apartment over a candle store in Ashland. Their new home smells pleasantly dreamy at all hours. Megan doesn't get any acting work, but she does find a job teaching theater at a local high school, and Noah works in the scene shop at the Angus Bowmer Theatre, building sets. For a while, things are good. The constant confusion, fear, and unreality of his former life fades into a dream of soft colors and inviting scents. The sense of being watched recedes, and his past seems less like something that's happened to him and more like vivid scenes in a book he once read, a borrowed nightmare. Love and a simple life. This is the real magic.

But years pass with increasing speed. Leaves drop from the trees only to jump back up overnight, green and renewed, while Noah and Megan march out of youth and toward the gray, murky country of middle age. Somewhere in this montage of years, something slips away from them. By the time Noah is twenty-nine, his esophagus burns whenever he consumes anything with tomato sauce. His back and knees ache all the time for no reason. He carries a roll of Tums and a bottle of Advil everywhere he goes. Every time he turns a corner, he's exactly

where he expects to be. Geography holds no surprises
or inconsistencies. He's tired all the time, exhausted
by his job. Sometimes he catches himself looking at the
sky, wondering what Ashland would look like from above.
Would it be cold up there? Would he need goggles to see
his apartment building? He used to ride the night winds.
The sky was his, and so was Leannon. Or he was hers.
He knows it's wrong to miss a monster. And so he tells
himself he doesn't.

It might be easier if things were still good with
Megan. It's not like they're bad, per se. They don't
fight. They don't even argue. But they don't laugh or
smile or really talk much anymore. At the end of most
days, they spend their time together on opposite sides
of the couch, eating burgers or pizza and numbing out to
the paltry comforts of laugh-track sitcoms. They don't
ever talk about her father, or the Fellowship, or Noah's
past, and they rarely touch one another on purpose.

Sometimes he looks at Megan, so far away on her side
of the couch, and he wonders why she seems so unhappy.
He asks her from time to time, and she always shrugs and
turns the question back on him.

Are you happy? she says.

He feels numb and unlike himself and doesn't
understand why. He was saved. Why wasn't his salvation
enough? Why is he so disappointed whenever he turns a
corner and finds himself exactly where he's supposed to
be? Why has he started doodling city skylines on scraps
of paper?

And then, one night when he's thirty years old, Noah
wakes in the middle of the night to the sound of
scratching on glass: *skritch-skritch-skritch,* at his
bedroom window. Some part of him has been waiting for
this, had expected it sooner. He rises, heart racing, and
crosses the bedroom, but before he can pull the curtains

aside, his phone begins to ring. He hesitates before the window, hand on the curtains, momentarily disoriented. Megan stirs, and he reaches for the phone. He picks it up off the bedside table and reads a Texas number he doesn't recognize.

Hello? he says.

Who is it? Megan says, voice thick with sleep.

The voice at the other end is small and full of static like a fading radio signal, and he doesn't catch anything but the last two words, uttered in breathy panic: *little prince.*

Eunice? he says. *Eunice, hello?*

Noah? It's a man's voice now, much clearer, and sounding confused.

Who is this? Noah says.

He walks to the window to part the curtains, but whatever was out there is gone now. It's just him, Megan, and the voice on the phone saying, *Noah, this is Hubert. Something terrible has happened.*

Part Six

The Shunned House

I

I returned to Vandergriff on a Sunday in March 2013, riding coach near the wing of an American Airlines flight as it dipped below the clouds into the gray, wet, miserable reality of DFW airport. Weather-related complications kept us on the tarmac for nearly an hour, and I had to squeeze my Kindle to keep from screaming with frustration. It was only rain, for Christ's sake. Cars drove in rain all the time. What the fuck slowed down a *landed* plane?

Beside me in the window seat, Megan put a hand on my arm. "Bring it down a notch. You're about to white-knuckle that gizmo in half."

I set the Kindle back on my lap and gave Megan an apologetic look. She squeezed my arm. There was sympathy in her glance, but something else behind it. I looked away, through the window.

When we finally disembarked, Kyle met us at the baggage claim. We'd kept in touch via social media, but I hadn't seen him in person since my wedding, so his beer gut and salt-and-pepper hair took me by surprise. He pulled me into a bear hug and pounded me twice on the back.

"It's good to see you," he said. "Although the circumstances suck."

I reintroduced him to Megan, and she smiled as they shook hands. I tried to remember the last time I'd seen her smile at something other than a sitcom and failed. A muddled potpourri of jealousy and longing pinged in my chest.

Kyle insisted on carrying her bag to his Prius and loaded it into the back for her. He wanted her to sit up front, too, but she proved immovable on this point. She stretched out in the backseat and I rode shotgun. We crept out of the parking garage and into gridlocked traffic amid a heavy, view-obscuring thunderstorm.

I gestured at the endless lines of cars around us. "Sorry about this. You probably had better things to do today."

"Are you kidding?" Kyle said. "If I weren't here I'd be at home wrangling the kids while Donna's at her book club. Instead they're with my mom today. This is like a spa day for me."

Megan snorted in the backseat.

"How are your folks?" I said.

Kyle cleared his throat. "Mom tossed Dad out. For good this time."

"What for?" I said, trying to sound like I had no theories of my own. I had no proof Mr. Ransom had continued philandering after Sydney vanished, but a man who could fall in love with one teenage girl seemed likely to have fallen in love with others.

"No one thing in particular," he said. "At least, not that I know of. Mom seems a lot happier. Redid the whole house. It doesn't even feel like the place where I grew up anymore."

"And your dad?" I said.

"Living in a trailer park," Kyle said.

He went on for a bit, prompted by questions from me and Megan, talking about his marriage, his three kids, and, eventually, The Wandering Dark. He and Donna had bought the place from Mom in 2003 and rebuilt on the old bones, turning the attraction from a nightmare maze into a safari through the country of the undead. They rechristened it Zombie Mansion and it opened in unintentional tandem with the zombie craze kicked off by *28 Days Later* and *Shaun of the Dead*. They'd done well for a while, but, as my family had learned, in the haunting business, familiarity eventually breeds indifference, and Zombie Mansion had finally closed last year. Kyle had taken a job at a company that sold boxes and packing supplies, and Donna answered phones in an office.

"We still have the warehouse and everything in it," he said. "I'm brainstorming ways to bring it back." The words sounded hollow, as though even he didn't quite believe them. It would be hard to leave behind the stability of his current job. Adulthood gets us all in the end.

Things got quiet after that. Kyle turned the windshield wipers up to full speed. They made whiny sounds against the glass, and I could feel all of us trying to think of something—anything—to talk about that didn't involve the reason for our return to Vandergriff.

Megan finally made a gambit. "So, Kyle—I hear my husband used to date your wife?"

"For less than a month," I said, playing along. "And then Kyle—*my best friend*—stole her away."

"*Stole* is a strong way to put it," Kyle said.

"So is *best friend*," I said. We all laughed, and for a moment, I was happy to be home, in a car with my wife and my best friend, seeing the two of them get along, teaming up to make me the butt of a joke. It was a glimpse into the life I'd thought I would have when Megan and I had first gotten together, the one that had never quite materialized.

The feeling evaporated as we pulled into Eunice and Hubert's neighborhood. Well—to call it a neighborhood was an overstatement. The street on which Eunice's house stood was the first and only row of completed homes in the development. Skeletal, unfinished structures and empty, weed-filled lots lined the streets beyond. A faded sign on the street corner promised HOUSES AND LOTS STARTING AT $30,000.

"Sign looks old," I said as we drove in.

"It's been there for years," Kyle said. "The people bankrolling the project went out of business and nobody's come in to finish it. There used to be forklifts and cranes out there, but I guess someone bought those and took them. Now the rest of it sits and ages."

He parked in Eunice's driveway behind a family-friendly SUV that must have been Hubert's. Eunice's car, listed in the newspaper articles as a black 2009 Toyota Camry, was absent, probably still in police custody. The house was a two-story brick structure with wide front windows, a sloping lawn, and a view of an industrial park across from the development.

Kyle and I got out of the car to retrieve the suitcases and ran up the driveway ahead of Megan.

"Call me if you need anything," he said. "We can get a beer."

He ran back to the car, waving at Megan as she walked up the drive with a magazine open over her hair as a pitiful umbrella. I rang the bell, and Hubert threw open the door. He'd remained skinny and pale, but looked more haggard, his hair unkempt, dark bags beneath his eyes.

"Noah," he said, and pulled me into a tight hug despite my sopping clothes. "Thank God you're here."

2

Like the outside of the house, everything inside seemed calculated to communicate a message of suburban normality: the dining room with the glossy wooden table and straight-backed chairs; the matching china hutch; the pleasant, forgettable paintings of boats and landscapes alongside Sears family portraits; the pristine cream-colored carpet and white furniture in the living room. *Everything is fine here,* the house seemed to say through gritted teeth. *We are normal and happy, goddammit.*

Two children sat on the living room floor, playing with Lego bricks: Caroline, age ten, and her brother, Dennis, eight. Both glanced up as I entered. Dennis looked like a smaller, rounder version of his father, and Caroline looked achingly like her mother, with the same red hair and pale complexion, the same gangly limbs and weak chin. When Hubert introduced us, Dennis gave me a dazed nod, but Caroline glared, as though already suspecting me of some wrongdoing. Hubert offered us coffee, and we sat in the breakfast nook to drink it.

"What do you know?" he said.

"Sorry?" I said, an icy flush running through me as though I'd just been accused. I felt Megan's gaze fall upon me again. I didn't meet it, but instead stared into my coffee cup. The silence stretched out.

"Oh," I said, lamely, as if I'd misunderstood his original question. "Only what we've read online."

Taking turns, Megan and I repeated the public version of the story: the previous Monday, Eunice had gone to work, spent a full morning at her desk, and, according to her coworkers, "seemed fine." At noon, she left for lunch and never returned. Her car was found parked in the unfinished housing development a block from where we sat right now. Her purse was sitting in the middle of one of the unfinished houses. Everything—even the cash—was still inside. When police tried to get in touch with my mom, to see if she had heard from Eunice, they couldn't reach her by phone. They couldn't get an answer knocking at her front door, either. When they entered the house, they found the television on and a pot of coffee burning in the kitchen, but no one inside. Neither Mom nor Eunice had been heard from since.

When we finished, Hubert said, "Eunice works late a lot and sometimes forgets to check her phone. I didn't worry until the next morning, when I woke up and she wasn't home. I lost a whole day before it occurred to me that something might be wrong."

"Hubert, I'm sorry," I said.

"No, I'm sorry," he said, and hit the table. My coffee splashed over the side of the mug and puddled on the wood. "I made vows when I married your sister. I was supposed to take care of her." I patted his shoulder and he pulled me into a second, tighter hug. I let him crush me like a stuffed animal.

When he let go, he wiped his face with the back of his hand. "There were things I should have noticed."

"Like what?" Megan said.

"She stopped taking her medication. I found at least three months' worth in a shoe box in her closet."

"And you didn't notice any change in her?" I said.

"She seemed . . . peppier," he said. "More energetic. Sometimes she stayed up all night. But, Noah, I swear to God, I thought it meant she was happy. That maybe she would start writing again."

Caroline and Dennis came into the kitchen then and cut the conversation short. The rest of the evening was subdued. Megan and I played the parts of the clueless, worried family while we sat in the living room and watched animated movies. The kids sat on the floor and built a Lego house.

"That's pretty good," Megan said, as they finished the main walls and started on the roof.

"It's only a dumb house," Caroline said.

"When I was a kid, I could never make anything with Legos," I said.

"Were you dumb?" Dennis said.

"Dennis!" Hubert said, but I laughed.

"Yeah, I guess I kind of was."

Around nine, Hubert sent the kids to bed. They were bunking together in Caroline's room so that Megan and I could have Dennis's bed. It became apparent as soon as we entered the room that the kid was apeshit for Lego. A Bionicle poster hung over his bed, and shelves had been built into the walls to display all his completed kits.

As soon as we shut the door behind us, Megan said, "I still think we should get in touch with the Fellowship." She'd been voicing this same desire several times a day ever since we'd heard about Eunice and Mom.

"We already agreed we were done with Fellowship business," I said. "Years ago."

"That was in 2003. This is now. Maybe they can help."

I stood up and paced the room. I made a show of looking at Dennis's shelves of race cars, spaceships, supervillain lairs, airports, and houses, a gallery of instructions followed with painstaking care. This fastidiousness must have been something he'd inherited from his father. Eunice and I were both slobs.

"I'm not saying it isn't Fellowship business," I said, "but my family are missing and I don't want a bunch of people poking around in Hubert's and the kids' lives. And, anyway, suppose you're right. Suppose my family were abducted by monsters. There's nothing we can *do*. That's how it's been for everyone else in the Fellowship, and how it went with Sydney."

I turned away from Dennis's toys to face her. She sat on the bed, knees to her chest.

"Why didn't you want me to come home with you?" she said, voice small.

"I *did* want you to come," I said, struggling to maintain eye contact.

She sighed and held out a hand to me. "Come to bed."

Instead, I got my toiletries from my suitcase and went to shower.

Megan was asleep when I came back, but she'd left the nightstand lamp on for me. I got in the bed next to her and turned out the light.

It was true that I hadn't wanted her to come to Texas with me. Things had been strange between us for a long time now. She seemed unhappy, and when she looked at me, there was always a searching quality in her eyes. It reminded me of the way people in Vandergriff used to look at me in the years after 1999—like there was something untrustworthy about me. And in this case, she was right. Part of my desire to come alone was wanting time and space to myself to make sense of my family's disappearance, without feeling like I was under a microscope. But the other part of it had to do with the circumstances around the disappearances. The scratching at my bedroom window, the faded voice on the phone. Back when Megan and I lived in Chicago, the City usually called to me when I was alone. It would be much harder to be alone with Megan around and analyzing my every move.

But of course I couldn't tell my wife that without admitting to a whole boatload of other things I'd kept from her. So here we were, in Texas, where she wanted to involve the Fellowship, and couldn't quite understand why I didn't. Both of us in my nephew's bed, she with her frowning dreams, I wide awake.

I knew I wasn't going to sleep anytime soon. I got out of the bed, got dressed, and found my phone. I texted Kyle:

How about a late-night tour of Zombie Mansion?

His answer came almost at once: *Give me thirty minutes.*

3

I waited for Kyle on the front lawn. The night air was cool and humid, the grass still wet. It put me in mind of the ever-present humidity in Leannon's world. I couldn't escape that feeling of being observed, like the whole street was watching me.

"Are you out there?" I said, not sure to whom the question was addressed. "Can you see me?"

The street gave no answer, but the sense of being surveilled didn't recede. When Kyle's Prius pulled up, I wasted no time hopping in.

"Do you want to talk?" he said.

"No."

He turned on the radio, and we drove across town to my family's old warehouse. My first glimpse of the building was partial, illuminated by Kyle's brights: a hulking monument whose former gray exterior had been painted over with an elaborate mural. Gray and blue zombies wandered a hellish postapocalyptic landscape of ruined, smoky buildings, crashed cars, skeletal playground equipment, and a burnt-orange sky. It looked like the world's most elaborate piece of van art.

"Whoa," I said.

"Donna hates it," he said, "but I wanted to make a strong first impression."

"It does do that," I said.

We got out of the car, and he pulled a six-pack of Shiner Bock from the hatchback. I took a bottle while he unlocked the building. The Styrofoam skull from the Wandering Dark days was gone, and the guest entrance had moved to the other end of the building. We walked into the warehouse proper, where the workshops, offices, and break room remained more or less intact. He turned on the power from the "control room." The building lit up around us, and I experienced a heartsick pang. I finally felt *home*.

We left the rest of the six-pack in the break room fridge and went outside again, to the guest entrance, a black door at the top of a ramp. We drank beer as Kyle walked me through the attraction.

"The idea is that you're part of a group of survivors trying to navigate a city full of zombies," he said, as we walked down a narrow alley between two fences. Behind the chain-link on either side sat old, junked cars and rough suggestions of storefronts and office buildings. "So you have a bunch of 'infected' milling around on both sides, and they seem to be minding their own business, when suddenly an uninfected woman runs up on your right and starts begging for help. That gets the attention of the infected, and they swarm over the barrier, and sirens start blaring, and all bets are off. Not really, but you know what I mean."

The rest of the attraction consisted of a series of increasingly high-risk encounters with the undead. Visitors crawled through tubes, ascended steep ramps, and had to help each other across wide gaps. It was more intense than anything we'd ever considered during our ownership, a ropes course from Hell.

"Donna wanted to give people a reason to exercise," Kyle said, as we shuffled through a red plastic tube on all fours, careful not to spill our beer. "Like we'd be doing a public good." We emerged from the tube at the base of a wide, steep ramp with ropes tied to the top. We chugged our bottles empty and began our ascent.

As we made our way deeper in, the challenges grew more demanding and conversation ceased. My heart pounded and my clothes stuck to my body. I kept waiting for that familiar feeling, that strange mix of unease and excitement that signaled the onset of a trip to the City, but it never came. With each new challenge, each turn of a corner, I remained beside Kyle. We swung between elevated platforms, crossed monkey bars, and edged along balance beams at what seemed like unsafe heights. By the time we shot down the slide that deposited us at the exit, my lungs burned and I had a stitch in my side. I was also, for the first time in a while, completely blissed out. I lay on the mat at the bottom of the slide, breathing hard and letting my mind reel through nothingness.

When I came back to myself, I got up and followed Kyle back to the employee break room, where we finished the six-pack.

"Thank you," I said, when I caught my breath. "I needed that."

He clinked his bottle against mine. In the silence, temporarily free of anxiety, something occurred to me.

"Hey, do you have anything left over from The Wandering Dark?"

"We left the old monster labyrinth in place," Kyle said. "It was useful for moving zombies around."

"What about costumes?"

"We zombified most of the clothes," he said. "Cut them up, made them ragged and bloody." He stood, and I followed him to the costume shop. He pointed at a pile of cardboard boxes in a corner. "Stuff we couldn't use is in there."

I opened the box at the top of the pile. I pulled out a rumpled brown suit coat, a frilly blouse with shoulder pads, and a pair of cutoff jeans. I recognized each item, small pieces of my past, long forgotten, but they weren't what I was looking for. I dug through more boxes.

"If you tell me what you're after—" Kyle said.

But I found it in the fourth box, stuffed in by itself: patchy brown fur of varying shades, looking old and cheap in the bright lights, robbed of the dark majesty it possessed in its natural habitat. My second skin. My monster suit.

"I should have guessed," Kyle said.

I looked it over. "You didn't do anything to it."

"Of course not. It's yours. Messing with it would have been wrong. Anyway, what do we need a monster costume for at a zombie mansion?"

I held the costume in my lap on the drive back, running my fingers through the tousled, matted fur. I felt a little more whole than I had an hour before.

"Is it all right if we stop here?" Kyle said, pulling into a Walgreens parking lot. "I promised my dad I'd bring him some pinworm medication."

I followed him inside, where he found the medicine and we joined a surprisingly long checkout line. After about two minutes of listening to the woman at the head of the line debate the wording of a coupon with the cashier, the cashier directed us to the open pharmacy counter in the back. There, a bored-looking woman in a white coat rang up people's purchases. Something about her face—the way she held her mouth, as though sucking on sour candy—snagged on my memory, but I couldn't quite place her. I let it go and played on my phone as we trudged toward the register.

"Noah? Noah Turner?"

I looked up. The woman was half-smiling at me.

"Yes?" I said.

The smile bloomed. "It's been a long time," she said. She pressed a hand to the name tag on her chest: HI, MY NAME IS BRIN. Brin. My sister's first and only girlfriend. Brin, who had broken Eunice's heart so completely that Eunice had leapt into a suicidal depression. Fucking goddamn shitting Brin.

"I remember you, Brin," I said.

Her cheer faltered. "I heard about Eunice and your mom. If there's anything I can do—"

"You can ring my friend up," I said. "We're in kind of a rush."

Her gaze dropped, and I felt a brutal satisfaction at this small cruelty. Fuck her. I could tell Kyle was curious, but I pretended to be engrossed in my phone as he dug out his debit card and paid.

"What was that about?" he said, as we left the store.

"Is it okay if we don't talk about it?" I said.

"You're the boss." He unlocked the car, but before we could climb in, Brin jogged out of the store, coat billowing behind her.

"Hey!" she called.

"Want me to get rid of her?" Kyle said.

"I'll handle it. Wait in the car." I met Brin halfway across the lot. "What do you want?"

"Look, I understand why you wouldn't want to talk to me," she said. "The way I treated Eunice was inexcusable. And what came after—" She rubbed a hand on her face. "It's the single biggest regret of my life. Religion—especially the weird kind, which is what I had—is a hard thing to get out from under. It can talk you into all sorts of stupid, cruel behavior. It can make you afraid of yourself, and instead of dealing with that, I made it Eunice's problem." She touched her face again. "It took me a long time to come to terms with myself. I always wanted to reach out to Eunice someday, but then I heard she got married and had kids. I don't know. I thought I still had time to make things right."

"Me too," I said.

"Anyway, I'm sorry," she said. "If you or your family need anything—well here, let me give you my number." She pulled a pen and paper from her lapel pocket and scribbled it down. She started hurrying back inside as soon as I took it from her.

"Brin?" I said.

She paused.

"I wish I was brave like you," I said.

She waved and then disappeared back into the store. I climbed into the car.

"Everything okay?" Kyle asked.

"Fine," I said.

We drove to the trailer park where Kyle's father was living, a flat, grassless concrete grid named Meadow Lake. Kyle asked if I wanted to come with him to the front door.

"Dad would probably want to say hi if he knew you were in town," he said.

"No thanks," I said, trying not to sound rude.

I watched from the passenger seat as Kyle climbed the cinder-block steps to the corrugated metal box containing his father. When Daniel Ransom answered the door, I was momentarily taken aback. He'd become a dazed, shrunken, slumped man with wispy white hair, dwarfed by pajamas that were far too big. Life had not been kind to him, and I felt a moment of something like pity. It passed.

I looked away, focusing on the piece of paper Brin had given me. My face burned at the thought of going back to Eunice's house, sleeping in her son's bed, and pretending to be as clueless as everyone else.

4

Megan was still asleep when I returned. Exhausted, I fell into bed beside her and finally slept. I dozed straight into the following afternoon, and woke only when the sunlight through Dennis's bedroom window became impossible to ignore. I went downstairs and found the family in the kitchen. Hubert was scrubbing dishes at the sink and handing them to Dennis to put into the dishwasher. Caroline and Megan sat at the kitchen table, Megan drinking coffee and Caroline reading a thick paperback. Her red hair obscured much of her face. She looked so much like Eunice that I felt a little sick to my stomach.

"Good afternoon," Hubert said. "There's coffee if you want it."

"Sure," I said, moving to the pot to pour myself a mug.

"Rough night?" Megan said. The words hit me like a baseball between the shoulder blades, and it took effort not to hunch in reaction.

"Yeah," I said. "Trouble sleeping."

"Same," Hubert said. "I haven't had a good night's sleep since."

I took a seat at the table with Megan and Caroline, my mug cupped between my hands. "What are we up to today?" I said.

"Not much so far," Hubert said. "We were just trying to decide what to do with the rest of our afternoon and evening."

"I want to go to the zoo," Dennis said.

Caroline looked up from her book. "Are you joking? Why would you want to visit animal prison?"

"Animal prison?" Dennis said. It had apparently never occurred to him that animals might not want to live at the zoo.

"We don't have to go to the zoo," I said. "We can go to a park. Or a movie."

Caroline stood and grabbed her book. She walked out the door to the backyard and slammed it behind her.

Hubert leaned against a counter and crossed his long, skeletal arms. "She's having a hard time. I'll talk to her."

"Give her space," Megan said, sliding into the vacant chair. "Drink some coffee with me. Take a load off."

Hubert complied, happy to be told what to do. Dennis continued to frown over the idea of an animal prison.

I claimed to have forgotten my phone and ran back upstairs to Dennis's room, where I parted the curtains and opened the blinds just in time to see Caroline straddle the top of the back fence and disappear over it into the unfinished housing development beyond.

5

I snuck out the front door and took the long way around the block after Caroline. I found her sitting cross-legged on the concrete foundation of what had probably been intended as the first draft of a living room or kitchen. She stood up as soon as she heard me, ready to run.

"I come in peace," I said, holding up both hands. I moved into the room and left the doorway open, so she could flee if she wanted. It was a symbolic gesture—the open room meant she could take off in any direction she liked—but an effective one. She remained tense but stayed where she was.

I wandered around, looked out between the slats at the unfinished homes on either side. "Do you come out here a lot?" I said.

"Mom and Dad don't like it," she said. "They're afraid we'll get hurt."

"That wouldn't have stopped me when I was your age."

"Mostly I come to watch Dennis play and make sure he's safe."

"You look out for Dennis," I said.

She nodded.

"Your mom always looked out for me when we were kids. You know you look just like her?"

She still didn't relax. "How did you know I was out here?"

"Luck," I said. "I happened to look out the window upstairs and saw you climb the fence."

"I didn't do anything wrong," she said, with a defiant glare. I didn't argue, but waited. The indignation gradually bled out of her face. "For a little while, Mom seemed so happy—happier than I've ever seen her—but then one day she turned mean. Like whatever we said or did was the wrong thing. And Dad—she was awful to him. She called him weak, and a coward, and said she should never have married him. She did it in front of me and Dennis, like she didn't care if we heard. And Dad hunched his shoulders and took it until she was done."

She blinked a few times and swallowed hard, loud enough for me to hear.

"I should be nicer to him," she said.

"Me too," I said.

"Then she got even worse. Sometimes I would wake up in the middle of the night and see her pacing her office with her arms crossed and her head down. I kept hoping things would get better. But then

Mom started taking long walks by herself in the middle of the night. Sometimes I would sneak into Dennis's room to look out the window, and I would see her pacing out here, shaking her head. And then, one day, she and Grandma were gone."

She looked away for what she said next: "Sometimes when Mom was in her office, I could see something outside the window, watching her."

"What kind of thing?" I said.

She glowered at me. "A monster in a robe. It looked kind of like if the big bad wolf went out in Little Red Riding Hood's cloak. Mom never seemed to see it, but I do." She looked at me, saw something in my face, and then said: "You've seen it, too, haven't you?"

I considered denying it. But I felt a kinship with this kid—she reminded me of Eunice, yes, but also of me. Smart and scared and trying to sort through the half-truths and lies her family had told her up to now.

"I have," I said.

"Do you know where Mom and Grandma are?" she said.

I closed my eye, afraid I was going to be sick. This was all my fault. Leannon had warned me years ago, on my wedding night. She'd told me that my request to be left alone wasn't "how this works." She'd told me there were things I didn't understand. And now she'd proven it. She'd taken my whole family.

When I opened my eye again, I found Caroline watching me with grave concern.

"Can you bring them home?" she said.

"I'm not even sure how I would start," I said. But as soon as I said it, I realized that wasn't true. I knew exactly where to start. I didn't *have* to wait for the City to invite me in again. I might be able to get back there under my own power.

6

I left Caroline in the empty house and walked back around the block. Everyone was in the kitchen when I reentered Eunice's house, which made it easy to steal Hubert's car keys from the hook inside the front door and slip out again. I managed to get out of the driveway and down the street without anyone coming out the front door. I drove across town with my phone on silent, unaware of any missed calls or texts.

It was early evening by the time I got to Mom's house on the other side of town, the sun obscured behind thick storm clouds and bringing on premature night. The house loomed larger than I remembered, seeming both wider and taller, as though it had been growing like any other living thing on a steady diet of whatever houses ate. Its windows reflected the streetlight, like the black eyes of an insect.

There were no police cruisers in the driveway or on the street, but there was yellow tape across the front door. I ducked under it to try my key, which still fit the lock. I left the lights off once I was inside. I didn't want the neighbors to see anyone was here. Instead I swiped past any notifications on my phone's home screen and used its flashlight to look around.

The house had obviously been combed over for evidence and then abandoned. The cushions had been pulled from the couch, and all the kitchen cabinets hung open, the contents left on the counters and floor. It reminded me of Leannon's house after the earthquake.

Aside from the mess, little had changed. The same curtains hung in the windows and the same table sat in the dining room. The place smelled musty, the air stale, as though the inhabitants were past their sell-by date. I went upstairs to my old bedroom. With the tossed bed and laundry all over the floor, it looked as though nineteen-year-old Noah would return at any moment. The same posters hung on the wall, and the same stack of books sat on the nightstand: *The Bloody Chamber, Ghost Story, The Ceremonies,* and *Memnoch the Devil.*

I found a piece of paper that had been left on my desk to gather dust for over a decade:

> *Noah,*
>
> *I came back for an encore at The Wandering Dark tonight, but they told me it was your night off. Sorry I missed you. Anyway, if you want, you should come to a get-together with me and some friends tomorrow night. I'd love to talk more.*
>
> *xoxo—Megan*

I felt a guilty twinge and started to open up my missed notifications screen but stopped myself. I had to get through this next part before I could worry about Megan. I crouched in front of the desk and opened the bottom drawer. It was stuffed with old high school homework projects, spiral notebooks, and comic books. I shoved my fist past all the paper and groped until my fingers closed around what I was looking for. I pulled it out and looked at it in the dark bedroom: a small, smooth black stone. My key to Leannon's world, abandoned here eleven years ago, still right where I left it.

I closed my fist around it, squeezed my eye shut, and pictured Leannon's house in the black forest, the miasmatic sky and the thick, humid air.

I opened my eye and found myself still crouched in my old bedroom. It hadn't worked. Why hadn't it worked? Had all its power run out? Had its batteries died after years of disuse? I turned the stone over in my hand. It didn't look any different than I remembered it.

There went my one big idea. Still, I wasn't quite ready to give up and head back to Hubert and Megan and the kids.

I dropped the stone in my pocket and finished searching the room, but I found nothing helpful. Same with Eunice's old bedroom and the "home office" at the end of the hall, where Sydney's high school portrait still sat on top of a filing cabinet.

I went downstairs to canvas the first floor. Nothing seemed unusual or out of place in the kitchen or living room. The bed in Mom's room was stripped bare, all the clothes and shoes a mess on the closet floor.

I was about to give up my search when the beam of my light passed something small and brown, pressed up against the back wall. I knelt and saw a cardboard box, so old and faded that it was almost yellow. I pulled the top flaps apart. It contained a single, ancient three-ring binder, fat with aged yellow paper. A title page had been tucked into the plastic of the front cover, written in faded pencil, the letters blocky like the writing on the cover of an old *Superman* or *X-Men* comic:

The Nameless City
By Harry and Margaret Turner

It looked like something a kid might draw in study hall, and it told me a lot about my parents: the father I would never know, and the version of my mother who had died along with him. Playful people. Fun people.

A photograph had been taped beneath the title, the one described oh-so-many pages ago: my parents crouched next to the FREE HAUNTED HOUSE sign, smiling and proud of their creation. (This was, and remains, the only picture of my father that I possess, a cherished thing still kept tucked into its plastic sleeve.)

I took the binder back to the bed and opened it. As the cover promised, it contained the plans Mom and Dad drew before his death—the ones Sydney and I had wanted to get our hands on. Mom claimed to have thrown them out, but here they were, designs for a massive attraction revolving around three hotels: the Gilman, based on the seaside town of Innsmouth from H. P. Lovecraft's novella; the Glitz, an Overlook-style hotel with a hedge maze and brass fixtures; and Ma's, a bed-and-breakfast with a black wrought-iron fence and a cemetery in the backyard.

Radiating out from the nucleus of hotels was, as near as I could tell, an actual city, with office buildings, shops, and restaurants, all rendered in exacting detail. From page to page, though, the layout of the city changed. It was impossible to find an anchor point from which to map it consistently. I paged back and forth, but the more I looked, the more it all appeared to be random, just like the layout of the City as I had experienced it myself.

I didn't have much time to ponder the new discovery and how it might help my quest to cross over to Leannon's world. I heard the front door open and the sound of muffled voices in the entryway. Someone had come.

"Noah?" Megan called. "Come on out. We're here."

7

When I emerged from the living room into the entryway, I found Megan with Josh, Eli, Hector, Laura, and Sarah. Despite my requests, she'd called the Fellowship and brought them with her. They'd turned on the lights.

"How did you know where to find me?" I said.

"There were only two places I could think of that you might go," she said. "I made a lucky guess on the first try."

"I told you I didn't need the Fellowship's help," I said.

"Maybe not," Megan said, voice calm and reasonable and a little sad. "But I need answers." I could sense something cold and dangerous in her. I had no room to wriggle here.

"Why don't we all go into the living room?" Sarah said.

Everyone took seats on the couches and chairs, except for Megan and me. We stood in front of the television. As the group stared at me, I felt that crawling sensation I used to get as a teenager, that sense of being exposed, suspected. That sense of being the other, an interloper among normal people.

"What do you want to know?" I said.

"Treat it like a meeting," Sarah said gently. "Start at the beginning of this latest event and tell us what's happened."

I bit back my rage at being cornered like this. I launched into the story of the strange phone call and the scratching at the window the night Eunice and Mom disappeared. I told them about Caroline's revelation that she had seen one of these creatures. I told them I had decided to see if there was anything I could do about the disappearances, but admitted I was stuck. I showed them the binder from Mom's closet, but not the black stone. That I kept to myself.

When I had finished, no one spoke for a moment. The members of the group looked at one another or at their laps. Josh finally broke the silence.

"This is such bullshit."

"Bullshit?" I said.

No one would meet my eye. Even Megan, standing beside me, became suddenly interested in the carpet.

"My mother disappeared when I was eight years old," Josh said. "She was a freelance journalist in San Antonio. She investigated the underground vampire community—not real vampires, you know, just creepy Anne Rice junkies who played dress-up and drank blood. She was making a name for herself, a career. Do you know what she was investigating right before she went missing?"

"I have no idea," I said.

"Unsolved disappearances." He paused and looked at me, as if inviting me to comment. I gestured for him to continue.

"A lot of disappearances you can draw reasonable conclusions about," Josh said. "Sometimes there's a spouse or an ex with a history of violence, even if there's not enough evidence to charge or convict. Other times the missing person has a history of substance abuse or mental illness. Mom wasn't interested in those cases. She was interested in the strange ones. Like the kid who walked into a g-force simulator ride in Huntsville, Alabama—a closed room with only one door in or out—and who never walked out again. Or the man in Maine who vanished from his locked prison cell in the middle of the night."

"I suppose she had a working theory?" I said, unable to keep the annoyance out of my voice.

"If she did, I don't know about it," he said. "She was just getting started, calling around, following up on leads. Our phone was turned off at the time, so she had to walk to the pay phone down the street every time she needed to make a call. It wasn't unusual for her to make the trip two or three times a night when she was working. Only this one time, she left and never came back. The police looked. She made the news. Shows about unsolved mysteries have featured the story a few times. Still nobody has any answers. She's just gone. Most people think that phony vampires got her, but I know better."

"What does any of this have to do with me?" I said.

"After the rest of your family went missing last week, your name started something itching at the back of my mind. On a hunch I went digging through my mother's notes for that last, unfinished story, and do you know what I found?"

"No clue," I said.

"Notes about a woman named Deborah Turner. Sound familiar?"

I shook my head.

"Paranoid schizophrenic," Josh said. "Widowed, husband killed in Korea. Found walking on the side of the road one night in her night-gown. Tried to fight off the police when they approached, and kept talking about a city. Had a son named Harry. Your father's name, if I'm not mistaken."

I nodded. "He died right after I was born. And his mother not long after. My mother never talked about either of them."

Josh pulled off his trucker hat and ran a hand through thinning blond hair. "It's strange that your family has such an involved history with these creatures. Every other incident the Fellowship has studied appears to be isolated. Nothing hereditary."

"That's news to me," I said, and that was at least partially true. My grandmother, found by the side of the road? Talking about a City? Did that mean she'd been taken and somehow escaped? Did that mean it could be done after all?

"We let you into our group," he said. "We shared our stories. Most of us were at your wedding. We accepted your tale about the night your oldest sister vanished. We accepted your story about what happened the night Megan's father was arrested. We took all of this on faith because we were so hungry for any information about what happened to the people we loved. But it's *weird* how tied up your family is with these creatures. We've all had a bad feeling about you for a very long time, and now you're sneaking off at night and lying to Megan about what you know, and trying to prevent her from talking to us. So why don't you stop bullshitting and tell us the fucking truth for once?"

I shoved my hands in my pockets and tried to think of some new tactic, some way to turn their gazes from me. The fingers of my right hand worried at a scrap of paper, feeling its edges. I pulled it from my pocket. It was Brin's phone number. I stared at it, the gears in my mind temporarily halted.

I tore my gaze away from the paper to find them still waiting for an answer.

"I—" I started, then stopped and cleared my throat. I closed my eye and saw Brin's face in the parking lot, lined with years of pain. Brin, who'd been brave and honest with me. Who had taken responsibility for herself and owned what she'd done.

"Everything I've told you is true," I said, opening my eye to start again. "But you're right, it's not the whole truth. I first saw one of these creatures when I was six years old. It stood outside my window every night, scratching the glass until I finally confronted it."

"Then why aren't you missing?" Josh said.

"I don't know," I said. "But for the next twelve years, this creature was my playmate, my protector, and eventually, my lover."

I felt the group's skepticism turn to revulsion. Megan's nose crinkled as though she'd just smelled something foul.

"I didn't know what these creatures were, or what they did," I said. "The creature I knew hid all of these things from me. I was a lonely kid with a magic best friend. Once I met Megan, and all of you, my feelings started to change. I went to the monster's world using this stone"—I pulled the black stone from my left pocket and showed it to them—"and saw a person trapped there and turned into a monster. I heard the story of how Megan's father was held in thrall to one of these creatures, driven insane. I didn't want that to be me. I banished the monster from my life and started my relationship with Megan."

"If this thing was grooming you, the sex was just another part of it," Sarah said, voice gentle. "You were manipulated. It's not your fault."

"Why didn't you tell me?" Megan said. Her hands were balled into fists, and her gaze was steely and terrible.

"Because of the way you looked just now," I said. "And also because I'd just met you. Do you really go into a new relationship blabbing about all your exes?" But, I realized with a sickening lurch, I was still lying. Even now. I sighed and clenched the black stone in my fist.

"Goddammit, that's not all," I said. "Yes, the monster and I were together, and, yes, I banished her. And, yes, I hid it from you because I wanted you and didn't want to scare you off. But the real truth—the whole truth," I said, "is that I've had one foot in and one foot out of this world for as long as I've known you. I thought being with you, telling you and your friends some of the truth . . . I thought it would change me. I thought if I hid from this part of myself long enough, it would go away. I thought it would save me from ending up like your father. But despite knowing what my monster is and what she does, I still miss her. Despite the fact that she's hunted me and my family for apparently the last fifty-odd years—God help me—I still love her."

As soon as I spoke the words, the world went gray. I briefly heard the startled exclamations of the Fellowship, but the sound faded as the air grew thick and humid around me, like a wet blanket. I'd crossed over at last.

8

When I used the black stone in the past, I had always chosen my destination. This time, however, it seemed to choose for me. When the fog cleared and the world coalesced again, I stood in a facsimile of my mother's living room, dark and emptied of other people. Fog swirled around my feet as I crossed the room to hit the light switch. The overhead lamp turned on, but the darkness remained a physical presence, one that ate light like fire eats oxygen.

I walked to the back door, opened it, and gazed upon a field of black grass, thick with ebon kindnesses. A forest of shadowy trees stood some way off in the distance. I almost stepped outside, meaning to make my way to the forest, to Leannon's hut—but a sound stopped me. A low, muffled moan, coming from the room right off the living room. Mom's room.

I went back inside and opened her door. A dim pink glow lit the room. The crib and rocking chair made it look like a nursery, but the framed photos shellacking the walls belied that impression. The moan sounded again, this time from behind me. I turned around as my mother staggered into the room, wearing a nightgown and looking dazed. She'd lost weight since I'd last seen her, and looked skeletal in her billowing nightgown, aside from the perfectly round, protuberant belly. She was pregnant.

"Mom," I said.

She didn't answer, but braced herself on the crib railing and lowered herself to her knees. She retrieved another framed photograph from underneath the crib and sat up to look at it. The glass was caked with dust, but I could still make out Mom and Dad on what must have been their wedding day. Mom wore a green dress, and Dad wore a suit that looked a little too big on him.

Mom ran a hand across the glass of the frame and left streaks in the dust. She massaged her swollen belly and moaned.

I knelt beside her. "Mom?" Still she didn't respond. I laid one hand on her stomach. It wilted like a trash bag full of leaves, then trembled. I pulled my hand away right before something tore up through the fabric and out of the belly, narrow, black, and moving fast. I ducked away and bumped against the wall. Two black vines had sprung from my mother's belly. They flailed about like the forelimbs of a praying mantis, stiff and hunting. When the stalks found nothing to pierce or grab, they retracted back beneath the torn fabric of her nightgown.

Mom had no visible reaction to any of this. She remained hunched over her photo, making weak, sad noises in the back of her throat. I wanted to continue trying to rouse her, but I worried that if the black vines emerged again, I might not escape a second time. I got to my feet and staggered out of the room.

I climbed the stairs. The second floor of the house also looked like an inverse of the real thing, a hall lined with closed doors. The door at the end of the hall—Mom's usually vacant "office"—clicked open. I inched toward it, listening for sounds behind the other doors, wanting to be ready if one might fly open and spew unthinkable horrors. As I got closer, I heard music coming from the open door: "Tubular Bells," the theme from *The Exorcist*. It was one of several movie themes we used to play on the PA outside The Wandering Dark. I stepped through the open door.

This next chamber was something like an impromptu DIY music gig or black box theater. A woman on a small stage in front of a standing crowd of people in Halloween costumes. Smoke wafted across the stage and a strobe light flashed, making the movements of the woman on the stage otherworldly, somehow unreal. She wore a black tutu, a perfect complement to her ghostly skin and raven hair. I squinted, trying to get a clear picture of her in the staccato lights.

"Sydney," I said. Sydney, still a prisoner, but still alive, still *human*, all these years later. I could hardly believe it.

The person next to me—a fellow in a suit, cape, and domino mask with a long, pointed nose—turned and put a finger to his lips.

"Shh," he rasped. His mask had no string to affix it to his head. The shiny, metallic material looked soldered onto his face at the temples, emerging from lumps of scar tissue. The eyes behind the mask weren't dull like Mom's, or Sydney's, but bright and glassy, caught up in the performance.

Onstage, Sydney twirled and stretched, ghostly in the intermittent illumination. It was hard to pick out details. Was her hair graying? Were there lines on her formerly smooth face? She'd been seventeen when she disappeared in 1989. She'd be forty-one now. Had she been dancing without pause all these years?

There were thick black vines around Sydney's ankles and wrists, going taut and slack in time with her movements. Something offstage was pulling the strings.

"I'll come back for you," I said, and backed out of the room. The man in the welded-on mask whipped around to shush me again.

As soon as I stepped into the hall, the office door shut itself and Eunice's bedroom door swung open.

"Okay, I get it," I said, raising my voice. "Where are you?" I walked past Eunice's room to my own door. The knob wouldn't turn. I slammed my shoulder into it, but it was like running into concrete. I headed for the stairs, but when I arrived, I found them guarded by a seven-foot-tall iron gate. If my own door was any indication, there was no point in trying to scale it. There were no shortcuts to the end of this attraction. I'd have to see it through as its designer intended. I entered Eunice's room.

It was as untidy and cluttered as I remembered it, crammed with books, and a wooden desk pushed up beneath the window. Eunice slumped there, striking keys on a black, oily-looking typewriter. The clatter was loud and rhythmic in the eerie quiet, as if she were playing the machine like a piano. She wore the ragged remains of business casual clothes. Her red hair was tangled and matted. I approached slowly, chest tight. Long, multijointed black stalks had grown from various points in the desk, and lodged themselves in her arms, her legs, her stomach, and even her forehead. The stalks danced to the rhythm of Eunice's typing. It looked like she was being prepared for transfiguration.

Eunice pulled a page from the typewriter and added it to a stack on her right. I picked the pages up, and she stopped typing. She raised her head. She looked paler than I remembered, her eyes vacant. Her face sagged with something greater than exhaustion. Blood ran down her forehead where the black stalks had pierced her skin.

The front of the manuscript was a title page:

The Turner Sequence

I flipped to the next page and read:

The Turner Sequence I: Margaret

When Margaret enters the fluid waking dream of the City, that mix of memory and nightmare, she thinks

she's in the tiny apartment she shared with Harry
in the poorer part of Lubbock—that shabby one-
bedroom affair with ratty carpet and wood-paneled
walls, although you can hardly see the walls behind
the stacks of boxes that line the room—boxes full
of Harry's paperbacks and comic books and pulp
magazines.

Eunice wheezed, and I started, stepping away from her.

"Put . . . it . . . back." The voice came from her mouth but sounded nothing like her. "Not . . . finished."

I set the pages on the desk and left the room, not sorry to hear the door click shut behind me. Back in the hall, the door to my room finally swung open.

The moment I stepped in, the floor vanished beneath me, and I fell with an unheroic yelp, landing on my hands and knees on a hard wooden floor. Soft warm light lit the room around me, and the dark receded some. Canvases leaned against the walls, and dried plants and roots hung from the ceiling. I'd arrived in Leannon's hut. Leannon, wearing her wolf's face, sat slumped in the middle of the room, her back to me. She had her hairy arms wrapped around her knees.

I stood up. "I'm here," I said.

She didn't answer. I stomped across the room and grabbed her shoulder.

"Hey," I said, and stopped as she looked up at me, orange eyes vivid with distress and torment. She gripped my hand, and I had just enough time to read what she had scribbled across the floor before the whole world went white:

FRIEND
HELP

The Hound

In this nearly silent film, a pale woman with red hair and a red cloak carries a basket of flowers through a forest of tall, thin trees. She pauses upon reaching a clearing with three simple crosses planted in the earth. On a nicer day, sunlight might fall on this little cemetery, but today the sky is black with storm clouds. The woman lays a white lily on each of the graves, then sits down before them. Several times she looks as though she might speak, but opts instead for the quiet and the rumble of clouds overhead.

The clouds burst, and she pulls up her hood and hurries back the way she came. She reaches a small wooden house that stands at the edge of the forest, on the outskirts of a small village of wooden buildings. The roads are muddy and empty, all doors shut against the storm.

The woman's house is a single room with a packed dirt floor, a bed, a fire pit, and a small kitchen. She sits in a chair before the fire with a stack of paper in her lap, drawing with a hunk of charcoal. As the world outside darkens, she remains seated, sketching the same three faces again and again: a bald man with a dark beard, and two dark-haired children. The drawings improve with each successive draft, as if the woman is sharpening the focus in her mind's eye, summoning laugh lines, playful glints in the eyes, melancholy mouths. She doesn't move as she works, or shift for comfort. She occasionally closes her eyes, but never looks up and never changes her expression of studious, frowning concentration.

She draws until she runs out of paper, then flips the pages over and draws on the backs. When she comes to the end of this second series, she stands and stretches. She sets her pages on the bed and pulls a cloth purse from inside her dress. She starts to count its contents, but drops the money when a scratching sound begins outside her door.

The woman gasps, and the purse hits the floor with a muffled *clank*. The scratching ceases. The woman eyes the purse, as if wondering whether to recommence her counting, but then the scratching returns, audible above the drumming of the rain. The woman steps over her purse and opens the front door. The doorstep and the village roads appear empty, although it's hard to see through the pounding rain.

She starts to withdraw into the house, but something past the tree line catches her gaze: a pair of glowing orange eyes, clear and sharp even through the storm.

Rather than startle or shrink back, the woman tilts her head and furrows her brow. She's more curious than frightened.

She grabs her cloak and steps outside. Hood up, head down, she sloshes through the mud into the woods. Under the canopy of trees, she pulls the hood back and looks around. The orange eyes appear again, right in front of her face. She stands motionless as the figure unfurls from a crouch to its full height—at least a foot and a half taller than she is, draped in a long yellow cloak. The woman spreads her arms in a clear gesture of surrender. Gently—almost lovingly—the creature enfolds her in its long limbs and pushes off into the air, up through the trees and into the storm.

Rain pelts the woman's face and lightning flashes in the distance, momentarily brightening the sky—and then the sky changes from purple-black to a swampy green. The village has vanished, replaced with a sprawling mass of black towers and buildings that look like temples and mausoleums, but bigger and somehow more awful than anything ever erected on earth.

After this, the film begins to stutter, the narrative lost in a series of quick cuts and sensations: a mug of something thick and pungent; an incredible drowsiness accompanied by a sound like dry branches scrabbling across a concrete floor; sharp, unbearable pain and a tightness at the wrists and ankles; darkness, darkness, darkness.

Then, a different sort of pain. This part she remembers all too well, experiences from the inside. Her eyes open on a dark room, to the sound of cutting meat and an agony in her arms, legs, face, and chest, a feeling of something being taken—*sucked*—from her body and something else, thick and viscous, flowing in to replace it. Her body shakes and goes taut and she wishes for death, for anything to stop this pain—and then an unbearable itch spreads across the surface of her body. Her flesh tears, and clumps of fur burst from her skin. The world turns orange.

She tumbles out of the chair to which she has been strapped and lands on the floor, trembling. A line of wolf-faced monsters in colored robes enter the room and surround her. One of them—a gray wolf in blue—kneels and offers her a red robe. She pulls it on with shaking hands—no, not hands. Claws. She has claws now. She stands and the wolf in blue bares its fangs in a feral grin.

What follows is an orange smear of years during which the wolf is no longer anyone. She is driven by only a few impulses: *feed on their pain; capture workers; serve the City.* Various faces come and go, consistent only in their sadness, depression, grief, mental illness, and fear, each a crop to be harvested. Some people she only samples (a bad breakup here, death of a family pet there), and others she cultivates like gardens: the deeply depressed, the grief-stricken, the insane, the terminally ill. Some she feeds on for years, and others she takes to toil and dream darkly in the City. A select few—the strongest, most exquisite sufferers—are chosen for ascension and become wolves themselves.

To the wolf, their faces are all anonymous, easily forgotten—until she meets the Turners. It begins with Deborah, a woman teetering on the brink of madness. The wolf kidnaps her, but has second thoughts when she sees the woman's son, Harry. A small boy with dark hair, standing in his mother's bedroom in the middle of the night, terrified to be left alone. Something in the boy's face sounds against a deep, long-hidden memory within her. Another small scared boy whose face she can't quite place. For reasons the wolf doesn't quite understand, she lets Deborah go home, and leaves them in peace for years.

The wolf returns to Harry when he's grown, intending to feed upon him; his wife, Margaret; and his daughters, Eunice and Sydney. For years she dances at the edges of their perception, letting them catch glimpses and hints of her presence, heightening their pain and fear as Harry withers and dies. She delights as the family continues to fracture, but her work is interrupted once again when she meets another little boy: Noah Turner, age six, a perfect double of his dead father, standing behind his bedroom window and staring up at her with open fascination and no fear, able to see her whether she wants him to or not.

How long has it been since someone has seen her without terror and revulsion? Decades? Centuries? His curiosity and friendliness unlock something in her heart. She returns to him again and again. She spends her evenings in the atrium outside the boy's bedroom, using sidewalk chalk to copy pictures out of his storybooks onto the concrete. When she puts her paw on his hand and guides him through their first drawing together, she loses herself for a moment in a flash of bright white light, a sense of perfect flow.

When that moment ends, too soon, she sees what they have drawn together: a cartoonish likeness of the City. More important, she sees the drawing, the pavement, and Noah in full color. The orange tint of the world is gone.

It's the boy. Something about being near him brings back color and hints at other, bigger things out of her mind's reach. She starts working her way into his life. She steals his oldest sister away to the City and uses his confusion to wangle an invitation into his room. She sleeps in his bed, watches him grow up, teaches him to fly. In her time away from him she builds her little house in the black woods outside the City, a place not unlike her final human dwelling, and there she makes her first rough paintings, trying to hang on to her full-color vision.

She tells herself that she thinks of Noah as a tool or a pet, but jealousy burns within her as she watches him give an ebon kindness to Donna Hart and receive his first kiss in return. Perhaps, she realizes, the colors he brings into her world are a side effect of something deeper that has been quietly gathering for years.

She is full of fury as she saves Noah from the Gray Beast, and she finds a new level of clarity and color as she rediscovers her human shape, finds her human voice, and makes love to Noah for the first time. Love has called her out of the dark, and at last given her a name: Leannon.

For years, Leannon paints and makes love to Noah. She hides him from the City, keeps her colors, her human shape, her happiness. But of course this state of bliss cannot continue indefinitely. She withholds too much information from her young lover, ignores too many of his questions. He gets curious, distrustful, and finds the City on his own. When it sees him, it demands his life, as it demands the lives of all its visitors.

Leannon tries to protect Noah, even after he leaves her. She abducts countless others in his stead to try to appease her master, even as the color drains out of the world and her mind grows muddled. She forgets how to handle a brush or stretch a canvas. How to put on a human face, or smile. The City remains adamant, and she has more and more difficulty resisting its command. In a final, confused attempt that might be meant to save Noah or call for his help, she abducts Eunice and Margaret Turner in one night. She hopes that Noah will find his way here and rescue everyone, or that the City will be sated at least a little longer, gaining two new slaves in his place.

After the abduction, she sits on the floor in her house, her head in her paws, trying to hang on to the image of his face, the letters of his name. It's all slipping away. *She* is slipping away.

He does find a way back to her, uses the exact right words to open the door between the two worlds. And when he arrives—when his hand lands on her shoulder—she stops keeping secrets. She grabs him by the hand and finally shows him *everything*.

Part Seven

The Haunter
of the Dark

I

The avalanche of white light subsided. I'd seen everything I needed to see. Leannon started to release my hand, but I held on to her paw. I knelt next to her and folded her into my arms.

"I missed you so much," I said.

She returned the embrace and uttered a high-pitched whine from the back of her throat.

I stroked her back and scratched behind her ears. "It's okay. I'm here now."

2

After I made the deal, I went to Sydney first. The audience had left the little theater at the end of the upstairs hall, and the music had stopped. Sydney danced alone, to no tune, for no one. When I climbed up and untied the vines around her arms and legs, she collapsed into me and we both nearly tumbled off the stage. I fought to keep my balance and lowered her to the floor, her head on my bent knees. Her eyelids fluttered.

"Sydney," I said, stroking her matted hair. "Sydney, it's time to wake up."

Her eyes snapped open. "Daddy?" she croaked.

I nodded. It was easier this way.

"I don't understand," she said. She rubbed her eyes with balled-up fists, like a toddler. "Is this a dream?"

"Yes," I said. "And I need your help to wake us both up. Do you think you can walk?"

Arms around each other's shoulders, we hobbled down the stairs and into the living room. I sat next to her on the couch and held her hands.

"In another moment, you're going to wake up," I said. "But first I need you to drink something." I stood, took a steaming mug off the breakfast bar, and handed it to her. She sniffed it, and her brow creased.

"What is this?" she said.

"It's medicine," I said. "I know it smells funny, but you have to drink it all, okay?"

She took a deep breath, braced herself, then stopped as a loud *thump* sounded upstairs, followed by the sound of voices.

"What was that?" she said.

"Another part of the dream. You have to drink."

She tipped the mug to her lips and chugged its contents in a few short gulps. She put a fist to her mouth, like she was trying not to throw up. After the moment passed, she seemed more awake.

"How can you be here?" she said. "I watched you die."

"It's a dream," I reminded her. "And in dreams we're allowed to see one another as often as we like."

3

I went to Mom second. She still sat on the floor of the pink nursery, eyes shut tight. She clutched the photograph of her wedding day and cried. The vines that had been impersonating a pregnancy now lay around her like dead snakes.

"Mom, can you hear me?" I said.

She looked up at me and blinked. Like Sydney, she was confused.

"We can go now," I said, and offered her a hand.

She squeezed the photo to her chest and rocked back and forth. "I can't go," she said.

"Why not?"

"I fucked it all up," she said. "Everything. I lost my husband, my best friend, and my children. I told myself I was protecting them, but"— she shook her head—"I was pushing them away. I don't deserve to go home."

I squatted next to her. "I understand. It was easier to let us slip away and pretend that there was nothing missing, nothing wrong. It was easier than fighting and hoping and hanging on. But you held us together through sickness and poverty and disappearances and suicide attempts. You made The Wandering Dark, a place in our world that taught me to navigate this world. It's because of you that I get to bring everyone home. That means you, too, Mom."

She let me hug her then, leaned into my embrace and wrapped her arms around me. "I miss you all so much," she said. "I miss your father."

"I know," I said. "But the bad dream is almost over and the lights are about to come back on. I can't give you Dad back, but I can give you almost everyone else. I just need you to come out to the living room with me."

4

I went to Eunice third. Of those I freed, she was the only one I needed Leannon's help to extricate. She'd been stabbed by the black vines, strapped to the desk, ordered to write until her transfiguration, and Leannon had to seal the wounds so Eunice wouldn't bleed out. After Leannon rubbed in her special salve and left, Eunice sat at the desk, swaying slightly and staring into the middle distance.

I touched her arm, and she shrieked. I withdrew my hand. "I'm sorry," I said.

She continued to bob and list like a buoy on choppy waters. A tear ran down one of her cheeks.

"I have something for you," I said. I reached into my pocket and pulled out the paper with Brin's number on it. She took it almost mechanically, but it pulled her gaze from the middle distance and focused her eyes.

"Brin," she said, voice flat.

"She's working as a pharmacy tech in town," I said. "She always wanted to get in touch and make it up to you, but she didn't know the way back."

"Brin," she said again, sounding more herself. She smiled a little. "You always hated Brin."

"I also wanted to make things right with you, and I never knew how." I touched her arm again, and this time she allowed it, let me take her hand in mine. "Call Brin, or don't," I said. "But you deserve to be happy." I squeezed her hand. "And Caroline and Dennis miss you."

"Caroline. Dennis." The names had power, drew her a little closer to waking. She let me lead her down to the living room and accepted her mug of tea, but gave it a critical look before she drank.

"What's in this?" she said.

"It's an extract from a flower that only grows in this world. I call it the ebon kindness. It can put you into a trance, heighten suggestibility, and even alter your memories."

She slowed her drinking. "I'm not going to remember any of this," she said.

"It'll all fade like a bad dream," I said.

"Why? Why ask me to drink this?"

"It's part of the deal I made," I said. "You get to go home, but the memory stays here. Once you finish the tea, I'll help you forget."

"And what about you?" she said. "Who will make you forget?"

When I didn't answer, she seemed to understand the full import of what I wasn't saying. She grabbed my hand so hard it hurt.

"Hey," I said. "Who do I love most?"

"Little prince," she said. She set the mug down and grabbed my other hand, too. "Let me enjoy this moment with you," she said. "One more moment, please."

5

The sky in Vandergriff had turned pink at the edges when Eunice came staggering up the street to her own house. Her work clothes were torn where the desk had pierced her, crusted with dried blood and dirt. Her face was slack and pale in the predawn light, and although she would live, she still lacked most of her strength. She winced with each footfall, and hissed through gritted teeth.

Caroline and Dennis must have been looking out the window, alert in that way children sometimes are, knowing a thing before it's possible to know, because the front door flew open and they barreled across the lawn, faces red. They collided with Eunice so hard that she lost her balance and tumbled into a neighbor's yard, the grass still wet with yesterday's rain. They clung to her, faces buried against her body, voices muffled. Hubert followed soon after. He skidded in the grass, fell to his knees, and hit his family like a bowling ball.

"I can't believe it," he kept saying. "I can't believe it." He took Eunice's face in his hands, kissed her cheeks, her forehead, her eyelids. She wore an embarrassed, guilty look, enduring rather than enjoying her husband's attention. His euphoria would be short-lived. The Eunice who'd come home was not the same one who had left.

6

On the outskirts of Vandergriff, Kyle Ransom's Prius pulled into the driveway of his father's trailer. He walk-jogged up the path, in a hurry. He'd promised to come look in on his dad before work, but he was already running late.

He rapped "shave and a haircut" on the front door and waited. It usually took the old man a minute to get up and come to the door. Kyle checked the clock on his phone. When thirty seconds had passed with no answer and no sound from inside, he knocked again. Still no answer. Figuring that his father might be stuck on the toilet, Kyle pulled his keys from his pocket and unlocked the front door. He pushed inside.

"Dad?" he said, looking back and forth in the darkened trailer. "Everything all right?"

There was a strange smell in the air—something thick and pungent. It was somehow familiar, although he couldn't place it. It certainly wasn't anything he'd ever smelled in here before. He stood in the quiet for several more moments, breathing the heavy air, chasing the scent down the rabbit hole of his memory. It reminded him for some reason of Donna, and high school, and guilt at kissing her when she was still dating Noah.

Still trying to figure out what the scent was, he turned around, walked out of the empty mobile home, locked the door, got back into his car, and drove away. In the coming days, he would sound the alarm about his father's disappearance, and start a police investigation. But the police wouldn't look very hard, or find anything of value, and no one (including Kyle) would be able to muster much sorrow about any of it.

7

Across town, Sydney Turner woke in a strange, neatly kept room with books stacked on every surface. She sat up and caught sight of her reflection in the mirror on the back of the door: a middle-aged woman with streaks of white in her hair, her formerly perfect skin now lined around the mouth and eyes. She touched her face and saw pink welts around her wrists like bracelets of pain.

She lurched to her feet and hobbled out of the room. She walked down a hallway, then down some stairs, gripping the railing for balance.

"Hello?" she called. Her voice was rough and scratchy. She heard a *thump* from somewhere downstairs and hurried her pace to an empty living room. She called out again. "Hello?"

A door clicked open, and an old woman staggered out, eyes bleary. Her gaze sharpened as it landed on Sydney. The two women stared at one another, each trying to place the other. Sydney got there first.

"Mom?"

Margaret blinked a few more times. "Oh my god. Sydney?"

She rushed forward and pulled Sydney into a tight hug. Sydney tried to remember the last time her mother had hugged her. It must have been sometime around her father's funeral. Who was this aged stranger, squeezing her and crying? Surely not Margaret Turner. Maybe this was a dream, too. If so, it was a good one, where her permanent, lifelong anger began to dissolve under the deluge of her mother's weeping apologies. Sydney hugged her mother back. She had so many questions: How long had she been gone? What year was it? But for now, it was enough to be home, and alive, and crying with her mother.

I could almost leave the story here, at one of Eunice's favored "stopping places": the family reunited, safe and sound, even if their future appeared a bit ambiguous. And a part of me, so taken with the warmth and relief of the moment, is tempted to write "the end" and leave it. But I still have a little story left to tell. A little more happiness, a little more heartbreak, a few more questions to answer and loose ends to tie up. I'm not sure I have enough material to make a bow, but I'll do my best.

8

A little less than a year after my family came home, I snuck into a small ceremony at a hotel ballroom in Fort Worth. There weren't many guests, and most were people I didn't recognize, but there were a few Wandering Dark alums clumped near the back, along with Sally White and her husband. Their energy was so palpably warm and happy that I almost felt a part of it myself.

A moment after the groom and justice of the peace took their places at the altar, the string quartet near the front of the room began to play, the doors to the ballroom opened, and the bridesmaids emerged. Sydney and Caroline sailed up the aisle, as solemn and lovely as Tolkien's elves on the march to the Grey Havens. Sydney wore a long-sleeve dress and a blank expression and seemed to notice nothing as she stopped at her designated spot and turned to face the crowd. Caroline, though—as she turned toward the guests, our gazes locked across the room. She could see me. She shouldn't have been able to, but she could.

The quartet changed melodies, and Eunice emerged, arm in arm with Mom. Their walk up the aisle was a slow one for Mom, age sixty-six and still slightly limping after her tenure as an inhabitant of the City. I had a feeling she would limp a little for the rest of her life. She paused near the back aisle to smile at Sally. Sally, who didn't know what to make of this newly open version of Margaret Turner, smiled back and gave Mom a little shooing gesture. *On with the show.* The pause gave me plenty of time to study Eunice, stunning in a strapless seafoam green gown, her red hair gathered into a pile atop her head. She looked healthier than I'd seen her in years, her gentle glow somehow rendering the scars on her arms and face invisible. I wished for a way to stop time, to stretch the moment forever. As far as moments in which to get eternally entangled, I'd seen many worse.

Brin started sniffling about halfway through Eunice's procession. Dennis, at her side as the best man, offered her a pack of tissues, which she took gratefully. And then, much sooner than I would have ordained it, Eunice stood at the arch, beaming at her new spouse-to-be.

9

I lingered in the shadows at the reception, but Caroline kept shooting puzzled glances at me throughout the evening. I pretended not to notice. Instead, I watched Eunice and Brin dance, more or less hugging in the middle of the ballroom. I watched the way Brin cradled the back of my sister's head with one hand, the look of desperate love that crossed Eunice's face as she did it. I watched Sydney dance with Caroline and Dennis; she smiled when they looked at her, but frowned when she was left alone. Almost a year later and although she was home, she still wasn't quite whole. I wondered if she ever would be again.

I watched Eunice and Brin cut and serve cake. I watched Mom sitting at a table with Sally White and her husband. I could tell by the way Mom kept squeezing Sally's arm that it would be tough for Mom when this visit ended. She'd missed her best friend and had an almost compulsive need to make up for all the lost time.

I wished I could have joined my family in the center of the ballroom. I wish I could have told them that their days of being haunted and hunted were over. But I think they got the sense anyway, their evening full of laughter, drinking, music, and dancing. The Turners were a family again. My family, and I'd only had to nudge them a little to knit them back together.

Instead of interfering, I contented myself by breathing in the atmosphere from the edges of the room, and, as the evening wound down and the guests dispersed, and the newlyweds retired to their quarters, I tried not to be too disappointed, or afraid. I still couldn't help shuddering a little when Leannon appeared at my shoulder, wearing her human face, her red robe replaced by a blood-red dress.

"It was a beautiful ceremony," she said.

"Do you think it will work?" I said.

"Will what work?"

"The marriage. My family. Will they still be happy after tonight?"

"I don't know," she said. "But you've given them time, and a second chance. That's more than most anyone else gets. It will have to be enough."

I knew it was true even if I didn't like it.

"It's time to go," she said.

"Wait!"

Caroline must have sensed her window of opportunity closing, because she came running across the courtyard now, bridesmaid's gown fluttering around her.

Leannon and I traded a glance. She stepped back and gestured with a hand. *If you must.* Caroline stopped right in front of me, breathing hard. "I know you," she said. And then, as if doubting the proclamation, "Don't I?"

"Do you?" I said.

"It's like there's a fog in my head," she said. "But I remember Mom and Grandma were missing . . ." She put a hand to her temple and hissed. "And I remember your face. Noah." She continued rubbing her temple, as though teasing out the information. "Uncle Noah. You were there. Then Mom and Grandma were back. And Aunt Sydney, too. And you were gone. And sometimes I remember you, but then it's like I forget again." She squinted her eyes shut and then opened them wide. "You did something, didn't you? You saved us."

Her words startled me. Leannon and I had dosed all of my family with the ebon kindness. It didn't erase me, exactly, but it should have made it nearly impossible for them to think about me for very long.

"Try to forget you ever saw me," I said. "It'll keep you safe."

"What did you do, though?" she said. She pointed at Leannon. "And who is she?"

She was still asking questions as I took Leannon's hand, but the words faded as we crossed over.

10

I've waited until the end to tell this part because if I'm ever going to lose your sympathy, it will be here. I wanted you to see the other scenes with my family, to understand that I had good reasons.

Before I freed my family, I came back from the City to Mom's house alone. Megan and the Fellowship were still gathered in the living room, shouting at one another in their fevered excitement. I'd been gone for more than an hour, but, to my relief, they had waited. As soon as I reappeared, they quieted and regarded me with a sort of awe. I felt like Moses, descending Mount Sinai. Well, until Megan punched me in the jaw and I fell on the floor.

"You son of a bitch," she said. "You rotten motherfucker."

I didn't protest. I deserved any abuse—verbal or physical—that she wanted to heap on me.

"Obviously it worked," Eli said. He sounded a little excited, and also a little ashamed of how excited he felt. "Did you find your family?"

"Yes," I said, "but I can't get them free by myself. I'm still going to need your help."

"Why in hell would we help you?" Josh said, fiddling with the brim of his hat.

I rolled up onto my knees, rubbing my jaw. "I'm sorry if I gave you the impression you had a choice in the matter." I gestured over my shoulder as the monsters appeared.

There wasn't any blood, but there was plenty of screaming. I won't describe it here, but I'll remind you of the night I first saw Megan at Inferno. Picture the moment at the very end of that attraction, as the demons emerged from the walls and dragged all the howling, begging sinners to Hell.

When it was over, only Megan, Leannon, and I remained. Megan had dropped to her knees and covered her face with her hands. I wanted to comfort her, but that was no longer my place. Instead I waited until she got hold of herself again. She blinked a few times and seemed surprised to see herself still in Mom's living room.

"Why am I still here?" she said.

"I made a deal with them," I said, jerking a thumb at Leannon. "My family for the Fellowship. And you're my family, too."

Leannon made an impatient noise and stepped up beside me. She held out a mug of the ebon kindness tea. I took it and handed it to Megan. "All you have to do is drink this, and when you wake up tomorrow, you'll be back in our apartment, and you won't remember any of this."

Megan stared into the mug and ran one thumb along the rim. "I'll remember, and I'll come for them. I'll stop you. I'll find a way."

"You won't," I said, as gently as I could.

For a moment I thought she might make a scene or try to fight. That she might throw the tea in my face. Instead, she started to cry. I almost broke then. I might have told her that I was sorry. That of all the people I'd ever known, she deserved all this awfulness the least. I might have said that I still loved her, because I did. I just loved the rest of my family, Leannon, and the City more.

"I hate you," she said.

"Drink your tea," I said, amazed at the coldness in my own voice.

When she fell asleep, Leannon took her back to our apartment in Oregon. She passes out of my tale here, and I hope she finds some measure of peace away from me, my family, and the City. I hope, for both our sakes, that she doesn't penetrate the brain fog I've gifted her, and that our paths don't cross again.

In their lives, the Fellowship had only one another, and along with Mr. Ransom (an extra sacrifice made for Megan's freedom), they're still together now, held fast in beds of black vines. They got the answers they wanted, in the end, and paid for them. They're servants of the City, and toil in dark dreams, unable to wake.

I don't reject the choices I've made, or the cost. It's not so surprising, I guess. My monster suit always fit better than my regular skin. I was never a guardian, or a hero, but a creator and harvester of fear.

II

Leannon and I have just returned from the wedding and come upstairs to the room where I found Eunice last year. The desk where she wrote still sits here, the black vines swaying from its surface as though in a gentle wind. They've hung over me for the last several months as I've written this record, my overlong and inelegant version of Eunice's suicide notes. Tonight, their moment comes at last.

I'd like to tell you I sat back down tonight full of determination, ready to hold up my end of the bargain, but the truth is that my legs failed on the way up the stairs and Leannon had to carry me up and put me in the chair.

"Be brave now, *Leannon si,*" she whispered, and kissed my neck. "I'll be here."

The whole City feels silent but for the clack of my keys and my harsh, ragged breath. This is the second part of the deal I made, the final condition I must fulfill. In exchange for my family's safety and success, I will become a servant of the City. I now sit at the desk originally meant for Eunice, waiting to be transfigured into something wild and feral. I wait to join the work of feeding the City and populating it with dreamers.

My hope, as I type with unsteady hands, as the black vines begin to move more decisively, excited to begin their work, is that Leannon—my playmate, my best friend, and the love of my life—will be able to bring me back to myself, as I brought her back twice before. My hope is to wander the endless hidden streets, alleys, and offices of the City, to explore its many crevices and parse its dark secrets. My hope is to ride the night winds with Leannon forever.

There's always the chance that I won't be able to come back to myself like Leannon did. That I will be stuck as an unthinking animal, thinking only orange thoughts. If that happens . . . well. I've always been comfortable in the dark.

The desk is starting its work.

Oh god.

It hurts.

The Turner Sequence V: Harry

Although Harry sees the City, he never goes there. He goes someplace else.

It starts on his deathbed at Vandergriff Memorial Hospital. Nobody calls it that, of course. *Deathbed* is one of those clichés everyone utilizes in daily conversation—about what they'll remember, what they'll regret, what they'll recant—but when an actual deathbed appears, the term vanishes from the lexicon. No one speaks its name, because to speak its name speeds it along in its terrible work.

Harry's in so much pain now that he wouldn't mind if things sped along. This illness has been endless. At first, to pass the time, he drew designs for a haunted house he knows he won't be alive to build. It was fun to dream big, to give voice to the images that have nagged at his waking and sleeping thoughts since he was ten years old. A vast, sprawling City, eerily empty and darkly compelling for reasons he's never been able to articulate. He's always been afraid to talk about it, but now, under the guise of a game, he's been able to show it to Margaret, sharing it with someone at last.

His strength has waned, though, and he's too weak to draw anymore. Tonight, he lies alone in the dark after his family has gone home for the night, awake in bright, constant agony, and he whispers the term to give it power: *deathbed, deathbed, deathbed*.

For all the good it does. The end feels impossibly far away. The only upside of death's distance is that his family goes home at night and leaves him in peace. Family. A wife, two daughters, and now a son. The people he is supposed to love, but whose faces now trigger apathy, annoyance, or (when he feels sufficiently provoked) apoplexy. He wishes they would just stay home. He's sick of their wan, needy faces.

He used to be a warm, thoughtful person. He can point to specific moments of overwhelming happiness with these people in his past: his first kiss with his wife, Margaret, on a warm night in Searcy in 1968; Sydney's squeal of laughter as he pushed her on a swing at the park, her dark hair flying around her head; Eunice across the glass from a manatee at the Dallas World Aquarium, communing with the fat white beast while he held her aloft. He remembers all of it, but he doesn't feel any of it anymore. The doctors tell him that this is the tumor's work, distorting his personality, turning him into a fun-house-mirror version of himself, but he feels like this is the real Harry, the one from the shadows, emerging at last.

Now he lies in his bed, looking out the window, weak and hurting and repeating his mantra: *deathbed, deathbed, deathbed. Deathbed, deathbed, deathbed. Deathbed, deathbed, death—*

The sky outside the window lights up, a bright flash of blue that interrupts his thoughts. At first, he thinks it's lightning, but there's no rain, no thunder. He blinks, the afterimage bright against his eyelids. Maybe it's a hallucination. But it happens again, a bright blue pulse that bathes the whole world. He lifts the remote on his bed and presses the call button. No one answers.

He closes his eyes and listens for the telltale sounds of humanity out in the hall—rustle of papers, squeak of shoes on linoleum, hushed conversations—and hears none of it. He opens his mouth to call again, but the blue light floods the room, brighter than before, and for some reason this confirms what he already suspects. There's no one out there.

He disconnects himself from the various tubes and wires keeping him "comfortable." The effort winds him, but not as much as he suspected it might. He pushes the lever that lowers the bed's safety railing, and slides down into a heap on the floor. It hurts, but again, less than you might think.

He stands and shuffles into the hall, but instead emerges in the master bathroom of his house across town. His reflection gives him pause: he looks meatier, and still has a full head of hair. He wears jeans and a sweatshirt instead of his hospital gown. He doesn't feel great, but he certainly feels better than he did a few seconds ago. A garment bag hangs from the shower rod behind him. He unzips it and finds a white suit inside. The formal ghoul costume Margaret sewed for the Tomb.

There's a knock at the door, and Margaret opens it. She's dressed as the gravedigger, with a fake mustache pressed to her face.

"Why aren't you dressed yet?" she says.

"I lost track of—" He closes his eyes to clear his head.

"You okay?"

He nods. "Fine."

"Get a move on, space cadet. We're running late."

She closes the door. He disrobes and puts on the suit. After checking his reflection again, he leaves the bathroom, but instead of emerging into his bedroom, he finds himself in the tiny apartment he shared with Margaret during college—a one-bedroom unit with ratty carpet and fake-wood-paneled walls. Boxes full of his old paperbacks and comic books and pulp magazines line the room. His things are everywhere. The kitchen table is buried beneath his typewriter and stacks of school papers.

Thump.

The sound seems to come from the bedroom, and he leaves the overfull living room to investigate. He sees himself and Margaret in bed, both in their early twenties, as good-looking and healthy as they'll ever be. It's late, and the Harry in bed is asleep, wearing Margaret's sleep mask so she can leave the light on to read. Beside him, Margaret looks up from her copy of *The Haunting of Hill House* and leans over to kiss the sleeping Harry on the cheek. The Harry in bed continues to snore, unaware. The Harry watching touches his cheek and a pang of longing sounds against his heart.

The blue-white pulse blazes through the bedroom window. When he can see again, he's in a different bedroom, on a different night. At first his surroundings—the bed, the nightstand, the dresser—appear freakishly large. Then he looks down at his body and realizes that it's not the room that has grown. He's gotten smaller.

He's ten years old, and he's wandered into his mother's room in the middle of the night because he thought he heard her cry out. All he's found are rumpled covers in her bed. In the story he'll tell countless times over the course of his life, this is the moment when he turns and runs to the living room, to the telephone where he'll call for help. He'll admit that what he thought he heard must have been a nightmare, because when the police find his mother, barefoot, bruised, and dazed, she's nearly twenty miles from home. She would have been gone for hours if she walked that far. It's impossible that he heard her call for him.

But here's what actually happens: Harry walks to his mother's bed and finds it warm. As he runs his hand across the sheets, he brushes against something cool and hard. He lifts the object. It's a perfectly smooth black stone, and it gleams even in the dark. When Harry closes his fist around it, a hole opens in the world before him, smooth and round as the stone itself. Through it, he sees something he'll never forget: a vast, cyclopean mishmash of architectures, medieval castles bumping up against business buildings and sports stadiums beneath a green-black sky. Creatures fly through the heavens, little bat-like shapes against the miasma.

Again he hears it—his mother calling his name, shrieking it from far away: *Harry! Harry, please!*

He steps away from the hole in the world, tangles his feet, and falls over. The stone flies out of his hand as he catches himself with his palms, and the portal closes. He scrambles out of the room, heading for the telephone and adults who can solve the problem for him.

But as he runs out of the room, the blue light pulses before his eyes, and when he can see again, he sees himself, bald and bony in his hospital bed (*deathbed*), sleeping. A pregnant Margaret sits in the chair next to him, watching him with a hard-to-read expression on her face. She looks away from the sleeping Harry and at the binder in his lap, full of designs for a haunted house the size of a city. An expression of fascination crosses her face, and he knows, in that way you just know things in dreams, that somehow his vision of the City, the image he's been cursed by and fascinated with all his life, has somehow infected his family. The haunting won't end when he dies.

For the first time in months, he can feel around the corners of the tumor, and finds his true self, the one who cried at his daughters' births and longed for the pretty redheaded girl at the bookstore. His true self is ashamed. Ashamed that he opened his family up to this City and all its awful possibilities. Ashamed that he didn't listen to Eunice when she said she saw something at her bedroom window, didn't listen to Margaret when she showed him the

claw marks in the brick outside the house. Ashamed that
he didn't listen when the women in his life tried to tell
him something was wrong. Ashamed he pretended that things
were fine and normal when they were anything but.

He starts across the room toward Margaret, but as
he reaches her, the blue pulse flashes outside the
window and the scene changes again. He's still in the
hospital room, but now he's the Harry in the bed. The
pain is worse than ever, and his breath is ragged in
his own ears. He's vaguely aware of Sydney beside him,
holding his hand. He turns to her, because he has to
tell someone, has to warn them somehow. She looks so
frightened, so eager to please. He gathers his thoughts,
but it's difficult, like raking leaves in a high wind.

Eunice was right, he manages.

Daddy? she says.

Margaret, he says.

Sydney. It's Sydney, Daddy.

The drawings. The designs. It's all there. You have to,
he says.

Have to what? Sydney says.

It's seen us. It has our scent.

And then the scene changes again. He's still in the
hospital bed, but Sydney stands across the room, looking
sullen as Margaret hands him a newborn baby.

Noah. The baby's name is Noah. Harry's body is racked
with pain, but his mind is clear, and he's been given
a second chance to meet his son. Free of the tumor's
distortion, he has so much he wants to tell the boy, but
most important, maybe, is this: life makes monsters of
everyone, but it's always possible to come back. Pain
and death are real, but so are love, and family, and
forgiveness. But the words won't come. Instead he leans
forward and kisses Noah's forehead and hopes this tiny
pink blob of a person will grow up to understand.

The pulse flashes again outside the window, much
faster now, and when his vision clears, he appears to
be in the backyard of Spooky House, lying atop Margaret
on a mat. It's October 1968, and she's looking up at
him with those green eyes, trying to decide something,
and he knows it's something important, something big,
but before she can speak, the mat falls away beneath
them. No—it doesn't fall. It stays where it is. He and
Margaret are the ones moving, drifting up through space.
They're not the only ones, either. As he looks about, he
sees dozens of other people floating up, up, up, amid
cars, bags of garbage, dumpsters, dead leaves, sports
equipment, newspapers, cars, cats and dogs—anything
not bolted down rises through space. The sky strobes,
blue-white-blue-white-blue-white.

Margaret wraps her arms and legs around him, holding
on tight. They spin slowly up, like Superman and Lois
Lane dancing in the heavens. He wishes he could see
Sydney and Eunice again. He wishes he could see how
things turned out for them, whether they and their little
brother shrugged off the yoke he laid on their shoulders.
But this will have to do. This last moment with Margaret.

He kisses her, his funny, hot-tempered, and heartbroken
wife, and when he stops, he finds her crying.

Oh, Harry, she says. He understands. He feels it, too.
The weight of the years, of the pain, of all the things
they've both lost, things that even the death of gravity
can't carry away.

It's okay, he says. He kisses her again and again, her
cheeks, her temples, her chin, her flaming red hair. *It's
all okay. I love you, Margaret. Until the end of time and
whatever comes—*

Acknowledgments

Stephen King once said, "No one writes a long novel alone." I would like to second that, but amend it to say, "No one becomes a novelist alone." I've been helped along by a long list of teachers, professionals, relatives, and friends, and I'd like to extend thanks to a few of them now:

To my editors, Tim O'Connell and Anna Kaufman, for their endless enthusiasm, their incredible ideas, and their relentless determination to get this thorny labyrinth of a story just right. To the whole team at Pantheon Books for working their blue fairy magic on this manuscript to turn it into a real book: copy editor Susan Brown, production editor Kathleen Fridella, publicist Abigail Endler, marketer Julianne Clancy, interior designer Michael Collica, jacket designer Kelly Blair, and, of course, publisher Dan Frank.

To my incredible literary agent Kent Wolf, who saw something in this weird literary genre hybrid, and found it a perfect home. Thanks also to my film and TV coagents Lucy Carson and Kim Yau, who continue to take such good care of me over on the media side of things.

To my in-laws, Jim and Melany Harrelson, who gave me a quiet, beautiful place to finish work on this book and who are always delighted to hear any and all news from the literary world.

To my gifted and resilient wife, Rebekah, for encouraging and supporting this project, even as she endured a pulmonary embolism and the grueling process of diagnosing an autoimmune disorder. Her paintings sat next to my desk during the composition of this novel and were an endless source of inspiration.

To the Iowa Writer's Workshop, both the people who keep it running—Connie Brothers, Deb West, and Jan Zenisek—and my instructors: Ethan Canin, who reminded me that good fiction is about people; Lan Samantha Chang, who read my early pages and said she wanted to feel scared; Ben Hale, who gave no shortage of good technical advice; and Paul Harding, who always encouraged me to look for what was human and honest and true, even in a book full of haunted houses and monsters.

To my friends and colleagues at Iowa, who read early passages of this novel and provided useful criticism and encouragement: Jake Andrews, Kris Bartkus, Noel Carver, Patrick Connelly, Susannah Davies, Mgbechi Erondu, Sarah Frye, Jason Hinojosa, J. M. Holmes, Erin Kelleher, Maria Kuznetsova, Jennie Lin, Alex Madison, Magogodi Makhene, Kevin Smith, Lindsay Stern, Nyoul Lueth Tong, Monica West, and most especially, Joe Cassara and Sorrel Westbrook-Wilson, my novelist partners-in-crime.

To my writing teachers in Texas: Kristin vanNamen and Matthew Limpede of *Carve* magazine, as well as Tim Richardson, Tim Morris, and Joanna Johnson at the University of Texas at Arlington. Also teaching at UTA but deserving of a separate shout-out: Laura Kopchick, who put me on this path and continues to offer me opportunities whenever she can.

To the Barnes & Noble in Arlington, Texas, where I worked for eight years. I went to war on Harry Potter release nights, surreptitiously wrote my first real short story while cashiering, discovered innumerable new authors, and met my wife. I don't have a big family, but the staff at that store made me feel like I did.

And, to my parents, Rick and Patrice Hamill. Dad made up personalized bedtime stories for me every night, and Mom taught me how to pay attention to character and narrative structure. They started my love of storytelling, have always encouraged my writing, and I'll never be able to thank them enough.